PENGUIN

MALDOROR *and* POEMS

LE COMTE DE LAUTRÉAMONT was the pseudonym of Isidore Ducasse, a Frenchman born in Montevideo in 1846. He seems to have taken the name of Lautréamont from the title of a novel by Eugène Sue, inspired by the extreme arrogance of its Byronic hero. He came to France to complete his education, but died in Paris after only three years, in 1870. His sadism and his voluntary self-abandonment to fantasies from the depths of his mind led to his acclaim by the early surrealists, who considered him a spiritual ancestor.

PAUL KNIGHT was born in London in 1949 and educated at Finchley Grammar School, Trinity College, Cambridge, and Sussex and Edinburgh universities. He now teaches English at the University of Passau in Germany. His other translations include Dieter Wellershoff's *Winner Takes All* and the co-translation of Ernst Bloch's *Principle of Hope*.

COMTE DE LAUTRÉAMONT

*

MALDOROR *and* POEMS

*

Translated with Introductions by
PAUL KNIGHT

PENGUIN BOOKS

PENGUIN BOOKS

Published by the Penguin Group
Penguin Books Ltd, 27 Wrights Lane, London W8 5TZ, England
Penguin Putnam Inc., 375 Hudson Street, New York, New York 10014, USA
Penguin Books Australia Ltd, Ringwood, Victoria, Australia
Penguin Books Canada Ltd, 10 Alcorn Avenue, Toronto, Ontario, Canada M4V 3B2
Penguin Books (NZ) Ltd, Private Bag 102902, NSMC, Auckland, New Zealand

Penguin Books Ltd, Registered Offices: Harmondsworth, Middlesex, England

This translation first published 1978

043

Copyright © Paul Knight, 1978
All rights reserved

Printed in Great Britain by Clays Ltd, Elcograf S.p.A.
Set in Monotype Bembo

Except in the United States of America, this book is sold subject
to the condition that it shall not, by way of trade or otherwise, be lent,
re-sold, hired out, or otherwise circulated without the publisher's
prior consent in any form of binding or cover other than that in
which it is published and without a similar condition including this
condition being imposed on the subsequent purchaser

www.greenpenguin.co.uk

Penguin Books is committed to a sustainable
future for our business, our readers and our planet.
This book is made from Forest Stewardship
Council™ certified paper.

CONTENTS

INTRODUCTION TO *MALDOROR*

ISIDORE DUCASSE, who wrote the *Chants de Maldoror* under the pseudonym 'Comte de Lautréamont', was born in Montevideo on 4 April 1846, the son of a French consular official. From 1859 to 1862, Ducasse was a boarder at the Imperial Lycée in Tarbes, where he appears to have been a good scholar, distinguishing himself in arithmetic and drawing and showing aptitude for Latin verse translation, an exercise which he later came to detest, according to M. Paul Lespès, who was his classmate at the Imperial Lycée of Pau where, from October 1863 to August 1865, Ducasse was again a boarder. Lespès, interviewed in 1927, when he was eighty-one years old, recalled Ducasse as a silent, withdrawn boy, pale and long-haired, an admirer of Sophocles, Racine and Corneille as well as Edgar Allan Poe. Ducasse once showed Lespès some of his own poetry which the latter judged to be 'bizarre and obscure'. Yet, Lespès tells us, despite his dreamy, abstracted air, Ducasse was considered a 'good fellow' by the majority of the boys – an assessment which, in its naïve condescension, would certainly have brought an ironic smile to the lips of the author of *Maldoror*.

No record exists of Ducasse taking the Baccalauréat while at Pau, nor is much known of his activities between 1865 and August 1868, when the first book of *Maldoror* was published. According to A. Lacroix, Ducasse's first editor, he had come to Paris from South America intending to study at the Polytechnic or the College of Mining. In 1867, he was lodging at number 23 Rue Notre-Dame-des-Victoires. Lacroix goes on: 'He was a big, brown-haired young man, unshaven, nervous, of regular habits, and hard-working. He worked only at

7

night, sitting at his piano. He would declaim and work out his sentences, accompanying his prosopeias by chords thumped out on the piano.' This mode of composition, Lacroix continues, 'drove the other tenants to distraction'. There is no corroborating evidence for this account, published twenty years after Ducasse's death, though it has been eagerly seized on and fancifully embroidered by would-be biographers frustrated by the lack of solid information. Even the testimony of Lacroix cannot be accepted without reservation. As Marcelin Pleynet pointedly asks in his book on Lautréamont, why should Lacroix, who printed *Maldoror* without reading it and then refused to distribute the copies, treat the author with greater respect than he treated the work? Biographical information so far is scanty, and it does not get better. Lespès presents us with a picture, blurred through time, of a stereotype 'romantic' youth, wholly anonymous. Lacroix's account is not considered reliable. Yet that is virtually all there is. In the words of Edmond Jaloux: 'This man who is our contemporary is more unknown to us than Homer, Socrates, or Caligula.'

In the year or so before August 1868, we can assume that Lautréamont must have been working on *Maldoror*, the first book of which, a booklet of thirty-two pages costing thirty centimes, was published in August 1868, although it did not immediately appear on the bookshelves. In a letter to an unknown critic of 9 November 1868 Ducasse, signing himself 'the author', asks him to write a review of the first book, and we learn that it is now on sale, its distribution having been held up by 'circumstances beyond my control'. In 1869, probably in January, the first book is included in an anthology called *Parfums de l'âme*. And on 23 October of the same year, Poulet-Malassis announces in his *Quarterly Review of Publications Banned in France and Printed Abroad* the forthcoming publication of the *Chants de Maldoror* by the Comte de

Lautréamont. At the end of the same review, however, Poulet-Malassis states that the printer refused to hand over the copies just as they were about to go on sale. Given the extremely repressive atmosphere in Paris just before the Commune and the sensational and radical nature of the work, the printer's timorousness is at least understandable. Alarmed at this development, Ducasse wrote on the same day, 23 October, to his publisher Verboeckhoven, in an effort to reassure him of the moral intent behind the work. Although the letter is clearly dictated by the wish to have his work published, Ducasse's justification of his work is still interesting: 'Let me begin by explaining my position. I have written of evil, as Mickiewicz, Byron, Milton, Southey, A. de Musset, Baudelaire, etc., have all done. Naturally I have exaggerated the pitch along the lines of that sublime literature which sings of despair only to cast down the reader and make him desire the good as the remedy. Thus one is always, after all, writing about the good, only by a more philosophical and less naïve method than the old school, of which Victor Hugo and some others are the only representatives who are still alive . . .' 'It is the beginning of a publication which will only be completed later, after my death. Thus the moral of the end has not yet been drawn.' And Ducasse then offers, if the work is well received, to cut out certain sections which are 'too strong'. He ends this letter by saying that what he desires above all is to be judged by the critics.

Ducasse's publisher intended to sell Les Chants de Maldoror in Belgium and Switzerland. In a letter of 27 October, Ducasse tells him that the minds of Swiss and Belgian readers are 'better prepared than the French to savour this poetry of revolt'. Mentioning the effect of Naville's lectures in Lausanne and Geneva on the 'Problem of Evil', Ducasse implies that there is a similarity in their approach to this problem. He says he will send a copy of Maldoror to Naville, 'for I am taking up this strange thesis more vigorously than my predecessors'. Ducasse's clear intention here is to invoke a respected ally, to categorize and thereby make it appear respectable, to allay his publisher's anxieties about its possible repercussions.

In January 1870, the anthology *Fleurs et Fruits* of Evariste Carrance referred on its back cover to the *Chants de Maldoror* by the Comte de Lautréamont as a work which had recently been published. In July of the same year the *Revue populaire de Paris* announces the forthcoming publication of *Poems* by Isidore Ducasse (note that the pseudonym has been discarded).

Ducasse died on 24 November 1870. His death certificate simply states: 'The twenty fourth of November, eighteen hundred and seventy, two p.m., death certificate of Isidore Lucien Ducasse, man of letters, aged twenty-four, born in Montevideo (South America), died this morning at eight o'clock in his domicile, Rue du Faubourg Montmartre, 16 – single (no further information).' His life and his death are utterly consistent in their mysteriousness and impenetrability. In *Maldoror*, Lautréamont says: 'I know my annihilation will be complete.' And in the *Poems*: 'I will leave no memoirs.'

The death of this young man without connections whose family was living in South America could not be expected to arouse great interest, especially as his writing had not then made the impact it was to make later. There were also strong historical reasons why it should pass almost unnoticed. The people of Paris had other concerns. Paris was under siege by the Prussian army and the city was not expected to be able to hold out beyond mid-December. Strict rationing of fuel and food had been introduced. The mortality rate had jumped dramatically and between 6 and 12 November it was 112 per cent higher than normal. As an indication of how desperate things were, François Caradec mentions that on 24 November, the day of Lautréamont's death, dog meat sold at 2.50 francs a pound, while cats' meat cost 12 francs.

Ignorance of the circumstances of Lautréamont's death and of most of his life has opened the door to all kinds of speculation and a mystique has arisen around this mysterious, elusive individual. The search for Ducasse the man behind the work of Lautréamont the writer goes on, as if what is contained in *Les Chants* were primarily of autobiographical interest. There are moments when a personal note is sounded, as when Lautréamont writes with such intense hatred of a teacher, 'a pariah of civilization', that we sense he must have suffered this kind of tyranny. But these moments are very rare. The facts we know about his life hardly tell us anything about his personality or his character. We have none of that intimacy of knowledge which comes from personal letters, from the judgements and reminiscences of friends. No photograph of Ducasse exists, and his facelessness intrigued the Surrealists, who are to be credited for recognizing Lautréamont's importance and 'resurrecting' him in the nineteen twenties.

If the annihilation of the historical Isidore Ducasse is almost complete, the same cannot be said of his pseudonym, the writer, Lautréamont. The *Chants de Maldoror* remain and so, too, do the *Poems*, written under the name of Ducasse (why the return to his real name?). In the face of these texts the 'problem' of biography recedes into the background, the question of the historical personality is secondary; perhaps fortunately, the would-be critic is left with no option but to concentrate on what is essential: the reading of the texts, the examination of their complex interrelation.

Yet with the majority of texts the identity of the author is a simple, unquestioned fact. The name of the work and its author appear together on the binding in reassuring and indissoluble union, the relation of one to the other is taken for granted; it is quite simple, apparently: the author writes the text, signs it, and it is his. The work of Lautréamont shatters this expectation, anticipating the way in which the texts themselves call in question and undermine 'innocent' assumptions about the essential problems of fiction: the relation between the written text and the world (or 'reality'), between the writer and the reader; the arbitrariness of the fictional text, the dangers and absurdity of expecting an easily digestible meaning; the relation of literary forms and devices consciously and ironically played against one another; the question of originality. It is the problem of writing fiction which is continually posed in these texts.

Latréaumont was the title of a novel by the then extremely successful sensational novelist Eugène Sue. (Lautréamont refers to himself in *Maldoror* as a sensational novelist.) The adoption of the pseudonym can be construed as a self-protective measure to avoid being identified by the censor. Certainly, Maldoror has some features in common with the 'romans noirs' of writers such as Sue. But it is also a metamorphosis, an alias assumed by one who fully realizes that, in the eyes of literary orthodoxy, his work is a criminal act: 'He knew that the police, that shield of civilization, had for many years been looking for him doggedly and single-mindedly, and that a veritable army of informers and agents was continually at his heels. Without, however, managing to catch him. So did his staggering skill foil, with supreme style, tricks which ought indisputably to have brought success, and arrangements of the most cunning meditation. He had a particular gift for taking on forms which were unrecognizable to the experienced eye.' Maldoror, master of disguises, obsessively pursued by the police as the incarnation of evil: Lautréamont's text, with its bewildering and deliberate multiplicity of literary registers, initially banned, rejected, considered unreadable. The parallel is clear, the quotation one of many which could have been chosen to show the author's awareness of his text and its implications.

This awareness of the danger, the 'criminality', of the act of writing is evident from the first lines of the book, which address the reader. 'May it please heaven that the reader, emboldened and having for the time being become as fierce as what he is reading, should, without being led astray, find his rugged and treacherous way across the desolate swamps of these sombre and poison-filled pages; for, unless he brings to his reading a rigorous logic and a tautness of mind equal at least to his wariness, the deadly emanations of this book will dissolve his soul as water does sugar. It is not right that everyone should read the pages which follow; only a few will be able to savour this bitter fruit with impunity.' Marcelin Pleynet in his book on Lautréamont has shown how this opening passage is itself an inversion of the rhetorical topos of affected modesty, where the author traditionally begs the reader's indulgence and asks him to make allowances for his many deficiencies. Pleynet observes that 'almost immediately, Lautréamont calls his reader in question. Right from the first lines, he makes the reader face up to his limitations and inadequacies, and, far from seeking to win him, advises him to give up reading the book.' Yet by suggesting that there are some readers capable of 'savouring this bitter fruit with impunity', he cleverly plays on the reader's vanity, knowing that every reader will immediately wish to count himself among the select few. This 'warning' is followed by the image of the flight of cranes, which ornithologists have praised for the accuracy of its observation. It has been suggested that such passages describing the flight of birds are lifted from or heavily based on books on ornithology and are not the product of Lautréamont's own observation, so that the ornithological accuracy which experts have admired becomes less uncanny. This does not reduce the literary effect, and the image loses none of its force for not being part of Lautréamont's own experience; the original on which this passage might have been based is completely transformed by its inclusion here. Lautréamont, himself the most original of writers, expresses contempt for the obsession with originality and even says, in the *Poems* that 'plagiarism is necessary'.

The opening passage foretokens much of what is to come – it, too, is 'the precursor of the storm', for it is shot through with that indefinable menace so characteristic of Lautréamont. Here, too, we see what he means by the 'rugged and treacherous way': the writing, the arrangement of main and subsidiary clauses, is uncompromisingly complex, making strong demands on our attention. (This separation of verb from object, and the interpolation of seemingly endless sub-clauses and restrictions becomes more marked in the latter books and has the effect of keeping the reader in suspense, and at the same time underlining his, the writer's, despotic control. He will decide when the moment is right to end that suspense.)

Meanwhile, our absorption in the crane simile is so complete that we momentarily forget its apparent function: to remind the reader that he, like the wise crane veering away, should, 'because he is no fool, take another, a surer and more philosophic line of flight'. Here the simile has almost become an end in itself, independent of the purpose for which, ostensibly, it was introduced. Later, the simile will be subjected to a far more radical distortion: 'The lamb-eating vulture, lovely as the law of arrested chest development in adults whose propensity to growth is not in proportion to the quantity of molecules their organism can assimilate . . .', or: 'the beetle, lovely as the alcoholic's trembling hands'. These examples are similes in form only, in their use of the word 'as'. We are struck here by the grotesque dissimilarity between the terms of the comparison, between the word 'lovely' and the image to which it is annexed. This difference between the simile as Lautréamont uses it and the similes we are accustomed to in our reading experience is crucial. Every aspect of Lautréamont's writing is an ironical pointer back to conventional modes of writing which it displaces, distorts, questions. We are forced to reflect on the triteness of most of the similes we have ever come across: 'sentences which have been passed under the screw-plate and subjected to the saponification of obligatory metaphors'. There is an implicit contempt here for all that is automatic and predictable in writing. The simile, in common with numerous other literary forms and devices, has become fossilized, reduced to the level of an automatic gesture, so bland as to go almost unnoticed. It is a device to which the author often has recourse when he wishes to relax in his writing, a moment of self-indulgence at the reader's expense. With Lautréamont the simile is a complex of similarities and differences – the reader, far from being borne effortlessly along to the next point in the narrative, is shocked into awareness of the process taking place on the page before him. Lautréamont himself admits he is unable to understand this compulsive need for comparison: 'It is, generally speaking, a strange thing, this captivating tendency which leads us to seek out (and then to express) the resemblances and differences which are hidden in the most natural properties of objects which are sometimes the least apt to lend themselves sympathetically to curious combinations of this kind, which, on my word of honour, graciously enhance the style of the writer who treats himself to this personal satisfaction, giving him the ridiculous and unforgettable aspect of an eternally serious owl.'

Not just at the beginning, but throughout *Maldoror*, Lautréamont addresses the reader. The tone he adopts for these apostrophes, these intimate conspiratorial conversations, varies greatly, but always behind them lurks his witty, patronizing irony: 'Let the reader not be angry with me if my prose does not have the good fortune to appeal to him.' Thus the reader is initiated into the text with allegedly helpful advice from the author, made an accomplice in Lautréamont's criminal act. Lautréamont diagnoses the reader's hypothetical response, weighs the effect his text has had so far, and reaches, among others, this conclusion: 'Is it not true, my friend, that to a certain extent these songs have met with your approval? Now what prevents you from going all the way?' The process of contagion which the reader was warned against at the beginning of the book is going forward to the author's satisfaction. The reader is overcoming initial objections, resistances, shedding preconceived ways of looking at a text, coming to accept the text on and in its own terms and to recognize that it is 'within the order of possible things'. The process of manipulation has been completely successful. By the sixth book, Lautréamont is even prepared to make concessions like this to the reader: 'Since you advise me to end the strophe at this point, I am willing, this once, to accede to your wish.' Lautréamont regrets, or feigns regret, at the necessarily limited nature of the writer–reader relationship – he would wish it to be more physical! 'If only I could see the face of him who is reading me through these seraphic pages. If he has not passed puberty, let him approach. Hold me tight against you, and do not be afraid of hurting me; let us contract our muscles. More. I feel it is futile to continue. The opacity of this piece of paper, remarkable in more ways than one, is a most considerable obstacle to our complete union.'

How is *Maldoror* different? What is it about this work which demands a re-thinking of our approach? Lautréamont's letter to his banker of 12 March 1870 is a variation on the letter already quoted to his publisher. In it he says: 'It is something of the same genre as Manfred of Byron and

Konrad of Mickiewicz, but far more extreme.' This self-interpretation by Lautréamont points to a possible method which can be applied to *Maldoror*. This consists of looking at the way Lautréamont exploits the literary forms and modes of his genre – 'tics', as he calls them in the *Poems*, 'stage effects' in *Maldoror* – and then analysing the differences between these forms and modes in their 'innocent' state and the way in which Lautréamont reworks, distorts them. Then perhaps we will be able to see whether *Maldoror* is merely 'far more extreme' or radically different from other works of 'the same genre'.

Let us call the genre of Lautréamont's *Maldoror* the 'roman noir' or 'black novel'. It is clear that there are resemblances between *Maldoror* and the writings of Sue, Maturin, Radcliffe. In these novels the author needs to make no pretensions to realism and the action is packed with the supernatural, the unaccountable, the satanic. Maturin's *Melmoth the Wanderer* has been singled out as being especially close in spirit and intent to *Maldoror*. This novel, published in 1821, was much admired by Baudelaire and Balzac. Melmoth has sold his soul to the devil. In return he is given supernatural powers and a term of life far longer than most men, but still limited. The escape clause is this: he will be released from his part of the contract if he can find a man or woman to replace him and make the pact in his stead. The novel tells of his attempts, in various parts of the world, to find such a person. Melmoth is presented as a dark and menacing figure, inscrutable and sinister, contemptuous of the narrowness of human aspirations. Maturin endows Melmoth with a Satanic dignity, and his diabolical actions are represented as springing from a superhuman despair and regret at the irreversibility of his compact. Unable by any means to escape his fate, he waits with mixed terror and anticipation for his death and his inevitable damnation. Maldoror shares some of Melmoth's characteristics. Yet whereas Melmoth is seeking escape and redemption, Maldoror's mission is quite different: 'Stupid, idiotic race. You will regret having acted thus! It is I who tell you. You will regret it! My poetry will consist exclusively of attacks on man, that wild beast, and the Creator, who ought never to have bred such vermin. Volume after volume will accumulate, till the end of my life; yet only this single idea will be found, preoccupying my consciousness.' The identification of Lautréamont with Maldoror here is absolute, whereas Maturin is forced to recoil in horror from his 'hero'. In Maturin's novel, Melmoth is seen standing on a high cliff, contemplating a ship sinking amid the despairing cries of crew and passengers. Melmoth is unmoved by this, and this reaction is considered unnatural. Maldoror views a similar spectacle with equal calm until he notices a survivor swimming towards the shore. He then dispatches him with a single, well-aimed bullet. (Note how effective a killer Maldoror is in his human form: sudden, lethal, economical in his movements.) Other similarities of incident could be found, and it will be agreed that Maldoror and Melmoth have certain traits in common. But already it is clear that Maldoror is 'more extreme' than Melmoth. He is no tragic illustration of the dangers of the Faustian urge. He is the blasphemous, remorseless opponent of God and man: in him there is no trace of repentance, no hope of redemption. Maldoror cannot be conveniently classified in the long and honourable tradition of the 'romantic hero'. He treats the romantic aspiration for the divine and the transcendental with supreme irony. What else can he be aiming at when, in the first book, he talks of the dogs howling at the moon and his mother's words of advice: 'When you are in bed and you hear the barking of the dogs in the countryside, hide beneath your blanket but do not deride what they do: they have an insatiable thirst for the infinite, as you, and I, and all other pale, long-faced human beings do.

I will even allow you to stand in front of your window to contemplate this spectacle, which is quite edifying ... Like those dogs, I feel the need for the infinite. I cannot, cannot satisfy this need. I am the son of a man and a woman, from what I have been told. This astonishes me ... I believed I was something more.' Later, when Maldoror tells of his dream that he had become a hog, he says: 'At last the day had come when I was a hog! ... Not the slightest trace of divinity remained: I raised my soul to the excessive height of that unspeakable delight.'

Maldoror's attitude to God and man is one of utter and insolent defiance and he takes this revolt to unequalled extremes, further even than Baudelaire. There is nothing comparable in the intensity of this hatred, nor in the variety of the forms it takes, ranging from frenetic outbursts to cold, calculated jeering. Here, too, the identification with Lautréamont is complete, the passages in question being frequently in the first person. God is portrayed as a visitor of brothels, anxious to hush up his crime: 'They wanted to know what disastrous resolution could have made me cross the frontiers of heaven and come down to earth to indulge in pleasures which they themselves despised ... Tell them a bold lie, tell them that I have never left heaven'; as a murderer, a sadist (both of these qualities he shares with Maldoror), and a cannibal; as a besotted drunkard incapable and unworthy of holding the reins of the universe, drivelling; and here Lautréamont takes pity on him and puts in a few good words for him, to mitigate the circumstances (although it could also be the Creator himself who is speaking here): 'Oh, you will never know how difficult it can be to keep on holding the reins of the universe! Sometimes the blood rushes to one's head when one is seriously trying to conjure a last comet from nothingness, and with it a new race of spirits. The intellect, stirred to the depths, yields like a beaten man and, for once in its life, lapses into the aberrations which you have witnessed!' The stock of conceivable insults seems to have been exhausted, but we are reckoning without Lautréamont's inventive audacity: 'A final word ... it was a winter night. While the cold wind whistled through the firs, the Creator opened his doors and showed a pederast in.' Maldoror is in a continual struggle with God, on equal terms, as a feared and respected adversary. He can never be victorious in this struggle, but God is not strong enough to defeat him.

God also is a danger to the writer. Maldoror puts a piece of wood between his eyelids to keep awake and protect himself from 'God spying' – i.e. dreams which in their seeming illogicality can be unravelled, interpreted and used in evidence against the dreamer. When he dreams, the individual is not free, but unceasingly bombarded by weird uncontrolled images springing upon the screen of his consciousness. It seems strange that Lautréamont should reject the dream when his work itself has such a surrealistic, nightmarish quality. But the assertion of the writer's control over his material is all-important. When dreaming, the individual is a bemused spectator as images from his waking consciousness and subconscious succeed one another in an order over which he has no control. The writer is master of his own fictions; his selection and presentation depend only on himself, he is his own censor, a creator whose omnipotence rivals God's. Lautréamont rejects the passivity of the dream, and this rejection is at the same time a defiance of God, conscience and remorse: 'A pitiless scalpel probes among its undergrowth. Conscience utters a long rattle of curses; the veil of modesty is cruelly torn away. Humiliation! our door is open to the wild curiosity of the Celestial Bandit. I have not deserved this ignominious punishment, hideous spy of my causality! If I exist, I am not another. I do not acknowledge this ambiguous plurality in myself. I wish to reside alone in my inner deliberations. Autonomy . . . or let me be changed into a hippopotamus.'

The idea of the writer's independence and control is central to *Maldoror*: indeed Lautréamont's ironic sensitivity to the problem of being a writer of fiction is perhaps the essential distinguishing feature of his work. *Maldoror* presupposes the traditional novel with all its assumptions, deliberately breaks all its rules. It has to be read with these texts in mind, parallel with them, as a form of counter-fiction which is continually pointing back to them. The traditional novel cannot be abolished. But it can be subtly undermined, its forms can be experimented with, its philosophical structure and its pretensions exposed. For Lautréamont the writing of fiction does not subserve any higher ideal; it is its own end: 'Even if I had no true event to recount to you, I would invent imaginary tales and decant them into your brain.' Fiction is 'engendered by the stormy flood of a love resolved not to quench its thirst with the human race. A hungering love, which would devour itself, if it did not seek sustenance in celestial fictions: creating, in the long run, a pyramid of seraphim more numerous than the insects which swarm in a drop of water, he will weave them into an ellipse which he will whirl around himself.' This whirling ellipse is destined to come up again, and at the end of it is Mervyn (the name of the hero of Scott's *Guy Mannering*, a name which seems to epitomize the romantic hero). Mervyn is here the hero of the 'little novel' in the sixth book and symbol of the traditional novel. In an act of controlled and well-aimed violence, his body is released, speeds through the air, and splatters against the dome of the Pantheon (the literary Pantheon? What more appropriate symbol could be found?) There it remains, a dreadful warning. The significance of this act is unmistakable: the novel is dead, brutally murdered, but not decently buried; and Lautréamont invites us to 'go and see for yourself, if you do not believe me'.

Mervyn's death can be symbolically interpreted as the death of the novel; but at the same time it can be seen as the possibility of its rebirth. For it is only the death of one form of the novel, but a form so influential, so monopolistic, as to come to be identified with the novel as such – the monolithic nineteenth-century novel, safe and settled in its form, unquestioned vehicle of social and psychological 'reality', resting on a philosophical and formal base which Lautréamont skilfully collapses. 'It is my opinion that the synthetic part of my work is now complete . . . from now on my intention is to start upon the analytic part . . . Today I am going to fabricate a little novel of thirty pages; the estimated length will, in the event, remain unchanged . . . I believe I have, after some groping attempts, at last found my definitive formula. It is the best: since it is the novel.' This triumphant cry of discovery can only be ironic. But the words 'fabricate' and 'analytic' have to be stressed. For Lautréamont's 'little novel' is at the same time a critique: it takes all the ingredients of the traditional novel and binds them together in an absurd but supremely self-conscious melodrama which explodes the traditional novel from within and almost makes the symbolism of Mervyn's death superfluous. This 'little novel of thirty pages' is a *reductio ad absurdum* in which Lautréamont demonstrates his critical insight and his sense of humour. But the conclusion to be drawn from it is unmistakable: henceforward it is impossible to write in the manner of Flaubert and Balzac, Scott and Dickens.

The omniscience of the author is immediately called in question. Mervyn, that 'son of fair England', is sixteen years and four months of age. Lautréamont knows this not because he is the omniscient author whose assertion of a character's age is necessarily unassailable, but because he claims to be 'an expert at judging age from the physiognomic lines of the brow'. Later on, Lautréamont even feigns partial ignorance:

'He has reasons which have not come to my knowledge and which I consequently cannot communicate to you, for hinting that he cannot remain on good terms with his brothers.' By scrupulously admitting this self-imposed gap in his knowledge, Lautréamont, far from reassuring the reader of his honesty and good faith, literally disorientates him. The confession of the minutest ignorance is disturbing. For is it not the traditional novelist's claim to total knowledge which makes us believe him? Lautréamont's deviation from the rule here casts an ironic sidelight on this aspect of the traditional novel; here again the reader is confronted with the fictivity of the text. He may reflect that the novelist usually interrupts his narrative only for explanation, for psychological reflection. He is bemused by this ironical confession of ignorance. This is part of the process the reader was warned against at the beginning of *Maldoror*. He is being manipulated, his expectations are being turned against him, the ground is giving way under his feet. And in this little novel, where he might have expected to find refuge, the process is, if anything, intensified.

The characters are perfect stereotypes: Mervyn, the dreamy adolescent; his father, the retired naval commander, stern and imperious, utterly dominating his timid, ladylike wife; his brothers in their velvet breeches and red silk stockings, tiptoeing across the carefully-polished parquet-floor. Their conversation is grotesquely pompous and literary: 'My gentle master, if you will permit your slave, I shall go and look . . . for a phial of turpentine spirit which I habitually use when migraine invades my temples after I have returned from the theatre or when reading a stirring chronicle of British chivalric history throws my dream-laden mind into the bogs of drowsiness.' And Mervyn's mother hurries towards the stairs, though 'she does not run as quickly as a member of the lower classes'. The characters are as if hypnotized, filled with nameless dread at the heaviness and gloom which hang over

23

their house. Numerous other 'stage tricks' are introduced: the secret letter signed in blood, the rendezvous, attempted murder, a last-minute rescue, then the catastrophe; a 'sub-plot' in which God unsuccessfully sends one of his archangels, disguised as a crab, to rescue Mervyn; the absurd 'story within a story' of the three daisies which is meant to explain Aghone's madness, and which underlines Lautréamont's unaccountability, his freedom, along the way of the book, to fabricate 'celestial' (!) fictions. At the same time, the little novel is deprived of the last slim vestige of credibility. But whether we find the narrative credible or not, whether we are convinced by the little novel, is irrelevant: indeed if we look at the novel in these terms, we will not be cooperating with the author at all. He has already told us that 'I do not think the reader will have cause to regret it if he brings to my narration less the harmful obstacle of stupid credulity than the supreme service of profound confidence, examining lawfully and with secret sympathy the poetic mysteries, too few in number in his opinion, which I undertake to reveal to him as and when the opportunity arises . . .' Lautréamont's concern in writing the little novel is purely with form, specifically with the linear narrative form. He infiltrates that form, distorts and subverts it from within. The little novel at the end of *Maldoror* is 'counter-fiction' posing as fiction – a pose we have to see through.

Thibaudet described *Maldoror* as a 'frenetic monologue'. Lautréamont's work, however, does not lend itself to these easy critical formulations. (Adjectives such as 'volcanic', 'intense', 'dynamic', 'sinister', come to mind; but they are pale approximations, stammering confessions of impotence to describe this work. As for placing it, we lack categories; it is unique. And so in talking of this text one has to be content with such approximations.) Baudelaire, in his poem 'To the Reader' at the beginning of *Les Fleurs du Mal*, wrote: 'If rape, poison, the dagger and the conflagration have not yet embroidered their agreeable designs on the banal canvas of our pitiable destinies, it is because our soul, alas, is not bold enough.' The reader of *Maldoror* will be able to judge whether Lautréamont was bold enough. But it is important not to be blinded by the violence of this text, its rejection of all moral constraint. This false perspective has led some critics to interpret *Maldoror* either as a 'particularly intense expression of Byronic despair' or else as 'frenetic', 'pathological'. Both these judgements show a failure to grasp a whole dimension of this work: the dimension of controlled, ironic reflection on the interrelation of fiction and reality. For from the fourth book onwards we notice a change in Lautréamont's writing. The dialogue with the reader already mentioned is part of this significant change of emphasis. The narrative episodes are broken into: we are made aware of the presence of the writer. The identity of the narrator with Maldoror becomes more problematic. Our attention is increasingly drawn to the fact that, here, a text is being produced: 'Look at this old spider of the large species, slowly protruding its head from a hole in the ground at one of the intersections of the room. We are no longer in the narrative. It listens carefully to hear if any rustling sound is still moving its mandibles in the atmosphere. Alas! we have now come to reality as far as the tarantula is concerned . . .' Lautréamont merely asserts that the transition from narrative to reality has taken place. And who can contradict him? And note how the spider egocentrically attributes all rustling sounds to the movement of mandibles!

These examples could be multiplied. They are evidence of an extreme critical awareness of literary form as well as of a brilliant wit. They also anticipate the essential preoccupation of modern French fiction precisely with its relation to the nineteenth-century novel. In the works of so-called 'new novelists' such as Butor and Robbe-Grillet we find this same awareness of fictivity, this realization that the implicitly vast claims of the nineteenth-century novel to 'reflect' social and psychological reality can no longer hold good. And so the novel deliberately restricts itself, becomes increasingly inward-looking; the process of writing itself becomes the subject of fiction: the break with the tradition means a greater concentration on formal possibilities, a continual search for, and experimentation with, new structures.

In recent years, structuralist literary criticism has emphasized this neglected and extremely modern element in Lautréamont's *Maldoror*. This new critical reading is invaluable. Yet no critical essay, least of all this, can do justice to an inexhaustible work; the 'definitive interpretation' of Lautréamont will never be written. *Maldoror* has been called an oceanic text; it has also been called schizophrenic, adolescent, absurd, infantile, brilliant. André Breton said that it was 'the expression of a total revelation which seems to surpass human capacities'. Gide said that reading Rimbaud and the sixth book of *Maldoror* made him ashamed of his own works. That such a diverse text should provoke such varying responses is hardly surprising. The reader can turn to *Maldoror* and judge for himself: he will meet 'the best professor of hypnotism he has ever known'; he will cross 'uncharted, perilous wastelands' to reach what Philippe Sollers calls 'the limits of literature'.

MALDOROR

FIRST BOOK

I

MAY it please heaven that the reader, emboldened and having for the time being become as fierce as what he is reading, should, without being led astray, find his rugged and treacherous way across the desolate swamps of these sombre and poison-filled pages; for, unless he brings to his reading a rigorous logic and a tautness of mind equal at least to his wariness, the deadly emanations of this book will dissolve his soul as water does sugar. It is not right that everyone should read the pages which follow; only a few will be able to savour this bitter fruit with impunity. Consequently, shrinking soul, turn on your heels and go back before penetrating further into such uncharted, perilous wastelands. Listen well to what I say: turn on your heels and go back, not forward, like the eyes of a son respectfully averted from the august contemplation of his mother's face; or rather like a formation of very meditative cranes, stretching out of sight, whose sensitive bodies flee the chill of winter, when, their wings fully extended, they fly powerfully through silence to a precise point on the horizon, from which suddenly a strange strong wind blows, precursor of the storm. The oldest crane, flying on alone ahead of the others, shakes his head like a reasonable person on seeing this, making at the same time a clack with his beak, and he is troubled (as I, too, would be, if I were he); all the time his scrawny and featherless neck, which has seen three generations of cranes, is moving in irritated undulations which foretoken the quickly-gathering storm. Having calmly looked in all directions with his experienced eyes, the crane prudently (ahead of all the others, for he has the privilege of showing his tail-feathers to his less intelligent fellows) gyrates to change the direction of the geometric figure (perhaps it is a triangle, but one cannot see the third side which these curious birds of passage form in space) either to port or to starboard, like a skilled captain; uttering as he does so his vigilant cry, like that of a melancholy sentry, to repulse the common enemy. Then, manoeuvring with wings which seem no bigger than a starling's, because he is no fool, he takes another philosophic and surer line of flight.

2

READER, perhaps it is hatred you wish me to invoke at the outset of this work! What makes you think that you will not sniff – drenched in numberless pleasures, for as long as you wish, with your proud nostrils, wide and thin, as you turn over on your belly like a shark, in the beautiful black air, as if you understood the importance of this act and the equal importance of your legitimate appetite, slowly and majestically – its red emanations. I assure you, they will delight the two shapeless holes of your hideous muzzle, if you endeavour beforehand to inhale, in three thousand consecutive breaths, the accursed conscience of the Eternal One! Your nostrils, which will dilate immeasurably in unspeakable contentment, in motionless ecstasy, will ask nothing better of space, for they will be full of fragrance as if of perfumes and incense; for they will be glutted with complete happiness, like the angels who dwell in the peace and magnificence of pleasant Heaven.

3

I WILL state in a few lines that Maldoror was good during the first years of his life, when he lived happily. That is that. Then he noticed that he had been born evil: an extraordinary fatality! As far as he could, he hid his real character for a large number of years; but in the end, because of the concentration this required, which did not come naturally to him, the blood used to rush to his head every day; until, no longer able to bear such a life, he flung himself resolutely into a career of evildoing . . . a sweet atmosphere! Who would have thought so! Whenever he kissed a little pink-faced child, he felt like tearing open its cheeks with a razor, and he would have done so very often, had not Justice, with its long train of punishments, prevented him. He was no liar, admitted the truth and said that he was cruel. Human beings, did you hear that? He dares to say it again with this trembling pen. So it is a power stronger than will . . . Curse! Could a stone escape from the laws of gravity? Impossible. Impossible, for evil to form an alliance with good. That is what I was saying in the above lines.

4

THERE are those whose purpose in writing is, by means of the noble qualities of heart which their imagination invents or which they themselves may have, to seek the plaudits of other human beings. For my part, I use my genius to depict the delights of cruelty: delights which are not transitory or artificial; but which began with man and will end with him. Cannot genius be allied with cruelty in the secret resolutions of Providence? Or can one, being cruel, not have genius?

The proof will be seen in my words. You have only to listen to me, if you wish ... Excuse me, for a moment it seemed as if my hair was standing on end; but it is nothing, for I had no trouble in putting them back in place again with my hand. He who sings does not claim that his cavatinas are utterly unknown; on the contrary, he commends himself because his hero's haughty and wicked thoughts are in all men.

5

THROUGHOUT my life, I have seen narrow-shouldered men, without a single exception, committing innumerable stupid acts, brutalizing their fellows and perverting souls by all means. They call the motive for their actions fame. Seeing these spectacles, I wanted to laugh like the others but I found that strange imitation impossible. I took a knife with a sharp steel cutting-edge on its blade and I slit my flesh where the lips join. For a moment I believed I had achieved my object. I looked in a mirror at this mouth disfigured by an act of my own will. It was a mistake! The blood flowing from the two wounds prevented me from discerning whether the laugh really was the same as others'. But after comparing them for a few moments I saw clearly that my laugh did not resemble that of human beings, i.e. I was not laughing at all. I have seen men, ugly men with their eyes sunk in dark sockets, surpassing the hardness of rock, the rigidity of cast steel, the insolence of youth, the senseless rage of criminals, the falseness of the hypocrite, the most extraordinary actors, the strength of character of priests, beings whose real character is the most impenetrable, colder than anything else in heaven or on earth; I have seen them wearing out moralists who have attempted to discover their heart, and seen them bring upon themselves implacable anger from on high. I have seen them all now, the

strongest fist raised towards heaven, like a child already dis-
obedient towards its mother, probably incited by some spirit
from hell, eyes full of the bitterest remorse, but at the same
time of hatred; glacially silent, not daring to utter the vast
ungrateful meditations hidden in their breasts, because those
meditations were so full of injustice and horror; I have seen
them grieve the God of mercy in his compassion; and again
at every moment of the day, from their earliest childhood
right up to the end of their old age, I have seen them uttering
unbelievable anathemata, void of all common sense, against
everything which breathes, against themselves, and against
Providence; prostituting women and children, thus dishonour-
ing the parts of the body consecrated to modesty. Then, the
waters of the seas rise up, engulfing ships in their bottomless
depths; hurricanes and earthquakes level houses; plague and
all kinds of diseases decimate families. But men do not realize
this. I have seen them blushing, or turning pale for shame at
their conduct on this earth – rarely. Tempests, sisters of the
hurricanes; bluish firmament, whose beauty I refuse to
acknowledge; hypocritical sea, image of my own heart;
earth, who hold mysteries hidden in your breast; the whole
universe; God, who created it with such magnificence, it is
thee I invoke: show me a man who is good ... But at the
same time increase my strength tenfold; for at the sight of
such a monster, I may die of astonishment: men have died of
less.

6

ONE should let one's nails grow for a fortnight. O, how
sweet it is to drag brutally from his bed a child with no hair
on his upper lip and with wide open eyes, make as if to touch
his forehead gently with one's hand and run one's fingers

through his beautiful hair. Then suddenly, when he is least expecting it, to dig one's long nails into his soft breast, making sure, though, that one does not kill him; for if he died, one would not later be able to contemplate his agonies. Then one drinks his blood as one licks his wounds; and during this time, which ought to last for eternity, the child weeps. There is nothing better than his blood, drawn in the way I have just described, and still very warm, unless it be his tears, bitter as salt. Man, have you never tasted your own blood, when by chance you cut your finger? How good it tastes, do you not think? For it has no taste. Besides, can you not remember a day when, beset by gloomy thoughts, you put your cupped hands to your sickly face, wet with the tears falling from your eyes; that hand then moving as if by fatality towards your mouth which then drank the tears from that cup in long draughts – trembling all the while like the chattering teeth of a schoolboy looking sidelong at the one born to oppress him? How good they taste, do they not? For they taste like vinegar. One would think the tears of one's lover would be best; but the tears of a child are more pleasing to the palate. The child, incapable of deceit, because he does not know evil yet: your lover always betrays you, sooner or later ... I guess this by analogy, although I do not know what friendship, what love are (I will probably never accept either of these; at least not from the human race). Therefore, since you are not repelled by your blood and your tears, drink, drink confidently the blood and the tears of the adolescent. Blindfold him, while you rend his palpitating flesh; and having for hours listened to his sublime cries, like the piercing death-rattles which sound in the throats of the fatally-wounded on battlefields, and having, like an avalanche, then subsided, you will rush into the next room and pretend to come to his aid. You will untie his hands, their veins and sinews swollen, you will restore sight to his haggard eyes, as you start licking his blood and tears again. How genuine then your repentance is! The divine spark within, which so rarely appears, is revealed; too late! How the heart overflows with longing to be able to console the innocent whom we have made suffer: 'Youth, who have suffered such cruel pain, who could have committed this crime against you, this crime for which I can find no name! How unhappy you are! How you must be suffering! And if your mother knew of this, she would be no nearer that death so abhorred by the guilty, than I am now. Alas! what, then, are good and evil? Are they not one and the same thing by which in our rage we testify to our impotence, and our longing to attain the infinite, however senseless the means? Yes, let them be one and the same thing . . . for if they are not what will become of me on the day of judgement! Youth, forgive me . . . here before your noble and sacred face stands he who has broken your bones and torn your flesh, which is hanging from different parts of your body. Is it a delirium of my deranged mind, is it a secret instinct independent of all reasoning, such as that of the eagle tearing apart its prey, which impelled me to commit this crime? And yet I suffer as much as my victim! Youth, forgive me! Once we have left this transitory life, I want us to be entwined for eternity; to form one being, my mouth pressed against your mouth. Even thus my punishment will not be complete. Then you will tear me ceaselessly both with your teeth and your nails. I will adorn my body with heavily-scented garlands for this expiatory holocaust; and we will both suffer, I from being torn, you from tearing me. O blond-haired youth, with your gentle eyes, will you do now what I advise you? In spite of yourself, I wish you to do it, and you will set my conscience at rest.' Having spoken thus, you will have tortured a human being, and you will at the same time have been loved by the same being: this is the greatest happiness which can be conceived. Later, you can take him to the hospital. For the paralytic boy will be in no condition to earn his living. You will be called good, laurel crowns and gold medals will cover your bare feet when in your old age you are laid out in the large and ancient vault. O thou whose name I do not wish to write on this page consecrated to the holiness of crime, I know your forgiveness was as boundless as the universe. But I still exist!

7

I HAVE made a pact with Prostitution to sow disorder in families. I remember the night which preceded this dangerous liaison. Before me I saw a tombstone. I heard a glow-worm, big as a house, say to me: 'I will give you the light you need. Read the inscription. It is not from me that this supreme order comes.' A vast blood-coloured light, at the sight of which my jaws clacked and my hands fell inert, suffused the air as far as the horizon. I leaned against a ruined wall, for I was about to fall, and read: 'Here lies a youth who died of consumption: you know why. Do not pray for him.' Not many men perhaps would have shown such courage as I did. Meanwhile, a beautiful naked woman came and lay down at my feet. Sadly, I said to her, 'You can get up.' And I held out to her the hand with which the fratricide slits his sister's throat. The shining worm, to me: 'You, take a stone and kill her.' 'Why?' I asked. And it said to me: 'Beware, look to your safety, for you are the weaker and I the stronger. Her name is Prostitution.' With tears in my eyes and my heart full of rage, I felt an unknown strength rising within me. I took hold of a huge stone; after many attempts, I managed to lift it as far as my chest. Then, with my arms, I put it on my shoulders. I climbed the mountain until I reached the top: from there, I hurled the stone on to the shining worm, crushing it. Its head was thrust six feet into the ground, a man's height; the stone rebounded as high as six churches. Then it fell down again into a lake, and for a moment the water-level, eddying, dropped as the sinking stone created an immense inverted cone. The surface became calm again; the blood-red light ceased to shine. 'Alas! alas!' the naked woman exclaimed. 'What have you done?' I said to her: 'I prefer you to him. Because I pity the unhappy. It is not your fault that eternal justice has created you.' And she said: 'One day men will do me justice; I will say no more to you. Let me go and hide my infinite sadness at the bottom of the sea. Only you, and the hideous monsters who swarm in those black depths, do not despise me. You are good. Adieu, you who have loved me.' I, to her: 'Adieu, once more adieu! I will always love you. From today, I abandon virtue.' And that is why, oh you peoples of the earth, when you hear the winter wind moaning on the sea and by its shores, or above the large towns which have long been in mourning for me, or across the cold polar regions, say: 'It is not God's spirit passing over us: it is only the shrill sigh of Prostitution in unison with the deep groans of the Montevidean.' Children, it is I who say this to you. Then, full of mercy, kneel down. And let men, more numerous than lice, say long prayers.

8

IN the moonlight, by the sea, or in isolated parts of the country, when plunged in bitter reflections one can see everything take on yellow, vague, fantastic shapes. Tree-shadows, now quickly, now slowly, run, come back, and disappear again to return in different shapes, flattening out, sticking to the ground. In the days when I was borne along on the wings of my youth, this used to make me dream, this appeared strange to me. Now I have grown used to it. Through the leaves the wind moans its languorous notes, and the owl sings its solemn complaint, which makes the hair of those who hear it stand on end. Then dogs, driven wild, break their chains and escape from distant farms. They run all over the country-side, a prey to madness. Suddenly they stop and, wildly anxious, their eyes burning, they look around them on all sides. And just as elephants, in the desert, before they die, look up one last time at the sky, despairingly raising their trunks, not moving their eyes, so too these dogs' ears do not move, but, raising their heads, they swell out their dreadful necks and start barking in turns, like a hungry child yelling for food, or a cat who has ripped its guts open on a roof, like a woman about to give birth, or a plague-ridden patient dying in hospital, or a young girl singing a sublime air; at the stars in the north, at the stars in the east, at the stars in the south, at the stars in the west; at the moon; at the mountains which in the distance seem like giant rocks in the darkness; at the tops of their voices they bark at the cold air they are breathing, the cold air which makes the insides of their nostrils red and burning; at the silence of the night; at the screech-owls who brush against their muzzles in their oblique line of flight, as they carry off in their beaks a rat or a frog, living nourishment, sweet to the little ones; at the rabbits who scurry out of sight in the winking of an eye; at the thief, fleeing on his galloping horse after committing a crime; at the snakes stirring in the heath, who make their flesh creep, their teeth chatter; at their own barks, which frighten them; at the toads whom they crush with a quick, sharp movement of their jaws (why have they strayed so far from the swamps?); at the trees, whose gently-rustling leaves are as many mysteries that they cannot understand, which they want to fathom with their attentive, intelligent eyes; at the spiders hanging beneath their long legs, who climb up trees to escape; at the ravens who, during the day, have found nothing to eat and are returning with tired wings to their nests; at the craggy cliffs along the sea-shore; at the fires burning on the masts of invisible ships; at the muffled sound of the waves beating against the huge fish who, as they swim, reveal their black backs and then plunge down again into the fathomless depths; and against man, who makes slaves of them. After which, they start running again through the countryside, bounding across ditches, paths, fields, through weeds and over steep rocks, their paws bleeding. You would think they had caught rabies and were seeking a vast pool in which to quench their thirst. Their prolonged howls fill nature with dread. And then, woe to the belated traveller! These graveyard fiends will set upon him, will tear him to pieces and eat him, their mouths dripping blood; for they have sound teeth. The wild animals, not daring to approach and partake of the meal of flesh, fled out of sight, trembling. After some hours, the dogs, exhausted by running round, almost dead, their tongues hanging out, set upon one another and, not knowing what they are doing, tear one another into thousands of pieces with incredible rapidity. Yet they do not do this out of cruelty. One day, a glazed look in her eyes, my mother said to me: 'When you are in bed and you hear the barking of the dogs in the countryside, hide beneath your blanket but do not deride what they do: they have an insatiable thirst for the infinite, as you, and I, and all other pale, long-faced human beings do. I will even allow you to stand in front of your window to contemplate this spectacle, which is quite edifying.' Since that time, I have respected the dead woman's wish. Like those dogs, I feel the need for the infinite. I cannot, cannot satisfy this need. I am the son of a man and a woman, from what I have been told. This astonishes me ... I believed I was something more. Besides, what does it matter to me where I come from? If I had had any choice, I would rather have been born the male

39

of a female shark, whose hunger welcomes tempests, and of the tiger, whose cruelty is well-known. You, who are looking at me, go away, for the breath I exhale is poisonous. No one has yet seen the green wrinkles on my brow; nor the protruding bones of my face which are like the bones of some huge fish, or the cliffs along the sea-shore, or the steep alpine mountains which I often crossed when the hair on my head was of a different colour. And when on stormy nights I prowl around the habitations of men, my hair lashed by the wind of the tempests, my eyes aflame, isolated like a huge boulder in the middle of a path, I cover my face with a piece of velvet, black as the soot which gathers inside chimneys. No eyes may behold the ugliness which the Supreme Being, with a smile of omnipotent hatred, has set upon my face. Each morning, when for others the sun rises, spreading joy and health-bringing warmth through nature, no line of my face moves as, staring into the space which is full of darkness, crouching in the depths of my beloved cave, in a mood of despair which intoxicates me like wine, I tear my breast to shreds with my powerful hands. Yet I do not feel that I am the victim of some rabid fit! Yet I do not feel that I am the only one who suffers. Yet I feel that I still am breathing. Like a condemned man flexing his muscles and reflecting on their fate as he is about to mount the scaffold, sitting up on my bed of straw with my eyes closed I slowly move my neck from right to left, from left to right, for hours on end; I do not fall down stone dead. From time to time, whenever my neck cannot continue moving in any direction, whenever it stops before starting to turn the opposite way again, all of a sudden I look up at the horizon, through the rare gaps in the brushwood which covers the cave's entrance. And I see nothing! Nothing . . . unless it be the countryside dancing and whirling with the trees and the birds criss-crossing the air. This perplexes my blood and my brain . . . who is beating me on the head with an iron rod, like a hammer striking the anvil?

9

I PROPOSE, without emotion, to declaim the cold and serious strophe which you are about to hear. You, pay attention to its contents and beware of the painful impression which it will not fail to leave, like a brand, on your perplexed imaginations. Do not think that I am about to die, for I am no skeleton yet and old age is not yet stamped on my brow. Discard therefore any notion of comparison with the swan at the moment when its soul takes flight; see before you nothing but a monster, whose face I am glad you cannot perceive; though it is less horrible than his soul. However, I am not a criminal ... enough of this subject. It is not long ago since I saw the sea again and walked the decks of ships and my memories of this are as strong as if I only came ashore yesterday. Nevertheless be, if you can, as calm as I in reading these lines which I already regret offering you, and do not blush at the thought of what the human heart is. O octopus, with your silken look! whose soul is inseparable from mine; you most beautiful inhabitant of the terrestrial globe, who have at your disposal a seraglio of four hundred suckers; you in whom, linked indestructibly by a common accord, the sweet communicative virtue and the divine graces are nobly present, as if in their natural residence, why are you not with me, your mercury belly against my aluminium breast, both of us sitting on some sea-shore rock, to contemplate the spectacle I adore!

Old ocean, crystal-waved, you resemble proportionally the azure stains seen on the disfigured tops of mosses; you are an immense blueness on the body of the earth: I love this comparison. Thus, on seeing you first, a prolonged breath of sadness, which one would take for the murmuring of your delicious breeze, passes, leaving ineffable traces on the deeply-moved soul, and recalling to the minds of those who love you – though one does not always realize this – man's crude beginnings, when he first came to know sorrow, which has been with him ever since. I hail you, old ocean!

Old ocean, your harmoniously spherical form, which gladdens the stern countenance of geometry, reminds me only too well of man's small eyes, which are like the boar's in their minuteness and like the eyes of night-birds in the circular perfection of their contour. However, throughout the centuries, man has considered himself beautiful. For my part, I rather suppose that man only believes in his own beauty out of pride; that he is not really beautiful and he suspects this himself; for why does he look on the face of his fellow-man with such scorn? I hail you, old ocean!

Old ocean, you are the symbol of identity: always equal to yourself. You never vary essentially and, if somewhere your waves are raging, further away, in some other zone, they are perfectly calm. You are not like man who stops in the street to watch two bulldogs snarling and biting one another's necks, but who does not stop to watch when a funeral passes; who is approachable in the morning, in a black mood in the evening; who laughs today and cries tomorrow . . . I hail you, old ocean!

Old ocean, there is nothing far-fetched in the idea that you hide within your breast things which will in the future be useful to man. You have already given him the whale. You do not easily allow the greedy eyes of the natural sciences to guess the thousand secrets of your inmost organization. You are modest. Man brags incessantly of trifles. I hail you, old ocean!

Old ocean, the different species of fish to which you give nourishment have sworn no brotherhood among themselves.

Each species keeps to itself. Temperaments, shapes and sizes, which vary from species to species, satisfactorily explain what at first appears to be only an anomaly. The same is true in man's case, though he cannot plead the same excuses. If a piece of land is occupied by thirty million human beings, they feel obliged not to become involved in their neighbour's existence, rooted as they are to their own piece of ground. From great to small, each man lives like a savage in his lair, rarely venturing out to visit his fellow-creature, who is also crouching in his lair. The great universal family of men is a utopia worthy of the most mediocre logic. Furthermore, his ingratitude stands out against the spectacle of your fecund breasts; for one thinks of those many parents ungrateful enough to their creator to abandon the fruit of their wretched union . . . I hail you, old ocean!

Old ocean, your physical immensity can only be conceived if one tries to measure the active potency needed to engender the totality of your mass. You cannot be embraced in a single look. In order to contemplate you, the sights of the telescope must be turned in a continuous movement towards the four points of the horizon, just as a mathematician is obliged when doing an algebraic equation to examine individually all the various possible cases before arriving at an answer. Man eats nourishing substances and makes other efforts, worthy of a better fate, to appear huge. Let him puff himself out as much as he wishes, this adorable frog. Set your mind at rest, he will not equal you in size; at least, I suppose not. I hail you, old ocean!

Old ocean, your waters are bitter. Their taste is the same as the rancorous gall which criticism distils and pours on the arts, the sciences, everything. If someone is a genius, it condemns him as an idiot; if another has a beautiful body, then he is a frightful hunchback. Certainly, man should have a strong sense of his own imperfections, three-quarters of which are due to himself alone, in order to criticize them thus. I hail you, old ocean!

Old ocean, men, despite the excellence of their methods, though they are helped by scientific means of investigation, have not yet succeeded in measuring your vertiginous depths. Even the largest and heaviest sounding-lines have failed to plumb your inaccessible gulfs. Fish may: but not men. I have often wondered which is the easier to fathom: the depth of the ocean or the depth of the human heart! Often as I stood on ships' decks with my hand on my brow, while the moon swung fitfully between the masts, I have found myself grappling with this difficult problem, having set aside anything which could distract me from my object. Yes, which is the deeper, the more impenetrable of the two: the ocean or the human heart? If thirty years of experience of life can sway the balance from one to the other of these solutions, I will venture to say that despite the depth of the ocean, it cannot rank, as far as a comparison of this quality goes, with the depth of the human heart. I have had connections with men who were virtuous. They died at sixty, and not one of them failed to exclaim that 'he had done his best on this earth, that is he had practised charity: that is all, that was easy enough, anyone might do the same'. Who can understand how two lovers who idolized each other only the day before, separate over a misinterpreted word, one going east, one going west, with needlepoints of vengeance, hatred, love and remorse, and never see one another again, each one draped in his solitary pride. It is a miracle which recurs every day but is none the less miraculous. Who can understand how it is that we relish not only the general misfortunes of our fellows, but even the particular misfortunes of our closest friends, at the same time as being distressed about them? An unanswerable example to close the series: man hypocritically says 'yes' and thinks 'no'. That is why the wild boars of humanity have so much trust in one another and are not egoists. Psychology still has a long way to go. I hail you, old ocean!

Old ocean, your might is such that men have discovered it to their own cost. In vain do they deploy all the resources of their ingenuity . . . they are incapable of mastering you. They have met their match. I say that they have found something stronger than they. This something has a name. That name is: the ocean! The fear that you inspire in them is such that they respect you. In spite of this, you set their heaviest machines dancing with grace, elegance and ease. You make them execute gymnastic leaps right up to the sky, and admirable dives to the bottom of your domains: a circus acrobat would envy them. They are fortunate if you do not enfold them finally in your whirling, bubbling embrace, taking them on a trip – not by railway – to see your aquatic entrails, to see how the fish are, and above all, how they are themselves. Man says: 'I am more intelligent than the ocean.' That is possible; it is even quite true; but the ocean is more terrifying to him than he to the ocean: this does not need to be proven. This observant patriarch, contemporary of the first epochs of our suspended globe, smiles with pity as he witnesses naval battles among the nations. The hands of men have created hundreds of leviathans. The pompous orders given on deck, the cries of the wounded, the bursts of a cannon-fire, these are noises whose only function is to kill a few seconds. It seems that the excitement is over, the ocean's belly has swallowed everything up. Its mouth is formidable, it must be huge towards the bottom, in the direction of the unknown. And at last, to crown the stupid comedy, which is not even interesting, you can see a passing stork in the air, slowed down by fatigue, beginning to cry, though not slackening its wingspan: 'Well . . . how annoying! There were some black specks down there; I closed my eyes and they just disappeared.' I salute you, old ocean!

Old ocean, great celibate, when you survey the solemn solitude of your imperturbable realms, you are justly proud of your native magnificence and of the true praises which I so fervently bestow on you. Rocked voluptuously by the gentle effluvia of your majestic slowness – that most imposing of all the attributes with which the divine power has endowed you – you unroll in sombre mystery, along all your sublime surface, your incomparable waves, in calm awareness of your eternal power. At short intervals, they follow one another in parallel lines. No sooner does one subside than another comes to meet it, accompanied by the melancholy sound of the frothing foam, reminding us that all is foam. (Thus human beings, those living waves, die one after another, monotonously; but they make no foaming sound.) The bird of passage rests on the waves, then abandons himself to their movements, full of proud grace, until the bones of his wings have recovered their accustomed strength and he can continue his aerial pilgrimage. I wish that human majesty were only the incarnate reflection of your own. I am too demanding but my sincere wish glorifies you. Your moral grandeur, image of infinity, is as vast as the philosopher's reflections, as woman's love, as the divine beauty of the bird, as the meditations of the poet. You are more beautiful than the night. Answer me, ocean, will you be my brother? Swell more violently ... more ... still more, if you want me to compare you to God's vengeance. Lengthen your livid claws, as you clear a way over your own breast ... that is good. Unroll your frightful waves, hideous ocean, whom I alone understand, before which I fall, prostrate, at your knees. Man's majesty is a deception; he does not overawe me: but you do. Oh when you advance with your high and terrible crest, wild and hypnotic, surrounded by a court of sinuous coils of waves rolling on one another fully aware of all you are, while you utter from the depths of your breast, as if weighed down by an intense remorse whose cause I cannot discover, the perpetual suppressed moan which men so often fear, even when they contemplate you, in safety, trembling from the sea-shore, then I see that I cannot claim the illustrious right to call myself your equal. That is why, in face of your superiority, I would give you all my love (and no one knows the amount of love in my aspirations towards the Beautiful) if only because you make me think with sorrow on my fellows, who form the most ironic contrast with you, the most farcical antithesis that has ever been seen in the whole of creation: I cannot love you, I detest you. Why, then, do I return to you for the thousandth time to your welcoming arms which caress my flaming brow, your touch dispelling its feverish heat. I do not know your hidden destiny; everything about you interests me. Tell me, then, if you are the abode of the Prince of Darkness. Tell me ... tell me, ocean (only me, so as to cause no grief to those who till now have known only illusions), tell me if it is the breath of Satan that creates the tempests which whip your salt-water cloud-high. You must tell me, for I would rejoice to know that hell is so near to man. I intend this to be the last strophe of my invocation. Thus, one last time, I want to hail you and bid you goodbye. Old ocean, crystal-waved ... Free-flowing tears well up in my eyes, I have no strength to go on; for I feel that the moment has come for me to return to men, brutish in their appearance; but ... courage! Let us make a superhuman effort and, conscious of our duty, fulfil our destiny on this earth. I hail you, old ocean!

10

You will not, in my last hour, find me surrounded by priests. I want to die lulled by the waves of the stormy sea, or standing on a mountain-top ... my eyes looking upwards, no: I know my extinction will be complete. Besides, I would have no hope of mercy. Who is opening the door of my funeral chamber? I had said no one was to enter. Whoever you are, go away; but if you believe you notice some mark of sorrow or of fear on my hyena's face (I use the comparison although the hyena is more handsome than I, pleasanter to look at), if you believe this, then let me undeceive you: let him approach. It is a winter night on which the elements are dashing against one another on all sides, man is afraid, and the youth broods on some crime against one of his friends, if he is like I was in my youth. Let the wind, whose plaintive whistle has saddened mankind ever since the wind and mankind have existed, let it carry me on the bone of its wings, just before my last agony, across the world impatient for my death. I will still enjoy in secret the numerous examples of human malice (a brother, unseen, likes to observe his brothers' acts). The eagle, the raven, the immortal pelican, the wild duck, the migrant crane, awakened, chattering with cold, will see me passing by the light of the lightning, a horrible, happy spectre. They will not know the meaning of it. On earth, the viper, the toad's bulbous eyes, the tiger, the elephant; in the sea, the whale, the shark, the hammer-fish, the misshapen ray-fish, and the tooth of the polar seal, will wonder what this violation of the laws of nature is. Man, trembling, will press his head against the earth in the midst of his groans. 'Yes, I surpass you all by my innate cruelty which it was not for me to suppress. Is this the reason why you prostrate yourselves before me? Or is it because you have seen me, a new phenomenon, traversing blood-drenched space like a terrifying comet? (A shower of blood falls from my vast body, like the blackish cloud which the hurricane pushes before it.) Do not be afraid, children. I do not want to curse you. The harm you have done me is too great, too great the harm I have done you, to have been deliberate. You have gone your way and I have gone mine, both similar, both depraved. Given our resemblance of character, we must, necessarily, have met; the resultant impact has been fatal for us both.' Then men, taking courage, little by little will look up, stretching out their necks like the snail to see who is speaking thus. All of a sudden, their flaming, distorted faces, showing their terrible emotions, will grimace in such a way that wolves will shrink in fear. They will all rise at once like an immense spring. What imprecations! What voices breaking as they yell! They have recognized me. And now see how the animals of the earth are joining in with men, making their bizarre outcry heard; the hatred they both feel has turned against the common enemy, me; they are reconciled by universal assent. Winds who bear me up, carry me higher; I fear perfidy. Let us disappear gradually from their sight, witness, once again, of the consequences the passions bring in their wake, completely satisfied. I thank you, oh bat rhinolophe, for waking me with the beating of your wings, bat with the horse-shoe crested nose: I realize that it was, in fact, only, unfortunately, a passing illness, and I feel – with disgust – that I am recovering. Some say you were coming towards me to suck the little blood left in my body: why cannot this supposition be reality?

II

A FAMILY around a table with a lamp on it:

'My son, give me those scissors on that chair.'

'They are not there, mother.'

'Go and look for them in the other room, then. Do you remember the time, my dear husband, when we vowed to have a child in whom we would be born again a second time and who would be the comfort of our old age?'

'I remember, and God granted our wish. We have nothing

49

to complain of in our lot on this earth. Every day we bless Providence and its goodness. Our Edward has all his mother's charms.'

'And his father's manly qualities.'

'Here are the scissors, mother. I have found them at last.'

He resumes his work ... but someone has appeared at the front door, and has for some time been contemplating the scene before him.

'What does this sight mean? There are many people less happy than these. What shifts have they made to be able to love their existence so? Away, Maldoror, from this peaceful hearth! You do not belong here.'

He has withdrawn!

'I do not know what can have brought it about; but I feel my human faculties conflicting in my breast. My soul is ill at ease, and does not know why; the atmosphere is heavy.'

'Wife, my impressions are the same as yours; I am trembling with fear that some misfortune is going to befall us. Have faith in God; our supreme hope is in Him.'

'Mother, I can hardly breathe; my head aches.'

'You too, my son! I will wet your temples and forehead with vinegar.'

'No, dear mother.'

See, he leans back on his chair, tired.

'Something is going round and round inside me, which I cannot explain. Now the least object annoys me.'

'How pale you are! This evening will not pass without some catastrophe plunging all three of us into the lake of despair.'

I hear in the distance prolonged cries of the most acute pain.

'My son!'

'Oh mother, I am afraid.'

'Tell me quickly if you are feeling ill.'

'Mother, I feel no pain . . . I am not telling the truth.'

His father has not recovered from his astonishment: 'These are cries one sometimes hears in the silence of starless nights. Although we hear these cries, he who utters them is not near here; for one can hear groans at three leagues' distance, borne by the wind from one town to the next. People have often spoken to me of this phenomenon; but I have never had occasion to judge the truth of it for myself. Wife, you spoke to me of a catastrophe; never has greater woe existed in time's long spiral than the woe of him who now troubles the sleep of his fellows . . .'

I hear in the distance prolonged cries of the most acute pain.

'Please heaven his birth may not be a calamity for his country, which has driven him from her breast. He goes from land to land, abhorred everywhere. Some say he has been afflicted since childhood with a kind of original madness. Others assert that he is extremely and instinctively cruel, is himself ashamed of this, and that his parents died of sorrow. There are some who claim that he was branded with a surname in youth; that he has been inconsolable ever since, because his wounded sense of dignity saw in this fact a flagrant proof of the wickedness of man, which becomes apparent in his earliest years and increases later. That surname was the *vampire*!'

I hear in the distance prolonged cries of the most acute pain.

'They add that day and night, without relief or rest, horrible nightmares make him bleed from his mouth and his ears; that spectres sit at his bed's head and – impelled in spite of themselves by an unknown force, implacably persistent, in voices one moment gentle, another like the roars of battle – yell in his face this name, still tenacious, still hideous, which will only perish with the universe. Some even assert that love has reduced him to this state; or that these cries testify to his repentance at some crime buried in the night of his mysterious past. But the majority think that he is tortured by immeasurable pride, as Satan once was, and that he wants to be equal with God . . .'

I hear in the distance prolonged cries of the most acute pain.

'My son, these are exceptional confidences. I pity you for having heard them at your age, and I hope you will never imitate this man.'

'Speak, oh my Edward; answer that you will never imitate this man.'

'Oh beloved mother, to whom I owe my life, I promise you, if the holy promise of a child has any value, that I will never imitate this man.'

'That is good, my son. You must obey your mother, no matter what.'

The groans can no longer be heard.

'Wife, have you finished your work?'

'There are still a few stitches to be put in this shirt, though we have stayed up late this evening.'

'And I have not yet finished my chapter. Let us take advantage of the lamp's last gleams; for the oil is running out, let each one of us finish his work.'

The child exclaims: 'If God lets us live!'

'Radiant angel, come to me. You will walk through meadows from morning to evening; you will not have to work. My palace is built of silver walls, gold columns, and diamond doors. You will go to bed when you choose, to the sound of celestial music, without saying your prayers. When, in the morning, the sun shows its dazzling rays and the lark carries its song with it out of sight up into the sky, you can stay in bed until you become tired of it. You will walk on the most precious carpets; you will be constantly enveloped in an atmosphere composed of the perfumed essences of the most fragrant flowers.'

'It is time to rest body and mind. Rise up, mother, on your

muscular ankles. It is right that your stiff fingers should abandon this excessive work. We should avoid extremes.'

'Oh, how pleasant your life will be there. I will give you an enchanted ring; when you turn its ruby round, you will be invisible, like the princes in fairy-tales.'

'Put those daily weapons of yours into the cupboard while I, for my part, arrange my papers.'

'When you put it back in its normal position you will reappear as nature formed you, oh young magician. All this because I love you and aspire to make you happy.'

'Go away, whoever you are; take your hands off my shoulders.'

'My son, do not fall asleep, lulled by the dreams of childhood. Our evening prayer together has not begun, and you have not yet put your clothes tidily on your chair . . . on your knees! Eternal creator of the universe, you show your inexhaustible goodness even in the smallest things.'

'Do you not like clear streams where thousands of little red, blue and silvery fish dart? You will catch them with a net so fine it will itself be the bait, until it is full. You will see the shiny pebbles beneath the surface, more polished than marble.'

'Mother, look at these claws; I do not trust him; but my conscience is clear. I have nothing to reproach myself with.'

'You see us prostrate at your feet, overwhelmed by your greatness. If any proud thought has crept into our minds, we reject it immediately with the spittle of contempt and make you irremissible sacrifice of it.'

'You will bathe with little girls there, who will embrace you in their arms. When you have left the bath, they will tress you crowns of roses and carnations. They will have transparent butterfly wings and long undulating hair floating around their pretty foreheads.'

'Even if your palace were more beautiful than crystal, I

would not leave this house to follow you. I believe you are an impostor, since you speak so softly, for fear of being heard. To leave one's parents is a wicked deed. I do not intend to be an ungrateful son. As for your little girls, they are not as beautiful as my mother's eyes.'

'All our life is spent singing canticles to your glory. We have been your faithful servants up to now and such we will remain until the moment when we receive your command to leave this earth.'

'They will obey you at your slightest sign and will think of nothing but pleasing you. If you wish for the bird which never rests, they will bring it to you. If you wish for the snow-carriage which takes you to the sun in the twinkling of an eyelid, they will bring it for you. They would bring you anything you asked for! They would even bring you the kite, big as a tower, who was hidden in the moon and from whose tail birds of all kinds hang by a silken thread. Think of what you are doing . . . follow my advice.'

'Do whatever you wish. I do not want to interrupt the prayer by calling for help. Although your body vanishes whenever I try to ward it off, know that I do not fear you.'

'Before you, nothing is great, unless it be the flame from a pure heart.'

'Think of what I have told you, if you do not want to repent later.'

'Celestial Father, avert, avert the woes which may befall our family.'

'Will you not be gone, evil spirit?'

'Preserve this my dearest wife, who has consoled me in my dejection.'

'Since you refuse, I will make you weep and grind your teeth like a man on the gallows.'

'And this my loving son, whose pure lips have scarcely opened to the kisses of life's dawn.'

'Mother, he is strangling me . . . Father, help me. I cannot breathe . . . Your blessing!'

A cry of immense irony has risen in the air. See how the eagles, stunned, fall turning and turning from the clouds, literally thunderstruck by the column of air.

'His heart has stopped beating . . . And his mother dead too at the same time as the fruit of her womb, whom I can no longer recognize, he is so disfigured . . . My wife! . . . My son! . . . I recall a far-off time when I was a husband and a father!'

At this scene he had said that he would not be able to bear this injustice. If that power accorded him by the infernal spirits, or rather which he draws from within himself, is efficacious, then this child, before the night has passed, should no longer be.

12

HE who does not know how to weep (for he has always repressed the suffering within) saw that he was now in Norway. He was in the Folrol isles, looking for sea-birds' nests on sheer crevasses, and was astonished that the three-hundred-metre-long rope which holds the explorer above the precipice had been so well chosen for strength and soundness. He saw in this, whatever may be said, a striking example of human goodness, and could not believe his eyes. If it had been his responsibility to prepare the rope, he would have made little cuts in it, so that it would snap, and hurl the hunter into the sea!

'Grave-digger, do you not want to talk to me? A sperm-whale slowly rises from the ocean's depths, lifting its head above water to see the ship which is passing through these solitary regions. Curiosity was born with the universe.'

'Friend, it is impossible for me to exchange ideas with you. For a long time now the moonbeams have been shining on the marble tombstones. It is the silent hour when more than one human being dreams that he sees women in chains appear, trailing their winding-sheets, covered in blood-stains, like stars on a clear night. He who sleeps utters groans like those of a condemned man, until he awakes to find that reality is three times worse than dreams. I must finish digging this grave with my tireless spade, so that it is ready tomorrow morning. One cannot do two things at once, if one is doing serious work.'

'He thinks that digging graves is serious work! You think that digging graves is serious work!'

'When the savage pelican resolves to give its breast to be devoured by its young, with no other witness than Him who could create such love, although the sacrifice is great, this is an act which can be understood. When a young man sees a woman he would worship in the arms of a friend, he starts to smoke a cigar; he stays at home, and enters into indissoluble friendship with sorrow; this act can be understood. When a boarder at school is controlled for years which seem like centuries, from morning to evening and from evening to morning again by a pariah of civilization whose eyes are constantly fixed on him, he feels the tumultuous upsurge of lasting hatred rising like thick smoke to his brain, which seems about to burst. From the moment when he was thrown into that prison, to the approaching moment when he will leave it, an intense fever turns his face a sickly yellow, knits his brows, makes his eyes sink in their sockets. At night he broods because he does not want to sleep. During the day, his thoughts soar beyond the walls of the place of degradation until the moment comes when he escapes, or when, as if plague-ridden, he is thrown out of the eternal cloister. This act can be understood. Digging a grave often surpasses the forces of nature. How, stranger, can you expect the pick to go on digging this earth which first nourishes us then provides us with a comfortable bed, protected from the winter winds which whistle through these cold lands, when he who holds the pick – having all day been touching convulsively with his trembling hands the cheeks of those once living who are now returning to his realm – sees before him in the evening, written in flaming letters on each cross, the statement of that terrifying problem which man has not yet resolved: the mortality or immortality of the soul. I have not ceased to love God, the creator of the universe; but if after death we are no longer to exist why do I see most nights each grave opening and its inhabitants gently lifting the leaden lids, to go out and breathe the fresh air?'

'Stop your work. Emotion is sapping your strength; you seem weak as a reed; it would be utter madness to go on. I am strong; I will take your place. Stand aside, then; and let me know if I am doing anything wrong.'

'How muscular his arms are, and what a pleasure it is to watch him digging the earth with such ease.'

'You must not let your mind be tormented by useless doubt: all these graves scattered throughout the cemetery like flowers in a meadow – the comparison is not a true one – are worthy of measurement by the philosopher's serene compass. Dangerous hallucinations may come by day; but above all they come at night. Do not therefore be surprised at the fantastic visions which your eyes seem to perceive. During the day when the mind is resting, examine your conscience; it will tell you, certainly, that the God who created man and gave him part of His own intelligence possesses goodness without limits and after our earthly death will take His masterpiece to His breast. Grave-digger, why do you weep? Why these tears, like a woman's? Remember this: we are on this mastless vessel to suffer. It is man's merit that God has judged him capable of conquering his deepest sufferings. Speak and since, according to your wishes, there would be no more suffering, tell me, if your tongue is like that of other men, in what virtue, that ideal which everyone strives to attain, would then consist?'

'Where am I? Has not my character changed? I feel a powerful breath of consolation brush against my cool, calm forehead, like the spring breeze which revives old men's hopes. Who is this man who in sublime language has said things which no mere passing stranger could have uttered? What musical beauty there is in the incomparable melody of his voice! I would rather hear him speak than hear others sing. Yet the more I observe him the less candid his face appears to be. The general expression of his features contrasts singularly with these words which only the love of God could have inspired. His somewhat wrinkled forehead is marked with an indelible stigma. And this stigma which has prematurely aged him, is it a mark of honour or of infamy? Should those wrinkles be looked on with veneration? I do not know, I am afraid to know. Although he says what he does not believe, I think he has reasons for acting as he has done, moved by the few tattered shreds of charity which still remain in him. He is absorbed in reflections which are unknown to me, and he is redoubling his activity in a kind of labour to which he is unaccustomed. His skin is drenched in sweat; he does not notice. He is sadder than the feelings inspired by the sight of a child in its cradle. How sombre he is! . . . Where do you come from? Stranger, allow me to touch you, let my hands, which rarely grasp those of the living, trespass on the nobility of your body. Whatever happens, I would know what to hold on to. This hair is the finest I have ever touched in my life. Who would be so bold as to doubt my judgement of the quality of hair?

'What do you want with me? Can you not see I am digging

this grave? The lion does not wish to be disturbed when he is feasting on flesh. If you do not know that, I will teach you. Come on, hurry. Do what you wish.'

'What is now shivering at my touch, making me shiver too, is flesh, there is no doubt of it. It is real . . . I am not dreaming! Who are you, you who stoop here as you dig a grave, while I stand here doing nothing, like an idler living on others' bread? It is the hour for sleep, or for sacrificing one's repose to the pursuit of knowledge. In any event, no one is out of his house, or if he is, he has been careful to close the door, so as not to let in thieves. Everyone is enclosed in his room as best he can, while the ashes in his old fireplace can still manage to give off enough dying heat to keep the room a little warm. But you do not do what the others do. Your clothes indicate that you are from some distant land.'

'Although I am not tired, it is pointless to continue digging the grave. Now undress me; then put me into it.'

'The conversation we have just been having, the two of us, is so strange that I do not know how to answer . . . I think the gentleman is having a little joke.'

'Yes, yes, it is true, I was not serious; I do not know what I am saying any more.'

He collapsed, and the grave digger rushed to support him!

'What is wrong?'

'Yes, yes, it is true. I was lying. I was really tired when I put down the pick . . . it is the first time I have done this kind of work . . . do not take any notice of what I said.'

'My opinion of him is being confirmed more and more. He is someone who has known dreadful affliction. I pity him so much that I prefer to remain in the dark. And then he would not want to answer me, that is sure: to open one's heart in such an abnormal state is to double one's suffering.'

'Let me leave this cemetery; I will continue on my way.'

'Your legs are not strong enough to hold you. You would

get lost on the way. My duty is to offer you a simple bed. I have no other. Trust in me. Accepting my hospitality does not oblige you to reveal any of your secrets to me.'

'Oh venerable louse, you whose body has no wing-case, one day you will bitterly reproach me for not having loved your sublime understanding enough; perhaps you were right, since I feel no gratitude towards this man who is helping me. Oh lantern of Maldoror, where are you guiding his steps?'

'To my home. Whether you are a criminal who has not taken the precaution of washing his right hand with soap after committing his atrocious crime and whose guilt is revealed by close inspection of his hand; or a brother who has lost his sister; or some dispossessed monarch fleeing his realms, my truly imposing palace is worthy to receive you. It was not built of diamonds and precious stones, for it is only a poor cottage, crudely put together; but this famous cottage has a historic past, which the present renews and continues incessantly. If it could speak it would astound even you, who seem to be astonished by nothing. How often this cottage and I have seen coffins pass by containing bones soon to be more worm-eaten than the door I leant against. My countless subjects increase each day. I need no periodical census to ascertain this. Here it is the same as in life; everyone pays rates in proportion to the opulence of the dwelling he has chosen for himself; and if some miser should refuse to hand over his dues, then I have instructions to do as bailiffs do when I am dealing with his case: there is no lack of jackals and vultures who would enjoy a good meal. I have seen many drawn up under the flag of death – the once-handsome man; the man who remained handsome even after death; men, women, beggars, kings' sons; the illusions of youth, the skeletons of old men; genius; madness; idleness and its opposite; the false and the true-hearted; the mask of the proud, the modesty of the humble; vice crowned with flowers and innocence betrayed.'

'No, certainly I will not refuse your offer of a bed worthy of me, till dawn which will come soon. I thank you for your kindness Gravedigger, it is grand to contemplate the ruins of cities; but it is grander still to contemplate the ruins of human beings!'

13

THE brother of the leech was walking in the forest, slowly. He stops several times, opening his mouth to speak. But each time his throat contracts, drives back the abortive effort. At last he cries out: 'Man, when you come across a dead dog lying on its back against a sluice gate which will not let it through, do not, as others do, go up and pick out the worms crawling from its swollen belly, examine them in wonder, take out a knife and cut up a large number of them, saying as you do so that one day you will be no more than this dog. What mystery do you seek? Neither I nor the four fin-legs of the polar bear in the Boreal ocean have been able to solve the problem of life. Take care, night is approaching, you have been here since morning. What will your family say, and your little sister, seeing you arrive so late? Wash your hands, go on your way, to your home, your bed. Who is that being yonder on the horizon who dares to approach me, without fear, in crooked, agitated jumps; and what majesty, mingled with serene gentleness! His look, though gentle, is deep. His enormous eyelids play in the breeze and seem to have their own life. I do not know him. When I stare at his monstrous eyes, my body trembles – for the first time since I sucked the dry breasts of what is called a mother. There is, as it were, a halo of dazzling light around him. When he spoke, all nature was hushed, and felt a great shudder. Since it pleases you to come to me, as if drawn by a lover, I shall not resist. How beautiful he is! It hurts me to say it. You must be powerful; for you have a more than human face, sad as the universe, beautiful as suicide. I abhor you with all my being; and I would rather, from the beginning of the centuries, have had a serpent coiled about my neck than look on your eyes . . . What! . . . is it you, toad? . . . fat toad! . . . wretched toad! . . . Forgive . . . Forgive! Why have you come to this earth where the accursed are? But what have you done to your viscous, reeking pustules to look so gentle? When you came from on high by command from above, with the mission of consoling the different races of living beings, you struck the earth with the speed of the kite in your long magnificent flight; I saw you! Poor toad! How often did I think of infinity then, and of my own weakness. "Another who is superior to those of the earth," I said to myself. "By divine will. Why should I not be, too? To what purpose this injustice in divine decrees? He, the Creator, is mad; and yet, he is the strongest, his wrath is dreadful! Since you appeared to me, monarch of pools and swamps, arrayed in the glory which belongs to God alone, you have in part consoled me. But my stumbling reason founders before such greatness! Who are you? Stay . . . oh stay on this earth. Fold your white wings, and do not look up with such anxious eyes. If you must leave, let us leave together!" ' The toad sits on his haunches (which so resemble those of men) and, while slugs, lice and snails flee at the sight of their deadly enemy, he speaks in these terms: 'Maldoror, listen to me. Look on my face, calm as a mirror. I believe my intelligence is equal to yours. One day you called me the mainstay of your life. Since then I have not proved unworthy of the confidence you put in me. I am only a simple dweller among the reeds, it is true; but thanks to my contact with you, taking only what was beautiful in you, my mind has become more exalted, I can speak to you. I have come to you to haul you from the depths. Those who call themselves your friends are struck with consternation when they see you, pale and stooping, in theatres, in public places, in churches, or with your two sinewy thighs pressed against that horse which gallops only by night as it carries its phantom-master, wrapped in his long, black cloak. Abandon these thoughts, which make your heart as empty as the desert; they are more burning than fire. Your mind is so sick that you do not realize it; you think you are perfectly normal when you are uttering the most senseless words (though full of infernal grandeur). Wretch! what have you said since the day of your birth? O sad remnant of an immortal intelligence, which God created with so much love! You have engendered only curses more frightful than the sight of ravenous panthers. For my part, I would prefer to have my eyelids stuck down, to have a body without legs or arms, to have murdered a man, than to be you! Because I hate you. Why do you have this character which astonishes me? What right do you have to come to this earth and pour scorn on those who live on it, rotten wreck buoyed up by scepticism? If you do not like it here, you should return to the spheres from where you came. A city-dweller should not reside in a village, like a foreigner. We know that in space there exist spheres more spacious than our own, whose spirits have an intelligence of which we cannot even conceive. Well ... go there then. Leave this moving ground! Show at last your divine essence, which you have kept hidden until now; and as soon as possible, direct your rising flight towards your sphere, which we do not at all envy you, proud that you are! For I have not managed to discover whether you are a man or more than a man! Adieu, then. Do not hope to encounter the toad again on your way. You have been the cause of my death. I leave for eternity, to beg your forgiveness!'

14

IF it is sometimes logical to refer to the appearances of phenomena, this first song finishes here. Do not be severe on him who has as yet only been tuning his lyre; it makes such a strange sound! However, if you are impartial, you will already have recognized a strong stamp amid the imperfections. As for me, I shall resume my work, to bring out, without too great a delay, a second song. The end of the nineteenth century will have its poet (yet, to start with, he must not produce a masterpiece, but follow the law of nature); he was born on American shores, at the mouth of the Plata, where two nations, once rivals, are now striving to surpass each other in moral and material progress. Buenos-Aires, the Queen of the South, and Montevideo, the coquette, stretch out their hands in friendship across the silvery waters of the great estuary. But eternal war holds destructive sway over these lands, joyously reaping countless victims. Adieu, old man, think of me if you have read me: and you, young man, do not despair; for whatever you may believe to the contrary, you have a friend in the vampire. And counting the scab-producing sarcoptes-mite, you will have two friends!

SECOND BOOK

I

WHAT has become of Maldoror's first song, since his mouth, full of belladonna leaves, uttered it through the realms of anger, in a moment of reflection? . . . What has become of this song . . . We do not know exactly. It is not in the trees, nor in the winds. And morality, passing through that place, not foreseeing that it had found in these incandescent pages an energetic advocate, saw him making for the dark recesses and secret fibres of consciousness, with a firm straight step. This much at least we do know: since that time, toad-faced man can no longer recognize himself, often falling into fits of rage which make him seem like a beast of the forest. It is not his fault. For ages, his eyelids weighed down beneath resedas of modesty, he had believed himself to consist only of good, and a minimal quantity of evil. Revealing his heart with all its wicked plots to him, I bluntly taught him the reverse: that he consists of evil only, with a minimal quantity of good which legislators are hard pressed to prevent from evaporating completely. In this I am teaching him nothing new and I wish he would not feel eternal shame at these bitter truths of mine; but the realization of this wish would not conform to the laws of nature. In fact I am tearing the mask off his false and slime-covered face, dropping, like ivory balls into a silver bowl, the sublime lies with which he deceives himself: it is understandable, then, that he cannot summon a look of calm on to his face, even when reason disperses the darkness of pride. That is why the hero I present has brought upon himself implacable hatred, by attacking humanity, which thought itself invulnerable, through the breach of absurd philosophical tirades; these abound like grains of sand in his books, the comic qualities of which I am sometimes, whenever my reason abandons me, on the point of finding so droll – but tiresome. He had foreseen it. It is not enough to sculpt statues of goodness on the shelves of libraries where parchments are stored. O human being, here you are now, naked as a worm, in the presence of my sword of diamond! Abandon your method; the time for pride is past: prostrated before you, I offer up this prayer. There is someone who observes the smallest actions of your guilty lives. You are ensnared by the subtle network of his relentless perspicacity. Do not trust him when his back is turned; for he is watching you; do not trust him when his eyes are closed, for he is still watching you. It is difficult to conceive that you can have made the dreadful resolution to surpass the child of my imagination in matters of guile and wickedness. His least blows are fatal. If one is careful, one can teach him who does not know it that wolves and brigands do not devour one another: perhaps they are not in the habit of doing so. Therefore fearlessly entrust all care for your existence to him: he will guide it in the direction he knows so well. Do not believe in his apparent intention of making you better; for you are, to say the least, only of indifferent interest to him: even in saying this I am making allowances in your favour. What I have said does not approach the whole truth. But it is because he delights in doing evil to you, rightly convinced that you will become as wicked as he and that you will accompany him, when the time comes, into hell's gaping abyss. His place has long since been appointed, the place where an iron gibbet stands, with chains and halters hanging from it. When destiny brings him there, the dismal pit beneath the trap door will never have tasted more delicious prey, nor will he ever have contemplated a more fitting habitation. It seems that I am speaking in an intentionally paternal manner, and that humanity has no right to complain.

2

I AM grasping the pen which is going to compose the second song . . . an instrument torn from the wings of some red pyraugue! But what is wrong with my fingers? The joints remain paralysed, as soon as I want to start my work. Yet I need to write . . . It is impossible! I repeat that I need to write my thoughts. I have, like any other man, the right to submit to this natural law . . . But no, no, still the pen will not move! What is this? See the lightning flashing in the distance, across the countryside. The storm is crossing the sky. It is raining . . . Still it is raining . . . How it rains! The thunder has burst, it has beaten down on my open window, stretching me out on the floor. It has struck me on the forehead. Poor young man! Your face was already disfigured enough by premature wrinkles and the deformity of birth. It did not need this long sulphurous scar, too! (I have just assumed the wound has healed, but it will be some time before that happens.) What do the storm and the paralysing of my fingers mean? Is it a warning from on high to make me think twice about the risks I am running by distilling the saliva of my square mouth? But this storm did not frighten me. What would a legion of storms matter to me? These celestial policemen carry out their difficult duties with zeal, if I am to judge summarily by my wounded forehead. I do not need to thank the Almighty for his remarkable skill; he aimed the thunderbolt so that it cut my face exactly in two; from the forehead, where the injury was most critical, down to the neck. Let someone else congratulate him on his accuracy! But these storms attack one who is stronger than they. And so, viper-faced Eternal One, not content with placing my soul between the frontiers of madness and these frenzied thoughts which are slowly killing me, you had to decide, after mature consideration, that it befitted your majesty to make torrents of blood gush from my brow! But what can you hope to achieve? You know that I do not love you, that I in fact hate you. Why do you persist? When will your behaviour cease to be enshrouded in all the appearances of strangeness? Speak to me frankly, as a friend. Do you not suspect that your odious persecution of me is characterized by a naïve eagerness which is utterly ridiculous, though none of your seraphim would dare to point this out to you? What rage has taken hold of you? I want you to know that if you abandoned the pursuit and let me live in peace I would be grateful to you . . . Go on, Sultan, lick the floor and rid me of the blood which has stained it. The bandaging is finished: my brow has been stanched and washed with salt-water, I have wound bandelets around my face. There is not much to speak of: four blood-drenched shirts, two handkerchiefs. One would not think at first sight that Maldoror had so much blood in his arteries, for his face has only a waxen, corpse-like sheen. But there it is. Perhaps that is all the blood his body could contain, and it is probable that there is not much more left. Enough, enough, you greedy dog; leave the floor as it is; your belly is full. You must not go on drinking; for you would very quickly start vomiting. You have glutted yourself adequately, now go and lie down in your kennel; consider yourself swimming in bliss; for three immense days you will not think of hunger, thanks to the globules which you swallowed with visible and solemn satisfaction. And you, Leman, take a broom; I should like to take one, too, but I do not have the strength. You understand, do you not, that I do not have the strength? Put your tears back in their scabbard, or else I will think that you are not courageous enough to contemplate in composure the huge gash occasioned by a punishment which for me is already lost in the night of past time. You will go to the fountain and fetch two pails of water. Once you have washed the floor, you will take the linen into the next room. If the laundress comes back this evening, as she should, you will give it to her; but as it has been raining heavily for an hour and is raining still, I do not think she will leave her house; in that case, she will come tomorrow. If she should ask you where all this blood comes from, you are not obliged to answer her. Oh, how weak I am! No matter; I shall nonetheless be strong enough to raise my pen-holder, and courageous enough to work out my thoughts. What concern was it of the Creator's, that he should plague me with the thunderstorm as if I were a child? I shall nonetheless persist in my resolve to write. These bandelets are a nuisance, the air in my room is thick with blood . . .

3

MAY the day never come when Lohengrin and I pass one another in the street, brushing against one another like strangers in a hurry! Oh let me flee for ever far from this thought! The Eternal One has created the world as it is: He would have been very wise if, in the time strictly necessary to break a woman's skull with hammer-blows, He had forgotten his sidereal majesty for a moment to reveal to us the mysteries amid which our existence stifles like a fish flailing on the ship's deck. But He is great and noble; He prevails over us by the might of his conceptions; if He parleyed with men, all His disgraceful acts would be flung in His face. But . . . wretch that you are! Why do you not blush? It is not enough that the army of physical and moral afflictions which surrounds us should have been created: the secret of our shabby destiny is not even revealed to us. I know the Almighty . . . and He too

69

must know me. If we chance to be walking along the same path, His sharp eyes see me coming from afar: He crosses the road, to avoid the triple platinum dart which nature gave me for a tongue! You will do me the favour, O Creator, of letting me give vent to my feelings. Wielding my terrible ironics in my firm untrembling hand, I warn you that my heart will contain enough to keep on attacking you until my existence ends. I shall strike your hollow carcass; but so hard that I undertake to knock out the remaining portions of intelligence which you did not want to give to man, because you were jealous at the thought that he would become your equal and which, cunning bandit, you had shamelessly hidden in your bowels, as if you did not know that one day I would discover them with my never-closing eyes, take them away and share them with my fellows. This I have done and now they no longer fear you; now they deal with you on an equal footing. Come, kill me and make me repent of my boldness: I bare my breast and await you with humility. Appear, then, derisory spans of eternal punishments! Pompous displays of over-rated qualities! He has proved incapable of stopping the circulation of my blood which defies Him. Yet I have proofs that he does not hesitate to stop the breath of other human beings in their prime, who have scarcely tasted the delights of life. It is quite appalling, in my humble opinion! I have seen the Creator whetting His futile cruelty, kindling fires in which old men and children alike have died. It was not I who started the attack; it is He who forces me to turn around with my steel-cord whip, like a spinning-top. Does He not Himself provide me with the accusations I use against Him? My terrifying verve will not flag. It thrives on the senseless nightmares of my sleepless nights. All this has been written for the sake of Lohengrin; so let us return to him. Fearing that he would become like other men later, I had at first resolved to stab him to death once he had passed the age of innocence.

But I reconsidered and wisely abandoned my resolution in time. He does not suspect that his life was in danger for a quarter of an hour. Everything was ready, and the knife had been bought. It had a fine and delicate blade, for I like grace and elegance even in the instruments of death; but it was long and pointed. Just one cut in the neck, carefully piercing the carotid artery, would have been enough, I think. I am glad I acted as I did; I would have regretted it later. So, Lohengrin, do whatever you wish, whatever you please; lock me up for ever in a dark prison with scorpions as the only companions of my captivity, or pull out my eye till it falls to the ground, I shall never reproach you in the least; I am yours, I belong to you, I no longer live for myself. The pain you cause me will not be comparable to the joy of knowing that he who wounds me with his murderous hands is steeped in an essence more divine than that of his fellows! Yet it is still noble to give one's life for another human being and thus to keep alive the hope that not all men are wicked, since there has been one who overcame my mistrust and aversion and attracted to himself my bitter sympathy.

4

IT is midnight; there is no longer a single omnibus to be seen, from the Bastille to the Madeleine. I am wrong; here is one which has appeared suddenly, as if from under the earth. A few late passers-by are looking at it attentively; for it does not resemble any other. On the open top deck men are sitting, with fixed unmoving eyes like dead fish. They are hunched up tight beside one another and seem to be lifeless; apart from that, the number of passengers permitted by the regulations has not been exceeded. When the coachman whips his horses, you would think it was the whip moving his hand, not his hand moving the whip. Who can this group of strange, dumb people be? Are they moon-dwellers? There are moments when one would be tempted to believe so; but they are more like corpses. The omnibus, anxious to arrive at the last stop, tears through space, making the roads rattle ... It is disappearing! ... But a shapeless form is madly pursuing it, in its wake, amid the dust. 'Stop, I beg you, stop ... my legs are swollen from a day's walking ... I have not eaten since yesterday ... My parents have abandoned me ... I do not know what to do now ... I have made up my mind to go back home and I would be there soon if you would let me have a seat ... I am only a little boy, eight years old, I trust in you ...' It is disappearing! ... It is disappearing! ... But a shapeless form is madly pursuing it, in its wake, amid the dust. One of the men, cold-eyed, nudges his neighbour and seems to be expressing his displeasure at these silvery moans which reach his ears. The other imperceptibly nods his head in agreement, only to plunge again into motionless self-absorption, like a tortoise into his shell. Everything in the expressions of the other travellers indicates that their feelings are the same as the first two. The cries can be heard for two or three minutes, becoming shriller every second. Along the boulevard one can see windows being opened and the frightened face of someone with a candle in his hand who, having looked out into the street, slams the shutters to again, and does not reappear ... It is disappearing! ... It is disappearing! ... But a shapeless form pursues it madly, in its wake, amid the dust. Among all these stony faces, only a young man absorbed in reverie seems to feel any pity for the boy's misery. He does not dare to raise his voice on behalf of the child, who still thinks he can reach the omnibus with his aching little feet; for the other men are casting contemptuous, imperious looks at him and he knows he can do nothing against their will. Stunned, his head in his hands, his elbows resting on his knees, he wonders if this is an example of 'human charity'. Then he realizes that it is only an empty phrase which is no longer even to be found in the dictionary of poetry, and he freely admits his mistake. He says to himself: 'In fact, why should I be interested in this small child? Let us leave him behind.' Yet a hot tear rolls down the cheek of this adolescent who has just blasphemed. Uneasy, he passes his hand across his brow, as if to push away a cloud whose opacity darkens his intelligence. He is struggling in vain in the century into which he has been thrown; he feels that this is not where he belongs, and yet he cannot get out. Terrible prison! Dreadful fatality! Lombano, since that day I have been well pleased with you! I did not cease to observe you, while my face appeared to be as indifferent as that of the other travellers. With an impulse of indignation the adolescent gets up and wants to go away, so as not to participate, even unwillingly, in an evil action. I beckon him, and he comes to my side ... It is disappearing! ... It is disappearing! ... But a shapeless form pursues it madly, in its wake, amid the dust. Suddenly the cries cease; for the child has tripped over a stone protruding from the road's surface, and he has injured his head in falling. The omnibus has disappeared over the horizon and all that can be seen now is the silent street ... It is disappearing! ... It is disappearing! ... But a shapeless form no longer pursues it madly, in its wake, amid the dust. Behold a ragman passing, bending over the child with his dim lantern in his hand; he has more goodness of heart than all his fellows in the omnibus. He has just lifted up the child; you may be sure that he will heal him, that he will not abandon him as his parents did. It is disappearing! ... It is disappearing! ... But from where he is standing the ragman's piercing look pursues it madly, in its wake, amid the dust. Stupid, idiotic race! You will regret having acted thus! It is I who tell you. You will regret it! My poetry will consist exclusively of attacks on man, that wild beast, and the Creator, who ought never to have bred such vermin. Volume after volume will accumulate, till the end of my life; yet this single idea only will be found, ever present in my mind!

5

ON my daily walk I used to pass through a narrow street every day. Every day a slim ten-year-old girl would follow me along the street, keeping a respectful distance, looking at me with sympathetic, curious eyes. She was big for her age, and had a well-shaped body. Long, black hair, parted on her head, fell in separate tresses on to shoulders like marble. One day she was following me as usual; the sturdy arms of a woman of the people caught her by the hair, like a whirlwind catches a leaf, and slapped her twice, brutally, on her proud, silent face. Then she brought that straying consciousness back home. I tried in vain to appear unconcerned; she never failed to pursue me, though her presence had by now become irksome. When I took a different route, she would stop, struggling violently to control herself, at the end of the street, standing still as the statue of silence, and she would not cease looking before her until I was out of sight. One day this girl went on ahead of me in the street, and fell into step with me. If I walked faster to pass by her, she almost ran to keep the same distance between us. But if I slowed down so that there would be a large space between us, she slowed down too, and did so with all the grace of childhood. When we reached the end of the street, she slowly turned round barring my way. There was no time now for me to slip away; now I stood before her. Her eyes were swollen and red. It was easy to see that she wanted to speak to me, but did not know how to go about it. Her face suddenly turning pale as a corpse, she asked me: 'Would you be so kind as to tell me what time it is?' I told her I did not have a watch and walked rapidly away. And since that day, child of the troubled and precocious imagination, you have not seen in your narrow street the mysterious young man whose heavy sandals could be heard clattering along those winding roads. The appearance of this blazing comet will never be repeated; the mournful object of your fanatical curiosity will no longer flash on the façade of your disappointed observation. And you will often think, too often, perhaps always, of him who did not seem to be worried about the good and evil of this life, who went haphazardly away – with his face horribly dead, his hair standing on end, with a tottering gait, his arms swimming blindly in the ironic waters of ether, as if he were seeking there the bleeding prey of hope, continually buoyed up, through the immense regions of space, by the implacable snow-plough of fatality. You will see me no more, and I will no longer see you! . . . Who knows? Perhaps this young girl was not what she appeared to be. Perhaps boundless cunning, eighteen years' experience and the charm of vice were hidden beneath her innocent appearance. Young sellers of love have been known to leave the British Isles gaily behind them and cross the channel. They spread their wings, whirling in golden swarms in the Parisian light; and whenever they were seen, people would say: 'they are no more than ten or twelve years old'. But in reality they were twenty. Oh, if this supposition be true, cursed be the windings of that dark street! Horrible! horrible! the things that happen there. I think her mother struck her because she was not plying her trade skilfully enough. It is possible that she was only a child and, in that case, the mother is even more guilty. For my part, I refuse to believe this supposition, which is only a hypothesis and I prefer to see and to love, in this romantic character, a soul

revealing itself too soon . . . Ah, young girl, I charge you not
to reappear before me, if ever I return to that narrow street.
It could cost you dear! Already, boiling waves of blood and
hatred are rising to my head! No! No! I, generous enough to
love my fellows! I have resolved against it since the day of my
birth! They do not love me! Worlds will be destroyed,
granite will glide like a cormorant on the surface of the
waves before I touch the infamous hands of another human
being. Back . . . back with that hand! Young girl, you are no
angel, you will become like other women after all. No, no,
I implore you, do not reappear before my frowning squinting
eyes. In a moment of distraction I might take your arms and
wring them like linen which is squeezed after washing, or
break them with a crack like two dry branches and then
forcibly make you eat them. Taking your head between my
hands with a gentle, caressing air, I might dig my greedy
fingers into the lobes of your innocent brain – to extract, with
a smile on my lips, a substance which is good ointment to
bathe my eyes, sore from the eternal insomnia of life. I might,
by stitching your eyelids together, deprive you of the spec-
tacle of the universe, and make it impossible for you to see
your way; and then I should certainly not act as your guide.
I might, raising your virgin body in my iron arms, seize you
by the legs and swing you around me like a frond, con-
centrating all my strength as I described the final circle, and
hurling you against the wall. Each drop of your blood would
spurt on to a human breast, to frighten men and to set before
them an example of my wickedness. They will tear shreds
and shreds of flesh from their bodies; but the drop of blood
remains, ineffaceable, in the same place, and will shine like a
diamond. Do not be alarmed. I will instruct half a dozen
servants to keep the venerated remains of your body and to
protect them from the ravenous hunger of the dogs. No
doubt the body has remained stuck to the wall like a ripe

pear and has not fallen to the earth; but a dog can jump extremely high, if one is not careful . . .

6

How delightful this child is, sitting on a bench in the Tuileries garden. His bold eyes dart looks at some invisible object, far off in the distance. He cannot be more than eight years old, yet he is not playing happily and in a manner which would befit one of his years. He should at least be laughing and walking with some friend, but to do so would not be in character.

How delightful this child is, sitting on a bench in the Tuileries garden! A man, moved by a hidden design, comes and sits beside him on the bench. His manner is suspicious. Who is he? I need not tell you, for you will recognize him by his tortuous conversation. Let us listen to them, without disturbing them: 'What were you thinking of, my child?'

'I was thinking of heaven.'

'You do not need to think about heaven. It is quite enough to think about this earth. Are you tired of life, you who have only just been born?'

'No, but everyone prefers heaven to earth.'

'Not I. For since heaven, like earth, has been made by God, you may be sure that there you will meet the same evils as down here. After your death you will not be rewarded according to your merits; for if injustices are done you on this earth (and experience will la.er teach you that they are), there is no reason why, in the next life, they should not continue to be committed. The best thing you can do is not to think of God and to take the law into your own hands, since justice is denied you. If one of your companions offended you, would you not be glad to kill him?'

'But it is forbidden.'

'It is not as forbidden as you think. It is just a matter of not getting caught. The justice of laws is worthless; it is the jurisprudence of the offended party which counts. If you detested one of your companions, would you not be wretched at the thought of constantly having his image before your mind's eye?'

'That is true.'

'Such a companion would make you wretched for the rest of your life; for, seeing that your hatred is only passive, he will continue to sneer at you and hurt you with impunity. So there is only one way of putting an end to the situation; that is to get rid of one's enemy. This is the point I wanted to make, so that you would understand the basis on which our present society is founded. Each man, unless he is simply an imbecile, must take the law into his own hands. He who gains victory over his fellow-men is the cleverest and the strongest. Would you not like to dominate your fellow-men?'

'Yes, yes.'

'Then be the strongest and the cleverest. You are too young yet to be the strongest; but from today you can use guile, the finest instrument of men of genius. When the shepherd-boy David struck the giant Goliath's forehead with a stone from a sling, is it not wonderful to note that it was only cunning which enabled David to conquer his adversary and that if on the other hand it had come to a hand-to-hand fight, the giant would have crushed him like a fly? In open war you will never be able to conquer men, on whom you wish to impose your will; but with cunning you can fight alone against them all. You desire riches, palaces, fame? Or were you deceiving me when you declared these noble aspirations?'

'No, no, I was not deceiving you. But I would like to attain what I want by other means.'

'Then you will achieve nothing. Virtuous and well-meaning methods lead nowhere. You must bring into play more powerful levers, more cunningly contrived traps. Before your virtue has brought you fame, before you have achieved your goal, a hundred others will have time to leap-frog over your back and arrive at the winning-post ahead of you, so that there will be no more room left for your narrow ideas. One must be able to embrace more amply the horizon of the present time. Have you not heard for example of the immense glory victories bring? And yet victories do not simply happen. Blood must be shed, a lot of blood, to achieve them and to lay them at the feet of conquerors. Without the corpses and the scattered limbs you see on the plain where carnage is wisely practised, there would be no war and, without war, there would be no victory. You see that, when one wants to be famous, one has to dive gracefully into rivers of the blood of cannon-blasted bodies. The end excuses the means. The first thing you need to be famous is to have money. Now, as you have none, you will have to murder to acquire it; but as you are not strong enough to handle a dagger, become a thief until your limbs are big enough. That they may grow more quickly, I advise you to do gymnastics twice a day, one hour in the morning, one at night. In this way, you will be able to start your career of crime at fifteen, instead of waiting till you are twenty. Love of glory excuses everything and perhaps later when you are the master of your fellow-men you will do them almost as much good as you did them harm in the beginning! . . .'

Maldoror notices that the blood is boiling in his young interlocutor's head; his nostrils are swollen; his lips are flecked with a light white foam. He feels his pulse; it is beating very fast. Fever has taken hold of this delicate body. He fears the consequences his words will have; the wretch sneaks away, frustrated at not having been able to converse longer with the child. When even in mature years it is so difficult to master our passions, poised between good and evil, how hard it must be for so inexperienced a mind? How much more relative energy is required! The child will escape at the price of three days in bed. May it please heaven that his mother's presence should restore peace to this sensitive flower, the frail exterior of a fine soul!

7

IN a flowery grove the hermaphrodite sleeps a deep, heavy sleep, drenched in his tears. The moon's disc has come clear of the mass of clouds, and with its pale beams caresses his gentle adolescent face. His features express the most virile energy as well as the grace of a celestial virgin. Nothing about him seems natural, not even the muscles of his body, which clear their way across the harmonious contours of a feminine form. He has one arm around his head and another around his breast, as if to restrain the beating of a heart which can make no confidences, laden with the heavy burden of an eternal secret. Tired of life and ashamed of walking among beings who are not like him, he has given his soul up to despair and wanders alone, like the beggar of the valley. By what means does he live? Though he does not realize it, compassionate souls are watching over him near at hand, and they will not abandon him: he is so good! he is so resigned! Sometimes, he willingly talks with sensitive people, without touching their hands, keeping at a safe distance for fear of an imaginary danger. If he is asked why he has chosen solitude as his companion, he raises his eyes towards the sky, scarcely restraining tears of reproach against Providence; but he does not reply to this tactless question, which fills his eyes, otherwise white as snow, with the redness of the morning rose. If the conversation goes on, he becomes anxious, looks around him in all directions as if he is trying to flee from an approaching enemy, quickly waves good-bye and moves off on the wings of his reawakened sense of shame to disappear into the forest. He is generally taken for a madman. One day four masked men, acting on orders, fell upon him and bound him tightly, so that he could only move his legs. The rough thongs of the whip crashed down on his back as they told him to make his way without delay to the Bicêtre road. He started to smile as the blows rained down on him and spoke to them with such feeling and intelligence of the many human sciences he had studied which indicated great erudition in one who had not yet crossed the threshold of youth, and of the destiny of mankind, fully revealing the poetic nobility of his soul, that his attackers, chilled to the blood with fear at the act which they had committed, untied his broken limbs and, falling at his knees, begged forgiveness, which was granted, and went away, showing signs of a veneration which is not ordinarily accorded to men. Since this event, which was much spoken of, everyone has guessed his secret, but they pretend not to know it so as not to increase his suffering; and the government has granted him an honorary pension, to make him forget that there was a moment when, without preliminary investigation, they had wanted to put him by force into a lunatic asylum. He keeps half of the money for his own use; the rest he gives to the poor. When he sees a man and a woman walking along a path shaded by plane-trees, he feels his body splitting from top to bottom into two parts, and each new part going to embrace one of the walkers; but it is only a hallucination, and reason soon takes over again. That is why he mixes neither with men nor with women; for his excessively strong sense of shame, which arose with the idea that he was only a monster, prevents him from giving his burning love to anyone. He would consider it self-profanation, and profanation of others. His pride repeats this axiom to him: 'Let each remain among his own kind.' His pride, I say, because he fears that by sharing his life with a man or a woman, he will sooner or later be reproached, as if it were a dreadful crime, for the conformation of his body. So he shelters behind his self-esteem, offended by this impious supposition, which comes from him alone, and he persists in remaining alone and without consolation amidst his torments. There in a flowery grove the hermaphrodite sleeps a deep heavy sleep, drenched in his tears. The birds, waking, contemplate, enraptured, this melancholy figure, through the branches of the trees, and the nightingale will not sing its crystal-toned cavatinas. The presence of the unhappy hermaphrodite has made the wood as august as a tomb. Oh wanderer misled by your spirit of adventure to leave your father and mother from the earliest age; by the sufferings you have undergone from thirst, in the desert; by the homeland you are perhaps seeking, after long wanderings as an outlaw in strange lands; by your steed, your faithful friend, who with you has borne exile and the inclemency of the climes which your roaming disposition has brought you through; by the dignity which is given man by journeys through distant lands and unexplored seas, amid the polar ice-floes, or under the torrid desert sun, do not touch with your hand, like a tremor of the breeze, these ringlets of hair on the ground among the grass. Stand back several steps, and you will be acting more wisely. This hair is sacred; it is the wish of the hermaphrodite himself; he does not wish this hair, perfumed by the mountain breeze, to be kissed religiously by human lips, nor his brow, which shines at this moment like the stars of the firmament. But it is better to think of it as a star which has fallen from its orbit, passing through space and on to this majestic brow, which it surrounds with its diamantine brightness, like a halo. Night, casting off sadness, puts on all its charms to fête the sleep of this incarnation of modesty, this perfect image of angelic innocence: the gentle humming of insects is less audible. The branches of trees bend their bushy heights over him to protect him from the dew, and the breeze, plucking the strings of its melodious harp, sends its joyous harmonies through the universal silence towards those closed eyelids which are dreaming that they are present at the cadenced concert of the spheres. He dreams that he is happy, that his bodily nature has changed; or that at least he has flown off on a dark-red cloud towards another sphere inhabited by beings whose nature is the same as his! Alas! let this illusion continue until dawn wakes him! He dreams that flowers are dancing around him like huge mad garlands, imbuing him with their suave perfumes, while he sings a hymn of love in the arms of a human being of magical beauty. But what his arms are clasping is only twilight mist; and when he awakes, his arms will clasp it no longer. Do not awaken, hermaphrodite; do not awaken yet, I implore you. Why will you not believe me? Sleep . . . sleep on for ever. May your breast rise as you pursue the chimerical hope of happiness, I grant you that; but do not open your eyes. Ah! do not open your eyes! I want to leave you thus, so that I do not have to witness your awakening. Perhaps, one day, with the help of a voluminous book, I will tell your story in moving words, appalled by all that it contains and by the moving lessons to be drawn from it. Till now, I have not been able to; for every time that I wanted to, copious tears would fall on to the paper, and my fingers would tremble, but not from old age. But now I want to have the courage at last. I am shocked that my nerves are no stronger than a woman's and that I faint like a girl every time I reflect on your great misery. Sleep . . . sleep on; but do not open your eyes. Ah! do not open your eyes! Adieu, hermaphrodite: I will not fail to pray every day for you (if it were for myself, I should not pray). May peace be with you!

8

WHEN I hear a soprano uttering her vibrant and melodious notes, my eyes are filled with a hidden flame, flashes of pain shoot across them, and the burst of alarm-bell and cannonade resound in my ears. What can be the reason for this deep loathing of everything related to man? If those harmonies are played on the chords of an instrument, I listen in delight to the pearly notes wafting in cadence through the elastic waves of the atmosphere. Sense conveys to my hearing an impression so sweet as to melt nerves and thought. The magic poppies of an ineffable drowsiness envelop, like a veil filtering the light of day, the active power of my senses and the tenacious strength of my imagination. The story is told that I was born in the arms of deafness! In the first years of my childhood, I could not hear what was said to me. When, with the greatest difficulty, they had taught me to speak, it was not until after I had read on a sheet of paper what someone had written that I could in turn communicate the thread of my ideas. One day, woeful day, I had grown in beauty and innocence. Everyone admired the intelligence and goodness of the divine youth. Many a conscience blushed inwardly when it contemplated those clear features in which his soul was enshrined. No one approached him without veneration, for they had noticed in his eyes the look of an angel. But no, I knew only too well that the happy roses of youth would not flower perpetually, wreathed in capricious garlands, on his modest and noble brow, which all mothers used to kiss with frenzied devotion. It was beginning to seem to me that the universe, with its starry vault of impassible and tormentingly mysterious globes, was not perhaps the most imposing thing I had dreamt of. And so, one day, tired of trudging along the steep path on this earthly journey, trudging along like a drunkard through the dark catacombs of life, I slowly raised my splenetic eyes, ringed with bluish circles, towards the concavity of the firmament and I, who was so young, dared to penetrate the mysteries of heaven! Not finding what I was seeking, I lifted my eyes higher, and higher still, until I saw a throne made of human excrement and gold, on which was sitting – with idiotic pride, his body draped in a shroud of unwashed hospital linen – he who calls himself the Creator! He was holding in his hand the rotten body of a dead man, carrying it in turn from his eyes to his nose and from his nose to his mouth; and once it reached his mouth, one can guess what he did with it. His feet were dipped in a huge pool of boiling blood, on the surface of which two or three cautious heads would suddenly rise up like tapeworms in a chamber-pot, and as suddenly submerge again, swift as an arrow. A kick on the bone of the nose was the familiar reward for any infringement of regulations occasioned by the need to breathe a different atmosphere; for, after all, these men were not fish. Though amphibious at best, they were swimming underwater in this vile liquid! . . . until, finding his hands empty, the Creator, with the first two claws of his foot, would grab another diver by the neck, as if with pincers, and lift him into the air, out of the reddish slime, delicious sauce. And this one was treated in the same way as his predecessor. First he ate his head, then his legs and arms, and, last of all, the trunk, until there was nothing left; for he crunched the bones as well. And so it continues, for all the hours of his eternity. Sometimes, he would shout: 'I created you, so I have the right to do whatever I like to you. You have done nothing to me, I do not deny it. I am making you suffer for my own pleasure.' And he would continue his savage meal, moving his lower jaw, which in turn moved his brain-bespattered beard. Oh reader, does not this last-mentioned detail make your mouth water? Cannot whoever wishes also eat brains just the same, which taste just as good and just as fresh, caught less than a quarter of an hour before in the lake – the brains of a fish? My limbs paralysed, utterly dumb, I contemplated this sight for some time. Thrice I nearly keeled over, like a man in the throes of an emotion which is too strong for him; thrice I managed to keep my feet. No fibre of my body was still; I was trembling like the lava inside the volcano. Finally, my breast so constricted that I could not breathe the life-giving air quickly enough, my lips opened slightly and I uttered a cry . . . a cry so piercing . . . that I heard it! The shackles of my ears were suddenly broken, my ear-drum cracked at the shock of the sounding mass of air which I had expelled with such energy, and a strange phenomenon took place in the organ condemned by nature. I had just heard a sound! A fifth sense had developed in me! But what pleasure could I have derived from such a realization? Since then, no human sound has reached my ears without bringing with it the feeling of grief which pity for great injustice arouses. Whenever anyone spoke to me, I remembered what I had seen one day above the visible spheres, and the translation of my stifled feelings into a violent yell, the tone of which was identical to that of my fellow-beings! I could not answer him; for the tortures inflicted on man's weakness in that hideous red sea passed before my eyes roaring like scorched elephants and brushing with their burning wings against my singed hair. Later, when I knew mankind better, this feeling of pity was coupled with intense rage against this tiger-like stepmother whose hardened children know only how to curse and do evil. The brazen lie! they say that evil is the exception among them! That was long ago; since then I have not spoken a word to anyone. Oh you, whoever you may be, when you are beside me, do not let any sound escape your vocal cords; do not with your larynx strive to outdo the nightingale; and, for yourself, do not on any account attempt to make your soul known to me by means of language. Maintain a religious silence, uninterrupted by the least sound. Cross your hands humbly on your breast, and lower your eyelids. I have told you this, and since that vision revealed to me the supreme truth, too many nightmares have sucked my throat, by day and by night, for me to have any courage left to renew, even in thought, the sufferings I underwent in that infernal hour, the memory of which remorselessly pursues me. Oh! when you hear the avalanche of snow falling from the high mountain; the lioness in the barren desert lamenting the disappearance of its cubs; the tempest accomplishing its destined purpose; the condemned man groaning in prison on the eve of his execution; and the savage octopus telling the waves of the sea of his victory over swimmers and the shipwrecked, then you have to acknowledge it: are not these majestic voices finer than the sniggering of men?

9

THERE exists an insect which men feed at their own expense. They owe it nothing; but they fear it. This insect, which does not like wine but prefers blood, would, if its legitimate needs were not satisfied, be capable, by means of an occult power, of becoming as big as an elephant and of crushing men like ears of corn. And one has to see how respected it is, how it is surrounded with fawning veneration, how it is held in high esteem, above all the other animals of creation. The head is given it as its throne, and it digs its claws solemnly into the roots of the hair. Later, when it is fat and getting on in age, it is killed, following the custom of an ancient race, to prevent it from suffering the hardships of old age. It is given a magnificent hero's funeral, with prominent citizens bearing the coffin on their shoulders straight to the grave. Above the damp earth which the grave-digger is shrewdly moving with his spade, multicoloured sentences are combined on the immortality of the soul, the emptiness of life, the incomprehensible will of Providence, and the marble closes for ever on this life, filled with such toil, and which is now but a corpse. The crowd disperses, and night soon covers the walls of the cemetery with shadows.

But be consoled, human beings, for this grievous loss. Look at his countless family, which he so freely bestowed on you and which is advancing, that your despair should be less bitter, should be, so to speak, sweetened by these surly abortions, which will later grow into magnificent lice of remarkable beauty, monsters of wise demeanour. Under its maternal wing it has incubated several dozen beloved eggs in your hair, dried by the unremitting suction of these fearsome strangers. And now the time has come for the eggs to hatch. Do not fear, these youthful philosophers will soon grow, in the course of this ephemeral life. They will grow so much that they will soon make you aware of it with their claws and their suckers.

And yet you still do not know why they do not devour the bones of your head, why they are satisfied with ceremoniously extracting the quintessence of your blood. Wait a moment and I will tell you: it is because they do not have the strength. You may be sure that if their jaws conformed to the measure of their infinite desires, your brain, the retina of your eyes, your spinal column and all your body would be consumed. Like a drop of water. Take a microscope and examine a louse at work on a beggar's head; you will be surprised. Unfortunately these plunderers of long hair are tiny. They would be no good for conscription; for they are not of the size which the law requires. They belong to the short-legged lilliputian world, and the blind do not hesitate to classify them among the infinitesimally small. But woe to the sperm-whale that fought against a louse! Despite his size, he would be devoured in a trice. Not even his tail would remain to tell the news. An elephant can be stroked. But not a louse. I would not advise you to try this dangerous experiment. Beware, if you have a hairy hand, or even if it is only flesh and bone. Your fingers have had it, they are beyond hope. They will crack as if they were on the rack. By a strange enchantment, the skin disappears. Lice are incapable of doing as much evil as their imagination contemplates. If you find a louse, go on your way, do not lick its papilla with your tongue. An accident would happen to you. Cases have been known. Never mind, I am already content with the amount of harm it has done you, O human race; but I would like it to do you even more harm.

How much longer will you keep up the worm-eaten cult of this god, who is insensible to your prayers and to the generous sacrifices that you offer him as an expiatory holocaust? Can you not see that this horrible manitou is not grateful for the bowls of blood and brains which you lay on his altars, piously decorated with garlands of flowers. He is not grateful ... for earthquakes and tempests have been raging uninterruptedly since the beginning of all things. And nonetheless (this is a spectacle worthy of observation), the more indifferent he is, the more you admire him. It is clear that you are wary of his attributes, which he hides; and your reasoning is based on the consideration that a divinity of such extreme power can only show such disdain for the faithful who obey the commandments of his religion. For that reason different gods exist in each country: here, the crocodile, there, the prostitute. But when it comes to the louse, of holy name, the nations of the earth, one and all kissing the chains of their slavery, kneel together in the august sanctuary before the pedestal of this shapeless and bloodthirsty idol. Any people that did not obey its own grovelling instincts and made as if to rebel, would sooner or later disappear from the face of the earth like an autumn leaf, destroyed by the vengeance of the inexorable god.

O louse of the shrivelled-up eyes, as long as rivers pour their waters into the depths of the sea; as long as the stars gravitate along their fixed orbits; as long as the dumb emptiness has no horizon; as long as humanity tears its own sides apart with disastrous wars; as long as divine justice hurls its avenging thunderbolts down on this selfish globe; as long as man denies his creator and, not without reason, snaps his fingers at him, combining insolence and disdain, your reign over the universe will be assured, and your dynasty will extend its influence throughout the centuries. I salute you, rising sun, heavenly liberator, you, the invisible enemy of man. Continue to tell lewdness to couple with him in impure embraces and swear to him with oaths not written in powder that she will be his faithful lover until eternity. Kiss from time to time the dress of the great unchaste, in memory of the important services she does not fail to render you. If she did not seduce man with her lascivious breasts, it is improbable that you would exist, you, the product of this reasonable and logical coupling. O son of lewdness! tell your mother that if she abandons man's bed and thenceforward walks a solitary way, alone and without support, she will put your existence at risk. And let her fragrant womb, which has borne you for nine months, be stirred at the thought of the dangers which her tender fruit, so gentle and peaceful, but already cold and savage, would run as a result. Lewdness, queen of empires, keep before my hate-filled eyes the sight of your starving offspring's imperceptible growth. To achieve this goal, you know that you have only to stick more closely to man's sides. And you may do this without compromising modesty, since both of you have been married for a long time.

As for me, if I may be permitted to add a few words to this

hymn of glorification, I will say that I have had a grave built, forty square leagues in area, and of a corresponding depth. There, in its foul virginity, lies a living mine of lice. It fills the bottom of the pit, and thence it spreads out in wide thick veins in all directions. This is how I built this mine. I pulled a female louse out of the hair of man. I slept with it for three consecutive nights, then I threw it into the pit. Destiny saw to it that human fecundation, which would have been impossible in other similar cases, was successful this time; and after a few days, thousands of monsters, crawling in a compact mass of matter, first saw the light of day. This hideous mass became more and more immense in time, acquiring the liquid property of mercury, and branched out into several groups which at the moment sustain themselves by eating one another (the birth-rate being higher than the mortality-rate), unless I throw them as fodder a new-born bastard whose mother wished its death, or the arm of some young girl which I cut off during the night, after drugging her with chloroform. Every fifteen years, the generations of lice which live off men diminish noticeably and infallibly predict the approaching era of their complete destruction. For man, more intelligent than his enemy, has managed to conquer him. Then, with an infernal spade which increases my strength, I extract blocks of lice from this inexhaustible mine, break them up with axe-blows, and transport them into the arteries of cities. There they dissolve on contact with human temperature as in the first days of their formation in the winding galleries of the underground mine, they dig down into the gravel and spread like little streams into the dwelling-places of men like malign spirits. The watchdog gives a low bark, for it seems to him that a legion of unknown beings is penetrating the pores of the walls, bringing terror to the bed of sleep. Perhaps, at least once in your life, you have heard one of these wailing, prolonged barks. With his feeble eyes he tries to pierce the darkness of the night; for all this passes the understanding of his dog-brain. This humming irritates him, he feels he has been betrayed. Millions of the enemy swoop down thus on each city, like clouds of locusts. That will be enough for fifteen years. They will fight against man, and inflict sharp wounds on him. After this period, I will send others. When I am smashing the blocks of living matter, it may happen that one fragment is denser than another. Its atoms are striving furiously to break off from the agglomeration and go and torment mankind; but the cohesion of the whole is such that it resists all their efforts. In a supreme convulsion, they make such an effort that the block, unable to scatter its living elements, soars right into the air as if set off by gunpowder, then falls again, and buries itself firmly in the ground. Sometimes, a pensive peasant sees an aerolith vertically rending space, moving downwards towards a cornfield. He does not know where the stone comes from. Now you have, clearly and succinctly, the explanation of the phenomenon.

If the face of the earth were covered with lice as the seashore is covered with grains of sand, the human race would be destroyed, a prey to dreadful pain. What a sight! With me, motionless on my angel wings in the air to contemplate it!

10

O RIGOROUS mathematics, I have not forgotten you since your wise lessons, sweeter than honey, filtered into my heart like a refreshing wave. Instinctively, from the cradle, I had longed to drink from your source, older than the sun, and I continue to tread the sacred sanctuary of your solemn temple, I, the most faithful of your devotees. There was a vagueness in my mind, something thick as smoke; but I managed to mount the steps which lead to your altar, and you drove away this dark veil, as the wind blows the draught-board. You replaced it with excessive coldness, consummate prudence and implacable logic. With the aid of your fortifying milk, my intellect developed rapidly and took on immense proportions amid the ravishing lucidity which you bestow as a gift on all those who sincerely love you. Arithmetic! Algebra! Geometry! Awe-inspiring trinity! Luminous triangle! He who has not known you is a fool! He would deserve the ordeal of the greatest tortures; for there is blind disdain in his ignorant indifference; but he who knows you and appreciates you no longer wants the goods of the earth and is satisfied with your magical delights; and, borne on your sombre wings, wishes only to rise in effortless flight, constructing as he does a rising spiral, towards the spherical vault of the heavens. Earth only offers him illusions and moral phantasmagoria; but you, concise mathematics, by the rigorous sequence of your unshakeable propositions and the constancy of your iron rules, give to the dazzled eyes a powerful reflection of that supreme truth whose imprint can be seen in the order of the universe. But the order surrounding you, represented by the perfect regularity of the square, Pythagoras' friend, is greater still; for the Almighty has revealed himself and his attributes completely in this memorable work, which consisted in bringing from the bowels of chaos the treasures of your theorems and your magnificent splendours. In ancient epochs and in modern times more than one man of great imagination has been awe-struck by the contemplation of your symbolic figures traced on paper, like so many mysterious signs, living and breathing in hidden ways not understood by the profane multitudes; these signs were only the glittering revelations of eternal axioms and hieroglyphs, which existed before the universe and will remain after the universe has passed away. And then this man of vision wonders, leaning towards the precipice of a fatal question-mark, how it is that mathematics contains so much imposing grandeur and undeniable truth, whereas, when he compares it with mankind, he finds among the latter only false pride and deceitfulness. And then this saddened superior spirit, whose noble familiarity with your precepts has made him even more aware of the pettiness and incomparable folly of mankind, buries his white-haired head in his fleshless hands and remains engrossed in his supernatural meditations. He kneels before you and in his veneration pays homage to your divine face, the very image of the Almighty. In my childhood you appeared to me one May night by the light of the moonbeams in a green meadow beside a clear stream, all three equal in grace and modesty, all three full of the majesty of queens. You took a few steps towards me in your long dresses floating like mist and lured me towards your proud breasts like a blessed son. Then I ran up eagerly, my arms clenched around your white throats. I fed gratefully on your rich manna, and I felt humanity growing within me, becoming deeper. Since that time, rival goddesses, I have not abandoned you. How many mighty projects, since that time, how many sympathies which I had believed to be engraved on the pages of my heart as on marble, have been slowly effaced from my disillusioned reason by their configurative lines, as the oncoming dawn effaces the shadows of the night! Since that time, rival goddesses, I have seen death whose intention, clear to the naked eye, was to people graveyards, I have seen him ravaging battlefields fertilized by human blood from which morning flowers grow above human remains. Since then I have witnessed revolutions on this globe, earthquakes, volcanoes with their blazing lava, the simoun of the desert and tempest-torn shipwrecks have known my presence as an impassive spectator. Since that time I have seen several generations of human beings lift up their wings in the morning and move off into space with the inexperienced joy of the chrysalid greeting its first metamorphosis, only to die in the evening before sunset, their heads bowed like withered flowers blown by the plaintive whistling of the wind. But you remain always the same. No change, no foul air disturbs the lofty crags and immense valleys of your immutable identity. Your modest pyramids will last longer than the pyramids of Egypt, those anthills raised by stupidity and slavery. And at the end of all the centuries you will stand on the ruins of time, with your cabbalistic ciphers, your laconic equations and your sculpted lines, on the avenging right of the Almighty, whereas the stars will plunge despairingly, like whirlwinds in the eternity of horrible and universal night, and grimacing mankind will think of settling its accounts at the Last Judgement. Thank you for the countless services you have done me. Thank you for the strange qualities with which you enriched my intellect. Without you in my struggle against man I would perhaps have been defeated. Without you, he would have made me grovel in the dust and kiss his feet. If it had not been for you, he would have flayed my flesh and bones with his perfidious claws. But I have kept on my guard, like an experienced athlete. You gave me the coldness of your sublime conceptions, free of all passion. And I used it to reject scornfully the ephemeral pleasures of my short journey, and spurn the well-meaning but deceptive advances of my fellows. You gave me the dogged prudence which can be deciphered at every step of your admirable methods of analysis, synthesis and deduction. I used it to outdo the pernicious wiles of my mortal enemy and to attack him skilfully in turn, plunging into his entrails a sharp dagger which will forever remain buried in his body; for it is a wound from which he will never recover. You gave me logic which is, as it were, the soul itself of your teachings, full of wisdom, and with its syllogisms, the complex labyrinth of which makes it nonetheless intelligible, my intellect felt its audacious strength increasing twofold. By means of this terrible auxiliary, I discovered in mankind, as I swam towards the depths, opposite the reef of hatred, the black and hideous wickedness which lurked amidst the noxious miasmata admiring its navel. First I discovered in the darkness of his entrails that nefarious vice, evil! superior in him to good. With the poisonous weapon you lent me I brought down from his pedestal, built by man's cowardice, the Creator himself! He gnashed his teeth and was subjected to this ignominious insult; for he had as adversary one stronger than he. But I will leave him aside like a bundle of string, in order to fly down lower ... The thinker Descartes once observed that nothing solid has ever been built on you. That was an ingenious way of pointing out that not just anybody can immediately discover your inestimable value. In fact, what could be more solid than the three principal qualities above mentioned which rise up, joined in a single crown, to the august summit of your colossal architecture? A monument which is incessantly growing as discoveries are made daily in your diamantine mines, and with all the scientific researches carried out in your domains. O holy mathematics, may I for the rest of my days be consoled by perpetual intercourse with you, consoled for the wickedness of man and the injustice of the Almighty!

II

'O LAMP with the silver burner, my eyes perceive you in the air, companion of cathedral vaults, and they ask why you are hanging there. It is said that at night your light illuminates the rabble who come to adore the Almighty, that you show the repentant the way to the altar. Listen, that is very probable; but ... do you need to perform such services for those to whom you owe nothing? Let the columns of the basilica remain plunged in darkness; and when a blast of the tempest, on which the demon is borne whirling through space, penetrates with him into the holy place, spreading terror, instead of struggling courageously against the foul gust of the Prince of Evil, go out, suddenly, as he blows feverishly on you, so that he may select his victims unseen from among the kneeling believers. If you do that, you may say that I owe you all my happiness. When you shine thus, spreading your dull but adequate light, I dare not succumb to the promptings of my character and I remain standing beneath the sacred portico, looking through the half-open door at those who escape my vengeance by hiding in the bosom of the Lord. O poetic lamp! you who would be my friend if you could understand me, when my feet are treading the basalt of churches in the night hours, why do you begin to shine in a way which, I must confess, seems extraordinary to me? Your gleams are then tinged with the white hue of electric light; the eye cannot look at you; and you illuminate with a new and powerful flame every detail of the Creator's kennel, as if you were in the throes of holy wrath. When, having blasphemed you, I withdraw, you become imperceptible, pale and modest again, sure in the knowledge that you have accomplished an act of justice. Tell me now; would it be because you know all the windings of my heart, that when I happen to appear where you are keeping watch, you eagerly indicate my pernicious presence, drawing the attention of the worshippers to the direction where the enemy of man has just appeared. I am inclined towards this view; for I, too, am beginning to know you; and I know who you are, old witch, keeping watch so well over sacred mosques where your curious master struts like a cock's crest. Watchful guardian; your mission is a mad one; I warn you; the first time you point me out to my cautious fellow-beings by increasing the strength of your phosphorescent light (I do not like this

97

optical phenomenon which is not, by the way, mentioned in any textbook of physics), I will take you by the skin of your breast, hooking my claws into the scabs of your scurvy nape, and I will fling you into the Seine. I do not intend, when I leave you alone, that you should deliberately behave in a manner harmful to me. There I will allow you to shine as much as I please; there you will defy me with your inextinguishable smile; there, convinced of the ineffectiveness of your criminal oil, you will urinate bitterly.' Having spoken thus, Maldoror does not leave the temple and remains with his eyes fixed on the lamp of the holy place ... He believes there is a kind of provocation in the attitude of this lamp, which he finds in the highest degree irritating because of its untimely presence. He says to himself that if there is a soul enclosed in the lamp it is cowardly of it not to answer his honest attack with sincerity. He beats the air with his sinewy arms, wishing the lamp would change into man; and then it would have a hard time for a quarter of an hour, he could promise it that. But by what means can a lamp change into a man; it is unnatural. He does not give up, and goes in search of a flat stone with a filed-down edge on the floor of the wretched pagoda. He hurls it violently into the air; the chain is cut in the middle like grass by a scythe, and the implement of worship falls to the ground, spreading its oil on the tiles. He seizes the lamp to take it outside with him, but it resists and grows bigger. He seems to see wings at its sides, and the top part takes on the shape of an angel. The whole thing is trying to rise into the air and fly off; but he holds it back with a firm hand. A lamp and angel forming one and the same body, that is something one does not often see. He recognizes the form of the lamp; he recognizes the form of the angel; but he cannot separate them in his mind; in fact they are in reality cleaving to one another, and form only one free and independent body; but he thinks that some cloud has passed before his eyes; causing him to lose something of the excellence of his eyesight. Nevertheless, he prepares courageously for the struggle, for his adversary shows no fear. The naïve tell those credulous enough to believe them that the sacred portal closed of its own accord, turning on its anguished hinges lest anyone should witness the impious struggles whose changes of fortune were going to occur within the walls of the profaned sanctuary. The man in the coat, though serious wounds are being inflicted on him by an invisible sword, tries to bring his mouth near to the angel's face; he thinks only of that, and all his efforts tend towards this goal. The angel's energy is ebbing, and he seems to have a presentiment of his fate. He only struggles weakly now and one can see the moment coming when his adversary will be able to kiss him with ease, if that is what he wishes to do. Well, the moment has come. With his muscles he strangles the angel who can no longer breathe, pushing back his head and leaning on his odious breast. For a moment he is moved at the thought of the fate which awaits this celestial being whose friend he would gladly have become. But he says that he is the Lord's envoy and he cannot control his wrath. It is done; something horrible is going to return to the cage of time! He leans over and puts his tongue, dripping with saliva, on to the cheek of the angel, who is looking up imploringly. For some time, he moves his tongue up and down his cheek. Oh! . . . Oh . . . look . . . look! . . . the white and pink cheek has become black as coal! It is emitting putrid miasmata. It is gangrene; there is no longer any room for doubt. The gnawing evil spreads all over his face and from there ravages the lower parts; soon the whole body is nothing but one vast vile sore. He himself, terror-stricken (for he did not think that his tongue contained such strong poison), picks up the lamp and rushes out of the church. Once outside, he sees a blackish shape with burnt wings laboriously flying towards the regions of heaven. They look at one another as the angel climbs towards the serene regions of the good, whereas he, Maldoror, descends into the vertiginous abysses of evil . . . What a look! All that mankind has thought for sixty centuries, all that it has yet to think in the centuries to come, could easily be contained in that supreme adieu, so much did it say! But it is obvious that these were thoughts far higher than those which spring from human intelligence; first of all because of the two characters and then because of the circumstances. This look bound them in eternal friendship. He is astounded that the Creator can have such noble envoys. For a moment, he thinks that he has made a mistake and wonders if he ought to have followed the road of evil as he has done. His disquiet has passed; he persists in his resolution; and it is glorious, according to him, to conquer the Almighty sooner or later, in order to reign in his stead over the entire universe, and over legions of such beautiful angels. The angel makes it clear without speaking that he will reassume his original form as he flies nearer heaven; and he lets fall a tear which cools the brow of him who gave him gangrene; and gradually disappears, rising like a vulture amidst the clouds. The guilty one looks at the lamp, the cause of all the preceding events. He runs like a madman through the streets towards the Seine and flings the lamp over the parapet. It whirls around for a few seconds and then plunges down into the murky waters. Since that day, every evening from nightfall onwards a shining lamp can be seen which rises and floats gracefully on the water, passes beneath the arches just off the Pont Napoléon, bearing instead of handles two charming little angel's wings. It moves forward slowly on the water, passes beneath the arches of the Pont de la Gare and the Pont d'Austerlitz, and continues on its silent course along the Seine as far as the Pont d'Alma. Once there, it turns easily again to follow the course of the river, returning after four hours to its starting point. Its light, white as electric light, eclipses that of the gas-lamps bordering the banks between which she advances like a queen, solitary, inscrutable, with an inextinguishable smile, not bitterly spilling its oil. In the beginning, the boats gave it chase; but it foiled these vain efforts, escaped from all pursuits, diving like a coquette to reappear a long way further on. Now superstitious sailors stop singing when they see it, and row in the opposite direction. When you are crossing a bridge by night, be careful; you are bound to see the lamp shining somewhere or other; although it is said that it does not show itself to everyone. When a human being with something on his conscience crosses the bridge, its light suddenly goes out, and the man, terror-stricken, vainly and desperately peers at the surface and the mudbanks of the river. He knows what that means. He would like to believe that he has seen the celestial light; but no, he says that the light only came from the front of the boats or from the reflection of the gas-lamps; and he is right . . . He knows that he is the cause of the lamp's disappearance; and, plunged in sad reflections, he quickens his step to arrive at his house. Then the lamp with the silver burner reappears on the surface and continues on its way with elegant and capricious arabesques.

12

LISTEN, human beings, to the thoughts which came to me in my childhood when I awoke with my red verge: 'I have just awoken; but my thoughts are still dull. Each morning I feel a heaviness in my head. It is rare for me to be able to rest at night; for frightful dreams torment me when I manage to get to sleep. In the day my mind is weary with strange meditations, while my eyes gaze aimlessly into space; and at night I cannot sleep. When shall I sleep then? And yet nature needs to insist on its rights. Since I disdain her, she makes my face pale and makes my eyes glow with the bitter flame of fever. Besides, there is nothing I would like better than to be spared exhausting my mind by continual reflection; but even if I did not want to, my dismayed feelings would irresistibly drag me down this slope. I have noticed that the other children are like me; but they are even paler and their faces are distorted by permanent frowns, like grown men, our elder brothers. O Creator of the universe, I will not fail to offer you up this morning the incense of my childish prayer. Sometimes I forget it and I have noticed that on these days I feel happier than usual; my heart opens out, free of all constraint, and I breathe more easily the balmy air of the fields; whereas whenever I accomplish this painful duty, imposed on me by my parents, of addressing a song of praise to you every day, I am always bored by the tedious necessity of laboriously inventing new versions, and so I feel sad and irritated for the rest of the day; for it does not seem to me to be either logical or natural to invent what I do not really think, and then I seek isolation, immense solitudes. If I ask them for an explanation of this state of soul, they do not answer me. I should like to love and to adore you; but you are too powerful, and there is fear in all my prayers. If simply by the manifestation of your thought you can destroy or create worlds, my weak prayers will be of no use to you; if whenever you wish you can send cholera to ravage cities, or send death to carry away in its claws, indiscriminately, people of all ages, then I wish to have no truck with one so fearsome! Not that hatred dictates the thread of my arguments; on the contrary, it is your hatred I fear which, at a capricious command, may suddenly emerge from within you and become vast as the wing-span of the Andean condor. Your questionable amusements are beyond me, I would probably be their first victim. You are the Almighty. I am not disputing your right to that title, since you alone have the right to bear it and you are yourself the end and limit of your own desires, be their consequences disastrous or beneficial. That is precisely why it would be painful for me to walk beside you in your cruel, sapphire-inlaid tunic, not as your slave but with the risk of becoming your slave from one moment to the next. It is true that when you look into your soul to examine your sovereign conduct, if the ghost of a past injustice towards wretched mankind, which has always obeyed you as your most loyal friend, should raise up before you the motionless vertebrae of an avenging backbone, then, too late, your haggard eyes weep tears of remorse and then, your hair standing on end, you really believe in the resolution you make; which is: to suspend forever in the undergrowth of nothingness the inconceivable diversions of your tigerish imagination; an idea which would be ludicrous if it were not pitiable; but I also know that constancy has never fixed like strong marrow in your bones the harpoon of its eternal habitation, and that quite often you and your thoughts, covered in the black leprosy of error, relapse into the dismal lake of dark maledictions. I would like to believe that these maledictions are unconscious (although that would in no way dilute the deadliness of their venom) and that good and evil joined together burst in reckless leaps from your gangrened breast, like the mountain stream from the rock, by the secret spell of some blind force; but I have no proof that this is the case. Too often I have seen your vile teeth chattering with rage and your august face, covered with the moss of time, reddening like a burning coal because of some trivial misdemeanour of men; I have seen this too often to be able to stand for long before the signpost of this innocent hypothesis. And so, every day, my hands devoutly joined, I shall offer up to you my humble prayer, since it has to be. But, I implore you, do not include me among the objects of your providence; leave me out of consideration, like the worm which crawls beneath the ground. I would prefer to feed greedily on marine plants, washed by tropical waves on to the shores of wild and unknown islands in the heart of those foaming regions; I would prefer this to the knowledge that you are observing me and that your sneering scalpel is probing my consciousness. It has just revealed to you the totality of my thoughts, and I hope that you, in your prudence, will generously approve of the good sense ineffaceably stamped on them. Apart from these reservations about the more or less intimate relations between us, my mouth is ready at any hour of the day to exhale, like an artificial wind, the wave of lies which reverence for your halo rigorously requires of each human being, from the moment when bluish dawn breaks; seeking the light in the satin folds of twilight as I seek good deeds, spurred on by love of the Good. My years are not many and yet I already sense that goodness is nothing but a couple of sonorous syllables. I have not found it anywhere. Your character is easy to read; you make it too blatant. You ought to hide it more skilfully. Yet perhaps I am mistaken and you are doing it deliberately; for you know better than anyone else how you ought to act. Men pride themselves on imitating you; that is why holy goodness finds no tabernacle in their wild eyes: like father, like son. Whatever one should think of your intelligence, I am only speaking as an impartial critic. I would be delighted to be shown that I have been led into error. I do not wish to show you the hatred I bear you, which I lovingly brood on like a cherished daughter; it is better to hide it from your eyes and in your presence only to assume the appearance of a severe censor, with the duty of checking on all your foul actions. Thus you will break off all active intercourse with my hatred, you will forget it and you will destroy completely this maggot which is gnawing at your liver. Rather I would prefer you to hear words of reverie and meekness ... Yes, it is you who created the world and all that is in it. You are perfect. There is no virtue which you do not possess. You are very mighty, as everyone knows. May the entire universe sing your eternal hymn through every hour of time. May the birds bless you as they soar over the countryside. The stars are yours. Amen!' How astonished you will be to find me as I really am!

13

I SOUGHT a soul akin to mine, but I could not find one. I searched every corner of the earth; my perseverance brought no reward. Yet I could not remain alone. Someone had to approve of my character; someone had to have the same ideas as I. It was morning; the sun rose in all its magnificence on the horizon and before my eyes a young man also arose, whose presence made flowers grow as he passed. He approached me and, holding out his hand, said: 'I have come to you who seek me. Let us bless this happy day.' But I answered: 'Go away. I did not call you; I do not need your friendship.' It was evening; night was beginning to spread the veil of its blackness over nature. A lovely woman, whose form I could only just make out, was exerting a spellbinding influence over me, and looking at me with compassion; yet she did not dare to speak to me. I said: 'Come closer, that I may make out clearly the features of your face; for the light of the stars is not strong enough to show them, at this distance.' Then, with her eyelids lowered, she stepped chastely across the lawn in my direction. As soon as I saw her I said: 'I see that goodness and justice have dwelt in your heart. We could never live together. Now you admire my beauty, which has distracted more than one; but sooner or later you would repent of having given your love to me; for you do not know my soul.

Not that I would ever be unfaithful to you: to her who gives herself to me with such trust and abandon I will give myself with equal trust and abandon; but get this into your head and do not ever forget it: wolves and lambs do not look lovingly at one another.' What did I need, I who had rejected with such disgust the loveliest of mankind! What I needed I could not say. I was not yet in the habit of keeping strict note of my mental phenomena according to the methods recommended by philosophy. I sat down on a rock, by the sea. A ship had just set all sails to leave those parts: an imperceptible point had just appeared on the horizon and was gradually approaching, driven on by the gust of wind, and growing rapidly in size. The tempest was about to begin its assaults, already the sky was growing dark, until it became black, almost as hideous as the heart of man. The ship, which was a big man of war, had just dropped anchor to avoid being swept on to the rocks. The wind was whistling furiously from all directions, tearing the sails to shreds. Thunder was bursting amid the lightning-flashes, and could not drown the sounds of lamentation heard in this house with no foundations, this moving sepulchre. The rolling of these watery masses had not yet broken the anchor-chains; but their buffetings had opened a way for the water in the ship's sides. It was an enormous breach; the pumps are unable to bale out the flood of salt water which comes foaming and beating down on to the bridge like mountains. The ship in distress fires the cannon to give the alarm; but it sinks slowly . . . majestically. He who has not seen a ship sinking in a hurricane, and flashes of lightning alternating with the deepest darkness, while those who are in it are overwhelmed with the despair you know of, that man knows nothing of the accidents of life. At last a universal wail of immense pain goes up from the sides of the ship, while the sea redoubles its dreadful attacks. It is the cry of men who have no strength left. Each man wraps himself in the cloak of resignation and leaves his fate in God's hands. They huddle up together like a flock of sheep. The ship in distress fires the cannon to give the alarm; but it sinks slowly . . . majestically. The pumps have been going all day long. Vain efforts. Night, thick and implacable, has come to put the finishing stroke to this gracious spectacle. Everyone says inwardly that once he is in the water he will not be able to breathe; for as far as he can recall, he knows of no fishes among his ancestors. But he resolves to hold his breath for as long as possible, to prolong his life by two or three seconds; that is the avenging irony with which he wishes to confront death . . . The ship in distress fires the cannon to give the alarm; but it sinks slowly . . . majestically. He does not know that the sinking vessel causes a powerful circumvolution of waves; that murky undercurrents have joined the troubled waters and a force from below, the counterpart of the tempest raging above, is making the movements of the element nervous and spasmodic. Thus, despite the store of composure which he is gathering in advance, the future drowned man, after mature consideration, ought to feel happy if he can even prolong his life amid the eddying deeps by the space of half a normal breath for good measure. He will not be able to flout death, which is his supreme wish. The ship in distress fires the cannon to give the alarm; but it sinks slowly . . . majestically. I am wrong. It is no longer firing its cannon, it is not sinking. No! the cockle shell has been completely engulfed. O heaven! how can one go on living after experiencing such delights! I had just been given the privilege of witnessing the death-throes of several of my fellow-beings. Minute by minute I followed the vicissitudes of their agony. Now the bawling of some old woman, mad with fear, was at a premium. Now only the yelling of a child at breast prevented the steering orders from being heard. The vessel was too far away for me to hear distinctly the sound of groans carried on the gust; but I brought it nearer by an act of will, and the optical illusion was perfect. Every quarter of an hour, when a gust stronger than the others, uttering its mournful tones above the cries of fear-stricken petrels, broke up the ship in a longitudinal crunching movement, increasing the laments of those about to be offered as sacrifices to death, I dug a sharp metal point deep in my cheek and secretly thought: They are suffering more! In this way I at least had a point of comparison. I apostrophized them from the shore, hurling threats and imprecations at them. It seemed that they ought to hear me! It seemed that my hatred and my words, overleaping the distance, were abolishing the physical laws of sound and distinctly reaching their ears which had been deafened by the roaring of the angry ocean. It seemed that they ought to think of me, and breathe vengeance in impotent rage! From time to time I looked up towards the cities slumbering on firm land; and seeing that nobody suspected that a ship was going to sink some miles from the shore, with birds of prey for a crown and ravenous aquatic giants for a pedestal, I took courage again and hope returned to me: so I was certain of their destruction! They could not escape! To make assurance doubly sure, I had gone to fetch my double-barrelled rifle so that if some survivor was tempted to approach the rocks of the shore to escape imminent death, a bullet in the shoulder would shatter his arm and prevent him from carrying out his plan. At the moment of the tempest's greatest fury, I saw a head, its hair standing on end, frantically bobbing up and down in the water. The swimmer was swallowing litres of water and, buoyed up like a cork, was sinking into the deep. But soon he would reappear, his hair streaming, his eyes riveted on the shore; he seemed to be challenging death. His composure was admirable. A huge bleeding wound caused by the jagged point of a hidden reef had gashed his brave and noble face. He could not have been more than sixteen years old; for the peach-like down on his upper lip could just be made out by the flashes which lit up the night. And now he was only two hundred yards from the cliff. I could easily get a clear view of him. What courage! What indomitable spirit! How the determined set of his head seemed to flout destiny as he vigorously cleaved the waves which did not easily give way before him. I had made up my mind in advance. I owed it to myself to keep my promise; the last hour had tolled for all; none must escape. That was my resolution; nothing would change it . . . a sharp sound was heard, the head went down, and did not reappear. I did not take as much pleasure in this murder as one might think; it was precisely because I was sated with all this killing which I was doing out of pure habit; one cannot do without it, but it provides only a slight enjoyment. The sense is dulled, hardened. What pleasure could I feel at the death of this human being when there were more than a hundred who, once the ship had gone down, would provide me with the spectacle of their deaths and their last struggle against the waves? This death did not even have the appeal of danger; for human justice, rocked by the hurricane of this dreadful night, was slumbering within doors, a few steps from me. And now that the years are weighing down on me, I can sincerely speak this simple and solemn truth: I was never as cruel as men afterwards said I was; whereas many times their persistent acts of wickedness went on wreaking havoc for years on end. Then my rage knew no bounds; I was possessed by fits of cruelty and I became fearsome to anyone who came within sight of my haggard eyes – that is, if he was of my race. If it was a horse or a dog, I let it pass: have you heard what I have just said? Unfortunately, on the night of that tempest, one of those fits had come upon me, my reason had abandoned me (for normally I was just as cruel, but more cautious); everything which fell into my hands that night would have to die; I am not claiming that this excuses my misdeeds. The fault is not entirely with my fellow-creatures. I am only stating things as they are while I wait for the last judgement, which makes me scratch my head in advance ... What does the last judgement matter to me! My reason never abandons me, as I have just claimed in order to deceive you. And when I commit a crime, I know what I am doing: I did not want to do something else! Standing on the rocks as the hurricane lashed my hair and my cloak, I watched ecstatically as the tempest's might bore down on a ship beneath a starless sky. I followed all the peripeteias of this drama, from the moment when the vessel dropped anchor until the moment when it was swallowed up, a deadly garment which dragged into the bowels of the sea all those who had put it on as a cloak. But the moment was approaching when I myself was to be involved in these scenes of nature in tumult. When the place where the vessel had been struggling clearly showed that it had gone to spend the rest of its days on the ground-floor of the sea, some of those who had been carried off by the waves began to reappear on the surface. They held one another around the waist, in twos and threes; it was a good way of not saving their lives; for their movements became entangled and they went down like leaking jugs. What is this army of sea-monsters cleaving the water so rapidly? There are six of them; their fins are strong and they are forcing their way through the heaving seas. The sharks soon make an omelette without eggs of all the human beings moving their limbs on the unstable continent; they share it out according to the law of the strongest. Blood mixes with water, and the water mixes with the blood. Their wild eyes light up well enough the scene of carnage. Yet what tumult is that there, yonder on the horizon? You would take it for a whirlwind approaching! What flailing! I see what it is. A huge female shark is coming to partake of pâté de foie of duck and cold beef. She is wild with anger; for when she

arrives, she is starving. A struggle ensures between her and
the other sharks, fighting over the few palpitating limbs which
are floating here and there dumbly on the surface of the red
cream. She snaps and bites to the right and to the left, wound-
ing fatally all that she gets her teeth into. But there are still
three living sharks around her and she is obliged to turn in all
directions to foil their tricks. With increasing emotion, such
as he has never felt, the spectator follows this new kind of
naval battle from the shore. He is staring at the courageous
female shark, whose teeth are so strong. He no longer wavers,
but shoulders his rifle and, with his customary skill, lodges his
second bullet in the gills of one of the sharks as it appeared
above the waves. Two sharks remain who, seeing this, go to
it all the more eagerly. From the top of the rock the man with
the briny saliva flings himself into the sea and swims towards
the pleasantly-coloured carpet, holding in his hand the steel
dagger which he always carries with him. From now on each
shark has an enemy to deal with. He advances on his weary
adversary and, taking his time, buries the sharp blade of his
knife in its belly. The moving citadel easily accounts for her
last adversary. The swimmer is now in the presence of the
female shark he has saved. They look into each other's eyes for
some minutes, each astonished to find such ferocity in the
other's eyes. They swim around keeping each other in sight,
and each one saying to himself: 'I have been mistaken; here
is one more evil than I.' Then by common accord they glide
towards one another underwater, the female shark using its
fins, Maldoror cleaving the waves with his arms; and they
hold their breath in deep veneration, each one wishing to
gaze for the first time upon the other, his living portrait.
When they are three yards apart they suddenly and spon-
taneously fall upon one another like two lovers and embrace
with dignity and gratitude, clasping each other as tenderly as
brother and sister. Carnal desire follows this demonstration

of friendship. Two sinewy thighs press tightly against the monster's viscous flesh, like two leeches; and arms and fins are clasped around the beloved object, while their throats and breasts soon form one glaucous mass amid the exhalations of the sea-weed; amidst the tempest which was continuing to rage; by the light of lightning-flashes; with the foaming waves for marriage-bed; borne by an undersea current and rolling on top of one another down into the unknown deeps, they joined in a long, chaste and ghastly coupling! . . . At last I had found one akin to me . . . from now on I was no longer alone in life . . .! Her ideas were the same as mine . . . I was face to face with my first love!

14

A HUMAN body is dragged along in the Seine. In the circumstances, she flows solemnly. The swollen body is buoyed up on the water; it disappears beneath the arch of a bridge; but further on it can be seen again turning round and round like a mill-wheel and going under now and then. A boatman hooks it with a rod as it goes by and brings it back to earth. Before it is brought to the morgue the body is left on the bank for some time to revive it if possible. A dense crowd gathers around the body. Those who cannot see because they are at the back push those in front, as much as they can. Everyone says to himself: 'I would never have drowned myself.' They pity the young man who has killed himself; they admire him; but they do not imitate him. And yet he found it quite natural to take his life, judging that there was nothing on earth capable of satisfying him, and aspiring towards higher things. His face is distinguished, his clothes are expensive. Is he seventeen yet? That is dying young! The stunned crowd continues to gape at him. Night is coming on. Everyone moves quietly away. No one has dared to turn the drowned man over and make him throw up the water which fills his body. They are afraid of showing any feeling, and no one has moved, they all keep to themselves. One of them goes away singing discordantly an absurd Tyrolean air; another snaps his fingers like castanettes . . . Troubled by his dark thoughts, Maldoror, on horseback, passes near the place with the speed of lightning. He sees the drowned man; that is enough. Immediately, he brings his courser to a halt and gets down from the stirrup. He lifts up the young man with no sign of squeamishness, making him throw up large amounts of water. At the thought that this inert body could be revived by his hands he feels his heart leap and under this excellent impression his courage redoubles. Vain efforts! Vain efforts, I said, and it is true. He rubs his temples; he rubs this limb and that; he breathes into his mouth for an hour, pressing his lips against the unknown young man's. At last he seems to feel a slight beating of the young man's breast. The drowned man lives! At this supreme moment several wrinkles could be seen disappearing from the horseman's forehead, making him ten years younger. But alas! the wrinkles will return, perhaps tomorrow, perhaps as soon as he has left the banks of the Seine. Meanwhile the drowned man opens his lustreless eyes and thanks his benefactor with a wan smile; but he is still very weak, and he cannot move at all. How fine it is to save someone's life! And how many faults are redeemed by this action! The bronze-lipped man, preoccupied till then with snatching him from the arms of death, looks at the young man more attentively, and his features are not unfamiliar to him. He says inwardly that there is not much difference between the blond-haired young man who had just nearly drowned and Holzer. Look how effusively they embrace one another. It is nothing! The man with the pupils of jasper is anxious to maintain a harsh and undemonstrative appearance. Saying nothing, he takes his friend and puts him up behind him on the saddle, and the steed moves off at a gallop. O Holzer, who thought you were sensible and strong, do you not see, from your very own example, how difficult it is, in a fit of despair, to maintain the composure you boast of! I hope you will not cause me such grief again, and I for my part have promised you never to take my life.

15

THERE are moments in life when man with his louse-ridden hair casts wild staring looks at the green membranes of space; for he believes he hears, somewhere ahead, the ironic hoots of a phantom. He staggers and bows his head; what he has heard is the voice of conscience. Then with the speed of a madman he rushes out of the house, takes the first direction his wild state suggests and bounds over the rough plains of the countryside. But the yellow phantom never loses sight of him, pursuing him with equal speed. Sometimes on stormy nights, while legions of winged octopi, which look like ravens at a distance, hover above the clouds, moving ponderously towards the cities of men, their mission to warn them to change their conduct; on such nights the dark-eyed pebble sees two beings pass by, lit up by the flashes of lightning, one after another; and wiping a furtive tear of compassion which flows from its frozen eye, it shouts out: 'Yes, he certainly deserves it; it is only justice being done.' Having said that he reassumes his grim attitude and continues to watch, trembling nervously, the manhunt, and the big lips of the shadowy vagina from which immense dark spermatozoids flow unceasingly like a river and then soar up into the lugubrious ether, hiding all nature with the vast span of their bat's wings, including the solitary legions of octopi, now gloomy at the sight of these dumb inexpressible fulgurations. But all the

time the steeplechase between these two tireless runners is
going on, and the phantom hurls torrents of fire from his
mouth on to the singed back of the human antelope. If, while
he is accomplishing this duty, he comes upon pity trying to
bar his way, he gives in disgustedly to her supplications, and
allows the man to escape. The phantom makes a clicking
sound with its tongue, as if to tell itself that it is giving up the
chase, and then returns to its kennel for the time being. His is
the voice of the condemned; it can be heard even in the
furthest layers of space; and when its dreadful shrieking
penetrates the human heart, then man would prefer, as the
saying goes, to have death as his mother than remorse as his
son. He buries his head up to his neck in the earthy windings
of a hole; but conscience volatilizes this ostrich-trick. The
hole disappears, a drop of ether; light appears with its train of
beams, like a flight of curlews swooping down on lavender;
and man, his eyes open, is face to face with his pale and
ghastly self again. I have seen him making for the sea, climb-
ing a jagged promontory, lashed by the eyebrow of the surge;
and flinging himself arrow-like down into the waves. The
miracle is this: the corpse reappeared next day on the surface
of the ocean, which had brought this flotsam of flesh back to
the shore. The man freed himself from his body's imprint in
the sand, wrung the water from his drenched hair, and
silently, stoopingly, returned to the way of life. Conscience
judges our most secret thoughts and acts severely, and is never
wrong. Being powerless to prevent evil, it never ceases to
hunt man down like a fox, especially in the hours of darkness.
Avenging eyes, which ignorant science calls meteors, shed a
livid flame of light, revolving on themselves as they pass and
uttering mysterious words ... which he understands! Then
his bed is battered by the convulsions of his body, burdened
by the weight of insomnia, and he hears the sinister breathing
of night's vague rumours. The angel of sleep himself, having

been struck a mortal blow on the forehead from a stone whose thrower is unknown, abandons his task and re-ascends towards heaven. Now this time I am here to defend man; I, the scorner of all virtues; I, whom the Creator has never forgotten since the day when I knocked from their pedestal the annals of heaven where by some infamous intrigue his power and his eternity had been consigned, and I applied my four hundred suckers to his armpits, making him utter dreadful cries. They changed into vipers as his mouth uttered them and went and hid in the undergrowth, among ruined old walls, on the watch by day, on the watch by night. These cries crawled, endowed with countless rings and a small flat head, and wickedly gleaming eyes. They have vowed to stop at the sight of human innocence. But when men in their innocence are out walking in the tangles of the maquis, on steep slopes or on the dunes of the sand, they soon change their mind, something makes them want to go back. If, that is, there is still time; for, at times, men notice the poison creeping along the veins of their leg by means of an almost imperceptible bite, before they have had time to turn back and escape into the open. Thus it is that the Creator, admirably cool even in the presence of the most appalling sufferings, extracts from the very breasts of men the germs which are harmful to those who live on earth. Imagine his astonishment when he saw Maldoror changed into an octopus coming towards him with his eight monstrous tentacles, each one of which was a solid lash which could easily have encompassed a planet's circumference. Caught unawares, he struggled for some moments against the viscous embrace, which was getting tighter and tighter ... I feared some foul trick on his part; having fed copiously on the globules of his sacred blood, I suddenly pulled away from his majestic body, and went and hid deep in a cave, which has been my abode since then. After many fruitless searches, he was still unable to find me.

That was a long time ago; but I think he knows now where I live; he is wary of entering; the two of us live like monarchs of neighbouring lands, who know their respective strengths, cannot defeat one another, and are weary of the useless battles of the past. He fears me, and I fear him; each of us, though undefeated, has felt the savage blows of his adversary, and it is stalemate. However, I am ready to take up the struggle again whenever he wishes. But I advise him not to wait for the right moment for his hidden schemes. I will always be on guard, I will always keep my eye on him; let him not visit the earth with conscience and its torments. I have taught men what weapons to use to combat it successfully. They have not yet grown accustomed to conscience; but you know that, for me, it is as the wind-blown straw. And I treat it as such. If I wanted to use this opportunity to indulge in subtle poetic discussion, I would add that a straw is more to me than conscience; for straw is useful for the ox chewing the cud, whereas conscience has only its claws of steel to show. These claws suffered a painful setback the day they came before me. As conscience had been sent by the Creator, I did not think fit to allow it to bar my way. If it had come to me with the modesty and humility proper to its rank (which it ought never to have tried to rise above), then I would have listened to it. I did not like its pride. I stretched out my hand and ground its claws with my fingers; they fell as dust to the ground, beneath the pressure of this new kind of mortar. I stretched out my other hand and pulled off its head. Then I hunted that woman out of my house with a whip, and I never saw her again. I have kept her head as a souvenir of my victory ... Gnawing the skull of the head which I held in my hand, I stood on one leg, like a heron, beside a precipice on the side of a mountain. I was seen going down the valley, while the skin of my breast remained as still and calm as the lid of a tomb! Gnawing the skull of the head which

I held in my hand, I swam in the most dangerous gulfs, along by lethal reefs, and I dived deeper than any current, to witness, as a stranger, the combats of sea-monsters; I swam so far from the shore that it was out of my piercing sight; and hideous cramps, with their paralysing magnetism, prowled around my limbs as they cleaved the waves with their forceful movements, but they did not dare to approach. I was seen returning safe and sound to the beach, while the skin of my breast remained as still and calm as the lid of a tomb! Gnawing the skull of the head which I held in my hands, I mounted the steps of a high tower. I reached the platform, high above the ground. I looked out over the countryside and the sea; I looked at the sun, the firmament; kicking hard against the granite which did not give way, I challenged death and divine vengeance with a supreme howl of contempt and then hurled myself like a paving-stone into the mouth of space. Men heard the painful resounding thud which occurred as the head of conscience, which I had abandoned as I fell, hit the ground. I was seen descending, slow as a bird, borne on an invisible cloud, and picking up the head, so that I could force it to witness a triple crime, which I was to commit that day, while the skin of my breast remained as still as the lid of a tomb! Gnawing the skull of the head which I held in my hands, I made for the place where the guillotine is. Beneath the blade, I placed the smooth and delicate necks of three young girls. Executor of fine works, I released the rope with the apparent deftness of a lifetime's experience; and the triangular blade, falling obliquely, lopped off three heads which were looking at me sweetly. Then I put my own head beneath the weighty razor, and the executioner prepared to do his duty. Thrice the blade slid along the grooves with renewed force; thrice, my material carcass was moved to the very depths, especially at the base of my neck, as when one dreams that one has been crushed to death beneath a collapsing house. The stunned crowd let me pass and leave the gloomy square. It saw me opening up with my elbows its undulating waves, carrying the head straight in front of me, while the skin of my breast remained as still and as calm as the lid of a tomb! I said I wanted to defend man, this time; but I fear my apologia is not an expression of the truth; and consequently I prefer to remain silent. Mankind will applaud this prudence with gratitude!

16

THE time has come to draw in the reins of my inspiration and to stop for a moment along the way, as when one looks at a woman's vagina; it is wise to look over the ground I have covered, and then, having rested my weary limbs, to soar off with a bold leap. To cover such a stretch in a single breath is by no means easy; one's wings get very tired, flying high, without hope and without remorse . . . No, let us not lead any further the haggard pack of pickaxes and spades across the explosive mines of this impious song. The crocodile will not change a word of the vomitings from beneath his skull. So much the worse, if some lurking shade, excited by the praiseworthy object of avenging mankind whom I have so unjustly attacked, stealthily opens the door of my room, and brushing against the wall like a sea-gull's wing, buries a dagger in the side of the plunderer of heavenly wrecks! The atoms of clay may just as well be dispersed in this way as any other.

THIRD BOOK

I

LET us recall the names of those imaginary beings of angelic nature, creations of a single mind, who, in the second song, shone with a light of their own. Once born, they die, like the sparks whose swift extinction on the burning paper the eye can hardly follow. Leman! .. Lohengrin!... Lombano!... Holzer! for a moment you appeared on my charmed horizon covered in the insignia of youth; but I let you fall back into chaos, like diving bells. You will never come forth again. It is enough for me to keep the memory of you; you must give way to other substances, less beautiful perhaps, engendered by the stormy flood of a love resolved not to quench its thirst with the human race. A hungering love, which would devour itself, if it did not seek sustenance in celestial fictions: creating, in the long run, a pyramid of seraphim more numerous than the insects which swarm in a drop of water, he will weave them into an ellipse which he will whirl around himself. During this time, the traveller, who has stopped at the sight of a cataract, will, if he looks up, see a human being in the distance, borne towards hell's depths on a garland of living camelias! But ... silence! The floating image of the fifth ideal slowly takes shape, like the blurred nuances of the aurora borealis, on the vaporous fore-front of my intellect, where it takes on more and more of a precise consistency... Mario and I were going along the strand. Our horses, with straining necks, rent the membranes of space and struck sparks from the stones on the beach. The cold blast struck us full in the face, billowing out our cloaks;

and the hair of our twin heads was blowing in the wind. The sea-gull, by its cries and the beating of its wings, tried to warn us of the possible proximity of the tempest. It cried: 'Where are they going, at this mad gallop?' We said nothing; plunged in reverie, we let ourselves be borne along on the wings of this wild career; the fisherman, seeing us pass by, swift as the albatross, and believing that here, fleeing before him, were the two mysterious brothers, so called because they were always together, hastened to make the sign of the cross and hid with his petrified dog behind a huge boulder. Those who lived on the coast had heard strange things told of these two characters, who would appear on earth amid the clouds in times of great calamity, when a dreadful war threatened to thrust its harpoon into the breasts of two enemy countries, or cholera with its sling was preparing to hurl death and corruption into entire cities. The oldest beachcombers would frown gravely as they explained that these two phantoms, the vast span of whose black wings everyone had noticed in hurricanes, above sandbanks and reefs, were the spirit of the earth and the spirit of the sea, whose majestic forms would appear in the sky during the great revolutions of nature, and who were joined together by eternal friendship, the rarity and glory of which have astonished the endless cable of generations. It was said that, flying side by side, like two Andean condors, they liked to hover in concentric circles among the layers of the atmosphere nearest to the sun; that in those regions they lived on the purest essence of light; that with great reluctance they decided to direct their vertical flight down towards the orbit in which the fear-stricken human globe deliriously revolves, inhabited by cruel spirits who massacre one another on the fields where battle rages (when they are not treacherously and perfidiously killing one another with the dagger of hatred or ambition in the middle of towns), and who feed on beings as full of life as themselves, but lower down in the scale of existence. Or when, to urge men to repentance by the strophes of their prophecies, they firmly resolved to swim with huge and powerful strokes towards the sidereal regions where a planet moved amid the thick exhalations of greed, pride, imprecations and sneers which rose like pestilential vapours from its hideous surface; this planet seemed only as big as a bowl, being almost invisible because of the distance; and there, sure enough, there were many opportunities for them to regret bitterly their spurned and misunderstood kindness; and they went and hid in the bowels of volcanoes to converse with the enduring fires of lava which bubble in vats in the centre of the earth, or at the bottom of the sea, where their disillusioned gaze could linger pleasantly on the fiercest monsters of the depths, who seemed models of gentleness in comparison with the bastards of mankind. And then when the propitious darkness of night fell, they would rush out of the porphyry-crested craters and from the undersea currents, leaving behind them the stony chamber-pot where the constipated anus of the human cockatoo strains, till they could no longer make out the shape of the vile planet suspended in space. Distressed at their fruitless attempt, the spirit of the earth and the spirit of the sea embraced and wept, amid the stars who shared their grief, and beneath God's eye. Mario and he who galloped by his side were not unaware of the vague and superstitious rumours spread by fishermen as, with doors bolted and windows closed, they whispered to one another around the fireside of an evening; while the night wind, wishing to warm itself, whistles around the straw cabin, shaking with its force the fragile walls, surrounded at the base with shells brought in by the dying undulations of the waves. We were not speaking. What have those who love to say to one another? Nothing. But our eyes expressed everything. I told him to pull his cloak around him more and he remarked that my horse was moving too far from his: each of us was as much concerned for the other's life as for his own; we are not laughing. He tries to force a smile. But I notice that his face is deeply lined, and bears the terrible weight of reflection, which is constantly struggling with the sphinxes who, with their squinting eyes, baffle mortal intelligence in all its anguished endeavours. Seeing that his attempts are futile, he averts his eyes and bites his earthly rein, raging and foaming at the mouth and looking towards the horizon, which flees at our approach. In turn I try to remind him of his gilded youth, which need only advance like a queen in the palace of pleasures; but he notices how difficult it is for my thin mouth to utter these words, how the years of my own spring have passed, sad and glacial, like an implacable dream passing over banquet tables, satin beds where love's pale priestess sleeps, paid with the glitter of gold, the bitter pleasures of disenchantment, the pestilential wrinkles of age, the terrors of solitude and the torches of sorrow. Seeing that my attempts are futile, I am not surprised that I cannot make him happy; the Almighty appears with his instruments of torture in the resplendent aureole of his horror. I avert my eyes and look towards the horizon which flees at our approach ... Our horses were galloping along the shores, as if they fled the eyes of men ... Mario is younger than I; the dampness of the weather and the salt water which spurts up on us bring cold to his lips. I said to him: 'Take care! ... Take care! ... close your lips on one another; do you not see the sharp claws of the cold which will chap your skin, furrowing it with its smarting wounds?' He fixed his eye on my brow and answered with the movements of his tongue: 'Yes, I see these green claws, but I will not alter the natural position of my mouth to get rid of them. Since this appears to be the will of Providence, I wish to submit to it. Its will could have been less harsh.' And I exclaimed: 'I admire this noble revenge.' I wanted to tear out my hair, but he forbade me with such a stern look that I obeyed him respectfully. It was getting late, the eagle was returning to its nest amid the jagged mountain rocks. He said: 'I will lend you my cloak to protect you from the cold. I do not need mine.' I replied: 'Woe to you, if you do as you say. I do not want another to suffer instead of me, and especially not you.' He did not answer, because I was right; but I began to comfort him, because of the violent and hasty tone in which I had spoken. Our horses were galloping along the shore, as if they fled the eyes of men . . . I looked up, like the prow of a ship borne upon a huge wave and I said to him: 'Are you crying? Tell me, king of the snows and the fog. I see no tears on your face, lovely as the cactus flower, and your eyes are dry as the bed of the stream; but in the depths of your eyes I see a blood-filled vessel in which your innocence boils, bitten in the neck by a scorpion of the largest kind. A violent wind blows down on the fire beneath the cauldron, spreading the dark flames outside your sacred eyeball. I moved close to you, my hair near your rosy brow, and I smelt burning, because my hair had been singed. Close your eyes; for, if you do not, your face, burning like the lava of the volcano, will fall in ashes into the palm of my hand.' And he turned towards me again, heedless of the reins he was holding in his hands, gazing at me tenderly, raising and lowering his lily eyelids like the ebb and flow of the sea. He wished to reply to my bold question, and did so as follows: 'Do not worry about me. Just as the mists of rivers drift over hillsides and on reaching the top rise into the atmosphere to form clouds; so have your anxieties on my account increased imperceptibly without any reasonable grounds, forming the illusory shape of a desolate mirage in your imagination. I assure you there is no fire in my eyes, although I feel as if my skull had been plunged into a basin of burning coals. How could my innocent flesh be burning in the cauldron, since I can hear only weak and indistinct cries which are but the moans of the wind passing over our heads. A scorpion could not have taken up residence and fixed his sharp pincers in my torn sockets; rather I feel as if there are more powerful tentacles grinding my optic nerves. Yet I am of your opinion, that the blood which fills the cauldron was extracted from my veins by an invisible torturer as I slept at night. I waited a long time for you, beloved son of the ocean; my sleep-weakened arms engaged in vain combat with the One who had stolen into the vestibule of my house ... Yes, I feel my soul padlocked in the bolt of my body and it cannot get out and flee far from the shores lashed by human waves, no longer to witness the livid pack of miseries relentlessly pursuing the human lizards over the sloughs and pits of immense despair. But I shall not complain. I received life as a wound, and I have forbidden suicide to heal the scar. I want the Creator to contemplate the gaping crevasse for every hour of his eternity. That is the punishment I inflict on him. Our coursers slow down, their bodies trembling like the hunter set upon by peccaries. They must not start listening to what we are saying. By dint of attention, their intelligence would increase and they might understand us. Woe to them! for they would suffer more. Just think, in fact, of the boars of mankind: does it not seem that the degree of intelligence which separates them from other beings has only been granted at the irremediable price of incalculable suffering? Follow my example and dig your spur into your courser's side. 'Our horses were galloping along the shore, as if they fled the eyes of men.'

2

BEHOLD the madwoman dancing along, with a vague memory of something in her mind. Children chase after her and throw stones at her, as if she were a blackbird. She brandishes a stick and makes as if to chase them, then continues on her way. She has left a shoe behind her on the path, and does not notice it. Long spiders' legs move on her nape; they are none other than her hair. Her face no longer looks like a human face, and she bursts into fits of laughter, like a hyena. She utters scraps of sentences in which, when they are put together, few would be able to find any clear meaning. Her dress has holes in several places and moves jerkily to show her bony and mud-bespattered legs. She moves forward in a daze, her youth, her illusions and her past happiness, which she glimpses through her ruined mind's haze, all swept along like a poplar leaf by the whirl of unconscious powers. She has lost her former grace and beauty; the way she walks is mean and low, her breath reeks of gin. If men were happy on this earth, it would surprise us. The madwoman reproaches no one, she is too proud to complain, and she will die without revealing her secret to those who are interested in her, but whom she has forbidden even to speak to her. Children chase after her and throw stones at her, as if she were a blackbird. She has dropped a roll of paper from her breast. A stranger picks it up, shuts himself in his room all night, and reads the manuscript, which contains the following: 'After many years of barrenness, Providence blessed me with a child, a girl. For three whole days I knelt in churches and never ceased thanking Him who had at last granted my wishes. With my own milk I suckled the child, who meant more to me than my own life. She was endowed with all the good qualities of body and soul, and she grew quickly. She would say to me: "I would like to have a little sister to play with; ask the good Lord to send me one; and I, in return, will wreathe a garland of violets, mint, and geraniums." My answer was to sit her on my lap, press her to my breast and kiss her lovingly. She was already interested in animals and used to ask me why it was that the swallow merely brushed against the cottages of men with its wings, without ever daring to enter. But I would put my finger on my mouth, as if to tell her to keep silent on this grave question, the rudiments of which I did not wish to explain to her and perhaps over-excite her childish imagination with too vivid a sensation; and I was anxious to change the subject, which is a painful one for every being who belongs to the race which has imposed its unjust dominion on all the other animals of creation. Whenever she spoke to me of the graves in the cemetery, saying how there one could breathe the pleasant perfumes of cypresses and immortelles, I was careful not to contradict her; but I said to her that it was the town where the birds lived, that they sang there from morning till dusk, that the graves were their nests where, lifting up the gravelids, they slept at night with their family. It was I who sewed all the pretty little clothes she wore, as well as the lace-dress, with its thousand arabesques, which was reserved for Sundays. In winter, she had her special place by the hearth; for she considered herself an important person. In summer, the meadows felt the gentle pressure of her steps when she ventured out with her silk net on the end of a rush, chasing the wild, free humming-bird, and butterflies with their frustrating, zig-zagging motion. "What have you been doing, you little scamp, your soup has been waiting for you for over an hour?" But she exclaimed as she flung her arms around my neck that she would never go back there. The next day she was off again, skipping over the daisies and the mignonettes; among the sunbeams and the whirling flight of the ephemera; knowing only life's prismatic glass, none of its rancour yet; glad to be no bigger than the bluetit; innocently teasing the warbler, which does not sing as well as the nightingale; slyly putting her tongue out at the nasty raven which was looking at her in a fatherly way; graceful as a young cat in her movements. I was not to enjoy her company for much longer; the time was coming near when she would unexpectedly have to say good-bye to life's enchantments, abandoning for ever the company of turtle-doves, grouse and greenfinches, the babbling of the tulip and the anemone, the counsel of the marsh-grass, the sharp wit of the frogs, the coolness of the streams. I was told what happened; for I was not present at the event of which my daughter's death was the result. If I had been, I would have defended that angel at the cost of my blood . . . Maldoror was passing with his bulldog; he sees a young girl sleeping in the shade of a plane-tree, and at first he took her for a rose. It is impossible to say which came first to his mind: the sight of this young girl, or the resolution which followed. He undresses rapidly, like a man who knows what he is going to do. Stark naked, he flung himself upon the girl, lifting her dress to commit an assault upon modesty . . . in broad daylight . . . that will not worry him, you may be sure. But let us not dwell on this impure act. Discontented in mind, he hurriedly gets dressed again, casts a prudent glance towards the dusty pathway where no one is walking, and orders the bulldog to strangle a blood-bespattered young girl with a snap of his jaws. He points out to the mountain-dog the place where the suffering victim is breathing and shrieking, and withdraws from the scene, not wishing to be present as the sharp teeth enter the pink veins. It seemed to the dog that the execution of this order was harsh. He thought he was being asked to do what had already been done, and contented himself, this monstrous snouted wolf, with violating in turn the virginity of this delicate child. From her torn belly

the blood flows again along her legs, over the meadow ...
Her moans join the whining of the animal. The young girl
gives him the golden cross which adorned her neck, so that
he would spare her. She had not dared to show it to the wild
eye of him who had first thought of taking advantage of the
weakness of her age. But the dog knew well that if he dis-
obeyed his master, a knife-thrust from his sleeve would open
up his entrails without a word of warning. Maldoror (how
revolting to pronounce the name!) heard the agonized cries
of pain, and was astonished that the victim was so tenacious
of life that she was not already dead. He approaches the
sacrificial altar and sees the behaviour of his bulldog, gratify-
ing his base instincts, rising above the young girl, as a ship-
wrecked man raises his head above the waves. He kicks him
and cuts out one of his eyes. The maddened bulldog flees
across the countryside, dragging after him along a stretch of
the road, which, though it is short, is still too long, the body
of the young girl which is hanging from him and which only
comes free as a result of the jerky movements of the fleeing
dog; but he is afraid of attacking his master, who will never
set eyes on him again. He takes an American penknife from
his pocket, consisting of twelve blades which can be put to
different uses. He opens the angular claws of this steel hydra;
and armed with a scalpel of the same kind, seeing that the
green of the grass had not yet disappeared beneath all the
blood which had been shed, he prepares, without blenching,
to dig his knife courageously into the unfortunate child's
vagina. From the widened hole he pulls out, one after one,
the inner organs; the guts, the lungs, the liver and at last the
heart itself are torn from their foundations and dragged through
the hideous hole into the light of day. The sacrificer notices
that the young girl, a gutted chicken, has long been dead. He
stops his ravages, which had gone on until then with in-
creasing eagerness, and lets the corpse sleep, again, in the shade

of the plane-tree. The knife was picked up where it had been left, a few steps away. A shepherd, a witness of the crime whose author was never discovered, waited until long afterwards before telling the tale, until he had made sure that the criminal had reached the frontier and that he no longer had to fear the revenge which would be taken on him if he told the truth. I pitied the madman who had committed this appalling crime which the legislators had not foreseen and for which there were no precedents. I pitied him, because it is likely that his reason deserted him as he went to work with the twelve-bladed knife, ripping the viscera from top to bottom. I pity him because, if he was not mad, his shameful behaviour shows that he must be harbouring intense hatred against his fellow-beings, to swoop so savagely down on to the flesh and arteries of a harmless child, my daughter. I was present at the burial of the last remains, silently resigned; and every day I come and pray over a grave.' When he has finished reading this, the stranger's strength fails him and he faints. He comes to, and burns the manuscript. He had forgotten this memory of his youth (how habit dulls the memory!); and after an absence of twenty years, he had returned to this fateful land. He will not buy a bulldog! . . . He will not converse with shepherds! . . . He will not sleep in the shade of plane-trees! . . . Children chase after her and throw stones at her, as if she were a blackbird.

3

TREMDALL, for the last time, has touched the hand of him who is deliberately going away, always fleeing onwards, the image of man always pursuing him! The wandering Jew says to himself that he would not be fleeing thus if the sceptre of the earth belonged to the race of crocodiles. Tremdall, stand-

ing in the valley, puts his hand before his eyes to concentrate
the solar rays and make his sight more penetrating, while the
other touches the breast of space with his horizontal un-
moving hand. Leaning forward, the statue of friendship, his
eyes mysterious as the sea, he contemplates the traveller's
garters as (with the aid of a metal walking stick) they make
their way up the hillside. The earth seems to give way beneath
his feet and even if he wished, he could not hold back his tears
and his feelings: 'He is far away; I see his form making its
way along a narrow path. Where is he going, with that slow
and heavy step? He does not know himself ... Yet I am
convinced that I am not asleep: who is it approaching, and
going to meet Maldoror? How huge the dragon is ... bigger
than an oak. You would think that its whitish wings, joined
firmly to its body, had sinews of steel, such was the ease with
which they cleft the air. Its body begins with a tiger's head
and ends in a long serpent's tail. It was not accustomed to
seeing such things. What is that on his brow? I see a word
there, written in a symbolic language which I cannot decipher.'
With one last wing-beat, he repaired to a place near him
whose tone of voice I know. He said to him: 'I have been
waiting for you, as you for me. The hour is come. Here I am.
Read on my brow my name written in hieroglyphic signs.'
Scarcely had he seen the enemy coming than Maldoror
changed into an immense eagle, and prepared for the combat,
contentedly clacking his hooked beak, by which he means
that he will take it upon himself alone to eat the dragon's
lower parts. Now they are describing circles of diminishing
concentricity, as each weighs up the other's strengths. They
are wise to do so. The dragon seems to me to be stronger; I
should like him to gain victory over the eagle. I shall experi-
ence great emotions at this spectacle in which a part of my
being is involved. Powerful dragon, I will, if necessary, spur
you on with my shouts. For it is in the eagle's interest that he

should be defeated. Why are they waiting before they attack? I am in mortal terror. Come on, dragon, you attack first. You have just landed a sharp blow with your claw: that is not too bad. I can assure you that the eagle has felt it; the wind blows away his beautiful, blood-stained feathers. Oh! the eagle has plucked out one of your eyes with his beak, whereas you have only torn off his skin; you should have been looking out for that. Bravo! take your revenge, and smash one of his wings; there is no denying how strong and sharp your tiger's teeth are. If you could only approach the eagle as he whirls in space and swoops down towards earth. I notice that even when he is falling you are wary of this eagle. He is on the ground, he will not be able to get up again. The sight of all these gaping wounds intoxicates me. Fly around him at ground level and finish him off, if you can, with the blows of your scaly serpent's tail. Courage, my fine dragon. Dig your powerful claws deep into him, and let blood mix with blood to form streams in which no water flows. It is easier said than done. The eagle has just devised a new strategic plan of defence, occasioned by the unfortunate risks of this memorable struggle; he is wise. He is sitting solidly in an unshakeable position, on his remaining wing, on his haunches, and on his tail, which had previously served as a rudder. He defies attacks even more extraordinary than those which have hitherto been flung at him. Now he turns with the speed of the tiger, and does not seem to flag; now he is on his back with his two strong claws in the air, coolly and ironically weighing up his adversary. I must know who the victor will be; the combat cannot go on for ever. I am thinking of the consequences! The eagle is fearsome; he is making enormous leaps which shake the earth, as if he were about to take off; yet he knows that that is impossible. The dragon does not trust appearances. He believes that at any moment the eagle will attack him on the side where he has lost his eye... O wretch that I am! This is what happens. How could the dragon have let himself be caught by the breast? In vain he uses his strength and his cunning. I see that the eagle, clinging to him with all his limbs like a bloodsucker, is burying his beak, and indeed his entire neck, deeper and deeper in the dragon's belly. Only his body can be seen. He appears perfectly at ease; he is in no hurry to come out. No doubt he is looking for something, while the tiger-headed dragon utters groans which awaken the forests. Behold the eagle, as he comes out of that cave. Eagle, how revolting you are! You are redder than a pool of blood! Though you hold a palpitating heart in your beak, you are so covered with wounds that you can hardly stand upright on your feathered claws; and, without relaxing the tight grip of your beak, you are staggering beside the dragon which is dying in the throes of frightful pain. Victory has been hard to achieve; no matter, you have won it; one must at least tell the truth ... You are acting according to the laws of reason as, moving away from the dragon's corpse, you divest yourself of the eagle's form. And so, Maldoror, you are the victor! And so, Maldoror, you have defeated Hope! From this moment, despair will prey on your purest substance! From this moment you will return, with a firm step, to your career of evil! Although I have become, so to speak, dulled to suffering, the last blow you struck the dragon did not fail to have its effect on me. Judge for yourself if I am suffering! But you frighten me. See, see that man fleeing in the distance. The bushy foliage of malediction has grown on him, excellent soil; he is accursed and accursed. Where are your sandals taking you? Where are you going, tottering forward like a sleepwalker on a roof? May your perverse destiny be fulfilled! Maldoror, adieu! Adieu, until eternity, when we will not be together!

4

IT was a spring day. The birds were pouring forth their warbling songs, and human beings were going about their different duties, bathed in the holiness of toil. Everything was working towards its destiny: trees, planets, dogfish. Everything, that is, except the Creator! He was lying stretched out on the road, with his clothes all torn. His lower lip was hanging down like a heavy chain; his teeth had not been cleaned, and the blond waves of his hair were full of dust. His body, benumbed by heavy sluggishness, pinned down on the stones, was making futile attempts to get up. His strength had deserted him and he was lying there, weak as an earthworm, impassive as the bark of a tree. Floods of wine filled the ruts which had been hollowed out by the nervous jerkings of his shoulders. Pig-snouted brutishness covered him with its protective wings and cast loving glances at him. His legs, their muscles slack, swept across the ground like two flapping sails. Blood flowed from his nostrils: as he fell he had knocked his face against a post . . . He was drunk! Horribly drunk! Drunk as a bug which in one night has gorged three barrels of blood; his incoherent words resounded all around; I shall refrain from repeating them here, for even if the supreme drunkard has no self-respect, I must respect men. Did you know that the Creator was drunk? Have pity on that lip, soiled in the cups of debauch. The hedgehog which was passing stuck his needles into his back and said: 'Take that. The sun has run half its course. Work, you idler, and do not eat the bread of others. Just wait till I call the cockatoo with its hooded beak.' The woodpecker and the owl, who were passing, buried their necks in his belly and said: 'Take that. What are you up to on this earth? Is it to offer the spectacle of this lugubrious comedy to animals? But I promise that neither the mole, nor the cassowary, nor the flamingo will imitate you.' The ass, which was passing by, gave him a kick in the temple and said: 'Take that. What had I done to you to deserve such long ears? Even the crickets despise me.' The toad, which was passing by, spat a fountain of slime on to his brow and said: 'Take that. If you had not given me such big bulbous eyes and I had seen you in the state you are in now, I would chastely have hidden the beauty of your limbs beneath a shower of ranunculi, myosotis, and camelias, so that no one would see you.' The lion, who was passing by, inclined his royal head and said: 'For my part, I respect him, even though his radiance now seems to be eclipsed. You others, so proud and superior, are mere cowards, since you attacked him while he was asleep. How would you like to be in his place and to have to endure from passers-by the insults which you have not spared him'? Man, who was passing by, stopped before the unrecognizable Creator; and for three full days, to the applause of the crab-louse and the viper, he shat on his august face! Woe to man, for this insult; for he did not respect the enemy, sprawled out in a mixture of blood and wine; defenceless, and almost lifeless! Then the sovereign God, awoken at last by all these mean jibes, got up as best he could; staggering, he went and sat down on a stone, with his two hands hanging down like the consumptive's two testicles; and cast a glassy, lack-lustre glance over all of nature, which belonged to him. Oh human beings, you are enfants terribles; but let us spare, I implore you, this great being who has not yet finished sleeping off the vile liquor and who has not got enough strength left to stand up straight; he has slumped down on to the boulder, on which he is sitting like a weary traveller. Look closely at the passing beggar; he saw the dervish stretching out a thin and hungry hand and, without knowing to whom he was giving alms, threw a piece of bread into the hand of him who was begging for mercy. The

Creator expressed his gratitude with a nod of the head. Oh!
you will never know how difficult it can be to keep on hold-
ing the reins of the universe! Sometimes the blood rushes to
one's head when one is seriously trying to conjure a last
comet from nothingness, and with it a new race of spirits. The
intellect, stirred to the depths, yields like a beaten man and,
for once in its life, lapses into the aberrations which you have
witnessed!

5

A RED lantern, the flag of vice, hanging from the end of a
tringle, rocking its carcass, lashed by the four winds, above a
massive, worm-eaten door. A dingy corridor, smelling of
human thighs, led to a yard where cocks and hens, scrawnier
than their own wings, were looking for food. On the wall
which surrounded the yard, on the east side, several very
small openings had been made and were closed off by a metal
grating. Moss covered this main part of the building which
had no doubt once been a convent and was now used as a
residence for all those women who, every day, showed the
inside of their vagina to the clients in return for a little money.
I was on a bridge, the piers of which went down into the
muddy water of the moat. From its raised surface I con-
templated the old ramshackle building and I could observe
the minutest details of its inner architecture. Sometimes a
grating would rise with a creak, as if by the impulsion of a
hand which did violence to the metal; a man's head would
appear in the half-open space; then his shoulders emerged
with flakes of plaster falling on them, followed in this labori-
ous extraction by his cobweb-covered body. Putting his hands
like a crown on the filth of all kinds which pressed the ground
with its weight, his feet still caught in the twists of the

grating, he resumed his natural posture and went to dip his hands in a rickety bucket whose soapy water had seen entire generations come and go; then he made off as quickly as possible, away from these suburban side-streets, to breathe the purer air nearer the town-centre. When the client had gone, a completely naked woman came out in the same manner, and went over towards the same bucket. Then the cocks and the hens rushed up in a crowd from all parts of the yard, attracted by the smell of semen, forced her on to the ground despite her vigorous resistance, swarmed all over her body as if it were a dung-heap and tore at the flaccid lips of her swollen vagina with their beaks until the blood came out. The hens and cocks, sated, went back to scratch around in the grass of the yard; the woman, now clean, got up, trembling and covered in wounds, as when one awakes after a night-mare. She dropped the cloth she had brought to wipe her legs with; no longer needing the communal bucket, she went back to her lair to await the next client. At this sight I, too, wanted to enter that house. I was about to come down from the bridge when I saw, on the coping of the column, the following inscription in Hebrew characters: 'You who cross this bridge, do not go in there. There crime sojourns with vice; one day, the friends of a young man who had passed through the fatal door waited in vain for his return.' My curiosity overcame my fear; a few moments later, I was standing before a grating of solid, intercrossing metal bars, with narrow spaces between them. I wanted to look inside, through that dark screen. At first I could see nothing; but I was soon able to make out the objects in the dark room by means of the rays of the sun, which was setting and would soon disappear on the horizon. The first and only thing which struck my sight was a blond stick consisting of horns which fitted into one another. The stick was moving! It was walking in the room! Its jerking was so violent that the floor shook;

with its two ends it was making huge holes in the wall and seemed like a ram battering the gates of a besieged town. Its efforts were in vain; the walls were made of freestone, and when it hit the wall I saw it bend like a steel blade and rebound like an elastic ball. Then this stick was not made of wood! I noticed later that it coiled and uncoiled easily, like an eel. Although it was as tall as a man, it did not stand upright. Sometimes it would try and then its ends could be seen through the grating. It was leaping up wildly and violently, then falling to the ground again. It could not break down the obstacle. I began to look at it more and more carefully, and I saw that it was a hair! After its great struggle with the matter which surrounded it like a prison, it went and rested against the bed which was in the room, with its root on the carpet and its tip against the head of the bed. After a few moments of silence, during which I heard broken sobs, it raised its voice and spoke thus: 'My master has left me in this room and forgotten all about me. He has not come back to look for me. He got up from this bed on which I am lying, combed his perfumed hair and did not realize that I had already fallen to the ground. Yet if he had picked me up, there would have been nothing surprising in such a simple act of justice. He has abandoned me in the confines of this room after being enfolded in a woman's arms. And what a woman! The sheets are still damp from their warm, moist embraces and bear, in their untidiness, the stamp of a night of love ...' And I wondered who his master could be! And I pressed my face even harder against the grating! 'While all of nature was slumbering chastely, he coupled with a degraded woman in lewd, impure caresses. He demeaned himself so far as to allow those withered cheeks, despicable in their habitual shamelessness, to approach his august face. He did not blush, but I blushed for him. There is no doubt that he was happy to spend a night with such a spouse. The woman, struck by his majestic appearance, seemed to be enjoying incomparable delights, and kissed his neck madly.' And I wondered who his master could be! And I pressed my face even harder against the grating! 'During this time, irritant pustules began to appear and to grow in number as a result of his unaccustomed eagerness for fleshly pleasures; I felt them surrounding my roots with their deadly gall and imbibing with their suckers the generative substance of my life. The more they abandoned themselves to their wild, insane movements, the more I felt my strength diminishing. At the moment when their bodily desires were reaching the paroxysm of passion, I noticed that my root had slumped, like a soldier wounded by a bullet. The torch of life had gone out in me and I fell from his illustrious head like a dead branch; I fell to the ground, without courage, without strength, without vitality; but with deep pity for him to whom I had belonged; but with eternal sorrow for his wilful aberration!' And I wondered who his master could be! And I pressed my face even harder against the grating! 'If he had at least taken to himself the innocent breast of a virgin! She would have been worthier of him, and the degradation would not have been so great. With his lips he kisses that mud-covered brow, on which men have trampled, full of dust . . . he breathes in, with his shameless nostrils, the emanations of those two moist armpits! . . . I saw the membranes of the latter shrink in shame while, for their part, his nostrils shrunk from the infamous inhalation. But neither he nor she paid any attention to the solemn warnings of the armpits, to the dull, pale revulsion of the nostrils. She raised her arms higher and he, thrusting more strongly, buried his face deeper in their hollow. I was obliged to be a party to this profanation. I was obliged to be a spectator at this unspeakable contortion; to be present at the unnatural alloying of these two beings, whose different natures were separated by an immeasurable gulf . . .' And I wondered who his master could be! And I pressed my face even harder against the grating! 'When he was sick of breathing this woman, he wanted to wrench off her muscles one by one; but as she was a woman, he forgave her, preferring to make one of his own sex suffer. He called in a young man from an adjoining cell. This young man had come to spend a few care-free moments with one of these women; he was enjoined to come and stand one step from his face. I had been lying on the ground for a long time now. Not being strong enough to get up on my burning root, I could not see what they did. All I know is that the young man was hardly within arm's reach when bits of flesh began to fall at the feet of the bed and came to rest on both sides of me. They told me in hushed tones that my master's claws had ripped them off the ado-lescent's shoulders. The latter, after some hours in which he had struggled against one of greater strength, got up from the bed and withdrew majestically. He was literally flayed from head to foot; he trailed his skin, which had been turned inside out, over the flagstones of the room. He said that his own character was full of goodness; that he liked to believe that his fellow-beings were good too; for that reason he had agreed to the wish of the distinguished stranger who had called him in; but that he would never have expected to be flayed by such a torturer. By such a torturer, he added after a pause. At last he went towards the grating which com-passionately opened to ground level in the presence of this body deprived of an epidermis. Without abandoning his skin, which could still be useful to him, if only as a cloak, he was trying to escape from this cut-throat; once he left the room, I could no longer see if he had had the strength to reach the gate which led out of that building. Oh, how the hens and the cocks moved respectfully away from the long trail of blood on the drenched ground, despite their hunger!' And I wondered who his master could be! And I pressed my face harder against the grating! 'Then he who should have thought more of his dignity and his righteousness sat up and leant, with some difficulty, on his tired elbows. Alone, dark, disgusted, and hideous! He dressed slowly. The nuns, buried for centuries in the convent's catacombs, having been awoken with a start by the noises of that dreadful night, the crashing and the shaking in the cell above the vaults, now held hands, and came and formed a funeral circle around him. And while he looked for the ruined remnants of his former splendour; while he washed his hands with spittle, then wiping them in his hair (for it was better to wash them with spittle than not to wash them at all, after an entire night of vice and crime), they intoned the laments for the dead, which are sung when someone has been buried. And in fact the youth was not to survive the tortures inflicted on him by a divine hand, and his agonies came to an end during the nuns' songs.' I remembered the inscription on the column; I understood what had become of the pubescent dreamer whose friends had been waiting for him since his disappearance ... And I wondered who his master could be! And I pressed my face harder against the grating! 'The walls opened to let him pass; the nuns, seeing him soar into the sky with wings till then hidden beneath his emerald robe, returned to their places beneath the lid of the tomb. He has returned to his celestial dwelling, leaving me here; it is not fair. The other hairs are still on his head; and I am lying in this dismal room on a floor covered with clotted blood and bits of dried meat; this room is damned since he came in; nobody enters; yet I am locked in. It is all over now. I shall never again see the legions of angels marching in thick phalanxes, nor the stars moving in the gardens of harmony. Well ... let it be ... I shall be able to bear my woe with resignation. But I shall not fail to tell men what happened in this cell. I shall give them permission to discard their dignity like a useless coat, since they have my master's example before them; I shall advise them to suck the verge of crime, since another has already done so.' The hair stopped speaking... And I wondered who its master could be! And I pressed my face harder against the grating!... Immediately, thunder clapped; a phosphorescent light penetrated into the room. In spite of myself I stepped back, warned by an inexplicable instinct; although I had moved away from the grating, I heard another voice, but this time insinuating, quiet, for fear of being heard: 'Stop leaping up and down! Be quiet ... be quiet ... if anyone should hear you! I will put you back with the other hairs; but first wait for the sun to set on the horizon, that night may cover your steps... I have not forgotten you; but you would have been seen as you left, and I would have been compromised. Oh! if only you knew how much I have suffered since that moment! When I returned to heaven, my archangels surrounded me inquisitively; they did not want to ask me the motive for my absence. They, who had never dared to look up at me, cast looks of utter amazement on my downcast face as they tried to solve the riddle; although they could not see into the heart of this mystery, their whispered thoughts expressed the fear that an unusual change had come about in me. They were shedding silent tears; and they had a vague sense that I was no longer the same, that I was now inferior to my previous self. They wanted to know what disastrous resolution could have made me cross the frontiers of heaven and come down to earth to indulge in pleasures which they themselves despised. They noticed on my brow a drop of sperm and a drop of blood. The first had shot from the thighs of the courtesan! The second had spurted from the martyr's veins! Odious stigmata! Indestructible rosaces! My archangels found the flaming remnants of my opal tunic in the thickets of space, floating above the wide-eyed peoples of the earth. They could not piece it together again, and my body remains naked before their innocence; a memorable punishment for abandoned virtue. See the furrows which have hollowed out a bed in my discoloured cheeks: it is the drop of sperm and the drop of blood, slowly oozing down over my dry wrinkles. Reaching my upper lip, they make an enormous effort and penetrate the sanctuary of my mouth, attracted, like a lover, by the irresistible throat. They are suffocating me, these implacable drops. Until now I had considered myself the Almighty; but no; I must bow my head before remorse which cries out to me: "You are only a wretch!" Stop leaping up and down! Be quiet . . . be quiet . . . if anyone should hear you! but first wait for the sun to set on the horizon, that night may cover your steps . . . I have seen Satan, my great enemy, rouse himself from his larva-like torpor and, lifting up the bony tangle of his massive frame, harangue his assembled troops; as I deserved, he poured scorn upon me. He said he was very surprised that his proud rival, caught in the act by one of his perpetual spying missions which had at last met with success, could so debase himself as to kiss the dress of human debauch, after a long voyage over the reefs of ether; and that he should brutally torture and kill a member of the human race. He said that this young man, crushed in the machinery of my refined tortures, might have been a genius; might have consoled men on this earth for the blows of misfortune with wondrous songs of poetry and courage. He said that the nuns of the convent-brothel were no longer quiet in their graves; but prowled around the yard, gesticulating like automata, crushing buttercups and lilacs underfoot; that their indignation had driven them mad, but not so mad as to forget the cause of the malady which afflicted their brains . . . (See them advancing, dressed in their white shrouds; they do not speak; they hold hands; their dishevelled hair falls on their naked shoulders; a bouquet of black flowers in their bosom. Nuns, go back to your vaults. Night has not yet completely fallen; it is only evening twilight . . . Oh hair, you can see for yourself; on all sides I am attacked by the maddening feeling of my depravity!) He said that the Creator, who boasts of being Providence for all that exists, has behaved, to say the least, with great negligence, in presenting such a spectacle to the starry worlds; for he clearly expressed his plan to report to all the orbiting planets on how, by my own example, I maintain virtue and goodness in the immensity of my realms. He said that the great esteem in which he had held such a noble rival had vanished from his imagination; and that he would prefer to put his hand on a young girl's breast, although this is an act of execrable wickedness, than to spit in my face, covered in three layers of mingled blood and sperm; he would rather not defile his slimy spittle by such an act. He said he justly felt superior to me, not in vice, but in virtue and modesty; not in crime, but in justice; he said I should be strung up for my countless faults; that I should be burned slowly over a blazing fire and that I should then be thrown into the sea, provided the sea was willing to receive me. That since I boasted of being just, I, who had condemned him to eternal pain for a slight revolt which had not had grave consequences, then I ought to be severely just with myself, and judge my conscience impartially, laden as it was with heinous crimes! . . . Stop leaping up and down! Be quiet . . . be quiet . . . if anyone should hear you! I will put you back with the other hairs; but first wait for the sun to set on the horizon, that night may cover your steps.' He paused for a moment; although I could not see him at all, I judged from the length of the pause that a surge of emotion was heaving in his breast, like a whirlwind arousing a family of whales. Divine breast, defiled one day by the bitter touch of a shameless woman's nipples! Royal soul, which in a moment of forgetfulness abandoned itself to the crab of debauchery, to the octopus of weakness, to the shark of individual abjection, to the boa of amorality, and to the monstrous snail of imbecility! The hair and its master hugged one another close, like two friends who meet one another again after a long absence. The Creator continued, the accused appearing before his own tribunal: 'And what will men think of me, of whom they thought so highly, when they find out about the aberrations of my behaviour, my sandals' hesitant march over the muddy labyrinths of matter, the direction of the dark route I took over the stagnant waters and damp rushes of the pool where dark-footed crime, shrouded in fog, turns blue and roars ... I see that I will have to work hard to rehabilitate myself in the future and regain their esteem. I am the Almighty; and yet in one respect I am inferior to the men I created with a grain of sand! Tell them a bold lie, tell them that I have never left heaven, where I am constantly enclosed, with all the cares of the throne, among the marbles, the statues and the mosaics of my palaces. I appeared before the celestial sons of mankind and I said to them: "Hunt evil away from your cottages, and let the cloak of good come in to your hearths. He who lays a hand on one of his fellow-men, fatally wounding him in the chest with a murderous knife, let him not hope for any mercy from me, let him fear the scales of my justice. He will go and hide his sorrow in the woods; but the rustling of the leaves through the grove will sing the ballad of remorse in his ears; and he will flee those parts, stung in the hips by bushes, holly, and blue-thistles, his rapid steps caught up in the supple creepers, bitten by scorpions. He will make for the pebbles of the beach; but the rising tide with its spray and its dangerous surge will tell him that it is not unaware of his past; and he will rush blindly towards the clifftops, while the strident equinoctial winds, whistling down into the natural caves of the gulf and the huge holes gouged in the rock-face, bellow like the huge herds of buffalo on the pampas. The lighthouses will pursue him to the northern limits with their sarcastic lights, and the will o' the wisps of the maremma, simple burning lights dancing in a fantastic style, will make the hairs of his pores shiver and make the iris of his eyes green. Let modesty thrive in your huts, and may it be safe in the shade of your fields. Thus will your sons become handsome and bow down in gratitude to their parents; if not, sickly and stunted as the scrolls of parchment in libraries, they will be led to revolt, and will step forward and curse the day of their birth and the lewd clitoris of their mother. How can men be brought to obey these strict laws if the legislator himself refuses to be bound by them? . . . and my shame is as immense as eternity.' I heard the hair humbly forgive him for confining him, since his master had acted from discretion, and not from carelessness; and the last pale ray of the sun which gave me light disappeared into the ravines of the mountain. Turning towards it, I saw it coil round, like a shroud . . . 'Stop leaping up and down! Be quiet . . . be quiet . . . if anyone should hear you! He will put you back with the other hairs. And now that the sun has set on the horizon, cynical old man and soft strand of hair, creep away from the brothel, while night, spreading its shadow over the convent, covers the lengthening of your furtive steps over the plain.' Then the louse, suddenly emerging from behind a promontory, says to me, brandishing its claws: 'What do you think of that?' But I did not want to reply. I withdrew and came back on to the bridge. I effaced the original inscription, and replaced it with this: 'It is painful to keep such a secret, like a dagger, in one's heart; but I swear never to reveal what I witnessed when, for the first time, I entered this terrible dungeon.' I threw the knife I had used to carve out these letters over the parapet. And making a few rapid reflections on the character of the Creator who was in his infancy and who was destined, alas! to make mankind suffer for quite a while (eternity is long) whether by his own acts of cruelty or by the ignoble spectacles of the chancres caused by a great vice, I closed my eyes like a drunken man at the thought of having such a being as my enemy, and sadly went on my way through the mazes of the streets.

FOURTH BOOK

I

A MAN, a stone, or a tree is going to begin this fourth song. When the foot slips on a frog which it has crushed, one has a feeling of disgust; but when one merely brushes against the human body with one's hand, the skin of one's fingers cracks like fragments of a block of mica smashed by hammer-blows; and just as, on ship's deck, the heart of a shark, though it has been dead for an hour, goes on beating with dogged vitality, so too our entrails are stirred to the depths long after that touch. Such is the horror which man inspires in his fellow-beings! Perhaps in suggesting this I am mistaken; but it may be that I am right. I know, I can conceive of a malady more terrible than the puffiness of the eyes which comes from long hours of meditation on the strange character of man: but I am still seeking it . . . and I have not been able to find it! I do not think I am less intelligent than the next man, but who would dare to declare that I have succeeded in my investigations? What a lie his lips would be telling! The ancient temple of Denderah is one and a half hours' journey from the left bank of the Nile. Today countless swarms of wasps have taken possession of its gutters and cornices. They fly around the columns like the thick waves of a head of black hair. Sole inhabitants of the cold porch, they guard the entrance to the vestibule as if it were a hereditary right. I compare the buzzing of their metallic wings to the incessant crashing of ice-floes flung against one another when the ice breaks up in polar seas. But when I consider the conduct of him whom providence gave the throne of this earth, the three pinions of my sorrow make a far louder hum! When, after eighty years' absence, a comet reappears in some part of the heavens, it displays its brilliant nebulous trail for men and for crickets to behold. No doubt it is unaware of this long journey; the same is not true of me: sitting up in bed while the jagged shapes of a gloomy and arid horizon loom up in force from the depths of my soul, I give myself up to dreams of compassion, and I blush for man! The sailor, cut by the blasts of the north wind, hurries back to his hammock when he has finished his night watch: why am I not granted this consolation? The thought that I have wilfully fallen as low as my fellow-beings, that I have less right than the next man to bewail our fate, which remains shackled to the hardened crust of a planet, or the essence of our perverse souls, pierces me like a massive nail. We have seen whole families wiped out by fire-damp explosions; but the pain they felt must have been short, since death is almost instantaneous, amid the ruins and the noxious gases . . . I . . . I still exist, like basalt. In the middle as at the beginning of their lives angels still look the same: yet it is ages since I looked myself. Man and I, confined within the bounds of our understanding, as often a lake is amid a circle of coral islands, instead of joining forces to defend ourselves against chance and misfortune, avoid each other, and, trembling with hate, take opposite roads, as if we had stabbed one another with the point of a dagger. You would think that each one realizes the scorn the other feels for him; motivated by a feeling of relative dignity, we are anxious not to mislead our adversary; each one keeps to himself and is aware that peace, if it were proclaimed, would be impossible to keep. Well, then, let it be! Let my war against man go on for eternity, since each recognizes his own degradation in the other . . . since we are both mortal enemies. Whether I am destined to win a disastrous victory or to succumb, the struggle will be good: I alone against mankind.

I shall not use weapons made of wood or iron; I shall spurn all the minerals of the earth; the powerful and seraphic resonance of the harp will be a formidable talisman in my hands. In several ambushes man, the sublime monkey, has already pierced my breast with his porphyry lance: a soldier does not show his wounds, however glorious they may be. This terrible war will bring sorrow to both sides: two friends stubbornly seeking to destroy one another, what a scene!

2

Two columns, which it was not difficult, far less impossible, to take for baobobs, could be seen in the valley, bigger than two pins. In fact, they were two huge towers. Now though, at first sight, two baobobs do not look like two pins, or even like two towers, nevertheless, by adroit use of the strings of prudence, one may affirm, without fear of error (for if this affirmation were accompanied by the least scrap of such fear, it would be no affirmation; although a single name expresses these two phenomena of the soul whose characteristics are sufficiently well-defined as not to be easily confused), one may affirm that a baobob is not so very different from a column that comparison between these two architectural forms should be forbidden ... or geometrical forms ... or both ... or neither ... or rather high and massive forms. I have just discovered, I do not deny it, the epithets appropriate to the nouns column and baobob: and I want you to know that it is not without a feeling of joy mingled with pride that I make this observation to those who, after raising their eyelids, have made the very praiseworthy resolution to look through these pages, while the candle burns if it is night, while the sun casts its light, if it is day. And yet, even if a higher power were to command us, in the clearest possible terms, to cast this judicious comparison, which everyone has been able to relish with impunity, into the abyss of chaos, even then, and especially then, let us not lose sight of this main axiom, that the habits acquired over years through books and contact with one's fellows, and the innate character of each individual, which develops in rapid efflorescence, all these would impose on the human mind the irreparable stigma of relapse into the criminal use (criminal, that is, if we momentarily and spontaneously take the point of view of the superior power) of a rhetorical figure which several people despise, but many adore. If the reader finds this sentence too long, let him accept my apologies; but let him expect no grovelling on my part. I may acknowledge my mistakes; but I will not make them more serious by my cowardice. My reasoning will sometimes jingle the bells of madness and the serious appearance of what is, after all, merely grotesque (although, according to some philosophers, it is quite difficult to tell the difference between the clown and the melancholic man, life itself being but a comic tragedy or a tragic comedy); however, each of us is free to kill flies and even rhinoceri from time to time as a relaxation from too demanding labours. The speediest way of killing flies, though it may not be the best, is this: you crush them between the first two fingers of your hand. The majority of writers who have gone into this subject have calculated, apparently convincingly, that it is preferable in several cases to cut off their heads. If anyone should reproach me for speaking of such an absolutely trivial subject as pins, I should like him to note, without bias, that the greatest effects are often produced by the smallest causes. And without straying more from the setting of this piece of paper, can one not see that the laborious piece of literature which I have been composing since the beginning of this strophe would perhaps be relished less if it were based on a problem in chemistry or internal pathology. Besides, in nature there are all kinds of tastes; and when at the beginning I compared the columns to the pins with such exactitude (certainly I did not think I would one day be reproached for it), I based this on the laws of optics which have proved that the further away from an object one stands, the smaller the image of its reflection on the retina.

Thus it is that what our mind's tendency to farce takes for a wretched attempt at wit is simply, in the author's own mind, an important truth, solemnly proclaimed! Oh that mad philosopher who burst into laughter when he saw an ass eating a fig! I am not making this up; ancient books have recounted in the fullest detail this wilful and shameful derogation of human nobility. I cannot laugh. I have never been able to laugh, though I have tried to do so several times. It is very difficult to learn to laugh. Or rather I think that a feeling of loathing for this monstrosity is an essential feature of my character. Now I have witnessed something even more outrageous: I have seen a fig eating an ass! And yet I did not laugh; honestly, not a muscle on my face moved. The need to cry took such violent possession of me that my eyes shed a tear. 'Nature! Nature!' I cried, sobbing. 'The hawk tears the sparrow to pieces, the fig eats the ass, and the tapeworm devours man.' Before deciding to go on, I wonder if I have spoken of the way to kill flies. I have, have I not? And yet it is equally true that I had not previously spoken of the destruction of rhinoceri. If certain of my friends were to claim the contrary, I would not listen to them and I would bear in mind that praise and flattery are two great stumbling-blocks. However, in order to appease my conscience as far as possible, I cannot help observing that this dissertation on the rhinoceros would carry me beyond the limits of patience and composure and would probably (let us even be so bold as to say certainly) daunt the present generation. To think of not speaking of the rhinoceros after the fly! At least as a passable excuse I ought to have mentioned (but I did not!) this un-premeditated omission, which will not surprise those who have studied in depth the real and inexplicable contradictions which abide in the lobes of the human brain. Nothing is unworthy of a great and simple understanding; the least phenomenon in nature, if there is anything mysterious about it, can be an inexhaustible subject of reflection for the wise man. If someone sees an ass eating a fig or a fig eating an ass (these two circumstances do not often occur, unless it be in poetry), you may be sure that after reflecting for two or three minutes on what course to adopt, he will abandon the path of virtue and start laughing like a cock! Yet it is not exactly proven that cocks deliberately open their mouths to imitate men and to grin anxiously. I am applying to birds the same word grimace that we use for men. The cock does not change his nature, not because he is unable to do so, but because he is too proud. Teach them to read and they refuse. No parrot would go into such raptures at its own ignorant and in-excusable weakness. Oh execrable debasement! how like a goat one looks when one laughs! The smooth calmness of the brow has disappeared and given way to enormous fish-eyes which (isn't it deplorable?) ... which ... start to shine like lighthouses! It will often happen that I solemnly make the most clownish statements ... I do not consider this a sufficiently decisive motive for me to open my mouth wide! I cannot help laughing, you will reply; I accept this absurd explanation, but then let it be a melancholy laugh. Laugh, but cry at the same time. If you cannot cry with your eyes, cry with your mouth. If even that is impossible, urinate; but I warn you that some kind of liquid is necessary here, to counteract the dryness that laughter, with its creased features, bears in its womb. For my part, I shall not be put out by the ludicrous chuckles and strange bellowings of those who always find fault with a character which is not like their own, because it is one of the countless intellectual variations which, without departing from his primordial model, God created for the guidance of this bony frame of ours. Until our times, poetry has taken the wrong path; rising up to the sky or crawling along the ground, it has failed to recognize the principles of its existence and has with good reason been scorned by honest people. It has not been modest ... and modesty is the noblest quality which can exist in an imperfect being! I wish to display my good qualities; but I am not hypocritical enough to hide my vices. Laughter, evil, pride and madness will appear in turn along with sensibility and the love of justice, and will be an example, to the utter astonishment of all men: everyone will recognize himself in my work, not as he ought to be, but as he is. And perhaps this simple ideal which my imagination has conceived will yet surpass all that has been held most magnificent and most sacred in poetry up to now. For if I let my vices seep through in these pages, people will believe even more in the virtues which shine through in them; and I shall put such high and glorious haloes around those virtues that the greatest geniuses of the future will be sincerely grateful to me. Thus hypocrisy will be categorically hunted out of my abode. And there will be impressive evidence of power in my songs, in the way I disdain received ideas. He sings for himself alone, not for his fellow-beings. He does not put the measure of his inspiration in the scales of human judgement. Free as the tempest, one day he ran aground on the indomitable strand of his terrible will. He fears nothing, unless it be himself. In his supernatural combats he will attack man and the Creator to his advantage, as when the sword-fish thrusts its sword deep into the whale's belly: accursed be him by his children and by my fleshless hand who persists in not understanding the implacable kangaroos of laughter and the bold lice of caricature! ... Two huge towers could be seen in the valley; I said so at the

beginning. Multiplying them by two, the result was four ...
but I could not see very clearly the necessity of this arith-
metical operation. I continued on my way, my face flushed
with fever, and cried out incessantly: 'No ... no ... I cannot
see very clearly the necessity of this arithmetical operation!'
I had heard the clanking of chains and groans of pain. May no
one find it possible, when passing through that place, to
multiply the towers by two, that the result may be four!
There are some who suspect that I love mankind as much as
if I were its own mother and had borne it nine months in my
perfumed womb; that is why I never go back to the valley
where the two units of the multiplicand stand!

3

A GALLOWS rose up from the ground. A yard above the
ground a man was hanging from his hair, with his hands tied
behind him. To increase his agony, and make him want any-
thing but to have his hands tied, his feet had been left to
dangle freely. The skin of his brow had been so stretched by
his hanging that his face, condemned by the circumstances to
the absence of its natural expression, looked like the stony
concretion of a stalactite. For three days he had endured this
torture. He shouted out: 'Who will untie my hands? Who
will untie my hair? I am dislocated by movements which
only separate my head further from the root of my hair.
Hunger and thirst are not the main reasons which prevent me
from sleeping. It is impossible for me to live for more than an
hour. Someone to slit my throat with a sharpened stone!'
Each word was prefaced and followed by vehement shrieks.
I darted from the bush behind which I was sheltering and
went towards the puppet or piece of lard hanging from the
yardarm. But now two drunken women came dancing along

from the other side. One was carrying a bag and two whips with ropes of lead and the other was carrying a barrel full of pitch, and two paint-brushes. The greying hair of the older woman blew in the wind like the tatters of a torn sail and the legs of the other one clacked like the beating of a tunny on the deck of a ship. Their eyes shone with such a strong black flame that I did not think at first that these two women belonged to my species. They were laughing with such selfish unconcern and their features were so loathsome that I did not for a moment doubt that I had before my eyes the two most hideous specimens of the human race. Once more I hid behind the bush, and kept quiet, like the acantophorus serracticornis, which only shows its head above its nest. They were approaching with the speed of the tide; putting my ears to the ground, the sound which I clearly heard brought me the lyrical clatter of their walk. When the two female orang-outangs arrived beneath the gallows, they sniffed the air for a few seconds. They showed by their absurd gestures the truly remarkable extent of their amazement at the result of their experiment, when they noticed that nothing had changed in these parts: the dénouement of death had not, in conformity with their wishes, occurred. They had not deigned to look up to see if the mortadella was still in the same place. One of them said: 'Is it possible that you are still breathing? You are hard to kill, my well-beloved husband.' And as when two choristers, in a cathedral, sing the alternate verses of a psalm, the second one answered: 'You do not want to die then, my gracious boy. Tell me how you have managed (surely it was by some spell) to scare off the vultures? Your body really has got so thin. The wind blows it like a lantern.' They each took a brush and tarred the hanging man's body . . . they each took a whip and raised their arms . . . I was admiring (it was absolutely impossible to do otherwise) the powerful accuracy with which the blades of metal, instead of sliding along the surface, as when one is fighting a negro and making vain efforts, as in a nightmare, to grab him by the hair, went, thanks to the pitch, right into the flesh, which was marked with furrows as deep as the bones' resistance would reasonably permit. I refrained from the temptation of taking pleasure in this excessively curious spectacle, which was less profoundly comic than one had the right to expect. And yet despite the good resolutions I had made in advance, how could I not acknowledge the strength of these women, the muscles of their arms? Their skill, which consisted in striking the most sensitive parts, will not be mentioned by me, unless my ambition is to aspire to total truth! Unless, putting my lips against one another (not everyone is unaware that this is the most common manner of bringing about this pressure), I prefer to maintain a tear-swollen and mysterious silence, the painful manifestation of which would be unable to hide, not only as well as but even better than my words (for I do not believe I am mistaken, although one must not, at the risk of failing to comply with the most elementary rules of cleverness, deny the hypothetical possibilities of error) the baleful results caused by the rage which sets the dry metacarpi and the strong joints to work: even if one were to take the viewpoint of the implacable observer and experienced moralist (it is almost quite important that you should know that I do not at least entirely admit this more or less fallacious restriction), even then doubt would not be able to spread its roots in this matter; since I do not at the moment suppose him to be in the hands of a supernatural power and he would inevitably perish, though not suddenly perhaps, due to the lack of a sap which fulfilled the simultaneous conditions of being nutritious and free of poisonous matter. It is understood (if not, then do not read me) that in saying this I am merely introducing the timid personality of my own opinion: yet far be from me the thought of renouncing rights which are indisputable! And I

most assuredly do not intend to take exception to this state-
ment in which the criterion of certitude glitters, that there is a
simpler means of reaching agreement; this would consist,
I express it in but a few words, which are worth more than a
thousand, in not discussing anything; and this is far more
difficult to put into practice than the generality of men would
like to think. Discuss is the grammatical word, and many
persons will find that they should not contradict what I have
just set down on paper without a voluminous dossier of
proofs. But the matter is significantly different, if one may
allow one's instinct to use rare sagacity in the service of cir-
cumspection, when it formulates judgements which, I can
assure you, would otherwise be so bold as to coast the shore
of braggadocio. To close this incident, which has been
deprived of its vein-stone by an act of frivolity as irremediably
deplorable as it is fatally interesting (a fact which everyone
will certainly attest to, once he has sounded out his most
recent memories), it is good, if one's faculties are in perfect
equilibrium, or better if the scale of imbecility does not out-
weigh by too much the scale on which the noble and mag-
nificent attributes of reason are placed, that is to say, to be
clearer (for hitherto I have merely been concise, a fact which
several will not even admit, because of my longueurs which
are only imaginary, since they achieve their goal, which is to
track down with the scalpel of analysis the fleeting appearances
of truth, even in their last entrenchments), if the intellect still
sufficiently predominates over the defects with which habit,
education and nature have weighed it down and choked it, it
is good; I repeat for the second and last time, for, by dint of
repetition, one would end up in most cases by understanding
each other, to return with my tail between my legs (if it is
even true that I have a tail) to the dramatic subject wedged in
this strophe. It is wise to drink a glass of water before I
attempt to continue my work. I prefer to drink two rather

than do without. Thus, when a runaway negro is being pursued through the forest, each member of the party hangs his rifle from the bindweed and they all meet in the shade of a thicket to quench their thirst and stay their hunger. But the halt only lasts a few seconds, the chase is eagerly taken up again, and the wild cries of the pursuers are soon heard once more. And just as oxygen is recognized by the property which it unassumingly possesses of lighting up a match which is still flickering in places, so will the accomplishment of my duty be recognized by the haste with which I return to the matter in hand. When the two females were no longer able to hold the whip, which exhaustion forced them to drop, they wisely called off this gymnastic labour which they had been engaged in for nearly two hours, and withdrew with an expression of joy on their faces which was not without menace for the future. I went towards the man who was calling out to me for help (for his loss of blood was so great that weakness prevented him from speaking and my opinion, although I was not a doctor, was that a haemorrhage had set in in his head and in his loins), and, having freed his hands, I cut his hair with a pair of scissors. He told me that one evening his mother had called him into her room and ordered him to undress and spend the night in her bed, and that then, without waiting for his answer, motherhood had stripped off its clothes and had made the most indecent movements in front of him. Then he had left the room. Moreover by his persistent refusals he had brought upon himself the anger of his wife who had lulled herself into the hope of a reward if she could get her husband to use his body to satisfy the old woman's passions. They had plotted and resolved to hang him from a gibbet in some unfrequented region, and there to let him perish by degrees, wretched and exposed to all kinds of dangers. It was only after numerous and serious reflections that they had at last hit upon this clever torture which had only been brought to an end by my unhoped-for intervention. Each expression was accompanied by signs of the most heartfelt gratitude and this was not the least merit of his confidences. I carried him to the nearest cottage; for he had just fainted, and I did not leave the ploughmen until I had given them my purse that they might attend to the wounded man and until I had made them promise to be as consistently compassionate to the poor wretch as if he were their own son. And I in turn told them what had happened and went towards the gate to set off again along the path; but after I had gone a hundred yards I came back to the hut again and, addressing its simple owners, I shouted: 'No ... no ... do not think that that surprises me!' This time, I went away for good; but I could not get a proper foothold: another man might not have noticed this! The wolf no longer passes beneath the gibbet erected one day by the hands of a wife and a mother, as when his charmed imagination would take the path towards an illusory meal. When he sees that black hair blowing in the wind on the horizon, he starts and, without losing any time, takes flight with incomparable speed. Should one see in this psychological phenomenon an intelligence superior to the common instinct of mammals? Without certifying or even anticipating anything, it seems to me that the animal realized what crime was. How could it fail to understand, when human beings have rejected the rule of reason to such an unspeakable extent leaving only savage vengeance in the place of this dethroned queen!

4

I AM filthy. I am riddled with lice. Hogs, when they look at me, vomit. My skin is encrusted with the scabs and scales of leprosy, and covered with yellowish pus. I know neither the water of rivers nor the dew of clouds. An enormous mushroom with umbelliferous stalks is growing on my nape, as on a dunghill. Sitting on a shapeless piece of furniture, I have not moved my limbs now for four centuries. My feet have taken root in the ground; up to my belly, they form a sort of tenacious vegetation, full of filthy parasites; this vegetation no longer has anything in common with other plants, nor is it flesh. And yet my heart beats. How could it beat, if the rottenness and miasmata of my corpse (I dare not say body), did not nourish it abundantly? A family of toads has taken up residence in my left armpit and, when one of them moves, it tickles. Mind one of them does not escape and come and scratch the inside of your ear with its mouth; for it would then be able to enter your brain. In my right armpit there is a chameleon which is perpetually chasing them, to avoid starving to death: everyone must live. But when one party has completely foiled the cunning tricks of the other, they like nothing better than to leave one another in peace and suck the delicate fat which covers my sides: I am used to it. An evil snake has eaten my verge and taken its place; the filthy creature has made me a eunuch. Oh if only I could have defended myself with my paralysed hands; but I rather think they have changed into logs. However that may be, it is important to state that my red blood no longer flows there. Two little hedgehogs, which have stopped growing, threw the inside of my testicles to a dog, who did not turn up his nose at it: and they lodged inside the carefully washed epidermis. My anus has been penetrated by a crab; encouraged by my sluggishness, he guards the entrance with his pincers, and causes me a lot of pain! Two medusae crossed the seas, immediately enticed by a hope which was not disappointed. They looked attentively at the two fleshy parts which form the human backside, and, clinging on to their convex curve, they so crushed them by constant pressure that the two lumps of flesh have disappeared, while two monsters from the realm of viscosity remain, equal in colour, shape, and ferocity. Do not speak of my spinal column, as it is a sword . . . Yes, yes . . . I was not paying attention . . . your request is a fair one. You wished to know, did you not, how it came to be implanted vertically in my back. I cannot remember very clearly; however, if I decide to take for a memory what was perhaps only a dream, I can tell you that man, when he found out that I had vowed to live disease-ridden and motionless until I had conquered the Creator, crept up behind me on tiptoe, but not so quietly that I did not hear him. For a short moment, I felt nothing. This sword was buried up to the hilt between the shoulder-blades of the festive bull, and his bones shuddered like an earthquake. Athletes, mechanical experts, philosophers and doctors have tried, in turn, all kinds of methods. They did not know that the evil man does cannot be undone! I forgave them for the depth of their native ignorance, and acknowledged them with a slow movement of my eyelids. Traveller, when you pass near by me, do not address the least word of consolation to me, I implore you. You will weaken my courage. Leave me to kindle my tenacity at the flame of voluntary martyrdom. Go away . . . let me not inspire in you any act of piety. Hatred is stranger than you think; its action is inexplicable, like the broken appearance of a stick in water. Such as you see me, I can still make sorties as far as the walls of heaven at the head of a legion of murderers, and then come back and, resuming this posture, meditate again on noble projects of vengeance. Adieu, I shall delay you no longer; and, so that you may learn a lesson and keep out of harm's way, reflect on the fatal destiny which led me to revolt, when I was perhaps born good! You will tell your son what you have seen; and, taking him by the hand, you will make him admire the beauty of the stars and the wonders of the universe, the robin's nest and the temples of the Lord.

And you will be surprised to see how amenable he is to your paternal advice, and you will reward him with a smile. But as soon as he knows he is unobserved, take a look at him and you will see him spitting his slime on virtue; he has deceived you, he who is descended from the human race, but he will deceive you no longer; thenceforward you will know what is to become of him. Oh unfortunate father, prepare, to accompany the steps of your age, the ineffaceable guillotine which will cut off the head of a precocious criminal, and the sorrow which will show you the way which leads to the grave.

5

WHAT is the shadow which casts the projection of its horned silhouette with incomparable power on to the wall of my room? When I put this dumb raving question to myself, the sobriety of my style is striving less for majesty of form than to give a picture of reality. Whoever you are, defend yourself; for I am going to hurl at you the sling of a terrible accusation: those eyes are not yours . . . Where did you get them from? One day, I saw a blonde woman pass by me; she had eyes like yours: you plucked them out. I see you want people to believe that you are beautiful; but no one is fooled; and I even less than the others. I am telling you this so that you do not take me for a fool. A whole group of scavenger birds, lovers of the flesh of others and defenders of the value of hunting, lovely as the skeletons which take the leaves from Arkansas panoccos, hover around your brow, like submissive and favoured servants. But is it a brow? It is not difficult to hesitate before answering this question. It is so low that it is impossible to check the small number of proofs for its doubtful existence. I am not telling you this for fun. Perhaps you have no brow, you who cast the image of your buoying movement, like a dimly reflected symbol of a fantastic dance, on the wall? Who scalped you then? If it was a human being whom you locked away in a prison for twenty years and who then escaped to prepare a revenge which would be a fitting reprisal, he did as he ought to do, and I applaud him; the only thing is, he was too lenient. Now you look like a Red-Indian prisoner, at least (let us note this as a preliminary point) by your expressive lack of hair. Not that it could not grow again, as physiologists have shown that, in the case of animals, even brains that have been removed eventually reappear; but my thoughts, stopping at this simple affirmation, which is not, as far as I can see, unmixed with enormous delight, do not even in their boldest extremes go as far as reach the bounds of a wish for your recovery; on the contrary, my thoughts operate on the basis of an extremely suspect neutrality which regards what for you is merely a temporary loss of hair as the presage of greater woes to come (or at least wishes it to be so). I hope you have understood me. And even if, by an absurd but sometimes unreasonable miracle, chance allowed you to find the precious skin which your enemy has religiously and vigilantly kept as the intoxicating souvenir of his victory, it is almost extremely possible that, even if one had only studied the law of probability in its relation to mathematics (now we know that analogy can easily bring the application of this law into other domains of the understanding), your justifiable but somewhat exaggerated fear of a partial or total chill would not spurn the important, and even unique, opportunity which would arise so expediently, though suddenly, of protecting the different parts of your brain from contact with the atmosphere, especially in winter, by means of a head-piece which rightly belongs to you because it is natural and which you would besides be allowed (it would be incomprehensible if you were to deny it) to keep constantly on your head, without running the always unpleasant risks of infringing the simplest rules of elementary decency. You are listening attentively to me, are you not? If you go on listening, your sadness will be far from escaping from the inside of your red nostrils. But as I am very impartial and as I do not detest you as much as I ought to (tell me if I am mistaken), you lend an ear to my speech despite yourself, as if impelled by a superior force. I am not as evil as you: that is why your genius bows down before mine ... Really, I am not as evil as you. You have just cast a glance at that city on the mountainside. And now what do I see? All its inhabitants are dead! I have as much pride as the next man, perhaps even more. Well, listen ... listen, if the confession of a man who recalls having lived for half a century as a shark in the undersea currents along the coast of Africa interests you deeply enough to pay attention to him, if not with bitterness, at least without the irreparable fault of showing the revulsion you feel for me. I shall not throw the mask of virtue at your feet, but shall appear before you as I am; for I have never worn it (if that is an excuse); and from the first moments, if you examine my features closely, you will recognize me as your respectful disciple in perversity, but not as your formidable rival. Since I do not dispute the palm of evil with you, I doubt if another will do so; for he would first have to be my equal, which is not easy. Listen, unless you are but the weak condensation of a fog (you are hiding your body somewhere, and I cannot find it): one morning, I saw a little girl leaning over the edge of a lake to pick a pink lotus; she steadied herself with precocious experience; she was stretching towards the flower when her look met mine (it is true that on my part the look was not unpremeditated). She immediately staggered like the whirlpool the tide causes around a rock, her legs gave way beneath her and, wonder to behold, a phenomenon which occurred as truly as I am talking to you now, she fell to the bottom of the lake; strange to say, she did not pick any more nymphaeceae. What is she doing down there? . . . I did not trouble to find out. No doubt her will, having joined the ranks under the flag of deliverance, is fighting desperate battles against decay. But, oh my master, at your look the inhabitants of the earth are wiped out, like an anthill crushed beneath the elephant's heel. Have I not just witnessed an example which demonstrates this? See . . . the mountain is no longer full of joyful sounds . . . it is as forlorn as an old man. The houses still stand, it is true; but it is not a paradox to state, in hushed tones, that the same cannot be said for those who were inside them and no longer exist. Already the emanations from the corpses have reached me. Can you not smell them? Look at those birds of prey waiting for us to go away, so that they may begin this giant meal; there is an endless cloud of them coming from the four corners of the earth . . . Alas, they had already come, since I saw their rapacious wings tracing a spiral monument above you, as if to spur you on to speed up your crime. Does not your sense of smell perceive the least emanation? The impostor is nothing but . . . at last your olfactory nerves are disturbed by the perception of aromatic atoms rising up from the city, though you do not need me to tell you this. I would like to kiss your feet, but my arms clasp only transparent vapour. Let us look for this untraceable body which my eyes nonetheless perceive: it deserves the most numerous tokens of sincere admiration on my part. The phantom is mocking me: it is helping me to look for its own body. If I gesture to it to remain in its place, it makes the same gesture back. The secret has been discovered; but not, I must frankly say, to my greatest satisfaction. Everything has been explained, the most significant as well as the most trivial details; these last are too unimportant to bring to mind; as, for example, the plucking out of the blonde woman's eyes: that is almost nothing! Did I not recall that I, too, had been scalped, though it was only for five years (the exact length of time had escaped me) that I had locked a human being up in prison so that I might witness his suffering, because he had, rightly, refused me a friendship which cannot be granted to beings such as me? Since I pretend not to know that my look can bring death even to the planets revolving in space, he who claims that I do not possess the faculty of memory is not mistaken. What remains for me to do is to smash this mirror to pieces with a stone ... it is not the first time the nightmare of temporary loss of memory has taken hold of my imagination whenever, by the inflexible laws of optics, I happen to stand before my own unrecognizable image!

6

I HAD fallen asleep on the cliff. He who has unsuccessfully pursued the ostrich across the desert all day has had no time to take any food or to close his eyes. If it is he who is now reading me, he can guess how heavy was the sleep into which I fell. But when the tempest with the palm of its hand has vertically pushed a vessel to the bottom of the sea; if, on the raft, but one man of all the crew remains, broken by weariness and privations of all kinds; if, for hours which seem longer than the life of man, he is tossed like flotsam on the waves; and if, some time later, a frigate's long curved keel should plough through those desolate regions and sight the wretch's fleshless carcass on the ocean, bringing help which almost came too late, I think this shipwrecked man will be even better able to guess the extent to which my senses were deadened. Mesmerism and chloroform, when they take the trouble, can also produce such lethargic catalepsies. They are not at all like death; it would be a lie to say they are. But let us come straightaway to the dream, lest eager readers, starving for reading matter of this kind, begin to roar like a shoal of macrocephalic whales fighting among themselves for a pregnant female. I dreamt I had entered the body of a hog, that I could not easily get out again, and that I was wallowing in the filthiest slime. Was it a kind of reward? My dearest wish had been granted, I no longer belonged to mankind. For my part I understood this to be the correct interpretation, and I felt the deepest joy. And yet I actively inquired into this to see what deed of virtue I had done to deserve this remarkable boon from Providence. Now that I have gone over in my mind the different phases of my frightful prostration on the granite belly, during which, unknown to me, the tide flowed twice over this irreducible mixture of living flesh and dead matter, it is perhaps not unprofitable to proclaim that this degradation was only a punishment inflicted on me by divine justice. But who knows his inmost needs or the causes of his pestilential joys? The metamorphosis was always in my eyes the high and magnanimous resonance of the perfect happiness which I had long been awaiting. At last the day had come when I was a hog! I tested my teeth on the barks of trees; with pleasure I contemplated my snout. Not the slightest trace of divinity remained: I raised my soul to the excessive height of that unspeakable delight. Listen then to me, and do not blush, inexhaustible caricatures of the Beautiful, who take seriously the laughable brayings of your supremely despicable souls; and who do not understand why the Almighty, in a rare moment of excellent buffoonery which certainly did not transgress the great general laws of the grotesque, one day took amazing pleasure in peopling a planet with strange microscopic beings called humans, made of matter resembling pink coral. Certainly, flesh and bone, you have reason to blush, but listen to me. I do not invoke your understanding; it would spit blood at the horror you cause it: forget it, and be consistent with yourselves . . . There were no constraints there. Whenever I wanted to kill, I killed. I even wanted to quite often, and no one stopped me. The vengeance of human laws still pursued me, although I did not attack the race I had so calmly abandoned; but my conscience did not reproach me at all. During the day, I fought my new fellows, and the ground was often bespattered with many layers of congealed blood. I was the strongest, and I won all the victories. Biting wounds covered my body; I pretended not to notice them. The animals of the earth shunned me and I remained alone in my dazzling grandeur. What was my astonishment when, having swum across a river, leaving behind me lands which my fury had depopulated to find other countries in which to plant my customs of carnage and murder, I tried to walk on that flowery bank. My feet were paralysed; and no movement of any kind belied this enforced immobility. It was then, amid supernatural efforts to continue on my way, that I awoke and realized that I was turning back into a man. Thus Providence made clear to me, in a not inexplicable way, that she did not want my sublime projects to be realized even in a dream. Reverting to my original form was such a great grief for me that I still weep at nights. My sheets are constantly wet, as if they had been dipped in water, and every day I have them changed. If you do not believe me, come and see me. Then you will be able to check with your own experience not only the likelihood but the truth of my assertion. How often since that night spent in the open on the cliff have I not joined herds of hogs to take on my ruined metamorphosis as a right! It is time to give up these glorious memories, which only leave the milky way of eternal regrets in their wake.

7

It is not impossible to witness an abnormal deviation in the hidden or visible operations of the laws of nature. Indeed, if everyone takes the trouble of ingeniously investigating the different phases of his existence (not forgetting a single one, for it might be just that one which furnished the proof of what I am suggesting), it would not be without a certain astonishment, which in other circumstances would be comic, that he recalls that, on such a day, to speak first of objective matters, he witnessed a phenomenon which seemed to go beyond, and positively did go beyond, the common notions of observation and experience, such as showers of toads for example, the magic spectacle of which was not at first understood by scientists. And that on another such day, to speak in the second and last place of subjective matters, his soul presented to the inquiring gaze of psychology, I will not go so far as to say an aberration of reason (which, however, would be no less curious; on the contrary, it would be more so), but at least, so as not to cause offence to certain cold individuals who would never forgive me for the flagrant lucubrations of my imagination, an unusual state, quite often very grave, which indicates that the bounds which good sense prescribes for the imagination are, despite the ephemeral pact between these powers, unfortunately overstepped by the powerful force of the will, but also more often than not by the absence of its effective collaboration. To prove the point let us give two examples, the timeliness of which it is easy to appreciate: that is if one has attentive moderation as one's guide. I give you two: the outbursts of anger and the disease of pride. I warn him who reads me to beware of forming a vague and *a fortiori* wrong idea of the beauties of literature I am shedding like leaves before me in the excessively rapid unfolding of my sentences. Alas! I should like to develop my arguments and comparisons slowly and magnificently (but who is master of his own time?), so that everyone could understand if not my dread at least my stupefaction when, one summer evening, as the sun seemed to be setting on the horizon, I saw a human being swimming in the sea, with the large webbed feet of a duck instead of arms and legs and a dorsal fin proportionally as long and streamlined as a dolphin's, strong of muscle, and followed by numerous shoals of fish (in the procession, among other water-dwellers, I saw the torpedo, the Greenland ananark, and the horrible scorpaena), all of whom showed signs of the greatest admiration. Sometimes he would dive and his slimy body would reappear almost immediately two hundred metres away. The porpoises, who in my opinion have well deserved their reputation as swimmers, could scarcely keep up with this new kind of amphibian, and followed at some distance. I do not think the reader will have cause to regret it if he brings to my narration less the harmful obstacle of stupid credulity than the supreme service of profound confidence, examining lawfully and with secret sympathy the poetic mysteries, too few in number in his opinion, which I undertake to reveal to him as and when the opportunity arises, as it unexpectedly did today, inwardly imbued with the tonic scents of aquatic plants which the freshening wind blows into this strophe, which contains a monster who has appropriated the distinguishing features of the palimped family. Who speaks here of appropriation? Let it be known that man, by his multiple and complex nature, is not unaware of the means of extending its frontiers; he lives in the water, like the hippocamp; flies through the higher layers of the air, like the osprey; burrows in the earth, like the mole, the woodlouse, and the sublime maggot. Such is, in its more or less succinct form (but rather more than less), the exact criterion of the extremely invigorating consolation which I strove to conceive, when I thought that the human being whom I saw so far off swimming with his four limbs on the surface of the waves as the most magnificent cormorant had never done, had perhaps only acquired this novel change in the extremities of his arms and legs as a punishment in expiation of some unknown crime. It was not necessary for me to trouble my head attempting to manufacture in advance the melancholy pills of pity; for I did not know that that man, whose arms, one after the other, were beating the bitter waves, while his legs, with all the power of the nar-whale's spiral tusks, were forcing back the aquatic layers, had neither deliberately appropriated these extraordinary powers nor had they been imposed on him as a punishment. From what I learnt later, here is the simple truth: prolonged existence in this fluid element had imperceptibly brought about important but not essential changes in the human being who had exiled himself from the stony continents; these I had noticed in that object which a hurried and indistinct look had, in the primordial moments of his appearance (by an unspeakable act of thoughtlessness, the aberrations of which will be well understood by psychologists and lovers of prudence), made me take for a fish of a strange form but not yet described in the naturalists' classifications; but perhaps in their posthumous works, although I do not make the excusable claim of tending towards this supposition, imagined under conditions which are too hypothetical. In fact, this amphibian (since amphibian it is, the contrary cannot be proved) was visible only to me (leaving out of consideration the fish and the cetacea); for I observed that some peasants, who had stopped to contemplate my face, which was troubled by this supernatural phenomenon, and who were vainly trying to explain why my eyes were constantly fixed, with a persistency which seemed invincible but in reality was not so, on a point in the sea where they themselves could only see an appreciable but limited number of shoals of fish of all kinds, distended the apertures of their huge mouths almost as much as a whale. 'It makes us smile, but it does not make us turn pale, as it does him'; they said in their picturesque language. 'And we are not so stupid as not to notice that he is not exactly looking at the bucolic frolickings of the fish, but much farther into the distance.' So that, for my part, mechanically turning my eyes towards the spread of those two mouths, I said to myself that unless in the entire universe one found a pelican as big as a mountain or at least as big as a promontory (marvel, if you please, at this restriction which does not waste a single inch of ground), no beak of bird of prey or jaw of wild animal would ever be able to surpass or even equal each of these gaping, but too dismal, craters. And yet, though I am fully in favour of the positive use of metaphor (this rhetorical figure does far more service to human aspirations towards the infinite than those who are riddled with prejudices and false ideas – which comes to the same thing – are prepared to acknowledge), it is none-theless true that the risible mouths of these three peasants are still big enough to swallow three sperm-whales. Let us shrink this comparison somewhat, let us be serious and content ourselves with saying that they were like three little elephants which have only just been born. In a single stroke, the amphibian left a foamy wake one kilometre long behind him. In the brief instant when his forward-straining arm remains suspended in the air before plunging down again, his fingers, outspread and joined together by a fold of skin in the form of membrane, seemed to be soaring up towards the heights of space and grasping the stars. Standing on the rocks, I used my hands as a speaking-trumpet and exclaimed, while crabs and crayfish fled into the darkness of the most secret crevices: 'Oh you who swim faster than the winged frigate in its flight, if you still understand the meaning of these loud sounds which mankind utters as the faithful translation of its inner thoughts, deign for a moment to halt your swift movements and tell me briefly the phases of your true story. But I warn you that you do not need to address me at all, if your bold design be to arouse in me that feeling of friendship and reverence which I felt for you the moment I saw you for the first time moving through the waves with the grace and the strength of a shark on your indomitable and rectilinear pilgrimage.' A sigh, which made me shudder to the bone and made the rock on which the soles of my feet rested stagger (unless it was I who staggered, violently pierced by the sound-waves which brought such a cry of despair to my ears), could be heard even in the bowels of the earth; the fish dived beneath the waves with noise of an avalanche. The amphibian did not dare approach too close to the shore; but as soon as he had ascertained that his voice reached my eardrum distinctly enough, he slowed down the movement of his palmate limbs and lifted his wrack-covered head up from the roaring waves. I saw him bow his head, as if, by a solemn command, to summon the wandering pack of memories. I did not dare interrupt him in this holy and archaeological occupation; absorbed in the past, he looked like a rock. At last he spoke, as follows: 'The centipede is not short of enemies. The fantastic beauty of its countless legs, instead of attracting the admiration of other animals, is perhaps only a powerful stimulus to their jealous irritation. I should not be surprised to find out that this insect is exposed to the intensest hatred. I shall not disclose my place of birth to you; it is of no account in this story; but it is my duty to prevent the disgrace which would spring from my disclosure from befalling my family. After one year, heaven granted the wish of my father and mother (God forgive them!): two twins, my brother and I, were born. All the more reason for us to love one another. But it was not to be so. Because I was the more intelligent and handsomer of us two, my brother hated me, and made no attempt to hide his feelings: that is why my mother and father

lavished most of their love on me, since by my genuine and
constant friendship I was trying to appease a soul which had
no right to bear ill-will against his own flesh and blood. Then
my brother's fury knew no bounds, and he damned me in
our parents' hearts with the most unbelievable calumnies. I
lived for fifteen years in a dungeon, with maggots and foul
water for my only food. I shall not tell you the unspeakable
torments I endured during my long and unjust confinement.
Sometimes, at any moment of the day, one of my three
tormentors would take turns to come into my room, carrying
tongs, pincers and different instruments of torture. The cries
which the tortures wrung from me left them unmoved; my
abundant loss of blood made them smile. Oh my brother, I
have forgiven you, first cause of all my ills! Is it not possible
that one day, in your blind rage, you may see the light?! I
reflected much in my eternal prison. You can guess how strong
my hatred of mankind in general became. My progressive
enervation, my solitude of body and soul, had not yet
deprived me of reason to the point where I felt resentment
against those whom I had not ceased to love: the threefold
iron collar in which I was enslaved. I managed, by means of a
cunning trick, to regain my freedom! Disgusted by those who
lived on land and who, though they called themselves my
fellow-beings, appeared to resemble me in nothing (if they
found that I resembled them, why did they hurt me?), I made
my way towards the pebbles of the beach, firmly resolved to
kill myself if the sea should in any way remind me of my
previous unhappy existence. Would you believe your own
eyes? Since the day I fled from my father's house, I have not
had as much reason as you might think to complain of my
life in the sea with its crystal grottoes. Providence, as you see,
has given me in part the nature of a swan. I live in peace with
the fish and they provide me with all the food I need as if I
were their monarch. I shall whistle in a special way so as not

to set your teeth on edge, and you will see them all reappear.'
It happened just as he had predicted. He went on swimming
regally, surrounded by his train of loyal subjects. And though
after a few seconds he had completely disappeared from sight,
using a telescope I could still see him on the furthest limits of
the horizon. With one hand he swam and with the other he
wiped his eyes, made bloodshot by the terrible self-control he
had had to muster to approach the shore. He had done this
to please me. I threw the tell-tale instrument against the steep
and jagged rocks; it leapt from rock to rock, and its broken
pieces were swallowed by the waves. Such were the final
gesture and supreme adieu by which I bowed down, as in a
dream, before a noble and unfortunate mind. Yet everything
that happened was real, that summer evening.

8

EVERY night, swooping with the vast span of my wings into
the death-throes of my memory, I summoned up the memory
of Falmer. His blond hair, his oval face, his noble features, were
still imprinted on my imagination ... indestructibly ...
especially his blond hair. Away, away with that hairless head,
shining like a tortoise-shell. He was fourteen, I was only a
year older. Let that mournful voice be silent! Why does it
come to denounce me? But it is I who am speaking. Using
my own tongue to utter my thoughts, I notice that my lips
are moving and that it is I who am speaking. And it is I who,
as I tell a story of my youth, feeling remorse pierce my
heart ... it is I, unless I am mistaken ... it is I who am speak-
ing. I was only a year older. Who is he to whom I am refer-
ring? It was a friend I had in the past, I think. Yes, yes, I have
already told you his name ... I do not want to spell out these
six letters again, no, no. And there is no point either in

repeating that I was six years older. Even then my superior physical strength was all the more reason for helping him who had given himself to me across life's rough way, rather than ill-treating a being who was obviously weaker. Now I think he was weaker in fact . . . Even then. He was a friend I had in the past, I think. My superior physical strength . . . every night . . . Especially his blond hair. Bald heads have been seen by more than one human being; age, illness, sorrow (the three together, or separately) satisfactorily explain this negative phenomenon. That at least is the answer a scientist would give me, if I questioned him about it. Age, illness, sorrow. But I know well (I, too, am a learned man) that one day, because he had caught my hand as I was raising my dagger to stab a woman in the breast, I grabbed him by the hair with my hand of iron and sent him whirling through the air with such speed that his hair remained in my hand, while his body, hurtling with centrifugal force, went crashing against the trunk of an oak. I know well that one day his hair remained in my hand. I, too, am learned. Yes, yes, I have already said what his name was. I know well that one day I committed a dastardly deed, as his body was flung through the air by centrifugal force. He was fourteen. When in a fit of madness I run across fields, pressing to my heart a bleeding thing which I have long kept as a revered relic, the little children who pursue me . . . the little children and the old women who pursue me, flinging stones after me, utter these mournful groans: 'There is Falmer's hair.' Away, away with that bald head, shining like a tortoise-shell . . . A bleeding thing. But it is I myself who am speaking. His oval face, his noble features . . . Now I think in fact he was the weaker. The old women and the little children. Now I think in fact . . . what was I going to say? . . . now I think in fact he was the weaker. With my hand of iron. That impact, did that impact kill him? I am afraid of finding out the truth about what my eyes did not witness. In fact ... Especially his blond hair. In fact, I fled into the distance with a conscience thenceforward implacable. He was fourteen. With a conscience thenceforward implacable. Every night. When a young man who aspires to fame, bent over his desk on the fifth floor, at the silent hour of midnight, hears a rustling sound which he cannot account for, he turns his head, heavy with meditation and dusty manuscripts, and looks round in all directions. But nothing, no start, no sign, reveals the cause of what he so faintly hears, though hear it he does. At last he notices that the smoke of his candle, soaring up towards the ceiling, causes in the surrounding air the almost imperceptible rustling of a piece of paper pinned by a nail to the wall. On the fifth floor. Just as a young man who aspires to fame hears a rustling which he cannot account for so I hear a melodious voice saying in my ear: 'Maldoror!' But before correcting his error, he thought he heard a mosquito's wings ... leaning over his desk. Yet I am not dreaming; though I am lying on my satin-sheeted bed, what of it? I coolly make the shrewd observation that my eyes are open, though it be the hour of pink dominoes and masked balls. Never ... oh! no, never! ... did mortal voice give utterance to those seraphic tones, pronouncing with such sorrowful elegance the syllables of my name! The wings of a mosquito ... How kind and gentle his voice is. Has he forgiven me? His body smashed against the trunk of an oak ... 'Maldoror!'

FIFTH BOOK

I

LET the reader not be angry with me, if my prose does not have the good fortune to appeal to him. You will agree that my ideas are at least singular. And what you say, respectable man, is the truth; but a partial truth. Now what an abundant source of errors and confusion all partial truths are! Flocks of starlings have a way of flying which is peculiar to them, and seem to move according to a regular and uniform plan such as that of a well-drilled company of soldiers punctiliously obeying the orders of their one and only leader. The starlings obey the voice of instinct, and their instinct tells them to keep on approaching the centre of the main body, whereas the rapidity of their flight takes them incessantly beyond it; so that this multitude of birds, thus joined in their common movement towards the same magnetic point, incessantly coming and going, circling and criss-crossing in all directions, forms a kind of highly turbulent eddy, the entire mass of which, though not moving in any definable direction, seems to have a general tendency to turn in upon itself, this tendency resulting from the individual circling movements of each one of its parts, in which the centre, endlessly tending to expand but continually pressed down and repulsed by the opposing force of the surrounding lines which weigh down on it, is constantly tighter, more compact, than any one of these lines, which themselves become more and more so, the nearer they come to the centre. In spite of this strange way of eddying, the starlings nonetheless cleave the ambient air with rare speed and every second perceptibly gain precious ground as they move towards the end of their weary migration and the goal of their pilgrimage. Neither should you take any notice of the bizarre way in which I sing each of these strophes. But let me assure you that the fundamental accents of poetry retain unabated their intrinsic rights over my understanding. Let us not generalize about exceptional cases, that is all I ask: yet my character is in the order of possible things. No doubt between the two furthest limits of your literature, as you understand it, and mine, there is an infinity of intermediate points, and it would be easy to multiply the divisions; but there would be no point at all in that, and there would be the danger of narrowing and falsifying an eminently philosophic conception which ceases to be rational, unless it is taken as it was conceived, that is, expansively. So, observer of a thoughtful disposition, you can combine enthusiasm with inner coolness; well then, for me you are ideal ... and yet you refuse to understand me! If you are not in good health, take my advice (it is the best I can give you), and go take a walk in the country. A poor compensation, what do you say? When you have taken the air, come back to me. Your senses will be less weary. Do not cry any more; I did not want to hurt you. Is it not true, my friend, that to a certain extent these songs have met with your approval? Now what prevents you from going all the way? The boundary between your taste and mine is invisible; you will never be able to grasp it: which proves that this boundary itself does not exist. Reflect that in that case (I am only touching on the question here) it would not be impossible that you had signed a treaty of alliance with stubbornness, that pleasant daughter of a donkey, such a rich source of intolerance. If I did not know that you were no fool, I would not reproach you thus. It is not good for you to become encrusted in the cartilaginous carapace of an axiom you believe to be unshakeable. There are other axioms, too, which are unshakeable and which run parallel to yours. If you have a strong liking for caramel (an admirable practical joke on nature's part), no one will think of it as a crime; but those whose intellect, more dynamic and more capable of great things, is such that it prefers pepper and arsenic, have good reasons for acting in this way, without the least intention of imposing their mild rule on those who tremble at the sight of a shrew-mouse, or the telling expression of a cube's surfaces. I speak from experience. I have not come here to play an agitator's part. And just as rotifera and tardigrades may be heated to boiling point without losing any of their vitality, it will be the same with you if you can cautiously assimilate the sour suppurative serosity which slowly emerges from the irritation which my interesting lucubrations cause. Well, have they not managed to graft the tail from one rat's body on to another living rat's back? Try then, similarly, to transport the several modifications of my cadaverous reason into your imagination. But be cautious. At the moment, as I write, new tremors are being felt in the intellectual atmosphere: it is simply a matter of having the courage to face them. Why are you pulling that face? And even accompanying it with a gesture which it would take a long apprenticeship to imitate: you may be sure that habit is necessary in everything and since the instinctive revulsion you felt at the first pages has noticeably slackened off in intensity in inverse ratio to the attentiveness of your reading, like a boil which is lanced, it must be hoped, even though your head is still groggy, that your recovery will shortly enter its final phase. There is no doubt at all in my mind that you are already verging on a complete recovery; and yet your face is still very thin, alas! But . . . courage! you have an uncommon spirit within you, I love you, and I do not despair of your complete deliverance, provided you take a few medicines which will but hasten the disappearance of the last symptoms of the disease. First, as an astringent and tonic food, you will tear off your mother's arms (if she is still alive), cut them up into little pieces, and you will then eat them in a single day with not the slightest trace of emotion on your face. If your mother was too old, choose another surgical subject, younger, fresher, and consumptive, whose tarsal bones are good at springing from the ground when one is see-sawing: your sister, for example. I cannot help feeling pity for her fate, and I am not one of those in whom cold enthusiasm merely puts on a show of goodness. You and I will shed for her, for this beloved virgin (but I have no proofs that she is a virgin), two spontaneous tears, two tears of lead. That will be all. The most soothing potion I can suggest is a bowl full of granular and blenno-rhagic pus in which the following will previously have been dissolved: a hairy cyst from the ovary, a follicular chancre, an inflamed foreskin turned back from the gland by para-phimosis, and three red slugs. If you follow my prescription, my poetry will welcome you with open arms, as when a louse by its embraces cuts off the root of a hair.

2

I SAW an object on a mound before me. I could not clearly make out its head; but already I guessed it was not of any common shape, without however being able to state precisely the exact proportions of its contours. I did not dare approach this motionless column; and even if I had had the ambulatory legs of three thousand crabs (not to mention those used for prehension and the mastication of food) I would still have remained in the same place if an event, very trivial in itself, had not levied a heavy tribute on my curiosity, and made its dikes burst. A beetle was using its mandibles and its antennae to roll along the ground a ball, the principal element of which was excremental matter, and rapidly advancing towards the aforesaid mound, going out of his way to make his determination to take that direction quite clear. This articulated animal was not very much bigger than a cow! If anyone should doubt what I am saying, let him come to me, and I will satisfy the most incredulous amongst you with reliable eye-witness accounts. I followed at a distance, obviously intrigued. What did he intend to do with that big black ball? Oh reader, who are continually boasting of your insight (and not without reason), could you tell me? But I do not wish to put your well-known passion for riddles to such a severe test. Suffice it for you that the mildest punishment I can inflict on you is to point out that this mystery will not be revealed to you (it will be revealed to you) until later, at the end of your life, when you will open philosophic discussions with your death-pangs at your bed-side . . . and perhaps even at the end of the strophe. The beetle had arrived at the foot of the mound. I had fallen in behind it and was following it at the same pace, though I was still a long way from the scene of the action; for, just as stercoraceous birds, restless, as if they were always starving, thrive in the seas which lap the two poles, and only accidentally drift into temperate zones, so I, too, felt uneasy and began to walk forward very slowly. But what was the corporeal substance towards which I was advancing? I knew that the family of the pelicanides consists of four distinct genera: the gannet, the pelican, the cormorant, and the frigate-bird. The greyish shape which appeared before me was not a gannet. The plastic block I perceived was not a frigate-bird. The crystallized flesh I observed was not a cormorant. I saw him now, the man whose encephalon was entirely devoid of an annular protuberance! I vaguely sought in the recesses of my memory for the torrid or glacial country in which I had already observed this long, wide, convex, arched beak with its marked unguicular edge, curved at the end; these scalloped straight sides; this lower mandible with its sections separate till near the tip; this interstice filled with membraneous skin; this large, yellow and sacciform pouch, taking up all the throat and capable of distending considerably; and these very narrow, longitudinal, almost imperceptible nostrils in the groove at the base of the beak! If this living being with its pulmonary and simple respiration and body decked with hairs had been entirely a bird down to the soles of its feet and not just as far as its shoulders, it would not then have been so difficult for me to recognize it: an easy thing to do, as you will see for yourself. Only this time I shall spare myself the trouble; for to make my demonstration clear, I should need to have one of those birds placed on my own desk, even if it were only a stuffed one. Now I am not rich enough to buy one for myself. Following a previous hypothesis step by step I should immediately have determined the true nature and found a place in the annals of natural history for him the nobility of whose sickly pose I admired. With what satisfaction at not being completely ignorant of the secrets of his dual organism, and what eagerness to know more, I contemplated him in his permanent metamorphosis! Though he did not have a human face, he seemed to me as handsome as the two long tentacular filaments of an insect; or, rather, as a hasty burial; or, again, as the law of the restoration of mutilated organs; and, above all, as an eminently putrescible liquid. But, heedless of what was happening round about, the stranger kept looking straight ahead with his pelican-head. Some other day I shall resume the final part of this story. Yet I shall continue my narrative with sullen eagerness; for if on your part you are anxious to know what my imagination is driving at (would to heaven that it were only imagination!) for my own part I have resolved to finish all at once (and not twice) what I wanted to tell you. Although, nonetheless, no one has the right to accuse me of lack of courage. But when one finds oneself in such circumstances, more than one will feel the throbbing of his heart against the palm of his hand. A coasting ship's master, an old sailor and the hero of a dreadful story, has just died almost unknown in a little port in Brittany. He was the captain of a sea-going ship, working for a privateer, and was away from home for a long time at a stretch. Now after an absence of thirteen months he returned to the conjugal home at the moment when his wife, who was still confined, had just presented him with an heir whom he felt he had no right to acknowledge as his. The captain gave no sign at all of astonishment or anger; he coldly asked his wife to get dressed and to come for a walk with him along the town ramparts. It was January. The ramparts of St Malo are very high and when the north wind blows even the bravest men cower. The wretched woman obeyed, calm and resigned. When she returned, she became delirious. She died during the night. But she was only a woman. Whereas I, who am a man, in the face of no less a tragedy, I do not know if I had enough self-control to stop the muscles of my face from twitching! As soon as the beetle had reached the foot of the mound, the man raised his arm towards the west (in the precise direction where a lamb-eating vulture and a Virginian eagle-owl were engaged in combat in the sky), wiped from his beak a long tear-drop which scintillated like a diamond, and said to the beetle: 'Miserable ball! Have you not been pushing it for long enough? You have not yet satisfied your passion for revenge; and already this woman, whose arms and legs you tied together with pearl necklaces to form a shapeless polyhedron so that you could drag her by her tarsal bones through valleys and over paths, over brambles and stones (let me approach, to see if it is still she) has seen her bones gouged with wounds, her limbs polished by the mechanical law of rotatory friction, and mingling into a congealed unit, her body presenting instead of its original outlines and curves the monotonous appearance of a home-

geneous whole which but too much resembles, in the con-
fusion of its several crushed elements, the mass of a sphere!
It is a long time now since she died; leave these remains on
the ground and beware of increasing to irreparable pro-
portions the rage which is consuming you; this is no longer
an act of justice; for egotism, lurking in the teguments of your
brow, slowly, like a phantom, raises the sheets which cover
it.' The lamb-eating vulture and the Virginian eagle-owl,
carried away by the vicissitudes of their struggle, had now
approached us. The beetle trembled at these unexpected
words and what at any other time would have been an
insignificant movement this time became the distinguishing
mark of a fury which knew no bounds; for he rubbed his
hind legs dreadfully against the side of the elytra, making a
shrill noise: 'Who do you think you are, you pusillanimous
creature? It seems you have forgotten certain events in the
past; you have not kept them in your memory, my brother.
This woman deceived us, one after the other. You first, and
then me. It seems to me that this wrong must not (must not!)
disappear so easily from our memories. So easily! Your
magnanimous nature allows you to forgive. But do you
know, despite the abnormal condition of this woman's
atoms, reduced to a pulpy pâté (it is not now a question of
whether one would think, on a first investigation, that this
body has noticeably increased in density as a result of the
working of the two powerful wheels rather than by the
effects of my ardent passion), whether she is not still alive?
Hold your tongue, and leave me to my revenge.' He resumed
his activity, and went away, pushing the ball in front of him.
When he had gone, the pelican exclaimed: 'This woman, by
her magic power, has given me the head of a pelican and
changed my brother into a beetle; perhaps she deserves even
worse treatment than that which I have just described.' And
I, who was not sure that I was not dreaming, guessing from

what I had heard the nature of the hostile relations which, above my head, joined the lamb-eating vulture and the Virginian eagle-owl in bloody combat, threw my head back like a cowl to give my lungs the maximum freedom and elasticity and, looking upwards, shouted to them: 'You two up there, cease your strife. You are both right. For she promised her love to both of you; therefore she has deceived you both. But you are not the only ones. Besides, she has deprived you of your human form, making cruel sport of your most holy sorrows. And you would still hesitate to believe me? Besides, she is dead; and the beetle has subjected her to a punishment which has left an ineffaceable mark, despite the compassion of him who was first deceived.' At these words, they put an end to their quarrel, stopped tearing out each other's feathers and ripping off scraps of flesh: they were right to act thus. The Virginian eagle-owl, handsome as the memento which a dog leaves on the curb as it runs after its master, buried himself in the crevices of a ruined convent. The lamb-eating vulture, lovely as the law of arrested chest development in adults whose propensity to growth is not in proportion to the quantity of molecules their organism can assimilate, vanished into the higher strata of the atmosphere. The pelican, whose generous act of forgiveness had made a great impression on me because I found it unnatural, resuming on his mound the majestic impassivity of a lighthouse, as if to warn human mariners to pay attention to his example, and steer clear of the love of dark sorceresses, kept on looking straight ahead of him. The beetle, lovely as the alcoholic's trembling hand, disappeared on the horizon. Four more lives which could be erased from the book of life. I pulled a whole muscle out of my left arm, for I no longer knew what I was doing, so moved was I at this quadruple misfortune. And to think that I believed it was excremental matter. What a fool I am.

3

THE intermittent annihilation of human faculties. Whatever you might be inclined to suppose, these are no mere words. Or at least these are not words just like any others. Let him who thought that, by asking an executioner to flay him alive, he was doing an act of justice, raise his hand. Let him who would expose his breast to the bullets of death hold up his head with a smile of delight. My eyes will seek out the mark of the scar; my ten fingers will concentrate the totality of their attention on carefully feeling this eccentric's flesh; I will check to see if the spatterings of his brain have spurted on to the satin of my brow. The man who would love such martyrdom is not to be found in the entire universe, is he? I do not know what laughter is, never having experienced it myself. And yet how imprudent it would be to maintain that my lips would not widen if it were granted to me to see him who claimed that, somewhere, that man exists. What no one would wish for himself has fallen to my share by an unfair stroke of fate. Not that my body is swimming in the lake of sorrow. Let us pass on then. But the mind dries up with the strain of continual and concentrated reflection; it croaks like the frogs on the marsh when a flight of ravenous flamingoes and starving herons swoops down to the rushes' edge. Happy is he who sleeps peacefully in his bed of feathers plucked from the eider's breast, without noticing that he is giving himself away. I have not slept for more than thirty years now. Since the unutterable day of my birth, I have sworn implacable hatred to the somniferous bedplanks. It was my own wish; let no one else be blamed. Quickly, abandon the abortive suspicion. Can you make out the pale garland on my brow? She who wreathed it, with her thin fingers, was tenacity. As long as any trace of searing sap flows in my bones like a torrent of molten metal, I shall not sleep. Every night I force my livid eyes to stare at the stars through the panes of my windows. To be surer of myself, a splinter of wood holds my two swollen eyelids apart. When dawn appears she finds me in the same position, my body upright against the cold plaster of the wall. However, I do sometimes happen to dream, but without for a moment losing the unshakeable consciousness of my personality and my capacity of freedom of movement; you must know that the nightmare which lurks in the phosphoric corners of the shadow, the fever which feels my face with its stump, each impure animal which raises its bleeding claw; well, it is my own will which makes them whirl around, to give a staple food to its perpetual activity. In fact free will, a mere atom avenging itself for its weakness, does not fear to affirm with powerful authority that it does not count brutishness among its sons: he who sleeps is less than an animal castrated the night before. Although insomnia drags these muscles, which already give off a scent of cypress, down into the pit, never will the white catacomb of my intellect open its sanctuaries to the eyes of the Creator. A secret and noble justice, into the arms of which I instinctively fling myself, commands me to track down this ignoble punishment remorselessly. Dreadful enemy of my imprudent soul, at the hour when the lantern is lit on the coast, I forbid my wretched back to lie on the dew of the sward. Victoriously I repel the ambushes of the hypocritical poppy. Consequently, it is clear that in this strange struggle my heart has checked his plans, starving man who eats himself. Impenetrable as the giants, I have lived incessantly with my eyes staring wide open. It is obvious that, at least during the day, anyone can offer useful resistance to the Great Exterior Object (who does not know his name?); for then the will guards its defences with remarkable ferocity. But as soon as the veil of night mists comes down, even over condemned men about to be hanged, oh, to see one's intellect in the sacrilegious hands of a stranger! A pitiless scalpel probes among its undergrowth. Conscience utters a long rattle of curses; the veil of modesty is cruelly torn away. Humiliation! Our door is open to the wild curiosity of the Celestial Bandit. I have not deserved this ignominious punishment, hideous spy of my causality! If I exist, I am not another. I do not acknowledge this ambiguous plurality in myself. I wish to reside alone in my inner deliberations. Autonomy ... or let me be changed into a hippopotamus. Engulf yourself beneath the earth, anonymous stigma, and do not reappear before my haggard indignation. My subjectivity and the Creator, that is too much for one brain. When night spreads darkness over the passage of hours, who has not fought against the onset of sleep, in his bed soaking with glacial sweat? This bed, luring the dying faculties to her breast, is nothing but a tomb made of planks of squared fir. The will gradually gives way, as if in the presence of an invisible force. A viscous wax forms a thick layer over the crystalline lens. The eyelids seek each other like two friends. The body is now no more than a breathing corpse. Finally, four huge stakes nail all the limbs on to the mattress. And observe, I beg of you, that the sheets are but shrouds. Here is the cresset in which the incense of religion burns. Eternity roars like a distant sea and approaches with large strides. The room has disappeared: prostrate yourselves, humans, in the funeral chamber! Sometimes, vainly trying to overcome the imperfections of the organism in the midst of the deepest sleep, the hypnotized senses perceive with astonishment that it is now only a block of sepulchre-stone, and reason admirably, with incomparable subtlety: 'To get up from this bed is a more difficult problem than one might think. Sitting in a cart, I am being taken off towards the binarity of the guillotine posts. Strange to say, my inert arm has knowingly taken on the stiffness of a chimney stack. It is not at all good to dream that one is going towards the scaffold.' Blood flows in wide waves over the face. The breast repeatedly gives violent starts, heaves, and wheezes. The weight of an obelisk suppresses the free expression of rage. The real has destroyed the dreams of drowsiness! Who does not know that when the struggle continues between the ego, full of pride, and the terrible encroachment of catalepsy, the deluded mind loses its judgement? Gnawed by despair, it revels in its sickness, till it has conquered nature, and sleep, seeing its prey escape it, retreats, angry and ashamed, far away, never to return. Throw a few ashes on my flaming eyeballs. Do not stare at my never-closing eyes. Do you understand the sufferings I endure? (However, pride is gratified.) As soon as night exhorts humans to rest, a man, whom I know, strides over the countryside. I fear my resolve will succumb to the onset of old age. Let it come, that fatal day when I fall asleep! When I awake, my razor, making its way across my neck, will prove that, in fact, nothing was more real.

4

'BUT who can it be? ... but who is it who dares like a conspirator to trail the rings of his body towards my black breast? Whoever you are, eccentric python, by what pretext do you excuse your ridiculous presence? Are you tormented by vast remorse? For you see, boa, your wild majesty does not, I suppose, make any exorbitant claim to exemption from the comparison I am going to make between it and the features of the criminal. This foaming whitish slime is for me the sign of rage. Listen to me: do you know that your eye is far from absorbing a ray of heavenly light? Do not forget that if your presumptuous brain thought me capable of offering you a few words of consolation, then the only motive for your mistake must be an abysmal ignorance of physiognomic science. For as long, of course, as is necessary, direct the light of your eyes towards that which I, as much as the next man, have the right to call my face! Can you not see how it is weeping? You were wrong, basilisk. You will have to seek elsewhere the miserable ration of comfort which my radical incapacity denies you, despite the numerous protestations of my good will. Oh, what force which can be expressed in sentences fatally brought you to your downfall? It is almost impossible for me to get used to the argument that you do not realize that, by flattening the fleeting curves of your triangular head with a click of my heels, I could knead an unmentionable putty with the grass of the savannah and the crushed victim's flesh.

'Out of my sight immediately, pallid criminal! The fallacious mirage of utter dread has shown you your own spectre! Dispel these insulting suspicions, unless you want me in turn to charge you and bring a counter-accusation against you which would certainly meet with the approval of the reptilivorous serpent. What monstrous aberration of the imagination prevents you from recognizing me? Do you not recall the important services I did for you, as a favour to an existence which I had brought out of chaos, and, on your part, the forever unforgettable vow that you would not desert my flag, that you would remain true to me till death? When you were a child (your intellect was then in its finest phase), you would be the first to climb the hill with the speed of the izard to salute the multicoloured rays of the rising dawn with a motion of your little hand. The notes of your voice gushed forth from your sweet-sounding larynx like diamantine pearls resolving their collective personalities into the vibrant aggregation of a long hymn of adoration. Now you fling to your feet the forbearance which I have shown for too long. Gratitude has seen its roots dry up like the bed of a pond; but in its place ambition has grown to proportions which it would be painful to describe. Who is he who is listening to me, that he should have so much confidence in his own excessive weakness?

'And who are you, audacious substance? No! ... no! ... I am not mistaken; and despite the multiple metamorphoses you have recourse to, your snake's head will always gleam before my eyes like a lighthouse of eternal injustice and cruel domination! He wanted to take the reins of command, but he cannot reign! He wanted to become an abomination to all the beings of creation, and in this he succeeded. He wanted to prove that he alone is the monarch of the universe, and there it is that he is mistaken. Oh wretch! have you waited till this hour to hear the mutterings and the plots which, rising simultaneously from the surface of the spheres, come with wildly-beating wings to graze the papillaceous sides of your destructible eardrum? The day is not far off when my hand will strike you down into the dust which you have infected with your breath, and, tearing the noxious life from your entrails, will leave your body writhing and contorted to teach the appalled traveller that this palpitating flesh which strikes his sight with astonishment and nails his dumb tongue to his palate, must not be compared, if one keeps one's composure, with the rotten trunk of an old tree which has decayed and fallen! What thought of pity can it be which makes me stay here, in your presence? You should rather retreat before me, I tell you, and go wash your immeasurable shame in the blood of a newborn baby: such are your practices. They are worthy of you. So on ... keep walking straight ahead. I condemn you to become a wanderer. I condemn you to remain alone and without a family. Wander forever on your way, so that your feet can no longer hold you up. Cross the sands of the desert till the end of the world engulfs the stars in nothingness. When you pass near the tiger's lair, he will rush to escape so as to avoid seeing, as in a mirror, his character mounted on the pedestal of ideal perversity. But when overmastering weariness commands you to halt before the flagstones of my palace covered with brambles and thistles, be careful with your tattered sandals and pass through the elegant vestibule on tiptoe. It is not a futile injunction. You could wake my young wife and my infant son, sleeping in the leaden vaults which run along by the foundations of the ancient castle. If you did not take these preliminary precautions, they could make you turn pale with their subterranean howling. When your inscrutable will deprived them of life, they knew how dreadful your power was, and were in no doubt at all on that point; but they did not expect (and their last adieux to me confirmed their belief) that your Providence would prove so merciless! Be that as it may, cross rapidly these abandoned and silent rooms with their emerald panelling, but tarnished armorial bearings, in which the glorious statues of my ancestors are kept. These marble bodies are incensed with you; avoid their glassy looks. It is a word of advice from the tongue of their one and only descendant. See how their arms are raised in a provocative attitude of defence, their heads thrust back proudly. Surely they have guessed the wrong you have done me; and, if you pass within range of the chill pedestals which support these sculpted blocks, vengeance awaits you there. If there is anything you need to say in your own defence, speak. It is too late for weeping now. You ought to have wept earlier, on more fitting occasions, when you had the opportunity. If your eyes have at last been opened, judge for yourself the consequences of your action. Adieu! I am going to breathe the sea-breeze on the cliffs; for my half-suffocated lungs are crying out for a sight more peaceful and more virtuous than the sight of you!

5

OH incomprehensible pederasts, I shall not heap insults upon your great degradation; I shall not be the one to pour scorn on your infundibuliform anus. It is enough that the shameful and almost incurable maladies which besiege you should bring with them their unfailing punishments. Legislators of stupid institutions, founders of a narrow morality, depart from me, for I am an impartial soul. And you, young adolescents, or rather young girls, explain to me how and why (but keep a safe distance, for I, too, am unable to control my passions), vengeance has so sprouted in your hearts that you could leave such a crown of sores on the flanks of mankind. You make it blush at its sons by your conduct (which I venerate!); your prostitution which offers itself to the first comer, taxes the logic of the deepest thinkers, while your extreme sensibility crowns the stupefaction of woman herself. Are you of a more or less earthly nature than your fellow-beings? Do you possess a sixth sense which we lack? Do not lie, and say what you think. This is not a question I am putting to you; for since as an observer I have been frequenting the sublimity of your intelligence, I know how matters stand. Blessed be you by my left hand and sanctified by my right hand, angels protected by my universal love. I kiss your faces, I kiss your breasts, I kiss, with my smooth lips, the different parts of your harmonious and perfumed bodies. Why did you not tell me immediately what you were, crystallizations of superior moral beauty? I had to guess for myself the innumerable treasures of tenderness and chastity hidden by the beatings of your oppressed hearts. Breasts bedecked with rose-garlands and vetiver. I had to open your legs to know you, I had to place my mouth over the insignia of your shame. But (I must stress this), do not forget to wash the skin of your lower parts with hot water every day for, if you do not, venereal chancres will infallibly grow on the commissures of my unsatisfied lips. Oh! if, instead of being a hell, the universe had only been an immense celestial anus, look at the motion I am making with my loins: yes, I would have thrust my verge into its bleeding sphincter, shattering, with my jerking movements, the very walls of its pelvis! Misery would not then have blown into my blinded eyes from entire dunes of moving sand; I should have discovered the subterranean place where truth lies sleeping and the rivers of my viscous sperm would thus have found an ocean into which they could gush. But why do I find myself re-gretting an imaginary state of affairs which will never bear the stamp of final accomplishment? Let us not trouble to construct fleeting hypotheses. Meanwhile, let him who burns with ardour to share my bed come and find me; but I make one condition for my hospitality: he must not be more than fifteen years old. Let him not, on his part, think that I am thirty; what difference does that make? Age does not lessen the intensity of the emotions, far from it; and though my hair has become as white as snow, it is not from age: on the contrary, it is for the reason you know. I do not like woman! Nor even hermaphrodites! I need beings who are the same as me, on whose brows human nobility is graven in more distinct, ineffaceable characters. Are you sure that those whose hair is long are of the same nature as I? I do not believe so, and I will not abandon my opinion. Bitter saliva is flowing from my mouth, I do not know why. Who will suck it for me, that I may be rid of it? It is rising . . . it is still rising! I have noticed that when I suck blood from the throats of those who sleep beside me (the supposition that I am a vampire is false, since that is the name given to the dead who rise from their graves; whereas I am living), I throw up part of it on the following day: this is the explanation of the vile saliva. What do you expect me to do, now that my organs, weakened by vice, refuse to accomplish the functions of digestion? But do not reveal these confidences to anyone. It is not for my own sake that I am telling you this; it is for yourself and the others, that the influence of the secret I have imparted should keep within the bounds of duty and virtue those who, magnetized by the electricity of the unknown, would be tempted to imitate me. Be so good as to look at my mouth (for the moment I have no time to use a longer formula of politeness); at first sight it strikes you by its appearance; there is no need to bring the snake into your comparison; it is because I am contracting the tissue as far as it will possibly go, to give the impression that I am cold of temperament. But you really know that the diametrical opposite is true. If only I could see the face of him who is reading me through these seraphic pages. If he has not passed puberty, let him approach. Hold me tight against you, and do not be afraid of hurting me; let us contract our muscles. More. I feel it is futile to continue. The opacity of this piece of paper, remarkable in more ways than one, is a most considerable obstacle to our complete union. I have always had a perverse fancy for schoolboys and the emaciated children of the factories. My words are not the recollections of a dream, and I would have too many memories to disentangle if I were obliged to describe all those events which by their evidence could corroborate the veracity of my woeful statement. Human justice has not yet caught me in the act, despite the expertise of its policemen. I even murdered (not long ago!) a pederast who was not responding adequately to my passion; I threw his body down a disused well, and there is no decisive evidence against me. Why are you quivering with fear, young adolescent reading me? Do you think I want to do the same thing to you? You are being extremely unjust ... You are right: do not trust me, especially if you are handsome. My sexual parts perpetually offer the lugubrious spectacle of turgescence; no one can claim (and how many have approached!) that he has ever seen them in the normal flaccid state, not even the shoeblack who stabbed me there in a moment of ecstasy! The ungrateful wretch! I change my clothes twice a week; cleanliness, however, is not the principal motive for my resolution. If I did not act thus, the members of mankind would disappear after a few days, in prolonged struggles. In fact, whatever country I am in, they continually harass me with their presence, and come and lick the surface of my feet. But what power can my drops of sperm possess, that they attract everything which breathes through olfactory nerves to them! They come from the banks of the Amazon, they cross the valleys watered by the Ganges, they abandon the polar lichen on long journeys in search of me, they ask the unmoving cities whether they have glimpsed, passing along their ramparts, him whose sacred sperm sweetens the mountains, the lakes, the heaths, the promontories, the immensity of the seas! Despair at not being able to find me (I secretly hide in the most inaccessible places to inflame their ardour) drives them to the most deplorable acts. They stand, three hundred thousand on each side, and the roaring of the cannons serves as a prelude to the battle. Each flank moves at the same time, like a single warrior. Squares are formed and then immediately fall, never to rise again. The terrified horses flee in all directions. Cannonballs plough up the ground like implacable meteors. The scene of the battle is now but a field of carnage, when night reveals its presence and the silent moon appears through a break in the clouds. Pointing out a space of several leagues strewn with corpses, the vaporous crescent of that star orders me to consider for a moment, as the subject of meditative reflections, the fatal consequences which the inexplicable enchanted talisman that Providence granted me, leaves in its wake. Unfortunately it will take many more centuries before the human race completely perishes as a result of my perfidious snare. Thus it is that a clever but by no means bombastic mind uses, to achieve its ends, the very means which would at first appear to present an insuperable obstacle to their achievement. My intelligence always soars towards this imposing question, and you yourself are witness that it is no longer possible for me to remain within the bounds of the modest subject which I had planned to deal with at the outset. A final word . . . it was a winter night. While the cold wind whistled through the firs, the Creator opened his doors in the darkness and showed a pederast in.

6

SILENCE! a funeral procession is passing by you. Bend both your knee-caps to the ground and intone a song from beyond the grave (if you consider my words rather as a simple form of the imperative than as a formal order which is out of place, you will be showing your wit, which is of the best). It is possible that you will thus succeed in extremely gladdening the dead man's soul, which is going to rest from this life in a grave. As far as I am concerned, the fact is certain. Note that I do not say that your opinion might not to a certain extent be the opposite of mine; but what is extremely important is to have exact notions of the bases of morality, so that everyone should be imbued with the principle which commands us to do unto others what one would perhaps like to have done unto oneself. The priest of religions is the first to begin the march, holding in one hand a white flag, sign of peace, and in the other a golden emblem representing the genitals of man and woman, as if to indicate that these carnal members are, most of the time, all metaphor apart, very dangerous instruments in the hands of those who use them, when they blindly manipulate them for mutually conflicting ends, instead of bringing about a timely reaction against the well-known passion which causes almost all our ills. To the small of his back is attached (artificially, of course) a horse-tail with thick hair, which sweeps the dust of the ground. It means that we should not by our behaviour debase ourselves to the level of animals. The coffin knows its way and follows behind the floating tunic of the comforter. The parents and friends of the dead person, to judge from their position, have decided to bring up the rear of the cortège. It advances majestically like a vessel on the open sea, cleaving the waves, unafraid of the phenomenon of sinking; for at the present moment, tempests and reefs are conspicuous by their explicable absence. Crickets and toads follow the funeral, at some paces' distance; they, too, are not unaware that their humble presence at the obsequies of whoever it is will one day be counted in their favour. They converse in undertones in their picturesque language (do not be so presumptuous, permit me to give you this disinterested piece of advice, as to believe that you alone possess the precious capacity of conveying your thoughts and feelings), about him whom they had often seen running over the green meadows and plunging the sweat of his limbs in the bluish waves of the arenaceous gulfs. At first, life seemed to smile on him without any hidden intentions; and crowned him with flowers, magnificently; but since your intelligence itself perceives, or rather guesses, that he has been cut off at the bounds of childhood, I do not need, until the appearance of a truly necessary retraction, to continue the prolegomena of my rigorous demonstration. Ten years. A number that can be exactly counted on the fingers of both hands. It is a little and it is a lot. In the case which now preoccupies us I shall rely on your love of truth for you to pronounce with me, without a second's delay, that it is a little. And when I briefly reflect on these dark mysteries by which a human being disappears from the earth as easily as a fly or a dragon-fly, without a hope of returning, I find myself brooding with bitter regret on the fact that I shall probably not live long enough to explain to you what I cannot claim to understand myself. But since it is proven that by some extraordinary chance I have not yet lost my life, since the distant moment when, filled with terror, I began the previous sentence, I reckon that it will not be futile to compose here a complete confession of my total incapacity, especially when, as at present, it is a question of this imposing and intractable problem. It is, generally speaking, a strange thing, this captivating tendency which leads us to seek out (and then to express) the resemblances and differences which are hidden in the most natural properties of objects which are sometimes the least apt to lend themselves to sympathetically curious combinations of this kind, which, on my word of honour, graciously enhance the style of the writer who treats himself to this personal satisfaction, giving him the ridiculous and unforgettable aspect of an eternally serious owl. Let us therefore follow the current which is carrying us along. The royal kite has wings which are proportionally longer than a buzzard's, and a far more effortless flight: so he spends his life in the air. He hardly ever rests, and every day covers immense distances; and this vast movement is not at all a hunting exercise, nor the pursuit of prey, nor even a journey of discovery; for he does not hunt; but it seems that flying is his natural state, his favourite condition. One cannot help admiring the way in which he carries it out. His long narrow wings do not seem to move; the tail thinks it is directing operations, and it is not mistaken: it is moving incessantly. He soars without effort; he swoops as if he were gliding down an inclined plane; he seems to be swimming rather than flying. He speeds up his career, he slows down and remains hanging, hovering in the same place for hours on end.

One cannot perceive the least movement of his wings; you can open your eyes as wide as a furnace door, it will do you no good. Everyone will have the good sense to confess without demur (though a little grudgingly) that he cannot at first sight perceive the relation, however distant it might be, which I am trying to point out between the beauty of the royal kite's flight and that of the child's face, rising like a water-lily piercing the surface of the water; and that is precisely in what the unforgivable fault consists: the fault of permanent impenitence about the deliberate ignorance in which we wallow. This relation of calm majesty between the two terms of my arch comparison is already a too common and even a sufficiently comprehensible symbol for me to be surprised any more at what can only be excused by that very quality of vulgarity which calls down upon everything it touches a deep feeling of unjust indifference. As if we ought to wonder less at the things we see every day! At the entrance to the cemetery, the procession is anxious to stop; its intention is to go no further. The gravedigger puts the final touches to the grave; the coffin is lowered into it with all the precautions normally taken in such cases; a few shovelfuls of earth cover the child's body. The priest of religions, amid the deeply-moved audience, pronounces a few words to bury the boy even more in the imaginations of those present. 'He says he is very surprised that so many tears are being shed over such an insignificant act. Those are his exact words. But he fears he cannot adequately describe what he claims is an unquestionable happiness. If he had believed, in his innocence, that death was so fearsome, he would have renounced this duty, so as not to increase the rightful sorrow of the many relatives and friends of the dead child; but a secret voice warns him to give them some words of consolation, which will not be without effect, even if they only give them a glimpse of the hope of a reunion in heaven between the dead child and those who survived him.' Maldoror was racing along at full gallop and seemed to be heading for the walls of the cemetery. The steed's hooves raised a false crown of dust around its master. You cannot know the name of this horseman; but I do. He was coming nearer and nearer; his platinum face was beginning to be visible, although its lower half was completely enveloped in a cloak which the reader has taken care not to let slip from his memory, and which meant that only his eyes could be seen. In the middle of his speech, the priest of religions suddenly turns pale, for his ear recognizes the fitful gallop of the famous horse which never abandoned its master. 'Yes,' he added once more, 'I have great confidence that you will meet again; then we will understand better than ever before how to interpret the temporary separation of body and soul. Whoever believes that he is truly living on this earth is lulling himself with an illusion which it is essential to dispel, and quickly.' The sound of the gallop grew louder and louder; and as the horseman, hugging the horizon, came into the field of vision of the cemetery gate, rapid as a tornado, the priest of religions, in more solemn tones, resumed: 'You do not seem to realize that this child, whom sickness allowed to know only the first phases of life, and whom the grave has just taken to its breast, is undubitably living; but let me tell you that he whose equivocal outline you see riding on a sinewy horse, and on whom I ask you as soon as possible to fix your eyes, for he is now but a dot and will soon disappear into the heath, though he has lived long, is the only truly dead man.'

7

EVERY night, at the hour when sleep has reached its highest degree of intensity, an old spider of the large species slowly protrudes its head from a hole in the ground at one of the intersections of the angles of the room. It listens carefully, to hear if any rustling sound is still moving its mandibles in the atmosphere. Given its insect conformation, it can do no less, if it means to increase the treasures of literature with brilliant personifications, than to attribute the mandibles to the rustling sound. When it has ascertained that silence reigns all around, it draws out, one after the other, without the help of meditation, the several parts of its body, and advances with slow, deliberate steps towards my bed. And a remarkable thing happens! I, who can repulse sleep and night-mares, feel paralysed through my entire body when with its long ebony legs it climbs along my satin bed. It clasps my throat with its legs and with its abdomen it sucks my blood. As simple as that! How many litres of deep reddish liquor, the name of which you know well, has it not drunk, since it started going through this same procedure with perseverance worthy of a nobler cause. I do not know what I have done to it that it should act in this way towards me. Did I inadvertently tread on one of its legs? Did I take away some of its little ones? These two hypotheses, which are both highly suspect, do not bear serious scrutiny; it is even quite easy for them to make me shrug my shoulders and bring a smile to my lips, though one ought never to laugh at anyone. Take care, black taran-tula; if your behaviour does not have an irrefutable syllogism to justify it, one night I will awaken with a start, and with a final effort of my dying will, I shall break the spell by which you paralyse my limbs, and crush you between the bones of my fingers like a piece of pulpy substance. Yet I vaguely recall that I have given you permission for your legs to climb over my breast; and from there on to the skin which covers my face; that consequently I have no right to do violence to you. Oh, who will untangle my disordered memories? As a reward I will give him whatever is left of my blood; including the last drop, there will be at least enough to fill the bacchanal cup. He speaks, and takes off his clothes as he does so. He rests one leg on the mattress and, pressing down on the sapphire floor with the other in order to raise himself up, he is now in a horizontal position. He has resolved not to close his eyes, to await his enemy unflinchingly. But does he not make the same resolution each time and is it not each time frustrated by the inexplicable image of his fatal promise? He says no more, and sadly resigns himself to what is to come; for to him his oath is sacred. He swathes himself majestically in the folds of his silk, disdains to tie together the tassels of his curtains and, resting the wavy ringlets of his long black hair on the velvet of his pillow, touches the wound on his neck where the tarantula has got into the habit of residing as a second nest, his face breathing satisfaction all the while. He is hoping that the present night (hope with him!) will see the last performance of the immense suction; for his only wish is that his torturer should put an end to his existence; death, that is all he asks. Look at this old spider of the large species, slowly protruding its head from a hole in the ground at one of the intersections of the room. We are no longer in the narrative. It listens carefully to hear if any rustling sound is still moving its mandibles in the atmosphere. Alas! We have now come to reality as far as the tarantula is concerned and, though one could perhaps put exclamation marks at the end of each sentence, that is perhaps not a reason for dispensing with them altogether! It has ascertained that silence reigns all around; now look at it, drawing out, one after the other, without the help of meditation, the several parts of its body, and advancing with slow, deliberate steps towards the solitary man's bed. Briefly it pauses; but its moment of hesitation is short. It says that the time has not yet come for it to cease its tortures and that it must first give the condemned man some plausible reasons to explain what determined the perpetuality of his punishment. It has climbed up to beside the sleeping man's ear. If you do not wish to miss a single word of what it is about to say, exclude all the irrelevant occupations which block up the portico of your mind and be thankful at least for the interest I am showing in you by enabling you to be present at dramatic scenes which seem to me to be truly worthy of arousing your attention, for what could stop me keeping to myself the events I am recounting? 'Awaken, amorous flame of bygone days, fleshless skeleton. The time has come to hold back the arm of justice. We will not keep you waiting long for the explanation you desire. You can hear us, can you not? But do not move your limbs; today you are still under our magnetic power and your encephalic atony persists: it is the last time. What impression does the face of Elsseneur make on your imagination? You have forgotten it! And that Reginald, with his proud bearing, have you graven his features on your retentive brain? Look at him hiding in the folds of the curtains; his mouth is moving down towards your brow; but he does not dare speak to you, for he is more timid than I. I am going to recount to you an episode from your youth, and put you back on the path of memory...' A long time before this the spider's abdomen had opened up and from it two youths in blue robes had sprung out, each with a flaming sword in his hand, and they had gone to take up their position at the side of the bed, as if from that moment on to guard the sanctuary of sleep. 'The latter, who still has not taken his eyes off you, for he loved you very much, was the first of us two to whom you gave your love. But you often hurt him by the hardness and abruptness of your character. For his part he continually made every effort to avoid giving you any cause for complaint: no angel would have succeeded in this. You asked him, one day, if he would like to come swimming with you near the sea-shore. Like two swans, both at the same time, you plunged from the high cliff.

Eminent divers, you glided into the watery mass, your out-stretched hands joined. For some minutes you swam underwater. You reappeared far from there, your hair wet and tangled, streaming with salt water. But what mysterious event could have taken place underwater that a long trail of blood should be seen on the waves? Resurfacing, you continued to swim, and pretended not to notice the growing weakness of your companion. He was rapidly losing strength, and you only lengthened your strokes towards the misty horizon, which appeared as a watery blur. The wounded man was uttering cries of distress, and you pretended you were deaf. Reginald called out your name three times, so that its syllables echoed over the sea, and three times you answered with a cry of delight. He was too far from the shore to reach it and was vainly struggling to follow in your wake, in order to reach you and rest his hand on your shoulder for a moment. The fruitless pursuit continued for an hour, with his strength failing and yours perceptibly increasing. Giving up all hope of keeping up with you, he said a short prayer, and gave himself up into God's hands, then turned on his back as we do when we are floating, so that his heart could be seen beating violently against his breast. In this way he waited for death to arrive, that he might have to wait no more. At this moment your powerful limbs had disappeared from sight and were still moving away, rapid as a plummeting sound-line. A boat which had been casting nets came into those parts. The fishermen assumed that Reginald had been shipwrecked and hauled him, unconscious, into their little vessel. The presence of a wound on his right side was noted; every one of those experienced sailors expressed the opinion that no jagged reef or splinter of rock was capable of piercing a hole at once so microscopic and so deep. Only a cutting weapon such as a stiletto of the sharpest kind could claim the paternity of such a fine wound. He himself always refused to tell of the several phases of the dive into the bowels of the waves and he has kept his secret until now. Tears now flow along his rather discoloured cheeks, and fall on the sheets: recollection is often more bitter than the thing itself. But I shall feel no pity: that would be showing too much respect for you. Do not roll your wild eyes in their sockets. Remain calm. You know you cannot move. Besides, I have not finished my tale. Lift up your sword, Reginald, and do not so easily forget revenge. Who knows? Perhaps one day it could come and reproach you. – Later you imagined yourself afflicted with remorse, the existence of which must have been ephemeral; you resolved to atone for your sin by choosing another friend, whom you would revere and honour. By this expiatory means, you were to efface the stains of the past and lavish on him who was to become your second victim the affection you had not been able to show to the first. A vain hope; character does not change from one day to the next, and your will remained consistent with itself. I, Elsseneur, saw you for the first time and from that moment on I could not forget you. We looked at each other for a few seconds, and you started to smile. I lowered my eyes, for I saw a supernatural flame burning in yours. I wondered if, under cover of blackest night, you had not secretly descended to us from the surface of a star; for I must confess, now that there is no need for dissimulation, that you were not at all like the boars of mankind; but a halo of glittering rays surrounded the periphery of your brow. I would have wished to enter into intimate relations with you; but I did not dare approach the striking novelty of this strange nobility, and an unrelenting terror prowled around me. Why did I not listen to these warnings of conscience? Well-founded presentiments. Noticing my hesitation, you blushed in turn and held out your arms. I bravely put my hand in yours and after this action I felt stronger; thenceforward the breath of your intelligence had passed into me.

With our hair blowing in the wind and inhaling the breath of the breeze, we walked on through groves thick with lentiscus, jasmine, pomegranate and orange-trees, the scents of which intoxicated us. A boar in full flight brushed against our clothes as it rushed past, and a tear fell from its eyes when it saw me with you; I could not explain its behaviour. At nightfall we arrived at the gates of a populous city. The outlines of the domes, the spires of the minarets and the marble balls of the belvederes stood out with their sharp indentations in the darkness against the deep blue of the sky. But you did not wish to rest in that place, although we were overwhelmed with fatigue. We slunk along the lower part of the outer fortifications, like jackals of the night; we avoided the sentinels on watch; and we managed, by the opposite gate, to get clear of that solemn gathering of reasonable animals, civilized as beavers. The flight of the lantern-fly, the crackling of dry grass, the intermittent howls of a distant wolf accompanied us in the darkness of our dubious walk across the countryside. What were the valid motives for fleeing the hives of men? With a certain anxiety I asked myself this question; besides, my legs were beginning to give way under me, having borne me up for too long. At last we reached the edge of a thick wood, the trees of which were entwined in a mass of high, inextricable bindweed, parasite plants, and cacti with monstrous spikes. You stopped in front of a birch. You told me to kneel down and prepare to die; you granted me a quarter of an hour to leave this earth. Some furtive glances you had secretly stolen while I was not observing you during our long walk, as well as certain strange and unaccountable gestures, immediately came to mind, like the open pages of a book. My suspicions had been confirmed. As I was too weak to put up a struggle, you knocked me to the ground, as the hurricane blows down the leaves of the aspen. With one of your knees on my breast and the other

on the damp grass, while one of your hands clasped my two
arms in its vice, I saw your other hand take a knife from the
sheath which hung from your belt. My resistance was negli-
gible, and I closed my eyes. The dull thud of cattle's hooves
could be heard in the distance, the sound carried by the wind.
It was advancing like a train, goaded on by the herdsman's
stick and the barking jaws of a dog. There was no time to
lose, and you knew it; fearing you would not be able to
achieve your ends, since the unexpected arrival of help had
increased my muscular strength, and seeing that you could
only pin down one of my arms at a time, you merely cut off
my right hand with a flick of the steel blade. The hand,
precisely severed, fell to the ground. You took flight, while I
was blinded with pain. I shall not tell of how the herdsman
came to my assistance, nor of how long I took to recover.
Suffice it to know that this treacherous act which I had not
expected made me wish to seek death. I took part in battles,
to expose my breast to fatal blows. I won fame on the fields
of battle; my name struck fear into the very bravest, such
carnage and destruction did my artificial arm sow in the
enemy ranks. However, one day, when the shells were
thundering far louder than usual and the squadron of horse,
drawn away from their ranks, were whirling around like
straws beneath the tornado of death, a horseman, fearless in
his bearing, came towards me to fight for the palm of victory.
The two armies stopped fighting and stood rooted to the spot
in silent contemplation of us. We fought for a long time,
riddled with wounds, our helmets smashed. By common
accord, we ceased the struggle in order to rest and then to
take it up again with renewed ferocity. Filled with admiration
for his adversary, each one raises his visor: 'Elsseneur!'
'Reginald!' those were the simple words that our panting
hearts uttered, both at once. The latter, having fallen into
despairing and inconsolable gloom, had taken up arms as I

had done, and he too had been spared by the bullets. In what strange circumstances we were now reunited! But your name was not pronounced! He and I swore eternal friendship; but it was most assuredly different from the first two occasions, on which you were the main actor! An archangel from heaven, the Lord's messenger, commanded us to change into a single spider and come to suck your throat every night, until an order from on high should put an end to your punishment. For nearly ten years we have stayed by your bedside, and from today you are delivered from our persecution. The vague promise of which you spoke was not made to us but to the Being who is stronger than you: you yourself understood that it was better to submit to this irrevocable decree. Awake, Maldoror! The hypnotic spell which has weighed on your cerebro-spinal system for two lustra is broken.' He awakens as ordered and sees two celestial forms disappearing into the sky, holding hands. He does not attempt to go back to sleep. Slowly, moving one limb after the other, he gets out of bed. He goes over to his gothic fireplace, to warm his body by the embers of the fire. He is wearing only a shirt. He looks around for the crystal carafe, that he may moisten his dry palate. He opens the shutters of the window. He leans on the window-sill. He contemplates the moon which sheds on his breast a cone of ecstatic rays which flutter like moths with silver beams of ineffable softness. He waits for morning with its change of scenery to bring its derisory relief to his shattered heart.

SIXTH BOOK

I

YOU whose enviable composure can do no more than embellish your appearance, do not think it is still a matter of uttering, in strophes of fourteen or fifteen lines, like a third-form schoolboy, exclamations which will be considered untimely, the resounding clucks of cochin-china fowl, as grotesque as one could possibly imagine, if one took the trouble. But it is more advisable to prove by facts the propositions I am putting to you. Would you then assert that because I have insulted man, the Creator, and myself in my explicable hyperboles, and with such whimsicality, that my mission is accomplished? No; the most important part of my work is nonetheless before me, a task remaining to be done. Henceforward the strings of the novel will move the three characters mentioned above; they will thus be endowed with a less abstract power. Vitality will surge into the stream of their circulatory system and you will see how startled you will be when you encounter, where at first you had only expected to see entities belonging to the realm of pure speculation, on the one hand the corporeal organism with its ramifications of nerves and mucous membranes and, on the other, the spiritual principle which governs the physiological functions of the flesh. It is beings powerfully endowed with life who, their arms folded and holding their breath, will stand prosaically (but I am sure the effect will be very poetic) before your eyes, only a few paces away from you, so that the sun's rays, falling first upon the tiles of the roofs and the lids of the chimneys, will then come and visibly shine on their earthly and material hair. But they will no longer be anathemata possessing the special quality of exciting laughter; fictive personalities who would have done better to remain in the author's brain; or nightmares too far removed from ordinary existence. Note that this very fact will but make my poetry finer. You will touch with your own hands the ascending branches of the aorta and the adrenal capsules; and then the feelings! The first five songs have not been useless; they were the frontispiece to my work, the foundation of the structure, the preliminary explanation of my future poetic: and I owed it to myself, before strapping up my suitcases and setting off for the lands of the imagination, to warn sincere lovers of literature with a rapid sketch, a clear and precise general picture, of the goal I had resolved to pursue. Consequently, it is my opinion that the synthetic part of my work is now complete and has been adequately amplified. In this part you learnt that I had set myself the task of attacking man and Him who created man. For the moment, and for later, you need to know no more. New considerations seem to me superfluous, for they would only repeat, admittedly in a fuller, but identical, form, the statement of the thesis which will have its first exposition at the end of this day. It follows from the preceding remarks that from now on my intention is to start upon the analytic part; so true, indeed, is this that only a few minutes ago I expressed the ardent wish that you should be imprisoned in the sudoriferous glands of my skin in order to prove the sincerity of what I am stating with full knowledge of the facts. It is necessary, I know, to underpin with a large number of proofs the argument of my theorem; well, these proofs exist and you know that I do not attack anyone without good reason. I howl with laughter to think that you will reproach me for spreading bitter accusations against mankind of which I am a member (this remark alone would prove me right!), and against Providence. I shall not retract one of my words;

but, telling what I have seen, it will not be difficult for me, with no other object than truth, to justify them. Today I am going to fabricate a little novel of thirty pages; the estimated length will, in the event, remain unchanged. Hoping to see the establishment of my theories quickly accepted one day by some literary form or another, I believe I have, after some groping attempts, at last found my definitive formula. It is the best: since it is the novel! This hybrid preface has been set out in a fashion which will not perhaps appear natural enough, in the sense that it takes, so to speak, the reader by surprise, and he cannot well see quite what the author is trying to do with him; but this feeling of remarkable astonishment, from which one must generally endeavour to preserve those who spend their time reading books and pamphlets, is precisely what I have made every effort to produce. In fact, I could do no less, in spite of my good intentions: and only later, when a few of my novels have appeared, will you be better able to understand the preface of the fuliginous renegade.

2

BEFORE I begin, I must say that I find it absurd that it should be necessary (I do not think that everyone will share my opinion, if I am wrong) for me to place beside me an open inkstand and a sheet of vellum. In this way I shall be enabled to begin the sixth song in the series of instructive poems which I am eager to produce. Dramatic episodes of unrelenting usefulness! Our hero perceived that by frequenting caves and taking refuge in inaccessible places, he was transgressing the laws of logic by arguing in a vicious circle. For if, on the one hand, he was indulging his loathing of mankind by the compensation of solitude and remoteness and was passively circumscribing his limited horizon amid the stunted bushes, brambles and wild vines, on the other hand his activity no longer found sustenance to feed the minotaur of his perverse instincts. Consequently, he resolved to approach the great clusters of population, convinced that, among so many ready-made victims, his several passions would find objects of satisfaction in abundance. He knew that the police, that shield of civilization, had for many years, doggedly and single-mindedly, been looking for him, and that a veritable army of agents and informers was continually at his heels. Without, however, managing to catch him. Such was his staggering skill that, with supreme style, he foiled tricks which ought indisputably to have brought success, and arrangements of the most cunning meditation. He had a particular gift for taking on forms which were unrecognizable to the most experienced eyes. Superior disguises, if I speak as an artist. Truly base accoutrements, speaking from a moral standpoint. In this respect his talent bordered on genius. Have you not observed the slenderness of the charming cricket, moving with agile grace in the drains of Paris? It was Maldoror! Mesmerizing the towns with a noxious fluid, he brings them into a state of lethargy in which they are unable to be as watchful as they ought to be. A state which is all the more dangerous because they do not realize they are in it. Today he is in Madrid; tomorrow he will be in Saint Petersburg; yesterday he was in Peking. But to make a precise statement as to the place which this poetic Rocambole is at present terrorizing with his exploits is a task beyond the possible strength of my dull ratiocination. That bandit is perhaps seven hundred leagues from this land; perhaps he is a few paces away from you. It is not easy to kill off completely the whole of mankind, and the laws are there; but, with a little patience, the humanitarian ants can be exterminated, one by one. Now since the first days of my infancy when I lived among the first ancestors of our race and was still inexperienced in setting traps; since those distant times before recorded history when, in subtle metamorphoses, I would at different periods ravage the nations of the globe by conquests and carnage, and spread civil war among the citizens, have I not already crushed underfoot, individually or collectively, entire generations, the precise sum of which it would not be impossible to conceive? The dazzling past has given brilliant promises to the future: they will be kept. To rake my sentences together, I shall perforce use the natural method of going back to the savages, that I may learn from them. Simple and imposing gentlemen, their gracious mouths ennoble all that flows from their tattooed lips. I have just proved that there is nothing ridiculous on this planet. Adopting a style which some will find naïve (when it is so profound), I shall use it to interpret ideas which will not perhaps appear awe-inspiring! In this very way, throwing off the frivolous and sceptical manner of ordinary conversation and prudent enough not to put ... but I have forgotten what I was going to say, for I do not recall the beginning of the sentence. But let me tell you that poetry is everywhere where the oafishly mocking smile of man, with his duck's face, is not to be found. First of all, I am going to blow my nose, because I need to; and then, powerfully assisted by my hand, I shall pick up the penholder which my fingers had dropped. How can the Carroussel bridge maintain its relentless neutrality when it hears the harrowing cries which the sack seems to be uttering!

3

THE shops of the Rue Vivienne display their riches to wondering eyes. Lit by numerous gas-lamps, the mahogany caskets and gold watches shed showers of dazzling light through the windows. Eight o'clock has struck by the clock of the Bourse: it is not late! Scarcely has the last stroke of the gong been heard than the street, the name of which has already been mentioned, starts to tremble, and is shaken to its foundations from the Place Royale to the Boulevard Montmartre. Those who are out walking quicken their steps and thoughtfully retire to their houses. A woman faints and falls on the pavement. Nobody helps her up; everyone is anxious to get away from those parts . . . Shutters are closed with a slam, and the inhabitants bury themselves under their blankets. One would think that the bubonic plague had broken out. Thus, while the greater part of the town is getting ready to plunge into the revels of night, the Rue Vivienne is suddenly frozen in a kind of petrifaction. Like a heart which has ceased to love, the life has gone out of it. But soon the news of the phenomenon spreads to other parts of the populace, and a grim silence hovers over the august capital. What has happened to the gas-lamps? What has become of the street-walkers? Nothing . . . dark and empty streets! A screech owl, its leg broken, flying in a rectilinear direction, passes over the Madeleine and soars up towards the Trône, shrieking: 'Woe to us.' Now in that place which my pen (that true friend, who acts as my accomplice) has just shrouded in mystery, if you look in the direction where the Rue Colbert turns into the Rue Vivienne, you will see, in the angle formed by the intersection of these two streets, the profile of a character moving with light footsteps towards the boulevards. But if you come closer, in such a way as not to attract the attention of this passer-by, you will observe with pleasant surprise that he is young! From a distance one would in fact have taken him for a mature man. The total number of days no longer counts when it is a matter of appreciating the intellectual capacity of a serious face. I am an expert at judging age from the physiognomic lines of the brow: he is sixteen years and four months of age. He is as handsome as the retractility of the claws in birds of prey; or, again, as the unpredictability of muscular movement in sores in the soft part of the posterior cervical region; or, rather, as the perpetual motion rat-trap which is always reset by the trapped animal and which can go on catching rodents indefinitely and works even when it is hidden under straw; and, above all, as the chance juxtaposition of a sewing machine and an umbrella on a dissecting table! Mervyn, that son of fair England, has just had a fencing lesson from his teacher, and, wrapped in his Scotch plaid, is returning home to his parents. It is eight-thirty, and he hopes to be home by nine. It is a great presumption on his part to pretend to know the future. Who knows what unforeseen obstacle might stop him on the way? And however uncommon this circumstance might be, ought he to take it upon himself to consider it an exception? Should he not rather consider as an abnormal fact the capacity he has shown up to now to feel completely free of anxiety, and, so to speak, happy? By what right, in fact, would he claim to reach his abode unscathed when someone is in fact lying in wait for him and following his intended prey? (I would be showing little knowledge of my profession as a sensational writer if I did not, at least, bring in the restrictive limitations which are immediately followed by the sentence I am about to complete.) You have recognized the imaginary hero who for a long time has been shattering my intellect by the pressure of his individuality. Now Maldoror approaches Mervyn, to fix in his memory the features of the youth; now, backing away, he recoils like an Australian boomerang in the second phase of its flight, or rather like a booby-trap. Undecided as to what he should do. But his consciousness feels not the slightest trace of the most embryonic emotion, as you would mistakenly suppose. For a moment I saw him moving off in the opposite direction; was he overwhelmed with remorse? But he turned back with renewed eagerness. Mervyn does not know why his temporal veins are beating so violently and he hurries on, obsessed with a dread of which he, and you, vainly seek the cause. He must be given credit for the determination he shows in trying to solve the riddle. But why does he not turn round? Then he would understand everything. Does one ever think of the simplest means of putting an end to an alarming state of mind? When a loiterer goes through the outskirts of town with a salad-bowl full of wine in his gullet and a tattered shirt, if in some shady corner he should see a sinewy cat, contemporary of the bloody revolutions witnessed by our fathers, melancholically contemplating the moonbeams which fall on the sleeping plain, he slinks forward in a curved line and gives a sign to a mangy dog, which leaps. The noble animal of the feline race bravely awaits its adversary and fights dearly for its life. Tomorrow a rag-and-bone man will buy its electrifiable skin. Why did it not flee? It would have been so easy. But in the case which concerns us at the moment, Mervyn compounds the danger of his own ignorance. He has, as it were, a few exceedingly rare glimmerings, it is true, the vagueness of which I shall not now stop to demonstrate; yet it is impossible for him to guess the reality. He is no prophet, I do not deny it, and he makes no claims to be one. Arriving on the main arterial road, he turns right and crosses the Boulevard Poissonière and the Boulevard Bonne-Nouvelle. At this point along his way he goes into the Rue du Faubourg Saint-Denis, leaving behind him the platform of Strasbourg railway station, and stops before a raised portal, before reaching the perpendicular superposition of the Rue Lafayette. Since you advise me to end the first strophe at this point, I am quite willing, this once, to accede to your wish. Do you know that when I think of the iron ring hidden under a stone by a maniac's hand, an uncontrollable shudder runs through my hair?

4

HE pulls the copper knob, and the gate to the modern town house turns on its hinges. He strides across the courtyard, strewn with fine sand, and mounts the eight steps leading up to the front door. The two statues on each side, like guardians of the aristocratic villa, do not bar his way. He who has denied everything, father, mother, Providence, love, and the ideal, in order to think only of himself, has taken good care to follow the steps which went before him. He saw him enter a spacious ground-floor salon, with cornelian wainscoting. The son of the family flings himself on the sofa, and emotion chokes his speech. His mother, in a long flowing dress, smothers him with her loving attention, taking him in her arms. His brothers, younger than he, stand around the sofa, their hearts heavy; they do not know life well enough to be able to form a precise notion of the scene before them. At last the father raises his cane and looks with great authority at those present. His hands on the arm of his chair, he slowly gets up and, moving away from his accustomed seat, advances anxiously, though weakened by years, towards the motionless body of his first born. He speaks in a foreign language and they all listen to him in devout and respectful silence: 'Who did this to you, my boy? The foggy Thames will shift a notable amount of mud yet before my strength is completely exhausted. Protective laws do not seem to exist in this inhospitable land. If I knew who was responsible, he would feel the force of my hand. Though I have retired and am now far from the scene of maritime combats, my commodore's sword on the wall is not yet rusty. Besides, it is easy to sharpen the blade. Mervyn, be calm. I shall give orders for the servants to start tracking down him who, henceforward, I intend to seek and kill with my own hands. Wife, begone from here, go and weep in a corner; your eyes move me, and you would do better to close up the ducts of your lachrymal glands. My son, I implore you, come to your senses, recognize your family. This is your father speaking to you . . .' His mother stands apart and in obedience to her master's orders has taken up a book and is trying to remain calm in face of the danger facing the son to whom her womb gave birth. 'Children, go and play in the park and take care, as you admire the swans swimming, not to fall into the water . . .' The brothers, their arms dangling by their sides, remain silent; they all, with feathers of the Carolina fern-owl in their hats, velvet breeches to the knees and red silk stockings, take one another by the hand and leave the room, taking care to touch the parquet floor only with the tips of their toes. I am sure they will not have much fun, but will walk solemnly between the plane-trees. They are precociously intelligent. So much the better for them. 'All my loving care is in vain, I lull you in my arms and you are impervious to my supplications. Will you lift up your head? I will kiss your knees, if necessary. But no . . . his head falls back again, inert.' 'My gentle master, if you will permit your slave, I shall go and look in my room for a phial of turpentine spirit which I habitually use when migraine invades my temples after I have returned from the theatre or when reading a stirring chronicle of British chivalric history throws my dream-laden mind into the bogs of drowsiness.' 'Wife, I did not invite you to speak, and you had no right to do so. Since our lawful union, no cloud has come between us. I am content with you, I have never had a complaint to make against you; nor have you against me. Go and look in your room for the phial of turpentine spirit. I know there is one in the drawers of your dressing-table, there is no need to tell me. Hurry and mount the steps of the spiral staircase and then return to me with a look of gladness on your face.' But scarcely has this sensitive London woman reached the first step (she does not run as quickly as a member of the lower classes) than she sees one of her ladies-in-waiting coming down the stairs, her cheeks red with sweat, bringing the phial which perhaps contains the liquid of life within its crystal walls. The lady curtsies gracefully as she hands her the phial, and his mother moves towards the fringes of the sofa, where lay the sole object of her tenderness. The commodore, with a proud but kindly gesture, accepts the phial from his wife's hands. An Indian foulard is dipped in it, and Mervyn's head is swathed in orbicular windings of silk. He breathes the salts; he moves an arm. His circulation improves, and the joyous cries of a Philippine cockatoo, perching in the embrasure of a window, are heard. 'Who goes there? . . . Do not stop me . . . Where am I? Is this a coffin bearing up my heavy limbs? The wood seems soft. Is the locket with my mother's portrait in it still around my neck? Back, evil-doer with your hair awry. He could not catch me and was left with a piece of my doublet in his hands. Let the bulldogs off their chains, for this night a recognizable thief may break into our home while we are plunged in sleep. My father and mother, I recognize you, and thank you for your pains. Call my little brothers. I bought sugared almonds for them, and I wish to kiss them.' With these words, he falls into a deep lethargic state. The doctor, who had been hastily sent for, rubs his hands and exclaims: 'The crisis is over. Everything is all right. Tomorrow your son will wake up fit and well. Go now all of you to your respective beds, that I may remain beside the patient till the coming of dawn and the nightingale's song.' Maldoror, hidden behind the door, heard every word. Now he knows the character of those who live in this town-house, and will act accordingly. He knows where Mervyn lives, and wishes to know no more. He has noted in a pocket-book the name of the street and the number of the building. That is the main thing. He is sure to remember them now. He advances like a hyena, unseen, and slinks along the walls of the courtyard. He climbs the iron railing with agility, and for a moment his feet are caught in the iron spikes; in a leap, he is on the road. He creeps stealthily away. 'He took me for an evil-doer!' he exclaims. 'He is an imbecile. I should like to find a man to whom the accusation the sick boy has made against me does not apply. I did not tear off a piece of his doublet as he said. A simple hypnagogic illusion, brought on by fear. It was not my intention today to seize him; for I have far different designs on this shy youth.' Make your way towards the lake where the swans are. And I will tell you later why there is a completely black one among them, with an anvil on his body on top of which is the putrefying corpse of a great crab, and I will tell you also why he rightly inspires mistrust in his aquatic fellows.

5

MERVYN is in his room. He has received a letter. Who could this be writing to him? His perplexity was such that he forgot to thank the postman. The envelope has a black border, and the words are written in a hurried hand. Will he go take the letter to his father? And what if the signatory should expressly forbid it? Full of anxiety, he opens the window to breathe in the fragrance of the atmosphere; the sun's rays reflect their prismatic irradiations on to the Venetian mirrors and the damask curtains. He throws the missive to one side amongst the gold-edged books and the albums with their mother-of-pearl bindings, all strewn over the repoussé leather which covers the surface of his desk. He lifts the lid of the piano and runs his slender fingers along the ivory keys. The brass chords scarcely make a sound. This indirect warning induces him to pick up the vellum paper again; but it shrank away, as if offended by the addressee's hesitancy. Caught in this snare, Mervyn's curiosity increases, and he opens the piece of processed paper. Until that moment the only hand-writing he had seen was his own. 'Young man, I am interested in you; I wish to make you happy. I will take you as my companion and we will go on long peregrinations in the isles of Oceania. Mervyn, you know I love you, and I do not need to prove it. I am sure you will grant me your friendship. When you know me better, you will not regret the trust you have placed in me. I will protect you from the dangers to which your inexperience exposes you. I will be a brother to you, and you shall not lack good advice. For a more detailed explanation of my plans, be at the Carrousel bridge the day after tomorrow at five o'clock in the morning. If I have not arrived, wait for me; but I hope to be there at the right time. Make sure you do so too. An Englishman will not lightly pass by an opportunity to see clearly into his own affairs. Young man, I remain, until we meet, your humble servant. Do not show this letter to anyone.'

'Three stars instead of a signature,' exclaims Mervyn; 'and a bloodstain at the bottom of the page!' His tears fall profusely on the strange pages which his eyes have so eagerly devoured and which open to his mind an unlimited field of new and vaguely-apprehended horizons. It seems to him (but only since he has finished reading the letter), that his father is rather strict and his mother is too superior. He has reasons which have not come to my knowledge, and which I conse-quently cannot communicate to you, for hinting that he cannot remain on good terms with his brothers, either. He hides this letter in his breast. His teachers noticed that on that day he did not seem to be himself. His eyes were unusually dark and the veil of excessive reflection had descended on his peri-orbital region. Each teacher blushed for fear of not being able to reach the intellectual level of his pupil, and yet he, for the first time, neglected his exercises and did no work at all. In the evening the family came together in the dining-room, adorned with ancient portraits. Mervyn admires the dishes laden with succulent meats and odoriferous fruits but he does not eat; the polychromatic streaming of Rhine wine and the frothy ruby of champagne are both enshrined in tall, narrow Bohemian stone goblets, and, even at the sight of this, Mervyn remains indifferent. He leans his elbow on the table and remains absorbed in his thoughts like a sleep-walker. The commodore, his face brown and weather-beaten from sea-surf, whispers in his wife's ear: 'Our eldest has changed since the day of the crisis; even before then he was far too prone to absurd ideas; today he is dreaming even more than usual. I was not at all like that when I was his age. Pretend you do not notice anything. An effective remedy, material or moral, is called for here. Mervyn, fond as I know you are of travel books and natural history, I am going to read you a story which will not displease you. I want you all to listen attentively; it will be to everyone's advantage, most of all to mine. And the rest of you, my children, learn, by paying attention to my words, how to perfect the construction of your style and to understand the author's most subtle intentions.' As if this brood of adorable brats could have understood what rhetoric is! He speaks and, at a sign from his father, one of the brothers goes to the paternal library and returns with a volume under his arms. During this time the table has been cleared, the silver removed, and then the father takes up the book. At the electrifying sound of the word 'travel', Mervyn looked up and endeavoured to put an end to his untimely meditations. The book is opened in the middle, and the metallic voice of the commodore proves that he has remained capable, as in the days of his glorious youth, of controlling the fury of men and of tempests. Well before the end of this reading, Mervyn has leant back on his elbows again, unable to follow the reasoned development of sentences which have been passed under the screw-plate and been subjected to the saponification of obligatory metaphors. The father exclaims: 'This does not interest him; let us read something else. Read, wife. Perhaps you will be more fortunate than I in chasing away the chagrin which hangs over our son's days.' The mother no longer has any hope; yet she has picked up another book and the pleasant sound of her soprano voice echoes melodiously in the ears of her offspring. But after a few words she is overwhelmed with a disheartening sense of failure and she too gives up the rendition of the literary work. Her first-born exclaims: 'I am going to bed.' He retires, his eyes lowered, staring coldly down, without another word. The dog begins to let out a mournful bark, for he does not find this behaviour natural, and the wind from outside rushed fitfully through the longitudinal crack in the window, making the flame under the two rose-crystal cupolas of the lamp flicker. His mother puts her hands to her forehead, and his father looks up to the sky. The children cast frightened glances at the old mariner. Mervyn double-locks the door of his room and his hand moves quickly over the paper: 'I received your letter at midday, and hope you will forgive me for the delay in my reply. I do not have the honour of knowing you personally and I did not know whether I ought to write to you. But as impoliteness has no place in our home, I resolved to take up my pen and thank you warmly for the interest you are taking in one who is a complete stranger to you. God forbid that I should fail to show gratitude for the sympathy with which you overwhelm me. I know my imperfections but I am nonetheless proud. But if it is fitting to accept the friendship of an older person, it is fitting also that he should understand that our characters are not the same. In fact, you seem to be older than I, since you call me young man, and yet I have my doubts about your real age. For how can I reconcile the coldness of your syllogisms with the passion which emanates from them? I shall certainly not abandon the country of my birth to accompany you to foreign lands. That would only be possible on the condition that I asked the authors of my days for the permission which I eagerly await. But as you have enjoined me to keep the secret (in the cubic sense of the word) of this spiritually mysterious affair, I shall eagerly obey you in your incontestable wisdom. It would seem that you are reluctant that this affair should see the light of day. Since you appear to wish that I should have confidence in your person (a wish that, I am delighted to say, is not misplaced), be so good, I beg you, as to show an analogous trust in me, and not to affect to believe that I shall be so far from your way of thinking as not to be scrupulously punctual at our rendezvous the day after tomorrow at the appointed hour. I shall climb the wall which surrounds the park, for the iron gate will be closed, and no one will see me leaving. To speak frankly, there is nothing I would not do for you, who revealed your inexplicable attachment so suddenly to my dazzled eyes, amazed above all by such a proof of goodness, which I most assuredly would never have expected. Because I did not know you. Now I do know you. Do not forget the promise you have made me to be on the Carrousel bridge. Assuming I walk along it, I am more certain than I have ever been of anything that I shall meet you there and touch your hand, provided that this innocent demonstration, from a youth who only yesterday knelt at the altar of modesty, does not offend you by its respectful familiarity. Now is not familiarity permissible in the case of a powerful and ardent intimacy, when perdition is absolute and assured? And what harm would there be, after all, in my bidding you adieu as I go by, when, the day after tomorrow, whether it is raining or not, the clock strikes five? You yourself, gentleman, will appreciate the discretion with which I have conceived this letter; for I shall certainly not permit myself to say more on a loose sheet of paper which is liable to go astray. Your address at the bottom of the page is almost illegible. It took me almost a quarter of an hour to decipher it. I think you acted wisely in writing the words out in such a microscopic hand. I shall follow your example and refrain from signing this: we live in a time which is too eccentric for us to be in the least surprised at what could happen. I should like to know how you found out the place where, in glacial immobility, I live surrounded by long rows of deserted rooms, the vile charnel houses of my hours of ennui. How can I put it? Whenever I think of you, my breast heaves, resounding like the collapse of a decaying empire; for the shadow of your love forms a smile which perhaps does not exist: it is so vague, and moves its scales so tortuously. I surrender to you my vehement feelings, new slabs of marble, virgin to mortal touch. Let us be patient till the first light of morning dusk, and, in expectation of the moment which will fling me into the hideous embrace of your pestiferous arms, I bow down humbly before your knees, which I press.' Having written this tell-tale letter, Mervyn went out to post it, then returned and went to bed. Do not expect to find his guardian angel at his bedside. True, the fish's tail will only fly for three days; but, alas, the beam will be burnt just the same; and a conical-cylindrical bullet will pierce the skin of the rhinoceros, despite the snow-daughter and the beggar! For the crowned madman will have spoken the truth about the loyalty of the fourteen daggers.

6

I OBSERVED that I only had one eye in the middle of my forehead! Oh silver mirrors, set in the panels of vestibules, how many services you have done me by your reflecting power! Since the day when, for an hour, an angora cat gnawed at my parietal protuberance like a trepan puncturing my brain, having jumped suddenly on my back because I had boiled its young in a copper vat full of alcohol, since then I have not ceased to shoot the arrows of self-torment at myself. Today, beneath the weight of wounds which have been inflicted on my body in different circumstances, either by the fatality of my birth or by my own fault; overwhelmed by the consequences of my moral decline (some of which have already befallen me; who will predict those yet to come?); the unmoved observer of the acquired or natural monstrosities which adorn the aponeuroses and the intellect of him who speaks, I cast a long look of satisfaction on the duality of which I am composed ... and I find myself beautiful! Beautiful as the vice of congenital deformation of the male sexual organs, consisting in the relative shortness of the urethral canal and the division, or absence, of its lower wall, with the result that this canal opens at a varying distance from the gland and below the penis; or again as the fleshy wattle, conic in shape and furrowed by quite long transverse wrinkles, which rises from the base of the turkey cock's upper beak; or rather as the truth which follows: 'The system of scales, modes and their harmonic succession is not dependent upon natural invariable laws but is, on the contrary, the consequence of aesthetic principles which have varied with the progressive development of mankind and which will continue to vary'; and, above all, as a corvet armed with turrets! Yes, I maintain the exactitude of my assertion. I can boast that I have no presumptuous illusions, and I would gain no advantage from lying; therefore you should not in the least hesitate to believe what I say. For why should I inspire horror in myself, when I have the laudatory testimony of my conscience? I envy the Creator nothing; but let him allow me to go down the river of my destiny in an increasing series of glorious crimes. Otherwise, raising my brow to the height of his and glaring angrily at his face which obscures my view, I shall make him understand that he is not alone the master of the universe; that several phenomena directly deriving from a deeper knowledge of the nature of things speak in favour of the contrary view and formally contradict the viability of the unity of power. For we are both contemplating one another's eyelashes, you see ... and you know that the clarion of victory has sounded more than once on my lipless mouth. Adieu, illustrious warrior; your courage in misfortune wins you the respect of your bitterest enemy; but Maldoror will be with you soon again in contention for the prey called Mervyn. Thus the prophecy of the cock, when it caught a glimpse of the future in the candelabra, will be fulfilled. Please heaven that the giant crab will rejoin the caravan of pilgrims in time, and tell them in a few words the Clignancourt ragman's tale!

7

ON a bench of the Palais Royal, on the left side and not far from the lake, an individual, emerging from the Rue de Rivoli, has come to sit. His hair is tousled and his garments reveal the corrosive effect of prolonged poverty. He has made a hole in the earth with a piece of pointed wood and has filled the palm of his hand with earth. He brought this sustenance to his mouth and then flung it quickly away. He stood up again and, placing his head against the bench, tried to put his feet up in the air. But as this rope-walking position did not conform to the laws of gravity, he fell back heavily on to the bench again, his arms flailing, his cap covering half his face, and his feet touching the gravel very unsteadily, so that he was more and more precariously poised. He remains in this position for a long time. Towards the middle entrance at the north, beside the rotunda which houses the little coffee-room, the hand of our hero is pressed against the railing. He surveys the surface of the rectangle, with such thoroughness that nothing escapes him. His investigation complete, he looks around near by and sees, in the middle of the garden, a man staggering as he practises gymnastics on a bench on which he is endeavouring to steady himself by performing miracles of strength and skill. But what good are the best intentions, in service of a just cause, against the derangements of mental alienation? He approached the madman and kindly helped him to resume a normal and dignified position, held out his hand to him, and sat down beside him. He observes that his madness is only intermittent; his fit has passed; his inter-locutor replies logically to all his questions. Is it necessary to relate the meaning of his words? Why should I, at random, reopen, at a given page, with blasphemous eagerness, the folio of human miseries? There is nothing more fruitfully instruc-tive. Even if I had no true event to recount to you, I would invent imaginary tales and decant them into your brain. But the lunatic did not go mad for his own amusement. And the sincerity of his account is marvellously allied to the reader's credulity. 'My father was a carpenter in the Rue de la Ver-rerie . . . on his head be the death of the three Daisies and may the beak of the canary eternally gnaw the axis of his ocular bulb! He had contracted the habit of drunkenness; at those times, after he had been through all the bars, his rage became almost immeasurable, and he would hit out indiscriminately at everything in sight. But soon, in face of his friends' re-proaches, he reformed, and became of a taciturn disposition. Nobody could go near him, not even our mother. A secret resentment seethed within him at this notion of duty, which prevented him from behaving in his own way. I had bought a canary for my three sisters; for my three sisters I had bought a canary. They had put it in a cage above the door, and the passers-by would stop each time to listen to the bird's songs, admire its fleeting grace, and study its clever variations. More than once my father had given orders for us to get rid of the cage and its contents, for he imagined that the canary was mocking him as it offered him its ethereal cavatinas sung with a vocalist's talent. He went and took the cage down from the nail on the wall and slipped off the chair, blinded by rage. A slight graze on his knee was the reward for this attempt. Having spent several seconds pressing a chip of wood on the swollen part, he rolled down his trousers, and, much more cautious this time, took the cage under his arm and went towards the other end of the workshop. There, despite the cries and entreaties of his family (we were very attached to that bird who was, to us, the genius of the house), he crushed the wickerwork cage with his metal heels, while a jointing-plane which he whirled about his head kept those who were present at bay. Chance would have it that the canary did not die straightaway; the flurry of feathers was still alive, despite its bloody mutilation. The carpenter went out, slamming the door behind him. My mother and I tried to prolong the bird's life, which was about to ebb away; it was drawing to its close, and the movement of its wings presented us only the spectacle, the mirror, as it were, of the supreme convulsion, of death-throes. During this time, the three Daisies, perceiving that all hope would soon be gone, by common accord took one another by the hand, and the living chain went and crouched in a corner, pushing a barrel of fat some feet away beside our bitch's kennel. My mother kept on at her task, and was holding the canary in her fingers, trying to revive it with her warm breath. But I was running distraught through all the rooms, knocking against the furniture and the tools. From time to time one of my sisters would show her head at the bottom of the stairs to inquire after the fate of the unhappy bird, and she would then sadly withdraw. The bitch had come out of her kennel, and, as if she understood the enormity of our loss, was licking the dress of the three Daisies in a sterile attempt to comfort them. The canary now had only a few moments to live. One of my sisters in turn (it was the youngest) appeared in the penumbra formed by the rarefaction of light. She saw my mother turn pale, and the bird, having raised its head as the lightning flashed in a final convulsive gesture of its nervous system, fell back again between her fingers, for ever inert. She told her sisters the news. They did not make the slightest murmur of complaint, the slightest whisper. Silence reigned in the workshop. All that could be heard was the occasional sharp creak of the pieces of the cage, which, by virtue of the wood's elasticity, partly sprang back into their original position. The three Daisies did not shed a single tear, their faces lost none of their ruddy freshness. They just stood still. They crawled into the inside of the kennel and stretched out beside each other on the straw; while the bitch, a passive spectator of this procedure, looked at them in amazement. Several times my mother called them; they did not make a sound. Tired by the emotions they had just been through, they would probably be asleep! She searched in every corner of the house, but could not see them anywhere. She followed the bitch, who was pulling her by the dress, towards the kennel. This woman knelt down and put her head to the kennel door. The spectacle which presented itself to her, allowing for the unhealthy exaggerations of maternal fear, must have been very harrowing, by my reckoning. I lit a candle and held it out to her; in this way, not a single detail escaped her. She came out of the premature grave, her head covered in straw, and said to me: "The three Daisies are dead." As we could not take them out of there, for you must bear well in mind that they were tightly entwined together, I went to the workshop to look for a hammer with which to smash the canine abode. I immediately set about the work of demolition, and the passers-by could well believe if they had any imagination at all, that we were hard at work in the house. My mother, impatient at the delays which were, however, necessary, was breaking her nails against the wood. At last the operation of negative release came to an end. The kennel, now split, fell apart on all sides, and we took the daughters of the carpenter, one after the other, from the ruins, having had great difficulty in prising them apart. My mother left the country. I never saw my father again. As for me, they say that I am mad and I live by begging. What I do know is that the canary no longer sings.' The listener inwardly approves of this new example which bears out his disgusting theories. As if, because of one man whose crime was committed under the influence of wine, one had the right to accuse the whole of mankind! Such at least is the paradoxical reflection which he tries to take into account; but he cannot get out of his mind the important lessons to be learnt from this grave experience. He consoles the madman with affected words of commiseration and wipes away his tears with his own handkerchief. He takes him to a restaurant and they eat at the same table. Then they go off to a fashionable tailor where the protégé is bought clothes fit for a prince. They knock at the conciergerie of a big house in the Rue de Saint-Honoré, and the madman is installed in a sumptuous third-floor apartment. The bandit forces him to accept his purse and, taking the chamber-pot from under the bed, puts it on Aghone's head. 'I crown you king of the intellect,' he exclaimed with premeditated solemnity. 'At your least call I shall come running; take as much as you wish from my coffers; I am yours, body and soul. At night, you will put the alabaster crown back in its usual place, and you have my permission to use it; but by day, once dawn has lit up the cities, put it back on your head as the symbol of your power. The three Daisies will live again in me, not to mention that I will be a mother to you.' Then the madman took a few steps back, as if he were the plaything of a malicious night-mare; lines of joy crossed his grief-ridden face; he knelt in self-abasement at his protector's feet. Gratitude, like poison, had entered the crowned madman's heart. He wanted to speak, but his tongue was tied. He leant forward, and fell on the floor. The man with the bronze lips retires. What was his object? To find a thoroughly dependable friend, naïve enough to obey the least of his commandments. He could not have found a better one, chance had been kind to him. He whom he found on a bench, has not, since an incident in his youth, known the difference between good and evil. Aghone is just the man he needs.

8

THE Almighty had sent one of his archangels down to earth to save the youth from certain death. He will be forced to come down himself! But we have not yet reached that point in our story and I find myself obliged to shut up, because I cannot say everything at once: every stage-trick will appear in its due place, as soon as the thread of this work of fiction considers the moment right. To avoid recognition, the archangel had taken the shape of a great crab, as big as a vicuna. He was standing on the jagged point of a reef out in the middle of the sea, and was awaiting the moment when the tide would recede, so that he could make his descent to the shore. The man with lips of jasper, hidden where the beach curved out of sight, was watching the animal, holding a stick in his hands. Who would have wished to read the thoughts of those two beings? The first was well aware that he had a difficult mission to accomplish: 'And how shall I succeed,' he exclaimed, with the swelling waves beating against his temporary refuge, 'where the courage and strength of my master have more than once failed him? I am only a being of finite substance, whereas no one knows where he is from, or what is his final purpose. The celestial armies tremble at his name; and in the regions from which I have just come, there are those who say that Satan himself, Satan, the incarnation of evil, is not more dreadful than he.' The other made the following reflections; they found an echo even in the azure cupola which they defiled: 'He appears to be completely inexperienced; I shall swiftly settle his account. No doubt he comes from on high, sent by him who is so fearful of coming himself. We shall see, in the event, if he is as imperious as he seems; he is not an inhabitant of the terrestrial apricot; he betrays his seraphic origin by his wandering, irresolute eyes.' The great crab, who for some time had been surveying a limited stretch of the coast, perceived our hero (who then drew himself up to his full Herculean height), and apostrophized him in the following terms: 'Do not attempt to struggle, give yourself up. I have been sent by one who is superior to us both, to fetter you and make it impossible for the limbs which are the accomplices of your thoughts to move. Henceforward you will be forbidden to hold knives and daggers between your fingers, believe me; as much in your interest as in others. Dead or alive, I shall take you; my orders are to bring you back alive. Do not force me to have recourse to the power which has been vested in me. I shall behave with great tact; do not, on your part, attempt to resist. Thus I shall recognize, with alacrity and delight, that you have taken a first step towards repentance.' When our hero heard this harangue, bearing the stamp of such a profoundly comic wit, he had difficulty in keeping a serious expression on his rough and sunburnt features. But at last no one will be surprised if I add that he ended by bursting out laughing. It was too much for him! He did not mean any harm by it! He certainly did not wish to bring upon himself the great crab's reproaches! What efforts he made to contain his mirth! How often he pressed his lips against one another, so as not to appear to offend his stunned interlocutor! Unfortunately, his character partook of human nature, and he laughed as sheep do! At last he stopped! And just in time! He had almost choked to death! The wind bore this answer to the archangel on the reef. 'When your master stops sending me snails and crayfish to settle his affairs, and deigns to parley with me personally, a means will, I am sure, be found for us to reach agreement, since I am inferior to him who sent you, as you have so rightly said. Until then, any idea of a reconciliation appears to me premature and likely to produce an illusory result. I am far from underestimating the good sense of every syllable you speak; and as we are uselessly wearing out our voices by shouting to one another at three kilometres' distance, it seems to me you would be wise to descend from your impregnable fortress and swim to dry land where we shall be able to discuss in greater comfort the conditions of a surrender which, however justifiable it may be, is still a disagreeable prospect for me.' The archangel, who had not been expecting such good will, withdrawing his indented head from the crevasse, answered: 'Oh Maldoror, has the day at last come when your abominable instincts will see the extinction of that torch of unjustifiable pride which is leading you to your damnation. I shall be the first to recount this laudable change of heart to the phalanges of cherubim, delighted to welcome back one of their own. You yourself know, and have not forgotten, that there was once a time when you had the first place among us. Your name was on everyone's lips; at present you are the subject of our solitary conversations. Come then ... come and make lasting peace with your former master; he will welcome you back like a prodigal son, and will not notice the enormous amount of guilt you bear, like a mountain of moose-antlers piled up by Indians, in your heart.' He speaks, and his body emerges completely from the depths of the dark opening. He appears, radiant, on the surface of the reef; thus a priest appears when he is certain of retrieving a lost sheep. He is about to leap into the water, to swim towards the man who has just been forgiven. But the man with lips of sapphire had calculated his perfidious move. His stick has been violently hurled through the air; after skipping over many waves, it strikes the head of the beneficent angel. The crab, mortally wounded, falls into the water. The tide washes the floating wreck up on to the shore. He was waiting for the tide so that it would be easier for him to swim ashore. Well, the tide came. It lulled him with its songs and set him down gently on the shore: is not the crab happy? What more does he want? And Maldoror, stooping down over the sand on the beach, takes two friends in his arms, inseparably united by the vagaries of the waves' movements; the corpse of the great crab, and the murderous stick! 'I have not yet lost my skill,' he cries, 'all I need is practice; my arm has lost none of its strength, and my eyes are as sharp as ever.' He looks at the inanimate animal. He fears he will be brought to account for the blood he has shed. Where will he hide the archangel? And at the same time he wonders whether death was instantaneous. He put an anvil and a corpse on his back; he makes his way towards a vast lake, all the banks of which are covered and, so to speak, immured by an inextricable tangle of large rushes. He wanted at first to take a hammer, but it is too light an instrument, whereas with a heavier object, if the corpse gives any sign of life, he will put it on the ground and smash it to powder with blows of the anvil. No, it certainly is not strength his arm lacks; that is the least of his problems. Arriving in sight of the lake, he sees it peopled with swans. He says that it is a safe retreat for him; by means of a metamorphosis, without setting down his burden, he mingles with the rest of the company of birds. Observe the hand of Providence where one was tempted to say it was absent, and draw profit from the miracle of which I am about to speak. Black as a raven's wing, three times he swam among the group of palmipeds in their dazzling whiteness; three times that distinctive colour which made him look like a lump of coal failed to disappear. It is because God in his justice would not allow him to deceive even this flight of swans. So that he remained openly in the middle of the lake; but they all kept clear of him, and no bird approached his shameful plumage to keep him company. And so he confined his dives to a remote bay at one end of the lake, alone among birds as he had been among men. This was his prelude to the incredible event which took place in the Place Vendôme!

9

THE corsair with golden hair has received Mervyn's answer. Reading the strange page, he follows the intellectual anxiety of its writer, left as he was to the weak powers of his own suggestion. He would have done better to consult his parents before answering the stranger's protestations of friendship. No good will come of his being involved, as the principal actor, in this equivocal intrigue. But after all, he asked for it. At the agreed time Mervyn left the door of his house and went straight ahead, following the Boulevard Sebastopol to the Fontaine Saint-Michel. He takes the Quai des Grands-Augustins and crosses the Quai Conti; as he passes along the Quai Malaquais, he sees an individual walking parallel with him, going in the same direction along the Quai du Louvre, carrying a sack under his arm. This man appears to be scrutinizing him. The morning mists have dispersed. The two passers-by both come on to the Pont du Carrousel at the same time, one from each side! Though they had never met before they recognized one another! Truly it was touching to see the souls of these two beings, so different in age, coming together in the nobility of their feelings. Such at least would have been the opinion of anyone who had stopped at this spectacle which many, even if mathematically minded, would have found moving. Mervyn, his face covered in tears, was reflecting that he would find, so to speak at the entrance to his life, a precious support in future adversity. You may be sure that Maldoror said nothing. This is what he did: he took the sack from under his arm, unfolded it, unclasped it, and forced the youth's entire body down into the rough cloth envelope. With his handkerchief he knotted the top end. As Mervyn was uttering loud and piercing cries, he picked up the sack like a laundry-bag and smashed it several times against the parapet of the bridge. Then the patient, perceiving that his bones were snapping, became silent. A unique scene, which no novelist will ever again rediscover! A butcher was passing, sitting on top of the meat in his cart. An individual runs up to him, enjoins him to stop, and says to him: 'There is a dog in this sack; it has mange: put it down as soon as possible.' The butcher is glad to oblige. The man who hailed him sees, as he walks away, a young girl holding out her hand. To what heights of audacity and impiety can he go? He gives her alms. Tell me if you wish me to take you to the door of a remote slaughterhouse, some hours later. The butcher has returned, and said to his friends as he threw his load to the ground: 'Let us hurry up and kill this mangy dog.' There are four of them, and each one picks up the hammer which he normally uses. And yet they do not set about their work straightaway, because the sack is moving violently. 'What is coming over me?' one of them shouts, slowly lowering his arm. 'This dog is uttering cries of pain,' said another, 'you would think it knew the fate which awaits it.' 'They always do that,' a third answered, 'even when they are not sick as in this case, it is enough for their master to be away from home for a few days and they start howling in a manner which it is truly painful to endure.' 'Stop!... stop!...' the fourth shouted, before all their arms had risen in unison, ready, this time, to strike decisively at the sack. 'Stop, I tell you; there is a point here which has escaped us. What makes you so sure that this cloth sack contains a dog? I want to find out what is inside.' Then, despite the jibes of his companions, he untied the bundle and took out one after another the limbs of Mervyn! He had almost suffocated in his cramped position. He fainted when he saw the light of day again. A few moments later, he gave unmistakable signs of life. His rescuer said: 'Let this teach you, in future, to be cautious, even in your own work. You almost found out for yourselves that it does not pay to fail to observe this law.' The butchers fled. Mervyn, heavy-hearted and full of dire forebodings, returns home and shuts himself up in his room. Do I need to dwell on this strophe? Ah! Who will not deplore the events which have occurred? Let us wait until the end to pass an even harsher judgement. The dénouement is about to rush in on us; and, in tales of this sort, where a passion, whatever its nature, is given, and fears no obstacle as it makes its way, there is no occasion for diluting in a godet the shellac of eighty banal pages. What can be said in half-a-dozen pages must be said, and then, silence.

10

In order to construct mechanically the brain of a somniferous story, it is not enough to dissect the reader's understanding with all kinds of folly and brutalize it completely with renewed doses, so as to paralyse his faculties for the rest of his life, by the infallible law of fatigue; one must, apart from this, by means of a good mesmerizing fluid, ingeniously reduce him to a somnambulic state in which it is impossible for him to move, forcing him to close his eyes against his inclination by the fixity of your own. I mean, and I say this not to make myself clear but only to develop my thoughts which interest and torment you at the same time by their most penetrating of harmonies, that I do not think it necessary, to achieve the goal one has set before one, to invent a poetry completely outside the laws of nature, and the pernicious breath of which seems to overthrow even absolute truths; but, to bring about such a result (consistent, moreover, with the rules of aesthetics, if one reflected well on it), is not as easy as you think. That is why I will make every possible effort to do so! If death should put a stop to the fantastic movement of the two long gossamer-thin arms on my shoulders which I use in the lugubrious crushing of my literary gypsum, I at least want the reader, in mourning, to be able to say: 'You have to do him justice. He has made me very stupid. What might he not have done if he could have lived longer! He is the best professor of hypnosis I know!' These few touching words will be carved on the marble of my tomb, and my shades will be content! – I shall continue! There was a fish's tail moving at the bottom of a hole, beside a down-at-the-heel boot. It was not natural to wonder: 'Where is the fish? I only see the tail moving.' For precisely since one was implicitly admitting one's inability to see the fish, it was because it was not really there. The rain had left a few drops of water in the bottom of this funnel in the sand. As for the down-at-the-heel boot, there have been those who thought that it was left there deliberately by someone. By divine power the great crab was to be reborn from his disintegrated elements. He took the fish's tail from the well and promised to put it back on to its lost body again if it announced to the Creator his proxy's inability to tame the waves of the raging Maldorean sea. He gave it two albatross wings, and the fish's tail took flight. But it flew up to the renegade's abode, to tell him what was happening and betray the great crab. But the latter guessed the spy's designs and, before the third day had drawn to its close, pierced the fish's tail with a poisoned dart. The spy's gullet uttered a feeble sigh and it gave up the ghost before it hit the ground. Then an ancient beam in the roof of a château drew itself up again to its full height, springing back on itself and crying out aloud for vengeance. But the Almighty changed into a rhinoceros, told him that this death was deserved. The beam calmed down and went back to its place in the heart of the manor, took up its horizontal position again and called back to it the frightened spiders, that they might continue, as in the past, to spin their webs in its corners. The man with lips of sulphur learnt of his ally's weakness; that is why he ordered the crowned madman to set fire to the beam and reduce it to ashes. Aghone carried out this harsh order. 'Since, according to you, the moment has come,' he exclaimed, 'I have gone and taken out the ring which I had buried beneath the stone, and I have attached it to the end of the rope. Here is the bundle.' And he held out a thick rope, rolled up and sixty metres long. His master asked him what the fourteen daggers were doing. He replied that they remained loyal and were ready for any event, if need be. The desperado nodded his head as a sign of approval. But he evinced surprise and even anxiety when Aghone added that he had seen a cock split a candelabra in two with its beak, look closely at each of the parts and cry out, as it beat its wings in a frenzied movement: 'It is not as far as you think from the Rue de la Paix to the Place du Panthéon. Soon we shall see the lamentable proof of these words.' The great crab, mounted on a fiery steed, was hurtling at full speed in the direction of the reef which had seen the stick flung by the tattooed arm, the reef which was his refuge the first day he came down to earth. A caravan of pilgrims was making its way to visit this place, thenceforward hallowed by an august death. He hoped to reach it, to beg urgently for help against the plot which was being hatched and of which he had been informed. You will see a few lines further on with the aid of my glacial silence that he did not arrive in time to tell them what a ragman had recounted to him of the day when, hidden behind the scaffolding of a house being built, he had looked towards the Pont Carrousel, still stained with the damp dew of night. The bridge had witnessed with horror the matinal sight of an icosahedron sack being rhythmically kneaded against its limestone parapet, and its notion of the possible had been confusedly enlarged in ever widening concentric circles. Before he arouses their compassion with the memory of that episode, they will do well to destroy the seed of hope within themselves . . . To shake yourself out of your inertia, put the resources of your good will to use, walk beside me and do not lose sight of that madman, his head covered in a chamberpot, pushing along, with a stick in his hand, one whom you would have difficulty in recognizing unless I took the trouble to warn you and to recall to your ear the name pronounced Mervyn. How he has changed! With his hands tied behind his back he is walking straight ahead as if he were going to the scaffold, and yet he is guilty of no crime. They have arrived at the circular enclosure of the Place Vendôme. On the entablature of the column, leaning against the square balustrade more than fifty metres above the ground, a man has flung and uncoiled a rope which falls to the ground a few steps from Aghone. With practice, a thing is quickly done; but I can say that the latter did not take much time to tie Mervyn's feet to the end of the rope. The rhinoceros had learnt of what was going to happen. Bathed in sweat, he appeared, gasping, at the corner of the Rue Castiglione. He did not even have the satisfaction of joining combat. The individual, who was surveying the area from the top of the column, loaded his revolver, carefully took aim, and pulled the trigger. The commodore, who had been begging in the streets since the day when what he believed to be his son's madness had begun, and his mother, called the snow-daughter because of her extreme pallor, thrust forward and flung themselves in front of the rhinoceros to protect it. Vain attempt! The bullet went through his skin as if it were a tendril; one would have thought, with all the appearance of logic, that death must inevitably follow. But we knew that this pachyderm had been endued with the substance of the Lord. He withdrew in sorrow. If it were not decisively proved that he is too merciful to every one of his creatures, I should pity the man on the column. The latter, with a flick of his wrist, draws in the rope, which has been weighted in the manner described. Now out of the perpendicular, its swinging movements sway Mervyn, who is looking downwards. Suddenly he snatches up in his hands a long garland of immortelles which joins the consecutive angles of the base against which his head smashes. He carries off into the air with him that which was not a fixed point. Having piled a large part of the rope at his feet in the shape of superposed ellipses, so that Mervyn remains hanging half way up the bronze obelisk, the escaped convict, with his right hand, forced the youth into an accelerated motion of uniform rotation, in a plane parallel to the column's axis, and gathered up in his left hand the serpentine coils of the rope, which lay at his feet. The sling whistles through space; Mervyn's body follows it everywhere, always kept away from the centre by centrifugal force, always maintaining an equidistant and moving position in an aerial circumference independent of matter. The civilized savage gradually lets out the rope until he comes to the end, which he holds in his firm metacarpus, which bears a strong, but deceptive, resemblance to a bar of steel. He starts to run round the balustrade, holding on to the ramp by one hand. This operation has the effect of changing the original plane of the rope's revolution, and increasing its already considerable tensile force. Thereafter he turns majestically in a horizontal plane, having passed successively and by imperceptible degrees through several oblique planes. The right angle formed by the column and the vegetable string has equal sides. The renegade's arm and the murderous instrument merge in linear unity, like the atomistic elements of a ray of light penetrating a dark room. The theorems of mechanics allow me to speak thus; alas! we know that one force added to another force will produce a resultant consisting of the two original forces! Who would dare to assert that the linear cordage would not already have snapped, had it not been for the strength of the athlete and the good quality of the hemp? The golden-haired corsair, all at once and quite suddenly, stops running, opens his hand and releases the rope. The recoil of this operation, so opposite to those that had preceded it, makes the balustrade creak in its joints. Mervyn, followed by the rope, is like a comet trailing behind it its flaming tail. The iron ring of the running knot, glittering in the sun's rays, invites one to complete this illusion for oneself. In the course of his parabola, the condemned youth cleaves the atmosphere up to the left bank, goes past it by virtue of the impulsive force which I suppose to be infinite, and his body strikes the Dome of the Panthéon, while the rope coils itself partly around the upper wall of the immense cupola. On its spherical and convex surface, which resembles an orange only in its form, one can, at any hour of the day, see a dried skeleton hanging. When the winds blows it, they say that the students of the Quartier Latin, fearing a similar fate, say a short prayer: these are insignificant rumours which one is by no means obliged to believe, and which are only fit for scaring little children. It holds in its clenched hands a kind of large ribbon of old yellow flowers. One must bear the distance in mind, and nobody, despite the evidence of his good eyesight, can state that they are really the immortelles of which I have spoken and which were snatched from an imposing pedestal near the Nouvel Opéra in the course of a one-sided struggle. It is nevertheless true that the crescent-moon shaped garments no longer take the expression of their definitive symmetry from the quaternary number: go and see for yourself, if you do not believe me.

INTRODUCTION TO *POEMS*

THE *Poems* of Isidore Ducasse were published in June 1870. They made little immediate impact and were not rediscovered until 1919, when they were reprinted in the Dadaist review *Littérature*. Whereas *Maldoror* has come to be accepted, or at least tolerated as a brilliant aberration, the *Poems* have met with resistance and rejection, frequently from professed admirers of *Maldoror*. What is to be made of what Camus called the 'laborious banalities' of the *Poems*? Is Ducasse, at the same time as discarding his nom de plume, repudiating *Maldoror*?

These questions suggest that we are presented with a choice between *Maldoror* and the *Poems*, between Lautréamont and Ducasse, that one or the other of these texts must be the statement of the author's 'real' intentions, his 'real' philosophy. But in fact the need for such a choice is illusory. The *Poems* do not repudiate *Maldoror*, they complement and correct the earlier text. They ensure that the process of radical interrogation which begins in *Maldoror* does not end when that book is closed. The danger is that, however strong the impression left by *Maldoror*, its memory will, like that of all other books and events, be effaced, relegated to a compartment of consciousness where it will crumble and decay, perhaps less rapidly than other books we have read but just as inevitably. The *Poems* prevent this, reminding us that *Maldoror* is more than a gesture of defiance, revolt, blasphemy – it is, essentially, a process of infiltration of literary forms, of undermining from within a text, of ironic self-awareness. The *Poems* take up this process in another form. *Maldoror* is itself subjected to that process, just as a whole set of literary assumptions and concepts are called in question in *Maldoror*. With the *Poems*,

Lautréamont/Ducasse breaks out of the static and linear categories of beginning and end; this process, made explicit in the *Poems*, will only come to an end with the death of the author, or if he gives up writing altogether (though even then it can be taken up by others, it is not the prerogative of an individual writer alone): 'The phenomenon passes. I seek the laws.' *Maldoror* is, in every sense of the word, a phenomenon, a stage in the process. But this process aims far beyond the 'fabrication' of a single text: 'The science I am establishing is a science distinct from poetry. I am not writing the latter. I am trying to discover its source.'

By the author's own admission, the *Poems* are not poems. They are maxims, conclusions reached after a syllogistic process in which terms have been omitted, assertions which claim the status of self-evident truth: 'The maxim does not need to be proved. One point in an argument requires another. The maxim is a law which contains a number of arguments. The closer the argument comes to the maxim, the more perfect it becomes. Once it has become a maxim, it rejects the evidence of a transformation.' The adoption of the maxim form in vogue in the seventeenth and eighteenth centuries in France seems to underline the author's advocacy of classical values, his contempt for an age of uncertainty, experimentation, revolt. Ducasse diagnoses the disease of contemporary literature, exhaustively listing its symptoms:

Upheavals, anxieties, deprivation, death, exceptions in the physical and moral order, the spirit of negation, brutishness, hallucinations wilfully induced, torture, destruction, sudden reversals of fortune, tears, insatiability, servitude, wildly burrowing imaginations, novels, the unexpected, the forbidden, the mysterious, vulture-like chemical peculiarities which watch over the carrion of some dead illusion, precocious and abortive experiments, bug-like obscurities, the terrible monomania of pride, the inoculation of profound stupors, funeral orations, jealousies, betrayals, tyrannies, impieties, irritations, acrimonies, aggressive outbursts, dementia, spleen, reasoned terrors, strange anxieties which the reader would prefer to be spared, grimaces, neuroses, the bloody screw-plates by which logic is forced to retreat, exaggerations, lack of sincerity, catch-words, platitudes, the sombre, the lugubrious, creations worse than murders, passions, the clan of assize-court novelists, tragedies, odes, melodramas, extremes perpetually present, reason howled down with impunity, odours of milksops, mawkishness, frogs, octopi, sharks, the simoun of the deserts, all that is somnambulous, shady, nocturnal, somniferous, noctambulous, viscous ... it is time to react against these repulsive charnel houses which I blush to name, to react against everything which is supremely shocking and oppressive.

It will immediately strike every reader that all the vices so vehemently condemned here are to be found in plenty in *Maldoror*. It is passages such as this which have led some readers of *Maldoror* to interpret the *Poems* either as a rejection of that text or as a proof of its author's 'insincerity'.

The more we read *Maldoror* and the *Poems*, the more inappropriate and incommensurate this accusation of insincerity seems – it is difficult to see how the criterion of sincerity can usefully be applied to Lautréamont's work and in particular to the *Poems*, which is a continual process of contradiction, negation, replacement and correction. If, however, we insist on applying this criterion, Ducasse tells us that: 'I allow no one, not even Elohim, to doubt my sincerity.'

This process of correction takes three main forms in the *Poems*: the revision of *Maldoror*; the rewriting of passages from Descartes, Pascal, La Rochefoucauld, Vauvenargues and others; and then there is internal contradiction: what is asserted at one point is denied at another, and vice-versa; mutually contradictory propositions are presented with the same dogmatic self-assurance (so that the maxim, would-be vehicle of irrefutable truths, is also called in question, its claims to self-evidence revealed as spurious).

The murderous hostility to mankind which runs through *Maldoror* gives way, in the *Poems*, to what appears a more positive judgement. In *Maldoror*, Lautréamont had written: 'I have seen men surpassing the hardness of rock, the rigidity of cast steel, the insolence of youth, the senseless rage of criminals, the falseness of the hypocrite . . . I have seen them wearing out moralists who have attempted to discover their heart, . . . bringing upon themselves implacable anger from on high . . . prostituting women and children, thus dishonouring the parts of the body consecrated to modesty; . . . show me a man who is good . . . But at the same time increase my strength tenfold; for at the sight of such a monster, I may die of astonishment: men have died of less.' The revised version in the *Poems* reads: 'I have seen men wearing out the moralists who attempted to discover their heart, and bringing upon themselves blessings from above. They showed respect to childhood and to age, to all that breathes . . . , they paid homage to woman and consecrated to modesty the parts of the body which we refrain from naming. The firmament, whose beauty I acknowledge, the earth, image of my heart, were invoked by me, in order to represent myself as a man who did not believe himself good. The sight of this monster, had it ever proved to be real, would not have killed me with shock: it takes more than that to kill a man. All this needs no comment.' It is naïve to see in this second passage a 'development' from a pessimistic to an optimistic view of human nature. Ducasse explicitly warns against such an interpretation: 'If these sophisms were corrected by their corresponding truths, only the corrections would be true; while the work which had been thus revised would no longer have the right to be called false. The rest would be outside the realm of the true, tainted with falsehood, and would thus necessarily be considered null and void.' Here we are beyond the critique of literary forms and structures. The limitations of a mode of thinking which reduces the complexity of things to sterile antitheses are exposed. Those who are imprisoned in this thought-structure – who are not, at least momentarily, liberated from it by the reading of *Maldoror* and the *Poems* – will misinterpret both these texts, seeing in them the same kind of antitheses as between good and evil, true and false: 'Good is the victory over evil, the negation of evil. If one writes of the good, evil is eliminated by this fitting act. I do not write of what must not be done. I write of what must be done. The former does not include the latter. The latter includes the former.' For Ducasse, what must be done includes what must not be done. Good includes or contains evil: the two are not seen as diametrically opposite. A pseudo-logic is at work here, using pseudo-syllogisms; the conclusions reached in this process do not follow from the propositions on which they are allegedly based. The most dogmatic and self-assured statements are the least tenable. It is as if Ducasse is intentionally building a house in which the foundations inevitably give way when the roof is put on: 'Several certainties have been contradicted. Several falsehoods remain uncontradicted. Contradiction is the sign of falsehood. Non-contradiction is the sign of certainty.'

The *Poems* frequently contradict assertions from *Maldoror*. Whereas in the latter the novel was acclaimed as the 'best', the 'definitive formula', in the *Poems* it is condemned because 'the moral conclusion is lacking'. An apparently clear case of outright contradiction – or is it? Is it the overdue contradiction of a falsehood which has been uncontradicted up to now, or was the original proposition from *Maldoror*, despite the irony behind it, one of the several certainties which have been contradicted?

Pascal had written: 'In writing down my thoughts, they sometimes escape me; but that reminds me of my weakness, which at every moment I forget; and this teaches me as much as the thoughts I have forgotten, for I tend only to know my own insignificance.' For Pascal, the experience of writing is humbling, a blow to intellectual pride, because he cannot grasp his thoughts. It is a confrontation with his own insignificance, another reason for abandoning himself to God's inscrutable will. The same experience has the opposite effect on Ducasse, who rewrites Pascal's text as follows: 'When I write down my thoughts they do not escape me. This action reminds me of my strength which at every moment I forget. I learn as I link my thoughts together. But I am only moving towards the realization of one thing: the contradiction between my mind and nothingness.' Nothing could illustrate more clearly the absolute contradiction be-tween Ducasse's thinking and Pascal's. Ducasse justifies this form of revision, replacement, in these terms: 'Plagiarism is necessary. It is implied in the idea of progress. It clasps an author's sentence tight, uses his expressions, eliminates a false idea, replaces it with the right idea.' For Ducasse, the adoption of Pascal's style is an essential part of the refutation of his ideas. In the *Poems*, the process is not always one of simple refutation. An idea may also be taken as a starting-point and then extended, explored in several possible permutations (in accordance with Ducasse's dictum that 'to be well-wrought, a maxim does not need to be corrected. It needs to be de-veloped'). Vauvenargues – earlier acknowledged as the source of a 'quotation' – had written: 'One cannot judge life by a falser rule than death.' Ducasse writes: 'One can only judge the beauty of life by the beauty of death.' 'As long as my friends are alive, I will not speak of death.' 'One can only judge the beauty of death by the beauty of life.' Vauvenargues' maxim is neither affirmed nor rejected, but, typically, developed in several directions and at the same time deprived of its aura of certainty, finality. In the *Poems* there is nothing final, nothing exempt from correction, development, replacement. It is futile to try to pin Lautréamont/Ducasse down to a standpoint, a 'philosophy', however complex, because there is no standing still; the process goes on, and in it every statement is 'valid' only in its place, is sure to be developed, revised, effaced later: 'I do not need to bother about what I will do later. What I am doing now I had to do. I do not need to discover the things I will discover later. In the new science, everything comes in its place – that is its excellence.'

The *Poems* were Ducasse's last work (he died a few months after they were published). But because his work is essentially a process, and because this process is not, and cannot be, the possession of any individual, it goes on: 'Poetry must be made by all. Not by one.' Lautréamont/Ducasse's ironic consciousness of the possibilities and limitations of fiction, his playing with and manipulation of literary forms, his insistence on the 'fictivity' of his texts give his work much in common with that of such writers as Beckett, Joyce, Robbe-Grillet, and Butor who have taken the process begun by Lautréamont in many different directions. So many-sided is the work that there are many possibilities suggested by the work which have still to be exploited. *Maldoror* and the *Poems* have lost none of their impetus, their disquieting novelty. They remain a 'permanent publication'.

POEMS

I

THE poetic whines of this century are nothing but sophisms.

The first principles must be beyond dispute.

I accept Euripides and Sophocles; but I do not accept Aeschylus.

Do not show bad taste and lack of the most elementary decency towards the Creator.

Abandon incredulity: that will please me.

There are not two kinds of poetry; there is only one.

There is a far from tacit convention between author and reader by which the former says he is sick and takes the latter as his nurse. The poet consoles mankind! The roles have been arbitrarily reversed.

I do not wish to be decried as a poseur.

I shall leave no memoirs.

Poetry is not the tempest, nor is it the tornado. It is a majestic and fertile river.

Only by accepting the physical presence of night have we come to accept it morally. O Night Thoughts of Young, many is the headache you have caused me!

One only dreams when one is asleep. It is only words such as dream, the futility of life, the earthly journey, the preposition perhaps, the misshapen tripod, which have infiltrated this dank languorous poetry like corruption into your souls. There is only one step from the words to the ideas.

Upheavals, anxieties, deprivation, death, exceptions in the physical and moral order, the spirit of negation, brutishness, hallucinations wilfully induced, torture, destruction, sudden reversals of fortune, tears, insatiability, servitude, wildly burrowing imaginations, novels, the unexpected, the forbidden, the mysterious, vulture-like chemical peculiarities which watch over the carrion of some dead illusion, precocious and abortive experiments, bug-like obscurities, the terrible monomania of pride, the inoculation of profound stupors, funeral orations, jealousies, betrayals, tyrannies, impieties, irritations, acrimonies, aggressive outbursts, dementia, spleen, reasoned terrors, strange anxieties which the reader would prefer to be spared, grimaces, neuroses, the bloody screw-plates by which logic is forced to retreat, exaggerations, lack of sincerity, catch-words, platitudes, the sombre, the lugubrious, creations worse than murders, passions, the clan of assize-court novelists, tragedies, odes, melodramas, extremes perpetually present, reason howled down with impunity, odours of milksops, mawkishness, frogs, octopi, sharks, the simoun of the deserts, all that is somnambulous, shady, nocturnal, somniferous, noctambulous, viscous, speaking seals, the ambiguous, the consumptive, the spasmodic, the aphrodisiac, the anaemic, the one-eyed, hermaphrodite, bastard, albino, pederast, abortions from the aquarium, bearded women, the drunken hours of silent depression, fantasies, sourness, monsters, demoralizing syllogisms, excrement, those who do not think with the innocence of a child, desolation, that intellectual manchineel, perfumed chancres, thighs covered with camellias, the culpability of the writer who rolls down the slope of the abyss, despising himself with cries of joy, remorse, hypocrisy, vague perspectives which crush you in their imperceptible works, spitting on sacred axioms, vermin and their insinuating titillations, extravagant prefaces, such as those to Cromwell, those by Mlle Daupin and Dumas the younger, decay, impotence, blasphemy, asphyxia, suffocation, fits of rage – it is time to react against these repulsive charnel-houses which I blush to name, to react against everything which is supremely shocking and oppressive.

Your mind is perpetually unhinged, lured into, and trapped inside the darknesses created by the crude art of egoism and *amour-propre*.

Taste is the fundamental quality which epitomizes all others. It is the *nec plus ultra* of the understanding. By virtue of this faculty alone can genius maintain the health and balance of all the other faculties. Villemain is thirty-four times more intelligent than Eugène Sue and Frédéric Soulié. His preface to the *Dictionary of the Academy* will outlive the novels of Walter Scott and Fenimore Cooper, and all the novels conceivable and imaginable. The novel is a false genre, because it describes the passions for their own sake: the moral conclusion is absent. To describe the passions is nothing: it is enough to have been born with something of the nature of a jackal, a vulture, a panther. It is a task we do not care for. But to describe them and then subject them to a high moral concept, as Corneille did, is another thing. He who refrains from doing the former but remains capable of admiring and understanding those who do the second surpasses him who writes the former by as much as virtue surpasses vice.

A sixth-form teacher, simply by saying: 'Not for all the treasures in the universe would I wish to have written novels such as those of Balzac and Alexander Dumas' proves himself to be more intelligent than Alexander Dumas and Balzac. Simply by realizing that one should not write of moral and physical deformity, by this alone, a fifth-year pupil shows that he is stronger, more able, and more intelligent than Victor Hugo, if he had only written novels, dramas, and letters.

Alexander Dumas the younger will never, absolutely never, make a speech at a school prize-day. He does not know what morality is. It makes no compromises. If he did, he would have to cross out, in a single stroke, every word he has written up to now, starting with his absurd prefaces. Find me a jury of competent men and let them decide: I maintain that a good sixth-former is better than Dumas in anything you care to mention, including the filthy question of courtesans.

The *chefs d'œuvre* of the French language are school prize-day speeches, and academic speeches. In fact, the instruction of youth is perhaps the finest practical expression of duty, and a good appreciation of Voltaire's works (I stress the word appreciation) is preferable to those works themselves. Naturally!

The best novelists and dramatists would eventually distort the famous idea of good, if the teaching profession, that conservatory of clarity and precision, did not keep the younger and the older generations on the path of honest and hard work.

In its own name and in spite of it, I have come to disown, with implacable will and the tenacity of iron, the hideous past of whining humanity. Yes: I wish to proclaim the Beautiful on my golden lyre, having eliminated the goitral sadness and the stupid outbursts of pride which corrupt the swampy poetry of this century! I will crush underfoot the bitter stanzas of scepticism which have no right to exist. Judgement, in the full bloom of its strength, imperious and resolute, without for a second hesitating in the derisory uncertainties of misplaced pity, condemns them, fatidically, like an Attorney General. We must relentlessly be on our guard against purulent insomnia and atrabilious nightmares. I despise and execrate pride and the indecent delights of that extinguishing irony which disjoints the precision of our thought.

Some excessively intelligent characters – there is no reason to dispute it with palinodes of doubtful taste – flung themselves headlong into the arms of evil. It is the absinthe (savorous? no, I don't think so, but noxious) which morally destroyed the author of *Rolla*. Woe to its connoisseurs! Scarcely has the English aristocrat reached maturity than his harp is shattered beneath the walls of Missolonghi, having gathered on his way only the flowers which brood on the opium of gloomy disasters.

Though he was more gifted than ordinary geniuses, if there had been at his time another poet, gifted, as he was, with the same measure of exceptional intelligence, and capable of rivalling him, he would have been the first to admit the futility of his efforts to produce incongruous multitudes of maledictions; and to acknowledge that the sole and exclusive good worthy of being striven for is, by unanimous agreement, to win our esteem. The fact is that there was no one who could successfully compete with him. And this is a point that no one has ever made. Strange to say, even perusing the miscellanies and books of his age, no critic ever thought of mentioning the rigorous syllogism of the preceding sentence. And I, who surpass him in this, cannot have been the first to think of this. So full were they of stupor and apprehension, rather than reflective admiration, in the face of works written by a perfidious hand which nevertheless revealed imposing aspects of a soul which did not belong to the common mass, which was freely able to face the last consequences of one of the two least obscure problems which interest non-solitary minds: good and evil. It is granted only to a few to approach this problem, either in the one direction, or in the other. That is why, while praising without reservation the marvellous intelligence which he, one of the four or five beacons of humanity, shows at every moment, one must have numerous silent reservations about the unjustifiable application and use which he made of that intelligence. He should not have passed through the satanic realms.

The fierce revolt of the Troppmanns, the Napoleon the firsts, the Papavoines, the Victors Noirs, and the Charlotte Cordays will be kept at a good distance from my cold and severe look. In one quick movement I push aside all these major criminals with their different titles. Who do they think they are fooling here? I ask, I slowly interpose. Hobby-horses of penal colonies! Soap-bubbles! Ridiculous dancing-jacks! Worn-out strings! Let them approach, the Conrads, the Manfreds, the Laras, the sailors who resemble the Corsair, the Mephistopheles, the Werthers, the Don Juans, the Fausts, the Iagos, the Rodins, the Caligulas, the Cains, the Iridions, the megaerae à la Colomba, the Ahrimanes, the manichean manitous, bespattered with human brains, who ferment the blood of their victims in the sacred pagodas of Hindustan, the serpent, the toad and the crocodile, divinities, now considered abnormal, of ancient Egypt, the sorcerers and the demoniac powers of the Middle Ages, the Prometheuses, the mythological Titans thunderstruck by Jupiter, the evil gods vomited up by the primitive imagination of barbarian peoples – the whole noisy pack of paper devils. Certain of overcoming them, I grasp the whip of indignation and concentration, and, feeling its weight in my hand, I stand my ground and await these monsters as their preordained tamer.

There are a number of degraded writers, dangerous buffoons, jokers and clowns, sombre hoaxers, genuine lunatics, who deserve to be locked up in Bedlam. Their cretinizing heads, which have a screw loose somewhere, create gigantic phantoms which go down instead of going up. A scabrous exercise, a specious form of gymnastics. Away with the grotesque nonsense, quick as can be. Please withdraw from my presence, fabricators by the dozen of forbidden enigmas, in which I could not previously, as I can today, find the trivial solution at the first glance. A pathological case of dreadful egotism. Fantastic automata: point out to each other, my children, the epithet which puts them in their place.

If, beneath the plastic reality, they existed somewhere, they would be, in spite of their undoubted, but false, intelligence, the disgrace, the opprobrium and the shame of the planets where they lived. Imagine them all gathered together with beings of their own kind. There would be an uninterrupted succession of combats, such as bulldogs, forbidden in France, sharks, and hammer-headed whales cannot dream of. There would be torrents of blood in those chaotic regions full of hydras and minotaurs, from which the dove, terrified beyond all hope, flees as fast as its wings will carry it . . . They are a bunch of apocalyptic beasts, who know quite well what they are doing. There are the conflicts of the passions, mortal enmities, ambition, and through it all the howlings of a pride which it is impossible to read, which restrains itself, and of which nobody can even approximately sound out the reefs and the shallows.

But they will no longer impress me. Suffering is a weakness, when one doesn't need to do so, when one can find something better to do. But, suffocating in marshes of perversity, to exhale sufferings of deranged splendour, is to show even less resistance and less courage! With the voice and with all the solemnity of my great days, I call you to my hearth, glorious hope. Wrapped in the cloak of illusions, come and sit beside me on the reasonable tripod of appeasement. With a whip of scorpions I chased you, like an unwanted piece of furniture, from my abode. If you wish me to believe that, in returning, you have forgotten all the grief which my short-lived repentance caused you in the past, well, then bring along with you the sublime procession – hold me up, I am fainting! – of the virtues which I offended, and their everlasting atonements.

With bitterness I have to state that there are only a few drops of blood left in the arteries of our phthisic age. Ever since the bizarre and odious whinings of the Jean-Jacques Rousseaus, the Chateaubriands, and the Obermanns, wet nurses of chubby babies, and all the other poets who have wallowed in the filthy slime, up to the dreams of Jean-Paul, the suicide of Dolores de Veintemilla, Allan's Raven, the Pole's Infernal Comedy, the bloody eyes of Zorilla, and the immortal cancer, a carrion, lovingly painted once by the morbid lover of the Hottentot Venus, the incredible sorrows which this century has created for itself, in their deliberate and disgusting monotony, have made it consumptive. Wet through with tears in their intolerable torpor!

And so on, the same old story.

Yes, good people, I order you to burn, on a spade red-hot from the fire, and with a little yellow sugar for good measure, the duck of doubt with its vermouth lips, which, in the melancholy struggle between good and evil, shedding tears which are not heartfelt, creates everywhere, without the aid of a pneumatic machine, universal emptiness. It is the best thing you can do.

Despair, feeding, as it always does, on phantasmagoria, is imperturbably leading literature to the rejection, *en masse*, of all divine and social laws, towards practical and theoretical evil. In a word, in all its arguments, it glorifies the human backside. Let me speak! You are becoming evil, I say, and your eyes are taking on the colour of men sentenced to death. I will not retract what I have just said. I want to write poetry that can safely be read by fourteen-year-old girls.

True sorrow is incompatible with hope. However great this sorrow may be, hope rises a hundred cubits higher. But spare me these seekers, leave me in peace. Down with them, down, paws off, droll bitches, troublemakers, poseurs. That which suffers, that which dissects the mysteries which surround us, does not hope. Poetry which discusses necessary truths is less beautiful than that which does not discuss it. Extreme vacil-lations, talent misused, waste of time: nothing could be easier to demonstrate.

It is puerile to praise Adamastor, Jocelyn, Rocambole. It is only because the author takes it for granted that the reader will forgive his villainous heroes that he gives himself away, relying on the good to justify his description of the bad. It is in the name of those same virtues which Frank disdained that we wish to uphold it, oh mountebanks of incurable diseases!

Do not imitate those shameless explorers of melancholy, magnificent in their own eyes, who find hidden 'treasures' in their minds and in their bodies.

Melancholy and sadness are the beginning of doubt; doubt is the beginning of despair; despair is the cruel beginning of the different degrees of evil. To confirm this you need only read the *Confession of a Contemporary*. The slope is fatal, once you begin to go down it. You are bound to end with evil. Beware of that slope. Destroy the evil at its roots. Reject the cult of adjectives such as indescribable, unspeakable, brilliant, incomparable, colossal, which shamelessly lie to the nouns which they disfigure: for they are followed by lubricity.

Second-rate intellects such as Alfred de Musset may doggedly push one or two of their faculties further than the corresponding faculties of first-rate intellects, Lamartine, Hugo. We are witnessing the derailment of an old and worn-out locomotive. A nightmare is holding the pen. But the soul has twenty faculties. So don't talk to me of the beggars who have magnificent hats, and nothing else but sordid rags!

Here is a means of proving Musset's inferiority to the other two poets. Read *Rolla*, *Night Thoughts*, Cobb's *Madmen*, or, failing that, the descriptions of Gwynplaine and Dea, or the Tale of Theramene from Euripides, translated into French verse by Racine the Elder, to a young girl. She trembles, frowns, raises and lowers her hands with no apparent object, like a man drowning; her eyes glow with a greenish light. Read her the *Prayer For Us All*, by Victor Hugo. The effect is the diametrical opposite. The kind of electricity is no longer the same. She bursts into laughter, she asks you to read more.

Of Hugo's work, only the poems about children will survive, and they are not all good.

Paul and Virginie offends against our deepest aspirations to happiness. In the past, this episode which is riddled with gloom from beginning to end, especially the final shipwreck, used to set my teeth on edge. I would roll on the carpet and kick my wooden horse. The description of sorrow is an error. We should see the beauty in everything. Had this incident been recounted in a simple biography, I would not attack it. That would change its character altogether. Misfortune is ennobled by the inscrutable will of Him who created it. But man should not create misfortune in his books. That is only to see one side of things. Oh maniacal howlers that you are!

Do not deny the immortality of the soul, God's wisdom, the value of life, the order of the universe, physical beauty, the love of the family, marriage, social institutions. Ignore the following baneful pen-pushers: Sand, Balzac, Alexander Dumas, Musset, Du Terrail, Féval, Flaubert, Baudelaire, Leconte and the Grève des Forgerons!

Communicate to your readers only the experience of sorrow, which is not the same as sorrow itself. Do not cry in public.

One must be able to grasp the literary beauty even in the midst of death; but these beauties are not part of death. Death here is only the occasional cause. It is not the means, but the end, which is not death.

The immutable and necessary truths which are the glory of nations and which doubt vainly strives to shake have existed since the beginning of time. They should not be touched. Those who wish to create anarchy in literature on the pretext of change are making a serious error. They do not dare to attack God; they attack the immortality of the soul. But the immortality of the soul is itself as old as the crust of the earth.

What other belief will replace it, if it is to be replaced? It will not always be a negation.

If one recalls the one truth from which all others follow, God's goodness and His absolute ignorance of evil, sophisms break down of themselves. So too, and just as quickly, does the literature which is based on them. All literature which disputes eternal axioms is condemned to live by itself alone. It is unjust. It devours its own liver. The *novissima Verba* bring haughty smiles to the faces of snot-nosed fifth-formers. We have no right to interrogate the Creator on any subject whatsoever.

If you are unhappy, you must not tell the reader. Keep it to yourself.

If these sophisms were corrected by their corresponding truths, only the corrections would be true; while the work which had been thus revised would no longer have the right to be called false. The rest would be outside the realm of the true, tainted with falsehood, and would thus necessarily be considered null and void.

Personal poetry has had its day, with its relative sleights of hand and its contingent contortions. Let us gather up again the thread of impersonal poetry, rudely interrupted since the birth of the manqué philosopher of Ferney, since that great abortion Voltaire.

It appears beautiful and sublime, on the pretext of humility or pride, to discuss final causes, and to falsify their known and lasting consequences. Do not believe it, because nothing could be more stupid! Let us link up again the great chain which connects us with the past; poetry is geometry par excellence. Since Racine, poetry has not made a millimetre's progress. It has lost ground. Thanks to whom? To the Great Soft-Heads of our age. Thanks to the sissies, Chateaubriand, the Melancholy Mohican; Senancourt, the Man in Petticoats; Jean-Jacques Rousseau, the Surly Socialist; Anne Radcliffe, the

Spectre-Crazed; Edgar Poe, the Mameluke of Alcoholic Dreams; Mathurin, the Crony of Darkness; George Sand, the Circumcised Hermaphrodite; Théophile Gautier, the Incomparable Grocer; Leconte, the Devil's Captive; Goethe, the Suicide who makes you weep; Sainte-Beuve, the Suicide who makes you laugh; Lamartine, the Tearful Stork; Lermontov, the Roaring Tiger; Victor Hugo, the Gloomy Green Echalas; Misckiewicz, the Imitator of Satan; Musset, the Fop who didn't wear an intellectual's shirt; and Byron, the Hippopotamus of Infernal Jungles.

From the beginning of time doubt has been in the minority. In this century it is in the majority. Through our pores we breathe in the dereliction of duty. This has only ever happened once; it will never happen again.

So clouded are the simplest notions of reason nowadays that the first thing third-form teachers do when they are teaching their pupils Latin verse – these young poets whose lips are still wet from their mother's milk – is to reveal to them in practice the name of Alfred de Musset. Well, I ask you! Fourth-form teachers set two bloody episodes for their pupils to translate into Greek verse. The first is the repulsive comparison of the pelican. And the second will be the dreadful catastrophe which happened to a ploughman. What is the use of looking at evil? Is it not in the minority? Why turn these schoolboys' heads towards subjects which, unable to understand them, men such as Pascal and Byron were driven mad by?

A schoolboy told me that his sixth-form teacher had set his class, day after day, these two carcasses to translate into Hebrew verse. These two blots on human and animal nature made him so ill for a month that he had to go to hospital. As we were friends, he asked his mother to ask me to come and see him. He told me, though somewhat naïvely, that his nights were troubled by recurring dreams. He thought he saw an army of pelicans swooping down on him and tearing his breast to pieces. Then they would fly off to a burning cottage. They ate the ploughman's wife and children. His body blackened with burns, the ploughman came out of the cottage and joined dreadful combat with the pelicans. Then they all rushed into the cottage which fell to pieces. And from the pile of ruins – without fail – he would see his teacher emerging, holding his heart in one hand and in the other a piece of paper on which could be made out the sulphurous lines of the comparison of the pelican and the ploughman as Musset had himself composed them. It was not at first easy to diagnose what kind of illness this was. I urged him to be meticulously silent, and not to speak to anyone, least of all his teacher. I shall advise his mother to keep him at home for a few days and will make sure she does so. In fact, I made a point of going there for several hours every day, and the illness passed.

Criticism must attack the form but never the content of your ideas, your sentences. Act accordingly.

All the water in the sea would not be enough to wash away one intellectual bloodstain.

GENIUS guarantees the faculties of the heart.

Man is no less immortal than his soul.

Reason is the source of all great thoughts!

Fraternity is not a myth.

Children, when born, know nothing of life, not even its greatness.

In misfortune, the number of our friends increases.

Abandon despair, all ye who enter here.

Goodness, your name is man.

Here dwells the wisdom of nations.

Every time I read Shakespeare, it seemed I was cutting in pieces the brain of a jaguar.

I shall write my thoughts methodically, according to a clear plan. If they are exact, each one will be the consequence of the others. This is the only true order. It indicates my object despite the untidiness of my handwriting. I would be debasing my subject, if I did not treat it methodically.

I reject evil. Man is perfect. Our soul never fell from a state of grace. Progress exists. Good is irreducible. Antichrists, accusing angels, eternal torment, religions, are the product of doubt.

Dante and Milton, hypothetically describing the infernal regions, proved that they were hyenas of the first order. The proof is excellent. The result is poor. Their works do not sell.

Man is an oak. There is nothing more robust in all of nature. The universe does not have to take up arms to defend him. A drop of water is not enough to save him. Even if the universe were to defend him, he would be no more dishonoured than that which does not save him. Man knows that his reign is without end, and that the universe has a beginning. The universe knows nothing: it is, at the very most, a thinking reed.

I think of Elohim as being cold rather than sentimental.

Love of a woman is incompatible with love of mankind. Imperfection must be rejected. There is nothing more imperfect than egotism *à deux*. In life, mistrust, recriminations, and oaths written in powder pullulate. We no longer hear of the lover of Chimène; now it is the lover of Graziella. No longer of Petrarch; now it is Alfred de Musset. At the moment of death, a rocky region near the sea, a lake somewhere, the forest of Fontainebleau, the isle of Ischia, a raven in a study, a Chambre Ardente with a crucifix, a cemetery where in the predictable and tedious moonlight, the beloved rises from her grave, stanzas in which a group of young girls whose names we do not know, take turns to make an appearance, giving the measure of the author, uttering their regrets. In both cases, all dignity is lost.

Error is the sorrowful legend.

By singing hymns to Elohim, poets, in their vanity, get into the habit of not bothering with the things of this earth. That is the great danger with these hymns. Mankind grows out of the habit of counting on the writer. It abandons him. It calls him a mystic, an eagle, a traitor to his mission. You are not the dove they seek.

A student could acquire a considerable amount of literary knowledge by saying the opposite of what the poets of this century have said. He would replace their affirmations with negations. If it is ridiculous to attack first principles it is even more ridiculous to defend them against the same attacks. I will not defend them.

Sleep is a reward for some, a torture for others. It is, for everyone, a sanction.

If Cleopatra's morality had been less free, the face of the

earth would have changed. But her nose wouldn't have become any longer.

Hidden actions are the most admirable. When I see so many of them in history I like them a lot. They have not been completely hidden. They have become known. And this little by which they have become known increases their merit. It is the finest quality of all that they wouldn't be kept hidden.

The charm of death exists only for the brave.

Man is so great that his greatness shows above all else in his refusal to admit that he is miserable. A tree does not know its own greatness. To be great is to know that one is great. To be great is to refuse to admit one's misery. His greatness rejects his miseries. The greatness of a king.

When I write down my thoughts, they do not escape me. This action reminds me of my strength which at every moment I forget. I learn as I link my thoughts together. But I am only moving towards the realization of one thing: the contradiction between my mind and nothingness.

The heart of man is a book which I have learnt to esteem.

Not imperfect, unfallen, man is no longer the greatest mystery.

I allow no one, not even Elohim, to doubt my sincerity.

We are free to do good.

Man's judgement is infallible.

We are not free to do evil.

Man is the conqueror of chimeras, the novelty of tomorrow, the regularity which makes chaos groan, the subject of conciliation. He judges all things. He is not an imbecile. He is not a maggot. He is the depository of truth, the epitome of certitude, the glory and not the scum of the universe. If he humbles himself, I praise him. If he praises himself, I praise him more. I win him over. He is beginning to realize that he is the sister of the angel.

There is nothing incomprehensible.

Thought is no less clear than crystal. A religion whose lies are based on it can trouble it for a few minutes, to speak of long-term effects. To speak of short-term effects, the murder of eight people at the gates of a capital city will trouble it – certainly – to the point where the evil is destroyed. Thought soon regains its limpidity.

Poetry must have for its object practical truth. It expresses the relation between the first principles and the secondary truths of life. Everything remains in its place. The mission of poetry is difficult. It is not concerned with political events, with the way a people is governed, makes no allusion to historical periods, *coups d'état*, regicides, court intrigues. It does not speak of those struggles which, exceptionally, man has with himself and his passions. It discovers the laws by which political theory exists, universal peace, the refutations of Machiavelli, the cornets of which the work of Proudhon consists, the psychology of mankind. A poet must be more useful than any other citizen of his tribe. His work is the code of diplomats, legislators and teachers of youth. We are far from the Homers, the Virgils, the Klopstocks, the Camoëns, the liberated imaginations, the ode-producers, the merchants of epigrams against the deity. Let us return to Confucius, Buddha, Jesus Christ, those moralists who went hungry through the villages. From now on we have to reckon with reason which operates only on those faculties which watch over the category of the phenomena of pure goodness.

Nothing is more natural than to read the *Discourse on Method* after reading *Bérénice*. Nothing is less natural than to read Biéchy's *Treatise on Induction* or Naville's *Problem of Evil* after reading *Autumn Leaves* or the *Contemplations*. There is no continuity. The mind rebels against rubbish, mystagogy. The heart is appalled at these pages some puppet has scrawled. This violence suddenly makes everything clear. He closes the book. He sheds a tear in memory of the barbaric authors. Contemporary poets have abused their intelligence. Philosophers have not abused theirs. The memory of the former will fade. The latter are classics.

Racine, Corneille would have been capable of writing the works of Descartes, Malebranche, Bacon. The spirit of the former is one with that of the latter. Lamartine, Hugo would not have been capable of writing the *Treatise on the Intellect*. The mind of its author is not equal to that of the former. Fatuity has made them lose the central qualities. Lamartine, Hugo, although superior to Taine, possess, like him – it is painful to admit this – only secondary faculties.

Tragedies excite the obligatory qualities of pity and terror. That is something. It is bad. It is not as bad as modern lyric poetry. Legouve's *Medea* is preferable to a collection of the works of Byron, Capendu, Zaccone, Felix, Gagne, Gaboriau, Lacordaire, Sardou, Goethe, Ravignan, Charles Diguet. Which one of you writers can produce works to compare with – what is it? What are these snorts of disagreement? – the Monologue of Augustus! Hugo's barbaric vaudevilles do not proclaim duty. The melodramas of Racine and Corneille, the novels of La Calprenède do proclaim it. Lamartine is not capable of producing Pradon's *Phèdre*; nor Hugo the Venceslas of Rotrou; nor Sainte-Beuve the tragedies of Laharpe or Marmontel. Musset is capable of producing proverbs. Tragedy is an involuntary error, it accepts the idea of struggle, it is the first step towards the good, it will not appear in this work. It maintains its prestige. The same cannot be said of the sophistries – the belated metaphysical gongorism of the self-parodists of my heroico-burlesque age.

The principle of all forms of worship is pride. It is ridiculous to address Elohim, as the Jobs, the Jeremiahs, the Davids, the Solomons, the Turquétys have done. Prayer is a false act. The best way of pleasing him is indirect, more consistent with our own powers. It consists in making our race happy. There are no two ways of pleasing Elohim. The idea of the good is one. That which is good in smaller things being also good in greater, I cite the example of the mother. To please his mother, a son will not tell her that she is wise, radiant, that he will behave in such a way as to deserve most of her praise. He acts otherwise. He convinces by his actions, not by protestations, he abandons the sadness which swells up the eyes of the Newfoundland dog. The goodness of Elohim must not be confused with triviality. Everyone is plausible. Familiarity breeds contempt; reverence breeds the contrary. Hard work prevents us from indulging our feelings and passions.

No thinking man believes what contradicts his reason.

Faith is a natural virtue by which we accept the truths which Elohim has revealed to us through conscience.

I know no other grace than that of being born. An impartial mind finds this adequate.

Good is the victory over evil, the negation of evil. If one writes of the good, evil is eliminated by this fitting act. I do not write of what must not be done. I write of what must be done. The former does not include the latter. The latter includes the former.

Youth listens to the advice of its elders. It has unlimited confidence in itself.

I know of nothing which is beyond the reach of the human mind, except truth.

The maxim does not need to be proved. One point in an argument requires another. The maxim is a law which contains a number of arguments. The closer the argument comes to the maxim, the more perfect it becomes. Once it has become a maxim, its perfection rejects the evidence of a transformation.

Doubt is a homage to hope. It is not a voluntary homage. Hope would never consent to be a mere homage.

Evil revolts against the good. It can do no less.

It is a proof of friendship not to notice the increase in our friends' friendship.

Love is not happiness.

If we had no faults we would not take so much pleasure in curing ourselves of them and in praising in others what we ourselves lack.

Those men who have resolved to detest their fellow-beings have forgotten that one must start by detesting oneself.

Those who never take part in duels believe that those who fight duels to the death are brave.

How the turpitudes of the novel crouch in the bookshop windows! Just as some men would kill for a hundred sous, it sometimes seems to a man who is lost that a book should be killed.

Lamartine believed that the fall of an angel would mean the Elevation of Man. He was wrong to believe so.

A banal truth contains more genius than the works of Dickens, Gustave Aymard, Victor Hugo, Landelle. With the aid of the latter a child who had survived the destruction of the universe would not be able to reconstruct the human soul. With the former it could. I suppose it would not discover the definition of sophism sooner or later.

Words expressing evil are destined to take on a more positive meaning. Ideas improve. The sense of words takes part in this process.

Plagiarism is necessary. It is implied in the idea of progress. It clasps an author's sentence tight, uses his expressions, eliminates a false idea, replaces it with the right idea.

To be well wrought, a maxim does not need to be corrected. It needs to be developed.

As soon as dawn comes, young girls go picking roses. A breath of innocence crosses the valleys, the capital cities, inspiring the most enthusiastic poets, bringing peace and protection to cradles, crowns to youth, belief in immortality to old men.

I have seen men wearing out the moralists who attempted to discover their heart, and bringing upon themselves blessings from above. They were uttering meditations as vast as possible, bringing joy to the author of our felicity. They showed respect to childhood and to age, to all that breathes and all that does not breathe, they paid homage to woman and consecrated to modesty the parts of the body which we refrain from naming. The firmament, whose beauty I acknowledge, the earth, image of my heart, were invoked by me, in order to represent myself as a man who did not believe himself good. The sight of this monster, had it ever proved to be real, would not have killed me with shock: it takes more than that to kill a man. All this needs no comment.

Reason and feeling counsel and supplement each other. Whoever knows only one of these, renouncing the other, is depriving himself of *all* of the aid which has been granted us to guide our actions. Vauvenargues said: 'is depriving himself of *part* of the aid.'

Though his sentence and mine are based on the personification of the soul in feeling and reason, the one I chose at random would be no better than the other, if I had written both. The one cannot be rejected by me. The other could be accepted by Vauvenargues.

When a predecessor uses a word from the domain of evil to describe the good, it is dangerous for his sentence to subsist alongside the other. It is better to leave the word's evil meaning unchanged. Before one can use a word from the domain of evil for the good, one must first have the right. He who uses for evil words from the domain of good does not have this right. He is not believed. No one would wish to use Gérard de Nerval's tie.

The soul being one, sensibility, intelligence, will, reason, imagination and memory can be introduced into our discourse.

I spent a great deal of time studying abstract sciences. Because one only has to communicate with a small number of people in such studies, I did not tire of them. When I began the study of man, I saw that these sciences were particular to him, that by flinging myself into these studies I was less able to change my condition than others who knew nothing of them. I forgave them their lack of interest! I did not believe I would find many fellow-students of this subject of man. I was wrong. There are more students of man than of geometry.

We die joyfully, provided no one talks about it.

The passions become weaker with age. Love, which should not be classified among the passions, becomes weaker, too. What it loses on one hand, it gains on the other. It is no longer so demanding towards the object of its desires, it does justice to itself: a certain expansion is accepted. The senses no longer excite the organs of the flesh. The love of mankind begins. On days when man feels he is an altar adorned with his own virtues, and recollects all the sorrows he has ever felt, the soul, in a recess of the heart where everything seems to be born, feels something which is no longer beating. I have just described memory.

The writer can, without separating one from the other, indicate the laws which govern each one of his poems.

Some philosophers are more intelligent than some poets. Spinoza, Malebranche, Aristotle, Plato are not Hégésippe Moreau, Malfilatre, Gilbert, André Chenier.

Faust, Manfred, Konrad are archetypes. They are not yet reasoning types. They are the archetypes of the agitator.

A meadow, three rhinoceroses, half a catafalque, these are descriptions. They may be memory or prophecy. They are not the paragraph which I am about to complete.

The regulator of the soul is not the regulator of a soul. The regulator of a soul is the regulator of the soul when these two kinds of souls are so commingled that it is possible to state that a regulator is only a regulatress in the imagination of a joking madman.

The phenomenon passes. I seek the laws.

There are men who are not archetypes. Archetypes are not men. One must not be dominated by the accidental.

Judgements on poetry are worth more than poetry itself. They are the philosophy of poetry. Philosophy, in this sense, includes poetry. Poetry cannot do without philosophy. Philosophy can do without poetry.

Racine is not capable of condensing his tragedies into precepts. A tragedy is not a precept. To one and the same mind, a precept is a more intelligent act than a tragedy.

Put a goose-quill pen in the hands of a moralist who is a first-class writer. He will be superior to poets.

Love of justice is, in most men, merely the courage to suffer injustice.

Hide, war.

Feelings express happiness, make us smile. The analysis of feelings expresses happiness, all personality apart; makes us smile. The former elevates the soul, dependently of space and time, to the conception of mankind considered in itself and in its illustrious members. The latter elevates the soul independently of time and space to the conception of mankind in its highest expression, the will! The feelings are concerned with vice and virtue; the latter is concerned only with virtue. The feelings are not aware of the course they follow. The analysis of feelings makes this known, and increases the strength of our feelings. With the former, all is uncertainty. They are the expression of happiness and sorrow, two extremes. With the latter, all is certainty. It is the expression of the happiness derived, at a given moment, from being able to restrain oneself amidst good and bad passions. In its composure it blends the description of the passions into a principle which informs its pages: the non-existence of evil. Feelings overflow when necessary, and also when it is not necessary. The analysis of feelings does not weep. It possesses a latent sensibility which takes us by surprise, helps us transcend our woes, teaches us to do without a guide, provides us with a weapon. Feelings, the sign of weakness, are not Feeling! The analysis of feeling, sign of strength, engenders the most magnificent feelings I know. The writer who is deceived by his feelings cannot be put on a par with the writer who is deceived neither by his feelings, nor by himself. Youth indulges in sentimental lucubrations. Maturity begins to reason clearly. Whereas once we only felt, we now think. We allowed our sensations to roam freely; now we give them a guide. If I consider mankind as a woman, I will merely say that her youth is on the ebb, that her maturity is approaching. Her mind is changing for the better. The ideal of poetry will change. Tragedies, poems, elegies will no longer take first place. The coldness of the maxim will dominate! In the time of Quinault, they would have been capable of understanding what I have just said. Thanks to certain faint glimmerings in reviews and folios in the last few years, I can understand it myself. My genre is as different from that of the moralists who merely state the evil without suggesting the remedy than theirs is from the melodramas, the funeral orations, the ode and the religious stanza. The sense of struggle is lacking.

Elohim is made in man's image.

Several certainties have been contradicted. Several falsehoods remain uncontradicted. Contradiction is the sign of falsehood. Non-contradiction is the sign of certainty.

A philosophy for the sciences exists. But not for poetry. I know of no moralist who is a first-rate poet. It is strange, someone will say.

It is a horrible thing to feel what is yours falling to pieces. One even only hangs on to it in the wish to find out if there is anything permanent.

Man is a subject devoid of errors. Everything shows him the truth. Nothing deceives him. The two principles of truth, reason and sense, apart from being reliable each for itself, enlighten each other. The senses enlighten reason by true appearances. And this same service which they perform for her, they also receive it from her. Each one takes it in turn. The phenomena of the soul pacify the senses, making impressions on them which I cannot assert to be unpleasant. They do not lie. They do not vie with each other in deception.

Poetry must be made by everyone. Not by one. Poor Hugo! Poor Racine! Poor Coppée! Poor Corneille! Poor Boileau! Poor Scarron! Tics, tics, and tics.

The sciences have extremities which touch. The first is the state of ignorance all men are in when born. The second is the ignorance attained by great souls. They have surveyed all that men can know, find that they know everything, and are yet in the same state of ignorance as when they set out. Theirs is a knowing ignorance, self-aware. Those who, having left the first ignorance behind, have some smattering of this sufficient knowledge, act as if they knew all the answers. The former do not trouble the world, their judgement is no worse than all the others'. The people and the clever determine the course of a nation. The others, who respect it, are no less respected by it.

To know things, it is not necessary to know the details. As they are limited, our knowledge is solid.

Love is not to be confused with poetry.

Woman is at my feet!

We must not, in describing heaven, use the materials of the earth. We must leave the earth and its materials where they are, in order to embellish life by its ideal. To speak in familiar tones to Elohim, to address him at all, is unseemly buffoonery. The best means of showing our gratitude towards him is not to trumpet into his ears that he is mighty, that he created the world, that we are worms in comparison with his greatness. He knows all that better than we. Men can refrain from telling him these things. The best means of showing our gratitude to him is to console mankind, to relate everything we do to mankind; to take it by the hand and treat it as a brother. It is more honest.

To study order, one must not study disorder. Scientific experiments, like tragedies, stanzas to my sister, gibberish about misfortune, have got nothing to do with life on earth.

It is not good for all laws to be known.

To study evil in order to extract the good from it is not the same as to study the good. Given an instance of good, I will seek its cause.

Up to now, misfortune has been described in order to inspire terror and pity. I will describe happiness, to inspire the opposite.

A logic for poetry exists. It is not the same as the logic of philosophy. Philosophers are not on a par with poets. Poets have the right to consider themselves above philosophers.

I do not need to bother about what I will do later. What I am doing now I had to do. I do not need to discover the things that I will discover later. In the new science, everything comes in its place – that is its excellence.

There are the makings of the poet in moralists and philosophers. The poet contains the thinker. Each caste suspects the other, developing its own qualities at the expense of those which bring it closer to the other caste. The pride of the latter proves incompetent to do justice to tenderer minds. Whatever a man's intelligence may be, the process of thinking must be the same for all.

The existence of tics having been established, we are not surprised to see the same words recurring more often than their due: in Lamartine, the tears which fall from his horse's nostrils, the colour of his mother's hair; in Hugo, the shadow and the madman are part of the binding.

The science I am establishing is a science distinct from poetry. I am not writing the latter. I am trying to discover its source. Across the helm which directs all poetic thought, billiards teachers will distinguish the development of sentimental theses.

The theorem is in its nature a form of mockery. It is not indecent. The theorem does not insist on being applied. The application we make of it debases it, becomes indecent. Call the struggle of matter against the ravages of the mind application.

To struggle against evil is to pay it too great a compliment. If I allow men to despise it, I hope they do not forget to say that that is all I can do for them.

Man is certain that he is not wrong.

We are not content with the life within us. We wish to lead an imaginary life in other people's minds. We strive to appear to be what we are. We make every effort to preserve this imaginary being, which is simply the real one. If we are generous, faithful, we are eager not to let it be known, we wish to attribute these virtues to this being. We do not get rid of them and then attach them to this being. We are brave in order to avoid the reputation of being cowards. A sign of our being's incapacity to be satisfied with the one without the other, to renounce either. That man who did not live to defend his virtue would be a scoundrel.

Despite the sight of our greatness, which has caught us by the throat, we have an instinct which corrects us, which we cannot repress, which exalts us!

Nature has perfections to show that it is the image of Elohim, faults to show that it is nonetheless only an image.

It is right that laws should be obeyed. The people understand what makes it just. It does not break the laws. Were we to make their justice depend on anything else, it is easy to cast doubt on it. Peoples are not subject to revolt.

Those who are out of order tell those who are in order that they are straying from nature. They believe they are right. One must have a fixed standpoint in order to judge. And where else is this standpoint to be found but in morality?

Nothing is less surprising than the contradictions in man. He is made to know truth. He seeks it. When he tries to grasp it, he is so dazzled and confused that no one would envy him the possession of it. Some wish to deny man's knowledge of truth, others to assert it. Each side uses such dissimilar arguments that they dispel his confusion. There is no other guiding-light than that which is to be found in nature.

We are born just. Everyone seeks his own good. It is the wrong way round. We must aim for the general good. The descent towards self is the end of all disorder, in war, in economics.

Men, having conquered death, misery and ignorance, have, in order to be happy, taken it into their heads not to think of these things. It is the only method they have devised to console themselves for so few ills. Most rich consolation. It does not cure the ill. It hides it for a short while. In hiding it, it gives the impression that it is being cured. By a legitimate reversal of man's nature, it is not the case that ennui, which is man's most deeply-felt evil, is his greatest good. It can contribute more than anything else to help him seek his redemption. That is all. Amusement, which he regards as his greatest good, is his least ill. More than anything else, he seeks in this the remedy to all his ills. Both are a counter-proof of the misery, the corruption of man, apart from his greatness. Man in his boredom seeks this multitude of activities. He has a notion of the happiness he has gained; finding it within himself, he seeks it in external things. He is content. Unhappiness is not in us, nor is it in other creatures. It is in Elohim.

Nature makes us happy in all states. Our desires represent to us an unhappy state. They add to our present state the afflictions of the imaginary one. Yet if we ever experienced these sorrows, we still would not be unhappy, we would have other desires corresponding to our new state.

The strength of reason appears greater in those who know it than in those who do not know it.

We are so far from being presumptuous that we would wish to be known all over the earth, and even by those who come after us when we are dead. We are so far from being vain that the esteem of five – let us make it six – people amuses and honours us.

The least thing consoles us. The greatest things afflict us.

Modesty is so natural in the heart of man that a worker carefully avoids boasting, yet wishes to have his admirers. Philosophers want theirs, too. And poets most of all! Those who write for glory wish to have the distinction of having written well. Those who read wish to have the distinction of having read. I, who write this, boast that I have this wish. Those who read it will do the same.

The inventions of man are increasing all the time. The goodness and malice of the world in general do not remain the same.

The mind of the greatest man is not so dependent that he is liable to be troubled by all the hurly-burly around him. It does not take the silence of the cannon to hinder his thoughts. It does not take the noise of a weather-vane or a pulley. The fly cannot gather its thoughts at present. A man is buzzing at its ears. It is enough to make it incapable of good counsel. If I want it to discover the truth, I will chase away this animal which keeps its reason in check, troubling this intelligence which governs realms.

The purpose of these people playing tennis with such concentration of the mind and movement of the body is to boast to their friends that they have played better than their opponent. That is the reason for their love of the game. Some sweat in their studies to prove to the mathematical experts that they have solved an algebraical problem which was no problem at all until then. Others expose themselves to dangers to boast of what they have achieved by what, in my opinion, are less spiritual means. The last group try desperately hard to see these things. They are certainly no less wise. It is above all to show that they know how worth-while it is. They are the least foolish of the whole lot. They know what they are doing. Perhaps the others would not be the same if they did not have this knowledge.

The example of Alexander's continence has made no more converts to chastity than that of his drunkenness has made teetotalers. People are not ashamed not to be as virtuous as he. They believe their virtues are not quite the same as the generality of men's when they see these same virtues practised by the great. They cling on to that which he has in common with them. However exalted they may be, they always have a point which connects them with the rest of mankind. They do not hover in the air, separated from our society. If they are greater than we, it is because they are flesh and blood as we are. They are on the same level, they stand on the same ground. At this extremity, they are as exalted as we, as children, a little more than animals.

The best means of persuading consists in not persuading.

Despair is the smallest of our errors.

Whenever we hear of a thought, a truth which is on everyone's lips, we only need to develop it and we find that it is a discovery.

One can be just, if one is not human.

The storms of youth precede the brilliant days.

Unawareness, dishonour, lubricity, hatred and contempt for men all have their price. Liberality multiplies the advantages of riches.

Those who are honest in their pleasures are also honest in their other dealings. It is the sign of a gentle disposition, since pleasure humanizes.

The moderation of great men limits only their virtues.

We offend men by praising them beyond their strict deserts. Many people are modest enough not to object in the least to being well thought of.

We must expect everything, fear nothing, from time, from men.

If merit and glory do not make men unhappy, then what we call misfortune is not worth their grief. A soul deigns to accept fortune, respite, if it can superimpose on them the strength of its feelings, the flight of its genius.

We admire great designs when we feel capable of great successes.

Reserve is the apprenticeship of minds.

We say sound things when we do not attempt to say extraordinary things.

Nothing which is true is false; nothing which is false is true. All is the contrary of dream, of illusion.

We must not think that those whom nature has made lovable are vicious. There has never been a century or a people which has inaugurated imaginary virtues and vices.

One can only judge the beauty of life by the beauty of death.

A playwright can give to the word 'passion' a meaning of utility. But he is then no longer a playwright. A moralist can give to any word whatsoever a meaning of utility. He remains a moralist just the same!

Whoever examines the life of a man will find in it the history of the species. Nothing has been able to vitiate it.

Do I have to write in verse to set myself apart from other men? Let charity decide!

The pretext of those who make others happy is that they are seeking their good.

Generosity shares in the joys of others as if it were responsible for them.

Order dominates among the human species. Reason and virtue are not the strongest.

Princes have few ungrateful subjects. They give all they can.

We can love with all our heart those in whom we find great faults. It would be impertinent to think that only imperfections have the right to please us. Our weaknesses attach us to each other as much as that which is not virtue could do.

If our friends do favours for us, we think that, as friends, they owe us them. We do not at all think that they owe us their enmity.

He who was born to command, would command, even on the throne.

When our duties have exhausted us we think we have exhausted our duties. We say that the heart of man can contain everything.

Everything lives by action. Communication between beings, the harmony of the universe, come from action. We find that this fecund law of nature is a vice in man. He is obliged to obey it. Unable to rest for a moment, we conclude he is in his place.

We know what the sun and the heavens are. We possess the secret of their movements. In the hands of Elohim, a blind instrument, an imperceptible spring, the world compels our homage. The revolutions of empires, the phases of time, the nations, the conquerors of knowledge, all this comes from a crawling atom, lasts only a day, destroys the spectacle of the universe through all the ages.

There is more truth than errors, more good qualities than bad, more pleasures than pains. We like to examine our character. We exalt ourselves above our species. We adorn ourselves with the esteem which we lavish on it. We think we cannot separate our own interest from that of mankind, that we cannot slander our race without compromising ourselves. This ridiculous vanity has filled books with hymns in favour of nature. Man is in disgrace with all those who think. It is a question of who can accuse him of the most vices. When was he not about to pick himself up, to piece together his virtues?

Nothing has been said. We have come too early. Man has existed for seven thousand years. In the matter of morals, as in everything else, that which is the least good is the most highly thought of. We have the advantage of working after the ancients, after the ablest of the moderns.

We are capable of friendship, justice, compassion, reason. Oh my friends! What then is the absence of virtue?

As long as my friends are still alive, I will not speak of death.

We are dismayed by our relapses, and to see that our misfortunes have corrected our faults.

One can only judge the beauty of death by the beauty of life.

The three full stops make me shrug my shoulders with pity. Does one really need that to prove that one is a man of wit, i.e. an imbecile? As if clarity was not as good as vagueness, in the matter of full stops!